The wait seemed like an eternity, but the front passenger door flew open and Martinez rolled out to the ground, sprung to a crouch, his gun panning the area from which she shot.

She stepped from behind the tree. "Lower the gun and drop it, carefully." Martinez appeared frozen in time, the back of his head as still as it had looked after she'd bloodied his nose. He slowly lowered his arms, but his hands looked to be joined and the gun not on the ground.

"Put the gun down." She hoped her voice did not betray the shaking of her arms.

Martinez began to turn.

"Move any further and I'll shoot."

He stopped. "No you won't."

The headlights splashed against the trees ahead rendering Martinez in eerie profile, like a suspect in a lineup, like the shadowed images of gunmen she'd practiced on at the firing range. This was no cardboard cutout, though. It was human life. He resumed his turn but as if in manual freeze-frame. Everything else faded to background, the hum of the engine the only sound. She aimed at his torso. The horrible implication of what he said finally sunk in. She *didn't* have it in her to kill him.

CAUSED & EFFECT

Bernie Bourdeau

ACKNOWLEDGMENTS

My first novel came to life with the help of a great many people, only a few of whom I have room to mention. Barbara Rogan is a fine novelist and a terrific writing instructor who convinced me early on that I could and should write this book. Jason Sitzes, a story editor whom I met through the knowledgeable professionals at Free Expressions Seminars, helped me whip the story pieces into shape. My copy editor, Rob Brill, took my vague notions of grammar and punctuation and converted them to English.

A number of NY state troopers, active and retired, helped me to understand procedures and protocols. Lee Lofland and the trainers at the Writers Police Academy added to that knowledge. Where I have the details right, these fine professionals deserve all the credit. Where I have them wrong I take full responsibility. Resorting to habits acquired in 20 years of lobbying, I never let the facts stand in the way of the story I have to tell.

Special thanks to my longtime critique partner Kelly Waite, and to my favorite cheerleader Annie Decker. Thanks also to my workshop group: Michelle, Sara, Alice, Annette, Laurie, and Emilia. It took some nerve writing a woman's point of view for my first effort. They helped me get her right and didn't laugh too hard at my early attempts bless them. Thanks to my good friend Sensei Allan for his help with the martial arts. Thanks to the many insurance fraud investigators I had the privilege to work with over the years, especially the now-retired Sam Lantz. Special thanks to the New York Insurance Associations, Inc. and the New York Alliance Against Insurance Fraud for allowing me to lead their fine organizations. What I know about insurance fraud derived from those associations.

Finally, a deep gratitude to my good friend Jay Martin, who pointed out that writing and publishing are commercial enterprises, and the business decisions about when and how to show my creations rest solely with me.

For Maggie

You believed even when I didn't.

CHAPTER 1

E ven from a distance, the guy looked as if he'd skittered in straight from Miss Muffet's crib. Linda Baldwin shifted in the spacious booth. A handful of premature Valentine's hearts dangled from the archway, partially obstructing her view. He stood near the rowdy bar crowd clustered by the overhead TV, trying to blend in, but not too deeply. Perhaps he feared being mistaken for one of them. His eyes scanned the backroom. The black V-neck sweater over a white collared shirt created the illusion he was bound for a photo shoot, not the backseat of a car. She'd bet a bundle this was her spider. *Come sit by my tuffet, lover.*

Linda fanned her face with the menu and undid the second button on her blouse, revealing a hint of lace. She opened her purse to remove a mirror and lipstick. The GPS blinked a reassuring green. She closed the bag and applied the lipstick. He approached.

Destiny. *Remember,* Destiny. She smiled at the irony of the name the shrinks had given her. If only they knew how long she'd waited for this day, dreamed about it, focused the dream into a narrow beam consuming everything in its path. Yes, she would be Destiny today. This *was* her destiny.

"Destiny?"

Linda nodded and returned the items to her purse. His face was too tanned for this time of year. His eyes flashed the color of her faded jeans. His fingers were long and tanned save for the circle of white skin on his ring finger. The scent of Polo invaded her nostrils.

"Jack?"

He slid into the booth and leaned forward against the pockmarked Formica table separating them. His eyes settled on the gap in her blouse. "Yeah. I'm glad we had a chance to meet."

"Me too. We got so much in common."

A server started toward the table. Jack waved her off. "Listen, they're strict about ID in this place and since you're 17…"

She forced a sheepish grin. "I was afraid to tell you before, in case you wouldn't meet me, but I can't lie now. I'm not 17 yet." She leaned forward and lowered her voice. "But I'm almost 16. When it comes to love, I don't think age matters, do you?"

Jack stared at her chest, licked his lips. "Not at all." He nodded toward the door. "I've got some wine coolers in my car."

She draped her ski jacket over her shoulders and followed him out back to the well-lit parking lot. Jack angled to the far corner where a black Crown Victoria with dealer plates blended into the shadow of a sprawling spruce. "Wow! You got a real nice car." She heard a beep and the car lights flashed once. Jack opened the passenger door for her. What a gentleman. He fondled her ass. She wanted to swing an elbow into his skull.

Once inside, Jack twisted the top off a wine cooler and handed it to her. He popped open a beer and clinked her bottle. "To a wonderful evening."

Linda wanted to toast, but not with the crap he'd brought. She raised the drink to her lips, pretended to sip, then slid the bottle in the cup holder. Jack took a long swig of his beer and placed his bottle next to hers.

Within five minutes, he'd unbuttoned her blouse, exposing the creamy bra she'd chosen for the occasion. His fingers peeled the fabric from her breasts and stroked her flesh. Panic sprouted. The shrinks had prepared her for a predator's hands on her body, but reality was quite different from what she'd imagined. How did hookers cope? Face it, she was letting a man who disgusted her do what he wanted in the hope of some payoff. She was little more than a whore. His fingers were ice. She shivered.

2

"You like that, baby? I make you shiver, huh?"

She wanted to knee him in the balls. *Calm down, Linda.* If she gave in now, she'd blow the whole sting. Prostitute or not, she was a professional. Her job to get Jack off the streets, behind bars where he belonged. "Oh, Jack," she moaned.

His hand grazed the waistband of her jeans; lingered on the button above the zipper. She gasped.

"I got you excited, baby?"

No. Jack would not get his finger or anything else between her legs. Everyone has her limits. Jack was a shrewd one, though, leaving no cyberspace evidence of his lust for underage girls. Linda had established her age at 15. Now to coax the magic words from Jack's lips. "Yes. Talk to me, Jack. Your voice is real sexy."

His hand continued along her zipper. Aggressive fingers rubbed her crotch through the denim. Beads of sweat formed on Jack's forehead. He sought her lips. She turned her head, the beer on his breath stirring a bad memory. Linda forced herself to moan again.

Jack responded, unbuttoning the waist and unzipping her jeans.

Roll the dice, Linda. Now! The giggle she'd practiced for weeks sounded genuine. "What do you want me to do?"

Jack whispered the words in her ear. His hand slithered inside her panties.

Out loud, Jack. She touched the hand, now resting on her pubic hair, her tolerance limit. Screw the sting; time to abort. "You said making love. Made me tingle. Tell me again."

A finger crept lower. She balled a fist to crush Jack's windpipe.

"Come on, baby. You know I want to fuck you almost as much as you want me."

Music to her ears, and loud enough for the recorder. *Closing time, Jack.* "Wait." Linda removed Jack's hand from her panties and arched her shoulders against the seatback, lifted her butt and lowered her jeans, exposing her bare thighs. "Get in the backseat. I have to get some…" She dropped her voice to an intimate whisper as she reached down for her bag. "You know, protection. This is exciting."

"No, I got one in my wallet." He grabbed her arm. "Let's go."

Like hell. She'd rather her own style of protection. "No, I got a special one. My girlfriends told me they're the best for your first time."

"First time?" Jack released her and nearly flew onto the backseat. Linda found her "special protection" and pointed the Glock at Jack, who sat naked from the waist down.

She chose her leather voice. "Your name's not Jack and mine's not Destiny. John Doe, my name is Trooper Baldwin. You, my friend, are under arrest for, among other lesser offenses, soliciting a sexual encounter with a minor. You have the right to remain silent. You have the right to an attorney." She completed the Miranda warning.

With her free hand, Linda reached in her bag and pressed the call button on her radio to summon her backup. She switched off the recorder and wondered how many troopers besides Ewing and her team would listen to the tape. In the unlikely event the case went to trial, the whole world would. No, when they shared the recording with Jack's lawyer, he'd be looking to save his client's ass from state prison. The county jail and a long probation would be a sweet alternative. Jack dressed in silence, shaking his head. She cuffed him and then dressed. She'd nailed the sex predator bastard and had an open-and-shut case, exactly what she'd envisioned when choosing law enforcement over a career as a lawyer.

***

The next day, Linda drove downtown at noon to meet with Assistant District Attorney Valerie Hoinski. She recognized the name from the newspapers as the ADA who handled many sex crime prosecutions and nearly all the high profile cases the DA chose not to touch. Within minutes of the introductions, Hoinski disclosed which category the case of Jack, aka Bradford Connor Tillinghast III, fell under.

Linda cut off Hoinski's summary of events. "Did you listen to the goddamned tape?"

"I listened, trooper."

"To the end?"

"Yes."

"Good. Now let me tell you about the part you missed. As a woman, I'm sure you'll appreciate this. The sleaze thought I was 15 or 16, and he had his hands all over my body. During the last minutes, his hand was in my pants. When he finally admitted he wanted sex, he was about to check on my virginity. Let me ask you, Val, can you feel what I'm describing? Come on, imagine. Make believe you're the one on the tape. I had the experience, Val. I bet if you did, you'd be thinking differently about this perp."

Hoinski refused to look at her. "I get your point."

"How? I haven't gotten there yet. Now I want you to imagine yourself as your own teenage daughter. Because you see, Val, Jack thought I was her: yours or someone else's teen daughter."

"What do you want from me?"

"How about a 25 charge you plea down to two years?" Penal Law section 130.25 covered third-degree rape. The act Jack schemed to commit provided up to four years in jail. Hoinski would get at least 18 months.

"I can't make the charge stick."

"You can. What you mean is you won't."

Hoinski continued looking anywhere but at Linda.

"OK, then how about *not* going down the 260.10 path you're headed?" Penal Law section 260.10 involved endangering the welfare of a minor with first offenses punished with the equivalent to a stern scolding.

"Where'd you get that?"

"Bad sign when the response is not a denial." Her mentor, Bert Bariteau, had predicted the outcome last night.

Hoinski finally looked at her. "Spoken like a true Bariteau protégé."

"How did you…"

"I know a lot about you, Trooper Baldwin. We share a mentor."

"Yeah? He teach you to pat sex predators on the back?"

Hoinski shook her head. "You and I are pawns in this particular game."

"You got to keep your clothes on, though."

"I know and I admire your courage. For what it's worth, I don't like this any more than you do."

5

"Then tell your boss no deal."

"I already did. He reminded me who the people elected and who signs my paycheck. I need the job. Besides, we do put away most serious sex offenders."

"At least those without connections."

"Bert trained you, and you're still thinking you're going to change the system?"

The question shouldn't have surprised Linda. "I don't *think* I'm going to change the system, Val. I am."

"Then I'm sorry for you, Linda. I am."

Linda stood to leave. "Don't be. Tell your boss he's not getting away with this. We busted our butts to make a good clean collar. My bosses won't stand for this shit. Someone above my pay grade is going to ream the DA a new asshole."

Hoinski shook her head. "If your sexist peckerhead boss thinks he's got any say in this, he's dreaming. He may be good buds with the boss, but friendship only goes so far."

Linda filed the tidbit on Captain Walker and the DA's relationship. "No, this will come from the top."

"You've got a lot to learn, Linda. You could start with protocol for speaking in court."

Linda grimaced. "Graney told?"

ADA John Graney had appeared at last night's arraignment and nearly bit Linda's head off afterwards.

"Forget Graney. The Honorable Shane Dolan called the boss first thing this morning. Did you really ask him?" Hoinski took a tablet from her desk and read to Linda. "'Your Honor, should I give Jack a ride back to the bar where he picked me up? If we hurry, maybe he can score before closing time.'"

"Close. Expletives deleted. Guy's rude. Never answered my question."

Hoinski stood, started around the desk. "Probably shocked speechless."

Linda pulled the door open and stepped into the hall. "Don't take this personally, Val, but when we finish with your boss and Dolan, they're going to wish they'd played this straight."

Hoinski took the door from Linda. "After you get over this, give me a call. I promised Bert I'd give you some career advice. Meantime, get a written commendation for your handling of this case put into your personnel file."

"Why?"

"Just do it." Hoinski pulled the door closed.

After she got over this? If women had cojones, Hoinski's would be brass. Outside the Albany County Courthouse, Linda allowed herself several minutes to cool off before calling Bert, who was also the father of her ex-boyfriend. Her junior year of college, she'd done a lengthy internship with Bert's lobbying firm and discovered she wanted no part of politics.

"Bad news, Kiddo." Bert took her call with the ceremony of an assassin.

"I just left your friend Val. Endangering, right?"

"Worse."

"She lied?"

"She doesn't know yet. This came down 10 minutes ago. Tillinghast walks, and on your back."

"Bullshit!"

"Afraid not."

"My bosses won't stand for that. Forget me. They'll look like fools."

"They got nothing to say about it, trust me."

"Where's this coming from?"

"Second floor."

The second floor of the state Capitol housed offices for the governor and his top staff. "Shit!"

"The family gave him a hundred grand last year alone. One other thing you should know. Before he went on the bench, Shane Dolan played step-and-fetch-it shyster for the Tillinghasts."

Though Dolan and the DA drove the cart, Linda focused on the State Police and governor about to betray her. "Can't argue with a hundred grand worth of logic, can you?"

"Not in my world. I can't blame you for being pissed off."

"Bert, pissed doesn't even begin to describe my feelings. Do me a favor and nail these fuckers."

"That's my girl. Brown will eat this up. He'll scoop the tabloids."

Alfred Brown was a columnist for the Albany Times Herald who often exposed government corruption. Bert had taught her to distrust all reporters, his only exception being Brown. She couldn't change the inevitable, but she could make life uncomfortable for a few days for the folks about to screw her.

Driving back to Troop G headquarters, she couldn't escape the whore feeling she experienced the night before in Jack's car. She went willingly, allowed a man to use her, all for a certain payoff. Now what did she have to show for her work? Nothing. The john paid the pimps and walked away. Hard to blame the outcome on the john. No, the problem was her pimps.

***

Linda stewed for two hours in her thoughts of pimps and whores, her anger rising by the minute. By the time the brass learned what Bert had gotten from his friend Jim Tonelli, the governor's chief of staff, Linda's anger approached the boiling point. She'd made her decision and knew exactly how to handle what came next.

The meeting took place in a windowless interview room with bare walls and overhead fluorescent light. Her report sergeant, Marty LeBeouf, and BCI Detective Mike Ewing, who'd organized the sting and recruited her, occupied two of the four metal folding chairs around the small square table.

Linda paused at the doorway. "Are we expecting anyone else?"

"Close the door and sit," LeBeouf said, his face taut. Like all the other males in the State Police hierarchy, LeBeouf said he wanted her to succeed. Unlike the others, he managed to convince her he meant it. His bio pegged his age at early 40s, like her mother. The gray hair suggested a decade older, her father's age. His physique and demeanor, more akin to the late-20s peacocks like Ewing, made the gray even more shocking.

"Captain Walker got a call from Judge Dolan this afternoon. He's not happy about the conversation." Ewing's tone suggested he shared Walker's sentiments. He was a kid compared to LeBeouf, the contrast underscored by the more relaxed dress of the detective. No more than five or six years older than she, cute, actually. She wondered if any of the people he arrested had ever asked *him* for ID. It figured Dolan would call Walker. She'd drawn an impression of Captain Theodore Walker as keeper of the sod in an organization still sensitive about male turf. Hoinski's remark confirmed the observation.

Dolan had some damned nerve, though. She brought him a pervert who preyed on young girls and during the entire arraignment, he eyed her, undressing her as if she appeared before him for prostitution. Then he sprung the predator to prey again with a "Sorry for the inconvenience" farewell. Bastard was lucky she curbed herself and stuck to an oral reaction. Now he had the balls to call the brass? Unbelievable. "I'm sorry, Detective. I made the remark in an emotional state. The words were ill advised. I won't repeat the mistake. The captain should tell Judge Dolan I recognize the gravity of my error. If need be, I will apologize in person."

They stared at her as if she'd just spoken in tongues. The two men exchanged eye contact before LeBeouf returned to her. "The DA has a problem with the bust."

"No."

"Yes, procedural stuff, mostly technical crap about intent. Not your fault."

"We'll be reviewing our protocols to address the DA's issues," Ewing added.

"Oh, good, I'm glad I did it right. I was afraid I might make a mistake."

"No, you did your part perfectly." LeBeouf's tension had eased.

"Then I wouldn't be out of line requesting a commendation for my personnel file?"

"Consider it done. You do understand the judge will dismiss all charges, right?" LeBeouf sounded wary.

"Of course. If we can't be sure of the guy's intent, we can't expect to convict him. I thought I knew. Guess I was wrong."

"We'll fix our protocols. Next time, you'll nail the guy." Ewing smiled.

"Well, about next time, it won't be me. I learned I'm not cut out for this."

"What are you talking about?" Ewing asked. "You did great."

"I'm not going into details, but the tape doesn't show what I endured from the scumbag. He made me so sick I nearly puked on him. Now, the thought of a sex predator even looking at me makes me a wreck. I hate to project the overwrought woman, but the emotion is so powerful, I just can't deal with the stress. Not advisable exposing me. Maybe I'll change, but for now, I'm sorry."

The two men were staring at each other when Linda stood and left the room. Like Val Hoinski, she needed this job. She'd worked too long and hard getting here to be dissuaded by Tillinghast, Dolan and their brethren. The good old boys would not drive her out. This was her life's work. Her destiny.

CHAPTER 2

He was mad at her. She'd walked nearly six blocks past the high school when she began to worry. She stopped. The first time, on Tuesday, she'd smiled and waved to him from the sidewalk. On Wednesday, she'd approached the curb and peeked inside his van. Yesterday she'd talked to him when he told her about the falls, a spectacular show of nature in early March, thanks to the snowmelt. She'd almost gotten in, but decided, hand on the door handle, the time wasn't right. That may have been a mistake.

Today would be their day. She'd made up her mind. If only he would show.

He likes you, Lilith. You can tell just by the way he watches you. He'll be here.

She resumed walking, slower now. The black panel van passed, and crept to the curb ahead of her. A surge of excitement ran through her as powerful as the spring runoff swelling the nearby Mohawk River. She reached the passenger door and glanced at her reflection in the tinted glass. Would he like the way she dressed today? The window retracted. She tugged at the straps of her backpack and cast her eyes down.

"Hey, cutie."

She looked up and smiled.

"I just drove by the falls. They're running hard. We should go."

11

"Gee, I don't know." He smiled at her, and she felt the itch that had been building all week, growing each time he was near. Her conscience made an ill-timed appearance dispensing advice: She shouldn't go. If anyone found out, her life would be hell, her reputation shot. She should fight the itch.

Yeah, whatever.

"You're a pretty girl, but you probably know that."

She patted her hair. The man called her pretty. The itch was winning. "Just to look at the falls?" she asked.

"Sure. There's a place no one else goes. We'll watch the falls, and then I'll drive you home."

She climbed in the passenger seat, dropping her backpack beside the door. The front cabin was roomy. A smoked panel obscured the back of the van.

Close up, the man was much more attractive than she had imagined. He might be only a few years older. He smiled, his charm pushing 10 on the enchantment meter. Even if it *was* wrong, nobody would find out. She pulled the door shut, the window rose, and the van rolled from the curb.

"Do I need my seatbelt?" He wasn't wearing his.

"We're not going far."

They rode in silence for a few minutes, but the man's smile vanished. The door locks clicked. He glanced repeatedly into the rear and side view mirrors. His wariness made her nervous. Had she made a mistake?

The man turned from his mirrors. His smile returned, his face relaxed. Whatever worried him was gone. "I didn't catch your name, cutie."

"Lilith."

"What grade are you, Lillian?"

"It's Lilith, and I'm a sophomore."

More silence and mirror checking. She studied his face, and realized, too late, she shouldn't have told him her grade. He probably thought a girl her age too immature for a man like him. Untrue, of course, but he couldn't know unless he gave her an opportunity to prove her maturity.

"So, you're like what, 17 or 18?" The van crossed a deserted parking lot overlooking the Mohawk several hundred yards downstream from the Cohoes Falls.

"Sixteen. Well actually, 15 going on." The van stopped at an ideal viewing location. The man killed the engine.

"You look older. I bet people tell you you're mature for your age."

She nodded, focused on the raging water. "Wow, you weren't kidding. The falls are awesome."

"They're beautiful, Lillian, but nowhere near as beautiful as you." He leaned toward her, put his arm around her shoulder.

A current rippled through her. "You think so? I'm beautiful?"

"I mean it. And sexy." He slid from the seat to his knees facing her. His lips sought hers. The suddenness of his move surprised her, and she turned her head. He nibbled on her earlobe, blowing softly in her ear. His breath smelled minty and his cheek scratched against hers. He tugged her skirt up. She'd expected this, but imagined doing it herself when the time was right.

"Wait." The fleeting image of a laughing face crossed her mind followed by the ping of red buttons on a white ceramic floor. The man nudged his shoulder between her knees, prying her legs apart. It was happening again, only this time in fast forward. She gasped. "No, please."

"God, you're beautiful." His fingers tugged at the waistband of her panties.

She tried to wriggle free but he had her pinned against the seat back. She pushed his shoulder, solid. She'd said no, but he didn't stop. The laughing face hadn't stopped either. Maybe this man thought her "please" meant she wanted him to continue. She couldn't have that on her conscience. "Stop. I don't want you-"

"Sure you do, Lillian. You came because you want me. Just like I want you. We're going to get what we both want."

At that moment, any doubt she harbored vanished. "You're right." She whispered in his ear. "This is what I hoped would happen."

Linda Baldwin had spent nearly seven years, hundreds of training sessions and thousands of hours of disciplined practice, all directed toward an unknown future moment in time.

Now.

Her fist smashed his Adam's apple. *He didn't see that coming, Lilith.*

The man exhaled. His head snapped forward, thumping her chest. She grabbed a handful of hair, yanked his head up. She speared an open palm under his chin driving his shoulders back against the dash panel. The man had yet to react before she'd slid the key ring from the ignition, grabbed her backpack, and slipped from the van. She straightened her clothes and pulled the gun from her pack.

She circled to the driver side, opened the door, waved the gun and shouted over the raging river's roar. "License and registration!"

"Jesus, don't shoot me." They were both shouting now. The words sounded shaky, like a deathbed confession even the speaker didn't believe. "I didn't do nothing."

"Got that right, asshole. Thirty seconds. I'm counting." Now came the real danger. If she didn't move fast and put on a convincing act, someone might call her bluff. "Nineteen, eighteen…"

"Shit! Hold on," he rasped.

It was the damned gun, which she handled with proficiency — on paper, anyway. She'd proven her ability to shoot down cardboard targets and human silhouettes. Her sensei had taught the awesome power of imagery, a technique she'd mastered so well she routinely subdued opponents nearly twice her size. But she could not envisage shooting a human being; not even this one.

The man produced the documents. The name read Steven Paquin. The paperwork was in order. The plates, however, did not match the registration. She stashed the papers in her backpack.

"Hey, I need them back."

"Out!"

"I don't think so."

She raised the gun to eye level. "Now!"

Paquin descended as if stepping on thin ice. "This is entrapment." He shouted, his words barely audible.

"Call the cops. You'll want to ditch the stolen plates first."

She returned the gun to her backpack. Paquin's bluster had faded to silence, but he watched intently as she zipped up the pack and strung it across her back. "I recorded our little encounter, Mr. Paquin, but today's your lucky day. I'm not calling the cops." No, should the local cops show, *she'd* land in deeper shit than he.

Paquin's right hand uppercut came as no surprise. She'd emboldened others by abandoning the gun. Linda looked forward to this part of her routine, left disappointed when a scumbag chose not to take a run at her. She dodged his fist and set herself to land a quick kick to his groin. Perverts who preyed on young girls deserved much more. Regrettably, most sex predators dodged a victim complaint, even fewer were prosecuted, and only a fraction convicted and punished. Although meager, a kick in the balls would have to do.

Her legs gave way. *What the hell?* She collapsed to her knees, realizing Paquin had used the punch to mask the kick that buckled her.

Paquin wrapped an arm around her neck, dragged her backwards. Linda's initial shock turned to terror when the side door of the van slid open revealing a makeshift bed. Panic overcame her, just as it had that afternoon, years ago.

Sensei Allan had spent seven years teaching her how to protect herself. A key tenet involved dealing with panic. On a cerebral level, she understood everything about its paralyzing effects, and devastating consequences. But panic knew her as well, peering into the darkest moments of her past, preserving the memories she'd tried to bury. She might school herself in martial arts, but if she failed to control panic, she would live out her life as the weak defenseless little girl she'd been in high school. From somewhere, Sensei's words penetrated the panic. *Calm. Think.*

Paquin paused. Linda seized the opportunity to get her legs under her. She swiveled her head, loosening his arm from her neck. She tried to pull away. Paquin jerked her back. She dropped her resistance, drove herself into the man. He stumbled back, as she landed two quick rabbit punches to his kidneys. He sprawled backward on the mattress. She pounced, slamming a knee in his groin. Paquin screamed and reached out for her. Linda brushed his arms aside and kneed him a second time. He groaned and fell silent.

"Did I make you feel like a man, Mr. Paquin?"

"Bitch."

She backed out of the van, shut the door, and jogged across the parking lot. At the street, she slowed to a walk and headed toward downtown and the city's lone taxi stand. Normally it would be a leisurely stroll basking in satisfaction of a job well done. But today, the shaking that started the minute she left Paquin would not leave. Her hands shook and her legs felt weak. Try as she might, she could not escape the terror of falling to her knees before a sex predator.

The trembling provided a timely reminder of the dangerous game she played. Though she stacked the deck in her favor, the sting was never a sure thing. It took an incident like this to remind her of the risks she took, professionally and personally. Insane. The time had come to stop the game. She walked several blocks considering the simplicity of her logic. Gradually, the trembling receded and the old spring returned to her step.

She stopped abruptly when an SUV glided to the curb across the street. The man behind the wheel stared at her. Having slipped back from Lilith mode, a few seconds passed before she realized what he was doing. She smiled at him. *See that man, Lilith, he's undressing you.* Linda glanced at her watch. She'd never done two in one day, but why not?

Stop the game? Who was she kidding? It never ended. There would always be adult men with unholy designs on underage girls. That's how the world worked. For a woman like herself, the realities made her choice simple: play the game, or become a spectator and pray for good to conquer evil. The folly of the proposition made her smile.

She waved at the man, stepped off the curb, started across the street, her eyes fixed on him. The window closed and the vehicle sped off. A horn blared. A Cohoes police cruiser had stopped not more than 10 feet away. She'd not seen the car coming.

A uniformed man emerged. Linda put her head down, turned, and started walking.

"Watch where you're going, young lady. You could have been hurt."

"Sorry, officer," she shouted, raising an arm and picking up her pace. She walked two blocks, not daring even a peek back, fearful the cop had decided to follow. She arrived at the taxi stand and ventured a look: no police. Relief flooded her while she waited inside for her ride.

Hey, Lilith, I don't think Mr. Paquin likes you. He called you a bitch.

For the first time that day, Linda laughed. A few minutes later, she realized the woman dispatcher eyed her, as if Linda had armed robbery in mind. She was grateful when the cab showed.

The taxi dropped her on North Mohawk Street. Linda ducked into an alley, crossed a second and emerged through a third onto Cataract Street, two doors from her apartment. The sight of a uniformed officer sitting on the hood of her Corvette stopped her.

"Nice car you got here, Miss Baldwin. Or should I say Trooper Baldwin?"

"The name's Linda."

"Your old man bought you the wheels, didn't he?"

"Why? You think I stole it?"

"Nice guy, your father. Most geniuses are off the wall, but he's like a regular person."

Her father was one of the world's most respected nanoscientists. He was also the world's greatest dad, a title that had nothing to do with the red Corvette convertible he'd bought her when she graduated high school. "Can I help you, officer? I believe the car is parked legally."

The man stood, wearing a "don't fuck with me" face, a permanent fixture she guessed. "Sergeant Rick Michaud and no, I don't want your help. That's why I'm here. If I wanted help, I'd be out at Troop G talking to Marty LeBeouf. Know the guy?"

"My report sergeant. So what?" How did he get LeBeouf?

"You state fucks make me laugh. You think small town cops are a bunch of dumb hicks?"

Not the Cohoes PD, which had a reputation as one of the finest small city forces in the country. "Nope."

"You go parading past Rosie, half a dozen times and you're not a student, she'll dime you every time. Yesterday was *your* day. Easy trail from there."

Linda pieced it together. The school crossing guard had seen the taxi a few times, grown suspicious and called Michaud, who visited the dispatcher and traced her to her neighborhood. Then what? Had to be her red Corvette convertible which she'd parked near the school one day when the cab failed to show. If the guard was as observant as Michaud claimed, she would have mentioned a red convertible. He must have run the plate, seen a familiar name, made a few phone calls, and pieced together a nice hypothesis. Accurate conjecture, but with no solid proof. "Congratulations. Now if you'll excuse me…" Linda started up the porch steps.

"My buddy, Bigwater, told me you were a wise-ass. He forgot to mention the dumb-ass part."

The name nearly made her stop and turn, but she didn't want Michaud to see the fear in her eyes. She opened the hall door.

"Listen, Baldwin, the only thing keeping me from calling your boss is I know your dad and I like him. Bought you one pass. You just used it. My advice would be to stop your game, but whether you take it or not, you keep it the fuck out of Cohoes or you'll wish you never met me. You hear me?"

Loud and clear. The door creaked shut behind her. Michaud had talked to Bigwater about her.

Shit!

CHAPTER 3

The radio squawked. "We got a disturbing the peace at Crooked Lake."

Linda set down the radar gun and reported her proximity. The dispatcher gave her the location. She turned on her flashers, pressed the pedal to the floor. The patrol car lurched toward Lakeshore Road. Five minutes later, she doused the flashers and bounced along a rutted single lane searching for the address.

She angled the car across the three parked in the dirt drive. The blare of hip hop assaulted her before she cut the engine. Another party happening, and as usual, Linda without invitation. She stepped from the car to a chill air smelling of decayed leaves, fresh-cut Christmas trees and cigarette smoke.

Disturbing the peace, the dispatcher had told her. How about inane lyrics set to asinine music? Hip hop, hip hop, beat that ho. As if there weren't enough violence aimed at women. Jesus! She stepped over a crusty patch of snow at the foot of the wooden steps and climbed the stairs.

She tapped the door, which swung in. A rush of cigarette smoke blew past her, surviving the pot sniff-test. Beer cans littered the coffee and end tables, surrounding two overflowing ashtrays. She counted six people, not one of whom noticed her presence. Understandable, for sure, because the six were three couples. A pang of envy passed through her.

On an overstuffed chair, a girl sat facing a boy, her pink blouse un-tucked from the black skirt hiked up to her waist. Her hips ground against him, her hands clasped behind his neck. His arms extended, hands covered by the skirt fabric mounded in his lap.

Another girl sprawled on the sofa. Her head rested in a boy's lap. Her back was bare except for the unclasped black lacy bra strap. A throw pillow covered the girl's head. The third pair sat on a love seat swapping a lit cigarette and a beer. A blanket covered them, a pile of clothes at their feet. Linda thought she recognized a cheerleader uniform beneath the underwear.

"Hi, guys. About the noise…" Linda shouted above the pounding rap music. One girl stopped grinding and another popped her head from under the pillow. The boy on the overstuffed chair reached back and the music stopped. A flurry of movement followed, frantic and brief. The half-dozen party animals covered and sat at attention. Deflation hung heavy. "Any of you old enough to buy beer?"

The kids exchanged glances, but no one answered, no one moved.

The girl with pink blouse moved her head close to her boyfriend's, her voice a hiss. "I told you it was…"

"Quiet, the officer wants to talk." The boy offered a grim smile.

What did she tell him? Something Linda should know about.

In the silence, an encrypted message flashed, and she was the only one without the secret decoder. She checked the anxious eyes flitting around the room and chose her target. She fixed her eyes on the girl from under the pillow, now sitting primly next to her boyfriend. She turned her head. Linda waited. Her gaze returned. "I asked you a question."

"It was just a-"

Her partner shook his head and nudged her. "Tiffany's 17."

"A what?"

"Little party," he said. "We're not hurting anybody. That's what she meant."

Linda kept her eyes fixed on the girl. "I wasn't talking to you, Sparky, so shut up. Finish the sentence, Tiffany. It was just a…"

The girl surveyed the room. She checked her hands, stole a glance at the boy, who put an arm around her shoulders, the cue Tiffany needed.

"Yeah, a little party. Jenna and Jeremy invited us. We didn't think we were bothering anybody."

"Really?" Linda saw no obvious evidence of drug use, but she'd bet a month's pay they were covering something.

Tiffany was ready to talk. It wouldn't take much. Isolate her, split the rest of the kids up and keep them guessing which set of lies their friends were using. She'd need backup. "OK, which one of you is Jenna, and who's Jeremy?"

"They're upstairs," the cheerleader's boyfriend said. "Are you a real trooper?"

"Shut the fuck up, John." Tiffany's guy shouted.

John's stating the question was the only surprise. Most folks thought it but said nothing. These kids were looking at her and thinking she was just a kid too. Why not? She could still pass for a teen. The uniform conferred an aura of maturity, undermined by the five-two and eyes of blue package that looked better suited for a high school art class.

The girls were thinking she'd picked a stupid costume to crash a party. The boys figured without a gun, they'd put her away. Hopefully they wouldn't do anything dumb. Lilith had enough excitement for one day. "OK, here's what we're going to do. You're all going to dress, show me some ID-"

Somewhere, a female voice screamed, "No, Jeremy. Don't." Linda's blood chilled. She pointed to John. "Jenna?"

"Yes." He nodded toward the staircase

Linda shouted, "Nobody leaves. I have your plate numbers. My partner is close by."

They might not buy the bluff, but she had to try. She spun around and took the steps two at a time. She placed a quick call for backup. A deep voice from down the hall said, "Yes, Jenna, we do it my way."

Linda rushed toward the sound.

"Jeremy, no. Please."

The desperation in the girl's voice fueled Linda's resolve. She stopped at a door where bedsprings squeaked. The handle refused to turn. "Open the door."

21

"We're busy," the deep voice shouted. Linda stepped back and kicked. The wood door splintered, crashed against the wall and recoiled. She stepped across the threshold and froze at the sight. A girl lay on the bed, legs up and spread, a black skirt bunched around her waist, red sweater and black bra beneath her chin. Beside her head lay a pair of black underwear.

For the second time today, an image of red buttons and torn black panties on white ceramic flashed in her mind. Bile rose in Linda's throat. She swallowed hard and the acid retreated. The young woman's head was jammed against the brass tubing of the headboard. A man wearing a polo shirt and nothing else knelt between her legs. His head turned, as if in slow motion. He glanced at Linda. One hand flew from the girl's breast. The other released the grip on her shoulder.

Linda opened her mouth to speak, but nothing came out. The words formed in her mind, but her brain had lost control of her vocal cords. Without warning, a powerful urge to leave the bedroom gripped her. The man stared at her.

A small water stain marked the wood planks covering the wall behind the bed, as if the framed Jesus minding the bed had shed tears. The girl lay motionless, her eyes darting between Linda and the man kneeling between her legs. They finally fixed on Linda, the fear in them a stark reminder that the uniform conferred a duty. "Off the bed! Pants on!"

The man stood, making her feel like Jack gazing up the beanstalk. Like Jack, she was eager to hack this one down.

The young woman pulled her sweater down, tugged her skirt back into place, and slid off the bed. The man said, "Come here, baby." Her eyes darted from Linda to the man buckling the belt on his jeans. She didn't move.

"How old are you, Jeremy?"

"Eighteen."

"Jenna?" The girl appeared frozen in place. "Jenna?" Nothing. "Jenna, can you tell me what happened?"

Jeremy moved to Jenna. He put his arm around her waist. "See, officer, Jenna loves to act. She does it all the time." Jenna jerked to attention at Jeremy's words. Pure terror registered in her face. He nudged Jenna. "You love to act. Ain't that right, baby?" Jenna pulled away from him. "Come on, Jenna, this ain't funny. The cop thinks I was trying to hurt you. Tell her it wasn't that way."

Jenna looked at Jeremy and blinked. She turned to Linda and shook her head, the shock and horror showing no sign of receding.

"Hands off, Jeremy. I want to talk to her alone. You stay put." She ushered Jenna into the hall near the top of the staircase where she could keep one eye on the splintered bedroom door. Where was her backup? She waited, watching Jenna for a sign of composure, her ears attuned to the hushed conversations floating up the stairs. Ten minutes passed and still no backup. Jenna was ready to talk.

"What's your last name, Jenna?"

"Jarosz."

"How old are you?"

"Almost 16."

Statutory rape. "Aren't you young to be hanging with this crowd?"

"Yeah? How old are you?"

The girl had a point: she was the victim. Linda was not here to judge. "Why don't you tell me what happened?"

"It's not my fault. I told Jeremy not to."

"You're right, this is not your fault."

They'd need to preserve the evidence. "When we finish here, I'll get you some medical attention."

"I don't need any. For what?"

"It's a precaution we take with victims."

"Victims?"

"What Jeremy did to you is a crime."

Jenna digested Linda's words, and blurted out, "He didn't fuck me."

Though Linda had witnessed the copulation, Jenna's response was no surprise. Denial was a common victim response in the early post-rape stages. "I want to help you through this, Jenna, but I'm going to insist you tell me the truth, even if it hurts."

The girl looked away. Linda pulled a small spiral-bound notebook and pen from her shirt pocket to record the interview. In the distance, a siren wailed. Tears began streaming down Jenna's cheeks. She sobbed. "I thought I was ready. I love Jeremy and I wanted to fuck him, but he scared me. I asked him to stop, but…"

Downstairs a deep voice boomed, "Good evening, my name is Trooper Bigwater." Jenna jerked her head back to Linda, terror in her eyes.

"It's OK. He's my partner." Bigwater! She'd be better off with a rattlesnake for backup. "I need to talk to him for a second." She shouted into the staircase. "Bigwater, up here."

He climbed halfway and stopped. "Ain't this just my luck?"

"Nice seeing you too, Bigwater. ID the kids. Find out who bought the beer and what they know about what was going on upstairs."

"What was that?"

"Statutory rape at the least. You got six downstairs?"

"Statutory between two kids? Bullshit if you ask me. You got six now."

Linda had graduated the academy with Bigwater and knew better than ask his opinion on sex crimes. "Someone left the party just when the fun was starting?"

"Cute little cheerleader, found her running down the road. Told her about all the perverts prowling dark places like Lakeshore Road."

"She got in your car anyway?"

"Fuck you, Baldwin."

"Grab her cell and keep her isolated for now. I may need her later. Lean on the other five hard before releasing them to a parent or legal guardian. They're covering up something that went down before I showed."

"I'll get right on it, *Detective* Baldwin."

"I'm serious. Take the Tiffany girl first. She'll be the one who talks if anyone."

"Here's a news flash, Baldwin. I don't take orders from you." He backed down the stairs. A few seconds later, his official voice drifted upward. "Listen up, folks. Here's what I want."

Linda called dispatch, requested a third unit, and tuned out Bigwater. She turned back to Jenna, who'd stopped crying. "You told Jeremy to stop. Then what?"

"He kept going. Next thing, he was in me. It hurt."

"OK, Jenna, these next questions are the most important ones. Did you want to have sex with Jeremy?"

"Well, I…"

"The truth, Jenna. Yes or no."

"Yes."

"At some point before engaging in sex, did he frighten you, causing you to change your mind?"

"You mean before he fucked me."

Linda nodded.

"OK, then, yes."

"When you decided not to have sex, did you tell Jeremy so and out loud?"

"Yes."

"Do you remember the exact words?"

Jenna thought a moment. "I think I said, 'No Jeremy, don't.'"

Audible downstairs, so Jeremy had certainly heard. "Then what did Jeremy do?"

"He fucked me."

"Do you mean Jeremy inserted his penis into your vagina after you told him no?"

"Yeah, that."

"Thank you, Jenna. We're through for now. Tomorrow, we'll do this again, same questions. I'll write everything down, and you'll have a chance to read your statement. When you tell me the words are right, I'll ask you to sign it. Do you understand what I'm saying about what will happen next?" Jenna nodded. "I'd like you to wait downstairs. I have to talk to Jeremy. I won't be long. Then we'll call your parents and have them meet us at the hospital."

"I'm not going to a hospital."

"I'm afraid you'll have to. If we want to make Jeremy accountable for what he did to you, we need to have you seen by a doctor."

"I still love him. I don't want to get him in trouble."

Linda felt for the girl. Love at 15 was a potent emotion, especially in young women. Jenna had to be a jumble of them, feelings that would likely shift over the next few days. The rape kit could not wait for Jenna to realize Jeremy had raped her, her love for him notwithstanding.

"Tell you what, Jenna. We'll get the test done, but we won't do anything without your OK. Will you do it?"

Jenna nodded. "I don't want any trouble for Jeremy."

She forced a smile. Jenna was growing up for a life of abuse. "I'm only investigating. I have your side of the story. Now it's Jeremy's turn. I'll be back soon."

Linda peeked around the bedroom door and found Jeremy pacing back and forth. She opened the door and stepped inside. "What's your last name, Jeremy?"

"Cronin." Worry showed on his face.

"Jeremy Cronin, you're under arrest for rape."

He digested the charges looking bewildered. The tension drained. He laughed. "What did you say?"

"You think this is a joke?"

"It *is* a joke. You want to know what we-"

"Shut up, Jeremy, and listen to me."

"We were just doing-"

"Listen to me!" Linda noted his clenched fists. Good for him. He wasn't going to take this lying down. "You have a right to remain silent, and you have a right to an attorney, but if you waive those rights, now that I've advised you of them, anything you tell me can be used to convict you. Do you understand?"

"Yeah, you cunts get to say you changed your mind and call it rape."

Did you hear that, Lilith? He expects you to take it lying down, like Jenna and all the other young women he's forced himself into. She took a quick step toward him. Jeremy raised an arm, fist still clenched. Her snap kick found his knee. He sucked air and keeled forward. She thrust her palm under his chin. A jolt rippled down her arm. Something cracked. He fell to his knees. She grabbed his wrist and twisted, forcing him to the side of the bed. With her free hand, she jammed his face into the brass. "A woman says no, that means no." Jeremy groaned. Linda leaned forward and whispered. "Did I make you feel like a man?"

She yanked his head back by the hair and examined his face. No cuts and no blood. That was good, though she hoped his skull throbbed as much as her elbow did. She cuffed his hands to the headboard behind his back. "I'll be back after I figure out where you're going to spend the night."

"You mean jail?"

Damn right, she meant jail. The kid deserved a whole night with Lilith, but he'd be a lot safer in the county jail. She descended the stairs to a clean living room where Jenna sat on a sofa staring into space. A full trash bag, neatly tied, sat on the front porch, where Bigwater stood talking to a man she guessed was one of the parents. A third patrol car, lights ablaze, sat idling behind Bigwater's.

"Jenna, do you want me to call your parents?"

Jenna snapped her head up, eyes wide. "No, let me." She pulled out a cell phone, wandered into the bathroom, and closed the door.

Bigwater returned to the living room. "What did the kids say?" she asked.

"Name, rank and serial number. Nothing went on upstairs and nobody knew where the beer came from."

"What did you get from Tiffany?"

Bigwater looked at her as if she were the village idiot. He tore out several pages of notebook.

"OK, I'll take those," she said

"No you won't. I'll file my own." A big grin spread over his face. "But I do have this." He reached into his shirt pocket, and extracted a single folded sheet of paper.

"What's this?"

27

"Special arraignment. Orders from above."

"Yeah? Who?"

"Doesn't matter. You know whose place this is?"

"Perp's name is Cronin. I assumed the camp belongs to his family."

"Bingo!"

"Meaning…?"

His grin turned to a snarl. "Let's get something straight, Baldwin. I haven't forgotten. I'm going to enjoy watching you twist. Your cheerleader's out back." He tossed a cell phone to Linda and stomped out the front door.

Bigwater was a dull toothache. Eventually it would require extraction. Linda started toward the rear of the camp, where a young woman in a white uniform stood, arms crossed, on an enclosed porch that faced a frozen lake. "You got my fuckin' phone? That asshole stole it." The girl pointed to the front door. "I'm calling my lawyer."

"What's your name?" The cheerleader wore a matching white skirt and blouse uniform with navy blue trim and lettering. The "SGH" stitched into the top served to accentuate an ample pair of breasts.

The girl stomped a sneakered foot. "I know my rights." Her emerald eyes sparkled and her auburn curls rippled when she set her jaw and tossed her head. Linda admired her spunk, but she needed the girl's help. She reached along her belt for the pouch holding the second pair of cuffs, pulled them out and allowed them to dangle at her side.

"What are those for?"

"These? I'm not sure. What did you say your name was?"

"Heather."

"That's it?"

"Gaines. Heather Gaines."

"I have a few questions."

"Why'd that jerk make me stay? I didn't do nothin'."

"Consuming beer when under the age of 21 is hardly *nothing*." Linda felt like a shit.

"How come you didn't arrest the others?"

"Well, you see, Heather, I'm a reasonable woman. They obeyed my order to stay put, so I was willing to let the beer slide. My partner got their stories, so I'm happy. Then there's you." Linda flipped the dangling cuff with her wrist.

"What do you want?"

"The truth. All your friends told us the same story. If yours lines up, we'll be square."

Tibbs Figueroa appeared at the front door. She'd graduated the academy with Tibbs and he'd become a friend, as good a one as she had these days. "Hey, Tibbs, back here." Linda rattled the cuffs and pointed at the couch Jenna had vacated. "Can I trust you to stay put on the sofa over there, Heather, or do I have to cuff you?"

Heather put her hands behind her back and hurried to the main room.

Figueroa shook his head as he approached. "Your good buddy, Bigwater, had some choice words for you, Linda."

"I'm shocked! Did you search?" Jenna emerged from the bathroom and wandered to the front door. Linda kept one eye on her.

"The place, them, and all three cars. No one objected, so I don't think it was drugs, if they were even hiding something."

"You had to see the reaction when I got here. Something they didn't want to talk about went down. I'm positive."

"OK, but I didn't see it. I'm going by what I observed. Hate to say so, but I agree with Bigwater."

"Talk to any of the kids?"

"Bigwater told me to lean on a Tiffany."

"And?"

"Strange. She seemed embarrassed talking to me about the party. Just beer and loud music?"

"Plus I caught them with their pants down." Jenna craned her neck outside and then stole a glance back at Tibbs and Linda. It seemed strange Jenna made no move to speak to Heather. "Walk with me, Tibbs."

Tibbs followed. "Ah, that explains Tiffany's reaction."

"I suppose." Her gut said otherwise.

Jenna bolted out of sight. Linda rushed to the porch. Below, Jenna sprinted to an idling car. Linda yelled to Jenna. The door slammed. The car drove off. She stepped back inside. "Heather, do you know where Jenna lives?"

"Off 20, I think. There's a small development behind the car wash."

"You want me to grab her now?" Tibbs asked.

"We got no cause. I wanted the hospital to collect a rape kit."

"Rape?" Heather shouted.

"Follow them, Tibbs. Make sure the driver knows you're behind, but no siren or lights. If they don't head in that general direction, pull them over, make something up, and call me. Go!"

Tibbs ran to the car.

Heather's face was somber. "Rape? Do you really think Jeremy, you know, raped Jenna?"

"Right now, I'm more interested in what happened downstairs."

Ten minutes later, Linda closed her notebook, and thanked Heather for her cooperation. She climbed the stairs to retrieve Jeremy, unshackled him from the bed, and allowed him to use the bathroom. Linda secured him in the backseat of the patrol car. Heather occupied the front passenger seat.

"Where are we going?" Jeremy sounded worried.

"I'm taking Heather home."

"What about me?"

"Heather, have you ever seen the inside of the county jail?"

"You can't just stick me in jail like that!"

Only because the decision wasn't hers. "Shut up. I'm in no mood to talk."

No one spoke the rest of the way to Heather's house. A few minutes after she left Heather off, Jeremy said, "This isn't the way to the jail."

Linda ignored the remark. She drove, recounting the statement Heather had given with only a minimal amount of added cajoling and bluster. Turned out the parties were Friday night rituals during basketball seasons. Jeremy had a key to the camp and boasted his father knew of the events and kept the refrigerator stocked with beer. He limited the affairs to four couples, and insisted they clean the place before leaving. An unspoken rule was only juniors and seniors could attend. Jenna was a sophomore, too immature to be dating a guy like Jeremy, according to Heather. The group was surprised when Jeremy brought "the kid," as Heather referred to Jenna. No one said anything because the place was his, but Jenna's presence was clearly a problem. Linda agreed with Heather, but kept the opinion to herself. The fact Jenna didn't belong didn't excuse Jeremy's deed. As for downstairs, either Heather was a convincing liar, or the scene Linda found was exactly that and nothing more. She leaned toward the liar explanation. People routinely lied to law enforcement, the only issue being the degree.

She glanced into the rearview mirror at Jeremy Cronin's expressionless face and thought about how the worried look on his face turned to relief when she'd accused him of rape: he'd laughed at the charge. That took balls. The expression before she charged him intrigued her, though. What worried him so much, that a rape charge relieved him? Jeremy's fear coupled with the first reaction downstairs left no doubt something other than underaged drinking went down. Throw in the heavyweight who engineered a late-night arraignment within minutes of Bigwater's arrival, and her level of certainty doubled. She might be a rookie, but she'd been around long enough to know a town judge didn't rise in the middle of the night for just any old perp.

Tibbs called to tell her he followed the car to the Jarosz residence, where the woman driver and Jenna got out and went inside. Tibbs followed and rang the doorbell. Mrs. Jarosz thanked him for his concern, said she knew what was best for her daughter, goodnight. Linda thanked Tibbs and hung up.

***

A man wearing jeans and a paint-speckled canary-yellow T-shirt answered her knock at the majestic 19th century mansion. Schodack Town

Justice, William Cassidy, according to Bigwater's note. He introduced himself, closed the door behind them, and sat on a knotty pine bench in the foyer. Cassidy's pointy nose and jet-black pupils reminded Linda of a weasel. She sensed her control of Jeremy slipping in the invisible presence of money and power. The judge cast a glance at the handcuffs. "What do you have, trooper?"

"Felony rape, statutory at the minimum, Your Honor."

"Those are serious charges. What do you have to say for yourself, Jeremy?"

"This whole thing is a big misunderstanding, Mr. Cassidy. I swear to you, nothing happened and I didn't hurt anyone."

"Your Honor, I witnessed a rape in progress and the victim confirmed as much to me."

"Do we have a sworn statement?"

"Not yet. I made the arrest based on my observation of the sexual activity and the victim's confirmation the intercourse was not consensual."

"That's a lie, Mr. Cassidy."

"Be quiet, Jeremy." Cassidy's tone was fatherly patient. "Fine, trooper. Bring the sworn statement in Wednesday evening at seven and we'll straighten this out. Meantime, I'm releasing Mr. Cronin to parental custody." He nodded toward Jeremy's shackled wrists. "You can take those with you. I'll keep an eye on him until his father gets here."

Linda stood motionless, her eyes fixed on those of the judge. Another Judge Shane Dolan. She'd learned, though. The bastard had made her apologize in person. Damn near choked on her own words. "Certainly, Your Honor." She unsnapped her key ring from her belt and unlocked the cuffs.

As soon as his wrists were free, Jeremy said, "She threatened to put me in jail, Mr. Cassidy."

The judge threw her a questioning look.

"I'm afraid the perpetrator misunderstood." Linda smiled. "That was unfortunate. Goodnight."

As she pulled the door shut behind her, Cassidy said "You played a great game tonight, Jeremy."

CHAPTER 4

L inda closed her eyes. She inhaled deeply. The scent engulfed rational thought. Strong, robust, hot. Hard to imagine adding a man to the recipe could heighten the seductive allure of a venti espresso. Well, she *could* think of one. She opened her eyes, leaned back, sinking further into the brown overstuffed chair. The line of Starbucks patrons, short when she'd arrived a few minutes earlier, now stretched to the door. She unfolded the newspaper and pulled out the sports section. The front-page photo of Jeremy shooting a basketball produced a bitter taste. The image reminded her of a similar picture of Bill, in the same newspaper the morning after Cohoes High won the state Sectional Championship. The bitterness receded.

The thrill she'd experienced the day after the game dwarfed that of a basketball championship. *Seven years ago, Linda.* Might as well have been a century.

"Is this seat taken?"

Linda looked up, startled. A squat man with hair sprouting from nose and ears squinted down at her. He wasn't a regular. "No."

He dropped onto the chair alongside hers. "You're reading about the Cronin kid. Ever seen him play?"

"No."

33

"Let me tell you something, the kid's a natural talent. My name's Eric, by the way." The guy sounded like Jeremy's agent.

"Oh yeah, a real talent." Linda sipped her coffee and read. "Red-hot Cronin leads Greenbush, title game a squeaker."

"Don't believe me, do you?" He leaned toward her. Linda smelled the coffee on his breath. "I was at last night's game. Kid scored 28 points, blocked five shots, and pulled down 14 rebounds with dozens of scouts in attendance. Impressive, I tell you." He leaned back, screwed up his mouth, and muttered, "Still cost me a bundle."

"You bet against Greenbush?" If Eric were such a big Cronin fan, why would he bet the opponent?

He glanced at her uniform and then past her, as if searching for someone at the counter. "No. I...I uh made a bet with a friend of mine. I had to give him seven points. Greenbush won by three, so I lost."

"Too bad. Well, I imagine Cronin will make news again." Charged with rape, if justice prevailed.

"He sure will." She should stop encouraging him. "The Sectional tournament starts Wednesday night. With Cronin, nobody's going to beat Greenbush. You going?"

"This Wednesday?"

Eric smiled. "Yeah. I got two tickets. We could go."

"Sorry. I'm busy."

"A date?"

Linda smiled and nodded. A hot one. "Red Hot Cronin" had scored a court date with her on Wednesday evening, right around game time. She and the BCI team would get Jenna's sworn statement, leaving little room for Jeremy, or Judge Cassidy to slither away. She'd caught a rapist in the act, and the system would nail the perpetrator. Eric had buried his face in the New York Times. Her espresso remained hot, and the memory of Bill lingered. Things were going her way.

***

Early Saturday afternoon, Linda leaned over BCI Detective Ewing's black metal desk, her hands resting on a top littered with paperwork. "What the hell did you expect? I told her I'd be bringing the statement, and you send over a couple macho studs who probably reminded her of the guy who raped her."

"They didn't remind her of anyone. Never got past the old lady. She said Jenna was sorry for the misunderstanding, they talked the matter over as a family, and the girl decided not to press charges."

The office was no larger than the walk-in closet housing her mother's formal wear. With the four-drawer metal file cabinet and single guest chair stacked with file folders, the space felt about as stuffed as her mother's closet as well. "You think the old man bought her off?"

Ewing shrugged. In a tone suggesting an inquiry of her familiarity with God Almighty, he asked, "You know who Eddie Cronin is?"

She knew now. Bigwater's warning prompted an early morning call to Bert who had filled her in on Jeremy's father, some of which she had known but forgot in the heat of the events. Edward "Slick Eddie" Cronin served as Rensselaer County Republican chairman. County judges and prosecutors across the river from Albany County held their positions courtesy of Eddie Cronin's endorsement. The Albany Times Herald editorial writers had coined the nickname Slick. Eddie wasted no opportunity to tell the world he despised the newspaper. The writers reciprocated. Eddie missed the advisory about getting in a pissing contest with people who bought ink by the barrel. "What's that got to do with justice?"

"Speaking of justice, Cronin wants his son's arrest reviewed, claims you used excessive force."

"Jeremy Cronin is what, six-four and 200 pounds. I'm five-two and 120."

"You don't deny the claim?"

"Define excessive."

"I thought so. You taking this case, personally, Baldwin? Handing out a bit of your own justice?" Ewing leaned back in his chair, hands behind his head, and stretched his neck. His eyes never left her.

"Personally? What're you talking about? I walked into the middle of a rape. An 18-year-old old man forced himself on a 15-year-old girl half his size. Worse, I think it was her first time. Got any idea what that feels like, detective? No? I didn't think so." Ewing motioned her to back up. Without realizing, she'd invaded his space. She backed away. "Sorry."

Unless she imagined things, Ewing's eyes were undressing her. "Fine. Investigate."

"We will."

"Tell Mr. Cronin I welcome the scrutiny. I wonder if he will."

"What's that mean?"

"I can prove Eddie supplied the beer to those kids."

"I read Bigwater's report."

"Yeah?"

"He's sharp. You might learn something from him."

"Oh, I already did. Why don't you ask him about it?" But Ewing didn't hear the response. His eyes drank her in. Damn, she wasn't imagining. Men had one-track minds. She folded her arms across her chest. "What are you looking at?"

"Jesus, Baldwin, are you always like this, or do you have a soft side?"

Linda stifled the urge to reach across the desk, grab him by the throat, and tell him affirmative on the soft side. "Do you use that line on *ALL* your troopers, or just the one's with tits?"

Ewing glared at her. "LeBeouf wants to see you when you're done here. You're done." He picked up the phone, punched some numbers, and waved her out.

Linda stepped from the office and closed the door. *Screw you Detective Sergeant Ewing.* If she discovered a soft side, Ewing would never see it. No chance in hell.

BCI usually had a full plate. No wonder Ewing was happy to clear the Cronin case. She'd just have to persuade LeBeouf to let her investigate. They got along well. She didn't foresee a problem.

LeBeouf was waiting when she arrived at his office. "I read your report. What do you think happened?"

"Think? I witnessed Jeremy Cronin raping Jenna Jarosz and arrested him. Then, Eddie Cronin called the Jarosz family last night or early this morning and bought them off. I think the sale was easy, given Jenna still thinks she loves Jeremy and doesn't want to make trouble for him."

"So we have a crime with no complaint, an uncooperative victim, and no physical evidence. You know what BCI calls that?"

"Yes. There *is* the matter of what I witnessed."

"Drop it."

"Did Figueroa or Bigwater report a suspicion the kids were hiding something?"

"No. What makes *you* think so?"

"The initial reactions were weird. One girl volunteered an answer to a question I didn't ask, and another told her boyfriend it was a mistake. In both cases, the guys cut them off and finished the sentence. Something wasn't right. I would have bet drugs, but the place and the kids were clean."

LeBeouf smiled. "Any chance the girls were ashamed you caught them bare-assed and engaged?"

"Might have been your generation, but not this one. Today, girls swap digital pictures in cyberspace you and I would find shocking. Modesty is a lost virtue. There's more to this. Why don't I-"

"Stay out of it? Good idea, because that's what you're going to do."

"Why?"

"One, we don't have a complaint. Two, Eddie Cronin's got you in his sights. I don't want you anywhere near him, his kid or anyone else involved in this incident. You hear me?"

"What about my hunch-?"

"You're not listening."

"Something went down. If we lean on the kids just a little, we can find out."

LeBeouf shook his head. "It's a manpower issue."

"I volunteer."

"Absolutely not! Maybe I'll have someone take a look."

"Yeah, and maybe my lottery numbers will come up this week."

LeBeouf stood, moved around the desk, perched himself on the front of it. "Did Ewing talk to you about the sting?"

"I haven't changed my mind."

"No, the drinking age sting."

"Isn't that the State Liquor Authority?"

"When the Legislature screams, it becomes everybody's problem. They passed the laws, now they want enforcement. The governor expects all agencies to pitch in. We promised the locals a body 20 hours a week. Ewing thinks an attractive young woman could charm store clerks to ignore her ID. The multi-agency task force is ramping up for a big sweep in a few weeks. Fines for storeowners and prosecution for parents."

"Like Eddie Cronin? Sign me up."

"Get off Cronin, would you? This is serious."

"Sure it is. We'll round up some adults and charge them with endangering the welfare of a minor. The same outrageous deal Val Hoinski had ready to offer Tillinghast, until her boss and Dolan deemed the penalty too harsh. If you're an adult, it's OK to try to screw a 15-year-old as long as you don't buy her beer to grease her pants. You want to tell me we're serious? Don't make me laugh."

"You've got to lighten up."

"Put Jeremy Cronin behind bars and watch my mood brighten."

"We need to give the local authority a name, and soon. Training starts next week. Ewing wanted you. Seriously, he didn't mention the sting?"

"He may have tried."

"Tried."

Linda recounted the soft side exchange with Ewing. "Guess he never got the chance. You want me to talk to him?"

"No. I want you in. I'll tell him."

"Well then, I guess I'm in."

She left LeBeouf. They were insane, all those males: Eddie, Cassidy, Walker, Ewing and LeBeouf. A little sweet talk, a dab of salve, a pinch of shuck, a dash of jive, a mountain of smoke, a few mirrors, and presto, the pesky little rape disappeared. Everyone pretended nothing happened. She'd seen it, though, and she wasn't part of their club. Jeremy Cronin scared up memories of another time she pretended a rapist was not. She'd made a simple vow after that.

Never again! *What do you think Lilith, shall I tell the basketball star you're in, or should we surprise him?*

CHAPTER 5

Before he met Amy Farraday, Enrique Martinez had no opinion of libraries. They were just institutions with no relevance to his daily life, much like Congress and the Catholic Church, two organizations in which he'd once placed great faith. Had someone predicted, two months ago, he would spend an evening in a library, Martinez would have smiled. Had anyone bet him his library visit would be to discuss a chick-lit book with a dozen women and he the only male, he would have doubled down.

The ball-busting bitch eyed him as she spoke. "Objects of pleasure, nothing more. That's the way men see women."

Martinez smiled, engaged her eyes and narrowed his. She turned her head. Pussy. No one stared down Enrique Martinez. No man. No woman. Nobody. Not anymore. He searched out Amy, sitting directly across from him in the circle of 15 metal folding chairs, only two unoccupied. On the other side of the glass door, a few patrons stood in line before the circulation desk while others browsed through racks of compact disc cases. Three walls of floor-to-ceiling bookcases covered with plastic tarps hemmed in the makeshift meeting space. The fourth wall held the door and a mural of downtown Troy circa 1900. The scent of fresh paint melded with the aroma of coffee from the pot on the rolling cart standing by the entrance.

The dozen women surrounding him represented an odd assortment. They sat listening to the discussion. Some, like the bitch, tried to monopolize the conversation. Most flipped pages and pointed to highlighted text. Some nodded agreement with a speaker. Others frowned

40

puzzlement. Their ages ranged from Amy, 29 this June 4, to about 60. A nondescript bunch, save Amy and the bitch. Unlike the bitch, who possessed a cover-girl face but a frame hard and angular with jutting edges to match her ice pick tone, Amy's pretty face came packaged with a body soft, curvy and pliant. She nodded to him. Someone began to say something.

Amy held up a hand. "One moment, please. We should give Rick the opportunity to answer Leslie's blanket assertion about males, if he chooses."

The bitch glared at Amy, and Martinez wondered whether she was a lesbian.

Why'd Amy want him to speak? This Leslie broad meant nothing to him. These days, only Amy called him "Rick" and got away with it. Back in high school, Zach Johnson and his boys hung the label "Rick the Spic" on him. He didn't like the name, but didn't know how to shed it. He knew better now. His Catholic upbringing foretold, "The meek shall inherit the earth." His father was meek — and got nowhere. No, if the timid *did* inherit anything, they'd find the Zach Johnsons had picked the place clean. That religious crap was a sop for losers.

"Rick?"

"What you say is true." He smiled at the bitch, turned his gaze back to Amy. "But only for *some* men. True, men find pleasure in the company of the right woman. Isn't that also true for women with the right man? I think it's wrong to call a woman an object of pleasure, nothing more." A warning light flashed in his brain. Amy had got to him. Nothing else explained those words. She beamed a smile. Good answer.

Martinez wondered if he might slip outside under pretense of a cigarette. He never smoked before or during a job. Amy didn't approve of his smoking, and he'd been weaning off, nearly killed the cravings. Five minutes, but would she be upset? He'd call the man, explain the delay. Amy's eyes read his mind. "Stay," they said, "this is important to me." Martinez settled into his chair, and into a growing anxiety.

"I think Leslie and Rick both make valid points." Amy the conciliator, the peacemaker forever ready to disarm a conflict. His cell phone vibrated in his lap and his shoulders twitched. He glanced at the display. Shit, the Russki. Third time since the meeting started, no doubt wanting confirmation of the job. Martinez's reputation was in jeopardy. He adhered to schedules and completed his contracts on time with never a hitch. He should have finished two hours ago, but he'd forgotten his promise to attend the book club.

Martinez had never dated a librarian, never been with a woman as smart as Amy, whose breadth and depth of book knowledge amazed him almost as much as her lack of understanding of the real world. Normally he did not tolerate ignorance. In Amy's case, he found her naiveté about the world endearing, made him feel like her protector. Amy was cute when she covered her ignorance with phrases and platitudes picked up in books, much like a deaf person might mask his condition by reading lips.

"Men and women are equals. If women will act that way, they'll be treated that way," Amy said.

People, particularly smart and sexy ones like Amy, surprised him by professing what they did not believe. The bitch spoke unadorned truth, depicting a world not as many women thought it should be. Most people didn't like the truth. They preferred the facts candy-coated or cloaked in a shroud of virtue. Sure, each person had his own standards. Why mankind felt compelled to adopt them remained a mystery. Moral suasion did not change natural law.

Amy was very much his kind of woman. The bitch probably realized the fact. That would explain why she baited him, trying to make him say something politically incorrect to justify throwing him out of the group. She had nothing to fear. He did not intend to take part in another one. Unless Amy asked.

Amy deftly steered the conversation away from the bitch's tangent and back to the book under discussion. The graceful ease with which she slipped from topic to topic reminded him of the way she stripped for him.

His presence at the book club meeting was strictly her idea. He stopped reading the novel at the point where the main character, a young woman, went on for three solid pages analyzing and interpreting an innocuous response her boyfriend had made. Martinez told Amy he should call the author, a woman naturally, and assure her no man ever said anything to a woman with three *lines* of hidden meaning, let alone three pages.

Amy had laughed, given him a book of short stories by Hemingway, a man's writer she'd said, but begged him to attend anyway. He knew why. For all their contrary claims, women were a lot like men. Amy wanted to boast about her sexual desirability to her women friends, like a 40-something man shows off his 20-something trophy wife to his male friends.

Tonight, Amy wore the three-quarter carat diamond stud earrings he'd given her and told anyone who admired them they were a gift from him. She probably didn't know her unadorned pierced ears attracted him at first sight, even more so than the bare ring finger. A wedding band on a woman's finger served as a stop sign. A married woman belonged to another man until the man said otherwise. Fooling with another man's wife was the equivalent to larceny. Enrique Martinez was no thief.

They'd met one morning shortly after the first of the year while in line at a coffee shop. He smiled. She smiled back. He'd planned to be in Albany for only a few hours: complete the contract, head back to the Bronx. He hated to deviate from plans and never did. That morning, though, he stopped to strike up a conversation with Amy. They talked for some time. He noticed her assessing him as they exchanged idle pleasantries. Maybe she was trying to reconcile the Martinez surname with the face most people mistook for Italian, blood inherited from his guinea mother.

He'd kept up his end of the conversation, his thoughts fixated on Amy's piercings. A woman pierced her body to hang jewelry in erotic places to attract a man. Men reacted as intended, but not because of the jewelry. No, the attraction lay in the woman's effort to make a man notice her. Amy's un-jeweled piercings, her naked orifices, drove him wild with desire. He'd known instinctively: if he hung diamonds from Amy's ears and she showed them off for him, he'd own her. Nothing was more erotic in a man's eyes than owning a beautiful woman. Many men denied the fact. Many men lied.

"Leslie is entitled to her opinion. Let's put the question to a vote." Amy's sharp tone snapped him to attention. He loved when she became assertive. The discussion had obviously ended with Leslie's reference to future club meetings. He sought out Amy's eyes but found them circling the room in a challenge. "Who thinks our meetings should exclude males? Show of hands." He recognized the tone of triumph. He loved giving Amy her way. No hand rose save the bitch's. "OK, then, two weeks, same time and same place. I chose the next book as a continuation of our man and woman relational theme. I think Bluebeard was Kurt Vonnegut's finest novel. You'll find the read interesting."

Martinez didn't know who Kurt Vonnegut was, but he thought Bluebeard was a pirate. What pirates had to do with men and women escaped him, though he expected Amy would enlighten him. He'd come to rely on Amy's insights, her bold frankness, her unflinching assessment of what satisfied her. He couldn't wait to get back to her apartment. He had never met a woman so blunt, so aggressive, and so assertive about how she expected a man to dominate her. Amy put his mother to shame in that regard, no mean feat.

***

"Did you like the Francis Macomber story?" Amy was sitting up in bed, her book now on her lap. Her favorite post-sex activity was reading. He lay on his stomach next to her, head centered over the Hemingway book. She must have noted his progress with the hunting story. She'd not spoken a word until he read the last page. With her reading glasses, book and faded blue cotton nightshirt, he found it hard to believe she was the same woman who'd had him nearly breathless, little more than an hour before. Amy had surprised him that first time in bed, a lioness, her needs primal and base. When finished, she slipped back into an intellectual. The woman amazed him.

"I don't like hunting." The year Enrique turned 15 his father had taken him on a hunting trip to the Adirondacks, where he'd witnessed a bunch of grown men slaughtering innocent animals and complaining about their bitchy wives. There was no sport in hunting. The animals didn't shoot back. Unlike the days men hunted and killed animals to survive, these men killed for fun. Most didn't even eat the meat. He'd thought at the time the men might better use their energy to straighten out their bitchy wives rather than slaughtering innocent animals just for kicks.

"But the story wasn't about hunting, was it?" Amy moved the book from her lap, removed her glasses and rolled to her side, her body snug against his.

"Right. More about marriage and murder." Hemingway wrote about a rich man and his beautiful but unfaithful wife who went big game hunting in Africa. While in the jungle, the wife screwed the guide, making no effort to hide the tryst from her husband, who then decided he'd had enough humiliation and would divorce her. Shortly afterwards, she shot him under circumstances, *sans* background, that looked like a hunting accident but cold-blooded murder otherwise.

Martinez reached to the nightstand for his vibrating cell phone. The Russki, again. He must be royally pissed by now. This would no longer wait. He absolutely must get to work, call in the completed job before the man got ideas about sending someone to look for him. He moved to get up.

Amy flung a leg over his. "Wait! What did you think?"

"It was a good story, but I didn't like the ending." When he read the part about the husband's hesitance to shoot a lion, he identified with the man. The first time he'd had a clear shot at a deer, he'd not fired the gun. When asked why, he made up a story about not being an expert shooter and worrying about only wounding the animal. His father patted his head. The following day, when his father returned from his beer run, he gave Enrique a packet of paper targets with animal and human figures, along with several boxes of ammunition. Martinez was content to spend the rest of the week honing his shooting skills. His father commented on the fact he used the human silhouettes exclusively.

"OK, let's pretend you're Enrique Hemingway and you get to write the ending." Amy rubbed against him. The story had aroused her. She would have to wait. He already had more explaining to do than he wanted.

"I would have the husband kill the guide and leave his wife alone in the jungle."

"An awfully righteous ending coming from a man who scoffs at morality." Amy's tone was now downright seductive.

What did she mean? "It's only justice."

She raised herself on one elbow, pulled her nightshirt off and flipped the garment over his head. "Let's imagine you're the guide in the story, and I'm Mrs. Macomber. There's been a tragic hunting accident, my husband is dead, and now you and I are alone in the jungle. What will you do with me?"

The scent of her on the shirt set his pulse racing. He realized the wrongness of Amy's fantasies was the allure that sucked him in. It mattered to him Francis Macomber's body was still warm. His wife had cuckolded him and then murdered him in cold blood. It was why he wanted the woman, wanted to turn her into his sex slave. Dammit! The Russki would just have to wait. Why not? He needed Martinez more than Martinez needed him. The Russki was a fool, just like the passel of Ivans he employed. "Stand up! Let me look at you, whore."

CHAPTER 6

F ans already packed the bleachers by the time Linda paid her admission and entered the gymnasium. The scent of fresh-popped popcorn brought back a memory of a game seven years ago when Bill starred in a stunning upset victory. Maybe she'd witness another one tonight.

The opposing basketball teams were warming up, as were the cheerleader squads. With her crop of auburn curls, Heather Gaines was easily identifiable, even in uniform. Heather stood to one side of a group of girls practicing jumps and flips. She followed Heather's gaze and spotted Jeremy Cronin. Linda walked the sidelines to the South Greenbush end of the court. She stopped and leaned against the padded wall. The tension was palpable and nearly as pungent as the perspiration odor seeping from the pores of the pack of grunting males.

Jeremy ran toward the basket, snagged a pass tossed up by a teammate, and jammed the ball through the hoop in one graceful motion. He wasn't Bill's caliber, but it *was* a sweet move. Jeremy's feet landed on the black end line.

"Nice, Jeremy."

He blinked. His jaw dropped.

Linda headed to the bleachers. A buzzer sounded. No doubt the place crawled with college scouts who had seen his skills and now wanted to find out if the kid could play under big-game pressure. Linda wondered the same. She climbed to an open space on the fifth row of seats, carefully stepping over and around spectators, coats, jackets, purses, cameras and other delicate electronics having no business lying on a bleacher seat. On the sidelines, the South Greenbush cheerleaders jumped and shouted, imploring the crowd to scream louder. They did a good job. The referee in the center circle threw up an arm and blew on his whistle, but the screaming drowned it. The official spoke to Jeremy and the other player inside the circle. The opponents shook hands. Throughout the proceedings, Jeremy's eyes scanned the bleachers. When they landed on her, Linda waved. It had been a long time since she'd seen a high school Sectional tournament game.

The noise level dropped several decibels. A young man wearing a single silver earring nudged Linda's arm with an elbow. "Check out the guy they sent to jump ball with Jeremy."

Linda smiled and nodded. Based on the peach fuzz on his chin and the fact he'd been screaming with the South Greenbush cheerleaders, she figured him for a student and wondered what he made of her.

Another young man, whose shaved head occasionally obstructed Linda's view of the court, leaned back. "They should call him Shorty. What's Jeremy looking for? He keeps looking up this way."

"Probably his girl. She usually sits behind the bench, but I ain't seen her," Earring said.

Jenna's absence at the big game was a positive sign. Perhaps she'd sorted out her emotions.

"Jenna or no Jenna, we're gonna kill Taconic." Baldy turned back to the court at the sound of the whistle.

The ref tossed the ball. Jeremy didn't jump. Taconic took possession. Twenty seconds later a Taconic player blew past a statue version of Jeremy Cronin and scored an easy layup.

"You see that?" Earring asked this of no one in particular. "What's wrong with Jeremy?"

Three minutes into the game, with South Greenbush trailing 8-0, the referee signaled a time-out.

Baldy turned. "Something's got into Jeremy."

"I thought you told me Cronin knew how to play." Across the court, Jeremy spoke to a coach. No, she wasn't through with this basketball star, regardless what his old man had engineered. The coach stood with his hands on his hips. Jeremy wiped sweat from his face with a towel.

"You go to school here?" Earring asked.

"No."

"Taconic?"

"Nope. Read about this Cronin kid and wanted to find out why all the fuss. I'm not impressed." The buzzer sounded. The coach patted Jeremy's back and pumped a fist. Jeremy returned to the court. The coach stared in Linda's direction.

"This ain't the real Jeremy. Something's… Hey, coach, don't leave now." Earring's words were barely audible over the crowd reaction to the cheerleaders' exhortations. He reached down and produced a bottle partially covered with a brown paper bag. He swigged from the bottle, swallowed and winked at Linda. "Want a hit?"

"Of what?"

"Jack."

In a world evolving at an alarming rate, some customs never changed. "No thanks."

"Suit yourself. You like weed? Me and Kenny got some for halftime."

"You do?" Her attention focused across the court. The coach stood behind the bench speaking to a man wearing jacket and tie seated in the second row. Linda recognized Eddie Cronin. Cronin nodded, and pulled a cell phone from his pocket. He spoke to the man, who then returned to his team. Eddie disappeared. The first quarter neared an end with South Greenbush trailing 18-4, when he returned. Jeremy had not scored or blocked a shot and grabbed only one rebound.

At the quarter break, Baldy and Earring moped. Baldy leaned back and stage-whispered. "I don't mind winning, Mark, but not like this."

Linda was about to interject a question, but Eddie Cronin crossed the court. He stood on the sideline and beckoned her. "Trooper Baldwin."

Baldy turned and scanned the crowd. "What's Jeremy's dad talking about? Ain't no trooper here."

She nudged Earring. "Save my place, I'll be right back."

Eddie smiled when she stood. She threaded her way down. A voice behind her said, "You gotta be shittin' me."

She reached the court and approached Eddie. When she got within bumping distance he took a step back. "Evening, trooper."

She stopped. "Wrong, Eddie. Tonight I'm just a basketball fan."

Cronin produced the cell phone, began punching numbers. "Hold on." He put the cell to his ear, smiled at her through clenched teeth and said, "She's standing here, next to me." A few seconds passed. Cronin said, "Thanks." He handed the phone to Linda. "A friend of yours wants to talk to you."

Linda wanted to tell Eddie where he could stick the device, certain she and Eddie shared no friends. Curiosity won. She snatched it. "Hello."

"Listen, Kiddo, I need a favor."

She nearly dropped the phone. She wanted to ask what connection Bert had to this slimy politician, but knew better. He was a lobbyist. No further explanation necessary. "I'm listening."

"I want you to leave the game. Immediately."

She began to comprehend the reality of what was happening. But how had Eddie known a request from Bert Bariteau would get him what he wanted? And why would Bert ask? "Why would I leave? It's a good game."

"Because I asked."

Aside from her father, only one person on earth could even make her *consider* a request based on that reason. "Why do you-?"

"It's for me, Kiddo, that's all."

Shit, Lilith, you can't even attend a basketball game in peace. "You *will* explain. Correct?"

"In due course. Things are not always as simple as they appear."

Except he hadn't witnessed Jeremy raping Jenna. Things didn't come much simpler. "OK. I'm leaving." She tossed the phone at Eddie who fumbled, but recovered before it fell to the court. The buzzer sounded. "You haven't heard the last of this."

Eddie smiled. "You know, when Bert first told me about you, I figured he exaggerated. I guess he didn't." He hustled across the court.

Why would Bert discuss her with the likes of Eddie Cronin? The teams took positions for the second quarter. Linda walked to the exit. She turned back as Jeremy grabbed an offensive rebound over the heads of two defenders, wheeled and stuffed the ball through the hoop for his first points of the game. If justice prevailed, he would foul out and Greenbush would lose.

She stood outside the gym breathing cool fresh air bearing a hint of spring. The cheering from inside filled the night. Jeremy might be skilled, but the scouts would surely wonder about his ability to play under pressure. This was his senior year, and he should have learned by now.

Seven years ago this month, Bill had played the varsity title game as a freshman with more confidence and awareness than she witnessed tonight from Jeremy. Bill made one clutch basket and steal after another to keep Cohoes close against a team everyone else expected to dominate the game. In the final two minutes, he took charge, almost as if his will alone controlled the flow of play.

The following day, the media gushed about his poise and skill, highly unusual for a first-year player. The news accounts reminded team supporters of the thrill Bill had given the night before with his play. He'd thrilled her, too, but that came the following afternoon at their tree.

The majestic oak stood at the bottom of Eagle's Nest ravine, a natural fissure separating her neighborhood from Bill's. The afternoon after the championship game, Bill had snuggled behind her, his hand on hers, tracing the initials he'd carved in a misshapen heart in the tree bark. He whispered in her ear. "I love you and I want to marry you when we grow up." She turned, took his hand and pulled him away from the tree.

They ran down a path gathering dried brush, twigs and grass. They piled the collection at the corner of an open space and knelt. Bill took her hand in his. Together they struck a match and steadied the hesitant flicker beneath the corner of a dry leaf. A tiny flame blossomed. Within minutes, the pile of dried tinder burned steadily: a perpetuation of a rite of spring the city's teens had celebrated forever.

They stood. His arms encircled and drew her close She responded. "I want to marry you, too." They remained locked in the embrace, hugging, kissing, whispering variations on their vows, oblivious to the stiffening breeze or the flames spreading out and away from them. By the time they noticed, the fire had raced beyond their control.

The inferno had burned for four hours, consuming most of the brush in the ravine, the smoke and ash drawing the attention of Cohoes firefighters as well as those of two neighboring communities. She and Bill had walked out of the conflagration posing as innocents, talking to the police and firefighters, asking if they could help.

Silly rites of spring! Silly childhood vows!

CHAPTER 7

The sign at the entrance to the South Greenbush campus read "Go Cats!" The varsity had extended the basketball season, thanks to a dramatic, come-from-behind win on Wednesday night. Jeremy Cronin was the hero, according to the newspaper. Linda shook her head. Three-pointers and rebounds didn't change the fact he raped Jenna. His family connections and star status created a bubble of protection she intended to burst. Even if she couldn't make Jenna talk, there were other ways to expose Jeremy.

She parked her Corvette and stepped out into the afternoon sunshine. Students streamed from the center doors of the sprawling building. Linda checked out several girls and breathed a sigh of relief. Her jeans, sweatshirt and sneakers would blend right in. Halfway across the parking lot, she stopped. On the periphery, his head in profile, Jeremy leaned against a light pole. A man facing him spoke with flying hands. Shit. Meeting Jeremy did not fit her plan. She changed direction to avoid him.

A shout drew her attention. The man jabbed at Jeremy's shoulder. Good. Maybe Jenna had an older brother and justice was near. Jeremy straightened but made no move to defend himself. The man grabbed Jeremy's arm and twisted it behind his back. Linda stopped. The man wrapped a forearm around Jeremy's neck. Classic chokehold. She broke into a sprint. "Let him go."

The man spun Jeremy around as if a toy, no easy feat given Jeremy's height and weight advantage. The fear in Jeremy's eyes turned to confusion when he recognized Linda. The man eyed her. He smiled. "Be a good little pussy and run along."

You hear what he called you, Lilith? His light olive skin made him look Hispanic but she detected no accent. He had brown hair, neatly trimmed and a rounded forehead that didn't fit the flattened nose.

She stepped up to him. He had about six inches and 60 pounds on her. "What did you say?"

He pushed Jeremy away. "You deaf?"

His breath smelled of tobacco. Her eyes focused on his hands, now at his sides. One hand moved with middle finger extended. Jeremy detected the move, too. He gasped. "She's a cop, man. I wouldn't..."

She seized the finger. She twisted with an adrenaline-spiked torque. The man's knees buckled and his torso turned. She slammed her shoulder into his back, pinning him against the light pole. She drew her knee back, and with all the force she could muster, rammed it into his ass. His groin met the pole with a satisfying thud. He yelped. She grabbed a handful of hair, yanked his head backward, then ground his face into the metal. "Did I make you feel like a man?" She stepped back, nerves wound tight, anticipating his next move. Jeremy bolted to the parking lot.

The man moved in slow motion. He straightened himself and placed his hands beside his head, his back to her. He remained still a long time. He finally moved, tugging a handkerchief from his pocket. He dabbed at his face and blew his nose. He turned, a trickle of blood appearing below his nose. "A police officer, you say?" His eyes scanned the lot. "Sorry, I didn't catch your name, officer." The man eyed her now, smiling.

"You didn't, but consider this your lucky day." Had she been a civilian, he might be in a coma or worse. His stare chilled her. His face reminded her of someone she knew, but couldn't name.

"So, you're a cop, eh?" His tone had shifted to that of a disappointed third-grade teacher. "A real young one. Beautiful, too. Don't be shy. Tell me your name." His stare had not relented. He'd not even blinked.

Despite everything she'd learned about eye contact and intimidation, she yielded to a compelling urge to lower her eyes. "Get out of here before I change my mind and charge you with sexual assault."

The man bowed at the waist. "Why thank you, beautiful police lady with no name. You're kind." He strolled off saying, "A cop. Well, well, well."

Linda continued to the school, her palms clammy from the man's words and tone, and the creepy stare that accompanied them. She should be angry with herself for losing control, but she wasn't. He wouldn't have done what he did if she'd been in uniform. True, he hadn't done anything, but his designs were obvious. Any man who felt free to stick a finger between a woman's legs because he thought she wasn't a cop deserved what he got—and more. No, the anger derived from the thought of similar assaults in which the man completed the deed, walked away without consequence and the woman suffered the shame.

They could tell her whatever they wanted about anger. They were wrong. Men did things that warranted anger. Why should she feign it? She would be living a lie if she masked her anger and pretended it was unjust. The man's actions pissed her off, to think otherwise tantamount to excusing his behavior. Anger sharpened her vigilance. She stepped up her pace toward the gym.

Heather wasn't at cheerleader practice, but Linda noticed a familiar face in the small group of girls near the top row of bleachers. She was the girl with head in boyfriend's lap at the party. Linda climbed. The girl's face turned ashen when Linda neared.

"Tiffany, right?"

"Am I in some kind of trouble?"

"No. I just want to talk to you." Linda ushered Tiffany to one side.

"Jenna told us we don't have to."

Jenna? "You mean Jeremy. Well, he's right. You don't." Linda pointed to her clothes. "I'm not a cop today and I have no beef with you. I'm trying to find out what happened that night."

"Do I need a lawyer? You're supposed to tell me, right?"

"You don't need one, and I only advise you of your rights when you're under arrest. You're not. I got a couple questions and you can help me make sense of what I heard at the camp."

"You mean about my answer, don't you?"

"Start there."

"I started to say it was just a mistake. I lied."

"Mistake?"

"Sucking my boyfriend, the guy I love, wasn't a mistake, even though my mom made me take that stupid purity vow."

Forcing a teen with raging hormones to take a vow of abstinence struck Linda about effective as screaming at a burning fire. Ice water worked better. "Did you think I would tell your parents?"

Tiffany nodded. "I don't need her in my face any more than she is. A blowjob isn't really sex, anyway."

"You running for President?"

"Huh?"

"Never mind. Look, Tiffany, I'm sure she's just worried about you."

"She had me when she was my age. Now she wants me to pay for her mistake. I hate her."

"Your secret's safe. Tell me what happened to Jenna."

"How would I know? I stayed downstairs. You went up. Why you asking me?"

"Come on, Tiffany, I'm not dumb. Girls talk. What did Jenna have to say?"

"She didn't tell me nothing."

"How long was she dating Jeremy?"

"Not long. About a month."

If Heather wasn't lying, that wouldn't have been Jenna's first time at the camp. Or maybe it was. If her parents forbade her, but Jeremy pressured, she would have eventually gone. The girl thought she loved him. Or she'd been before and Jeremy was simply impatient at the pace of the seduction. Or Heather lied. Why not, everyone else did. "Let's get back to downstairs."

Tiffany checked the time. "I think my mom's waiting for me."

"I have just a couple-" Something tapped her shoulder.

A man's voice said, "You're not a student." Linda turned. "Tiffany, do you know this individual?"

"Yes, Mr. Adams, her name is Linda." Tiffany stopped and looked Linda in the eye. The little twerp was about to blow her cover. "She's my cousin from New Jersey."

"I don't care where you're from, Linda. The sign says visitors must register and show ID at the office. Perhaps you missed it."

Hard to miss a notice typed in about 36-point font and plastered at eye level on each entrance door. Linda patted her pockets for the ID she'd deliberately left in the car. "I'll get my license, Mr. Adams. It's in my car."

"I'll escort you to the door," Adams said.

She reached the parking lot, got in her car and drove off. On her way home, she tried to make sense of what she'd learned at the school. Tiffany's too pat explanation was suspect. For one, she offered the explanation before Linda asked, almost as if she realized the lie she'd told that night didn't work and she needed a better one. Second, she didn't believe Tiffany didn't know anything about what happened to Jenna. The girl confided in *someone* after Jeremy's assault. School being gossip central, word would have spread. Tiffany lied. Why? Finally, Tiffany said Jenna told them they didn't have to talk. Linda presumed she meant Jeremy. Saying Jenna was a nervous mistake. What if it wasn't?

Throughout her musings about Tiffany, the image of the staring man kept returning. She should focus on why he attacked Jeremy. Yet her mind returned repeatedly to the discomfort she experienced looking into his eyes. How would she go about identifying him?

CHAPTER 8

Linda's phone rang as she readied for patrol. "Get in my office. Now!"

LeBeouf was on the phone when she appeared at his door. Silent, he motioned her to close the door and sit. When he finally spoke, he said, "She's here now." His eyes met hers. More silence save for the occasional noise escaping from the monologue LeBeouf was suffering. She was the subject of the speech and LeBeouf did not look pleased. What was going on? "I will, sir." He dropped the phone in the cradle. "Captain Walker says Eddie Cronin called."

"What's *he* want?"

"Wild guess, I'd say your ass."

Cronin's name reminded her: Bert still owed her an explanation. "Why so?"

"Jeremy has a dislocated shoulder. His basketball season is over."

"Gee, too bad."

"Eddie thinks you're responsible."

"I'm not." *He deserved it, though.* Jeremy wasn't telling him the truth if he believed her responsible. Why did Jeremy lie to his father? Linda thought of the man roughing up the kid and his bolting for the parking lot.

"The captain wants Eddie's charge checked out."

"Be my guest. There's nothing to find."

"You mean other than your acknowledgment you used excessive force in his arrest?"

"Ewing's words, sergeant, not mine."

"Did I order you to stay away from the Cronin kid?"

"Yes."

"Were you at Jeremy's game last Wednesday night?"

"No. I'm a Taconic fan. They happened to play Greenbush. I left after the first quarter. By the way, Cronin's not as good as the hype."

"Why were you at South Greenbush High on Friday afternoon?"

Oh, shit! "Friday? I had the day off. Let me think—"

"Cut the crap. You were seen questioning…" LeBeouf glanced down at the note he'd scribbled. "Tiffany Maillot: one of the guests at the Cronin camp. What did you want with her?"

"I thought she might want to hang out at the mall."

"Walker wants your ass out of here, and you're going to play smart ass? I'm thinking he may be right."

"I didn't go looking for Jeremy Cronin."

"Nobody's buying that. I'm a big supporter of yours, unlike others around here, but you can't survive doing shit like this. You ignored a direct order—"

"No I didn't. You told me to stay away from Cronin."

"Let me be clear about something. This incident's going in your file. Next one, you'll get a choice between resignation and termination. Do you understand?"

Dammit. They weren't going to drive her from her career, but she had no tolerance for a known rapist roaming the streets. "I'm clear. Does this mean you don't want to know about the man roughing up Jeremy?"

"So, you *did* contact Jeremy Cronin on Friday afternoon." He scribbled a note.

She should shut up, stop building the case for her firing. "He was about to get the shit kicked out of him. I intervened. Curious, he now shows up with a dislocated shoulder. How'd he say it happened?"

"I could be mistaken, but you sound like you're hounding the Cronins."

"No, but somebody should. I got a close look at the man I think responsible for Jeremy's shoulder. He's not someone Jeremy wants to be messing with."

"If someone does, it won't be you. I've got something else to keep you busy."

"Besides patrol and the beer sting?"

"You're off patrol."

"Why?"

"Mike needs your help."

"Bullshit! You want me at a desk where you can keep an eye on me." She probably should have thought some before blurting that out.

LeBeouf showed a fat smile. "Not true. I'm offering your services to Ewing on the M-A-I-A case."

"What's M-A-I-A?"

"The acronym for a big insurance company the mayor begged to build a new service center downtown. Now he calls about an accident claim. Says he suspects insurance fraud. What a surprise!"

The real surprise was the assignment. A BCI gig in the guise of a disciplinary action? Made no sense. "Who will I be working with?"

"Well, that's the problem. Nobody's working the case. Mike's pulling more manpower to work the homicides. I want you to help him out."

"Homicides? You mean there's been another? When? What happened?"

LeBeouf stood. "Talk to him."

Ewing's voice carried into the hall, the tone suggesting his conversation neared an end. She peeked inside and found him alone, back reclined on the chair, feet up on the corner of his desk. He waved her in. A smile broke over his face. "Great news, professor. Keep me posted." He replaced the phone, and lowered his feet to the floor. "How's the sting training going?"

"Fine." She sat. "LeBeouf wanted me to look at the insurance case."

"You?"

"My reaction, exactly. Based on his preface, I'm guessing you need a warm body to appease the mayor."

"I didn't say that."

"Just like I didn't say I used excessive force subduing a rapist."

Ewing grunted, reached across the desk to a stack of files. Thumbing through the tabs, he said, "The case is a bit cold. Accident happened nearly five months ago, early November, if I remember correctly. Yeah, here we go!" He pulled a file and flipped the folder open, glanced at the contents and handed it to her. "Not much. Albany police accident report, State Insurance Department Fraud Bureau report, contact info for the insurance company fraud specialist and a name, address and phone number of the last person who owned the car before the accident. Car disappeared."

"I'm working this alone?"

"You're not alone. You report to me and you don't move without my OK. You got that?"

"You bet. Maybe the car was totaled." She scanned the accident report. The physical damage section showed only minor damage.

Ewing pointed to two covered 10-ream cardboard boxes stacked in a corner behind him. "Oh, you inherited those, doctor bills. Should be interesting," he deadpanned. He turned his attention to his computer monitor. "I figure you start with the last known owner and then talk to the company fraud guy. Then let me know what you think."

"LeBeouf tells me you got another homicide?"

Ewing swung back around. "A near carbon copy."

BCI already had a two-week-old mob style homicide on its hands, the work of a pro. The victim was one Sergei Cszar, 27 years old and a recent graduate of the Mohawk Valley Chiropractic College. Cszar was a Russian citizen, in the country on an expired student visa, unemployed. "Similarities?"

"Hands tied, single bullet to the head, killed elsewhere and dumped within shouting distance of the first."

"And the vic?"

He flashed a sheet of paper. "Just in. Natasha Borisova, Russian citizen, in the U.S. on a student visa, recent graduate of the University at Albany, licensed clinical psychologist, unemployed."

"You said *near* carbon copy."

"This one was nude. Medical examiner says she'd had sex. Body bruises suggest it was not her choice."

An image of red buttons falling on white ceramic evaporated almost as quickly as it appeared. "Murder to cover the rape?"

"Doubtful. Without rape, it's a second professional hit. Wouldn't be the first time an executioner helped himself to some extra-contractual compensation."

She stood. "The two murders are connected, aren't they?"

"Possibly. But how?"

Linda picked up the file boxes. "Off business for a second. Why would an avid fan of a basketball team make a bet on the opposing team?"

"Most wouldn't. Why you asking?"

"Curious. Overheard some of the boys talking March Madness and didn't want to appear dumb. Under what circumstances?"

"Let's say his team is favored by a big margin, but he doesn't think they'll win by that amount. If he's right, he wins both ways. His team wins and he still collects the bet he made on the opponent."

"I see." She left the office. The bleacher conversation from the Taconic game came back to her. Baldy and Earring didn't mind winning, but not like that. How could they win if Greenbush was losing? She formed a theory of what the kids were hiding. But no, that was the Cronin incident and she dare not. *Jeremy, Jeremy, what were you up to? Besides rape?*

CHAPTER 9

After a couple uneventful weeks split between beer sting training and reviewing insurance medical forms, Linda thought she knew enough to ask a fraud investigator an intelligent question, perhaps two. Figueroa stopped Linda in the corridor by her desk. "Bigwater's entertaining some of the guys in the locker room with the story of how Eddie Cronin jerked your chain."

Linda wondered what other fictions Bigwater and the boys swapped about her in the privacy of the male sanctuary. *No, Lilith, you can't just charge in there and clean the place out.* "Bigwater's problem is he has no sense of humor. I figure it's because of the mini pecker I heard about."

"Where'd you hear that one?"

"Hey, you think you men are the only ones who compare."

Tibbs roared. "No shit?"

"Yeah, true, spread the word. Bunch of the women think the situation is funny. I think we should take pity."

"Whatever the size, I do know he's got a hard one for you. Says a buddy told him Cohoes cops got you under surveillance. You're out of control. What's that about?"

On second thought, Lilith... "The little weasel still in the locker room?" After she took care of Bigwater, she needed to find Michaud. He warned her not to cross his line again and she'd heeded the warning. Sergeant Rick just crossed hers. She clenched her fists and started to walk.

A hand seized her shoulder.

"Where you going, Linda?"

"Locker room."

"Won't you just prove what Bigwater's saying?"

"What? I'm out of control? I get my hands on Bigwater, he'll find out about control. I'll kick the shit out of him."

Figueroa looked at her for a moment. "Are you listening to yourself?"

So, Figueroa too. Screw him. "You believe him, don't you?"

"I'm a friend. I didn't say anything. I do think you could stand to calm down a bit."

"Gee, Tibbs, thanks for the advice. Now get lost."

His mouth opened, but nothing came out. He walked away saying, "Just remember whose side I'm on."

"Yeah, you made it clear." Any more people "on her side," she'd be buried within a month. Figueroa jammed the door open with his shoulder and left. *Another supposed friend gone for good, Lilith.*

He probably meant well, but he was dead wrong about her. She had plenty of reason for a little anger, but "out of control?" No way. She stayed out of the locker room to prove her point. Anger case closed.

She returned to her desk to begin work on the fraud case, a job repeatedly interrupted by speculation about her conversation with Figueroa. Damned Michaud.

Two hours later, Linda leaned back in the chair, stretched her arms, locked fingers, and tugged against the back of her head. The four-by-four cubicle, formed by a painted cinder block wall and two gray movable partitions, provided scant space for concentration. Phones rang nearly nonstop against the cacophony of voices shrilling over the partitions. The thick file folder on the desk may as well have been written in Chinese. It was all doctor mumbo jumbo, illegible handwriting and protocol codes and dollar signs and digits and decimals and payment-due dates. The insurance bullshit might render an insomniac comatose, but it took her mind off Bigwater and her argument with Tibbs.

Stapled to the inside cover of the file folder was a business card. Samuel Vance, Director of SIU, MAIA Insurance Company. The card included phone numbers, land, fax and cell, as well as email and company website. Below was a handwritten note. Joseph Arcuro, Valley View Apartments, 3809, Latham, NY. Cell phone (518) 555-6234. Vehicle identification number for a silver Town Car followed.

The aroma of fresh dripped coffee wafted by, good excuse for a break. When she returned, she dialed Arcuro. The three-chime response foretold the words of the synthetic woman. "We're sorry, but the number you have reached, 5-1-8-5-5-5-6-2-3-4, is no longer in service. No further information is available." The phone company still had a ways to go to make the computer sound like the live person it displaced.

Vance did not answer at his office. She left a voice message and then dialed his cell, which he answered on the second ring. "Mr. Vance, my name is Trooper Baldwin. I've been asked to investigate a complaint of insurance fraud made by the Mid Atlantic Insurance Agents Insurance Company."

Vance laughed. "Thanks for contacting me. The company name is a mouthful, so, around here, we use MAIA. Pronounced like the poet Angelou. You familiar with her?"

"Yes." In high school she'd read several of Maya Angelou's poems and even framed a line, which she kept on the bureau in her bedroom. *Courage allows the successful woman to fail—and learn powerful lessons from the failure—so that in the end, she didn't fail at all.*

Linda flipped through the notebook containing her observations and questions. Scant information, many questions. "I've been studying the file, and frankly…"

"Don't worry you don't understand. You're not supposed to. This is the work of professional criminals who specialize in covering tracks."

Vance had a distinct accent sounding like a cross between a Southern drawl and a Midwest nasal twang, a "drang" she decided. "You can't be sure."

"I am. If this case isn't a classic caused accident, I'll change my name to Elvis."

Linda wrote the words "CAUSED ACCIDENT" at the top of the first page in her notebook, and then asked Vance to explain.

"Listen, I have an appointment at 11 that will take up most of the afternoon. Can you meet me for lunch tomorrow?"

She checked her calendar and agreed to meet Thursday at an Italian restaurant two blocks from the Capitol.

Linda spent the balance of the day sifting through files and writing questions for Vance. Near the end of the day, Tibbs passed by just as the mail clerk dropped two envelopes on her desk, one from the Health Benefits office, the other, legal-sized, hand-printed in block letters with no return address.

He rolled a chair from the nearby desk and sat. "About this morning, I just want to say-"

"Forget about it, Tibbs. You're a friend. I let Bigwater get to me and shouldn't have." She opened the envelope and shook out three candid photos of herself in uniform.

"He can be annoying."

She peered inside then turned each photo over, looking for explanation. Nothing. Strange, and the longer she thought, creepy. She laid the pictures on the desk. "What do you make of this?"

"Sexy woman."

"Can I divert your one-track mind for just a moment? These came in an unmarked envelope with no explanation."

Figueroa tapped on a red splotch in the foreground of the third photo. "Your 'Vette?"

Linda leaned over and recognized through the blur, the red Acura that occupied the parking space in front of her apartment most days. "No, but my house."

He picked up and examined each photo. "They're like surveillance photos."

The pictures appeared in an action sequence: at the doorway, descending steps and on the sidewalk. "You thinking what I'm thinking?" she asked.

"Bigwater? I don't know. He likes to talk, but..."

"Interesting coincidence isn't it? He mentions surveillance and the photos arrive."

"OK, but why? He mentioned Cohoes PD. You never told me if there was anything to his story."

"There's usually a grain of truth to what Bigwater says. You have to watch out for the 99 percent-lie portion."

"What are you going to do?"

"Start with the Cohoes PD. Take a walk with me, would you." She started down the corridor. Tibbs followed. Outside, she led him from the building. "You follow high school basketball. Could a player of say, Jeremy Cronin's abilities affect the score of a game?"

"Is this coming from the person who loses her job for asking questions about Cronin?"

"It's theoretical, and you won't screw me."

"You think Cronin shaved points?"

"I never think about Cronin?"

Tibbs smiled. "A player of his skill level *could* affect a score, but many things make it unlikely. One, the coach controls who plays and how many minutes. More important though is lack of motive. The kid has a full ride at Duke, exposure to NBA scouts, and maybe a shot at the bigs. He's not risking his future for a few hundred or even a few thousand dollars. So, yeah, he *could*, but he wasn't."

She'd not shaken the image of the man, his unsettling stare, the ease with which he handled Jeremy. "Hadn't thought of that. Thanks. Dead end."

***

Linda sat on the hood of a Cohoes patrol car when Michaud exited the massive stone City Hall housing the police department. "You're late" she said as he approached.

"The chief got my ear. You know what that's like. So what's up?"

Linda watched his face as she recounted Bigwater's reference to his buddy and the Cohoes PD surveillance. "What did you tell him about me?"

"Nothing, and never would. When I found out you were a trooper, I called him and asked about you. Was that ever a mistake. He's been all over me about what we got on you."

"And you've told him nothing."

"I'm thinking maybe you two were lovers and you dumped him."

"He tell you that?"

"He won't tell me anything, but he's that kind of pissed at you. So what gives?"

"He doesn't like being shown up by a woman."

"Who does? What did you do?"

"One day at the academy I overheard a few guys discussing my anatomy and what they'd do with it. Bigwater got the biggest laugh when he said he'd make me smile, but he'd check my ID first. I walked into the room, sat across from him, and dropped my ID in my lap. I told him to come check if he had the balls. The guys burst out laughing. I stared at Bigwater. He has no sense of humor."

"Pretty lame, if you ask me."

"Next day, in self-defense training, the boys found out I'm a fourth-degree black belt. Bigwater was the last guy I took down. He lay spread eagle on the mat. I reached down to help him up and he called me a cunt."

"He's splayed and you're standing over him? Not too smart."

"As he discovered."

He put his hands over his groin. "Ouch! Hurts a guy just thinking. At least now I get it."

Linda handed him the three photos. "These aren't yours, are they?"

Michaud looked at them and laughed. "We make it a policy to not share surveillance photos with the target."

"And I'm not a target."

"Put it this way. If you were, the photos wouldn't look like these. Can I have them?"

"You want copies, OK, but why?"

"We take a dim view of anyone messing with our residents. You stay out of it. We'll talk to your neighbors."

"Good luck. I think I'm the only one on the street who speaks English."

"We call the place Little Moscow. I probably don't need to tell you this, but be careful."

"Will do."

"Goes for Watervliet too."

"Never go."

"Good. Chief tells me they may have a vigilante on their hands. Asked if we had a problem. I said nope." Michaud smiled, turned and walked back to City Hall.

I know, Lilith. We always finish what we started, no matter what.

When Linda reached home, she parked and spent the next two hours familiarizing herself with her neighborhood. She followed the alley that ran behind the house Michaud thought the photographer had used. To the north, the passage dead-ended at a hydroelectric power plant with no way out but a hundred-foot straight drop down a shale wall to the water. To the south, the lane crossed the foot of Front Street and became a narrow path descending to the weeds and brush that grew behind a series of abandoned mills. The wide paved ditches stretching from the mills to the riverfront surprised her. She recalled Bert's telling her textile manufacturers once dumped dyes and sewage directly into the Mohawk. All the ditches connected to passages under the mill buildings, and two tunneled beyond, under North Mohawk Street, emerging in a canal bed adjacent to the lightly traveled Harmony Street. She found no sign a vehicle had used the tunneled route. But on her return she noted that other than some weed sprouting sections of cracked concrete, the passage might have been a long driveway.

***

The next afternoon, after lunch with Vance, she drove the patrol car to Joseph Arcuro's last known address, trying to digest the most relevant of the technical information Vance had unloaded. Vance's dismay, though concealed, was no surprise. He expected a veteran BCI detective with insurance-fraud training.

During lunch she learned Vance's new chief financial officer, a recent Ivy League MBA, ordered him to pay the claim and stop the late payment penalty exposure. Vance refused and appealed his case to the CEO who sided with him. He told her state law imposed a two percent per month interest penalty on no-fault insurance payments made after 30 days. Fraud investigations turning up nothing exposed the company to the penalty for the length of the inquiry.

Vance did not say the CFO would blame him if they failed to prove fraud, but the message was clear. She assured him the State Police took the crime of insurance fraud seriously. If he didn't buy it, he was too polite to say. Vance surprised her too. The lanky redheaded man with the receding hairline could have been the ghost of her Grandpa Baldwin who'd died when she was in high school.

Linda's head swam in the technical jargon. A *staged* accident involved two vehicles, both in on the fraud. Linda guided the patrol car to Johnson Road. A *caused* accident also required two cars, only one involved in the scam. Vance claimed the caused label applied to the case in question. A *phantom* accident involved no cars.

A local fundamentalist group recently declared the Valley View Apartments complex "Sin City" for its swinging singles atmosphere. Staged, caused and phantom, three basic and generic auto-fraud schemes, each with scores of permutations, limited, according to Vance, only by the imagination of the perpetrators. They'd led her to Sin City.

The complex consisted of an access road flanked by a series of identical brick two-story buildings. Exterior concrete staircases rose to the second-floor entry doors from a sidewalk bordering a sea of yellow-striped blacktop. The Lexus parked on the side of Building 34 cut off her musings. Looked familiar. She detoured into the parking lot. No need to run those plates. The car belonged to her mother. Who'd she visit in Sin City?

Linda parked at Building 38. A sign revealed 3809 as second floor. She took the stairs two at a time, rang the bell and counted. Thirty seconds; no answer. She pushed again and thought she heard voices. She stepped back. A minute or so passed. A dead bolt clicked. The inner door opened, and through the screen, Linda saw the arms. The sculpted muscles reminded her of The Thinker, a statue she'd first seen on a visit to the Rodin museum in Philly.

"Can I help you?"

She pried her eyes from the arms and looked into his eyes, sultry brown. "I'm looking for a Mr. Joseph Arcuro." Why wouldn't her eyes move?

"That'd be me." A smile appeared.

"My name is Trooper Baldwin, and I'm investigating a car accident from last November involving a car for which you were the last owner."

An inkling of recognition flickered in his eyes. He addressed her breasts. "I'm in the business of buying and selling used cars. I move so many, I can't remember the ones from last month, let alone six months ago." His gaze wandered to her crotch.

"Well, get out your log and refresh your memory? You'll make my trip worthwhile."

Arcuro moved his eyes back to her breasts. He licked his lips. "Well, the problem, trooper, is I'm entertaining at the moment, if you know what I mean, so it's rather inconvenient." He looked into her eyes. "But why don't you stop by tomorrow around this time and we can visit?" He winked.

"Better yet, bring your records to Troop G headquarters tomorrow afternoon and ask for me." The scent of perfume reached her nostrils. Not just any perfume, though. The fragrance was the $700-an-ounce Nuit de Paris her mother purchased mail-order from France.

Arcuro stared. "Nice meeting you, Trooper Baldwin." Before he closed the door, she noticed a light-color blouse lying on the back of a sofa. The dead bolt clicked. Linda imagined an ivory blouse, silk, laced with French perfume, draped over the torso of a woman who shouldn't have been her mother, locked to a mythological Greek god, not her father.

She started the car and opened the windows. She stared at Arcuro's front door, her mind in a sprint, her stomach disagreeing with lunch. The circumstantial evidence was convincing. Little doubt remained when she factored in her own experience with her mother's capacity for betrayal. She considered and rejected a few possible actions, jammed the car into gear and drove off.

CHAPTER 10

Enrique Martinez unzipped the gym bag and removed the rifle stock. The first time he'd imagined doing something like this had also been about a woman. He would have spit at the thought, but the crime scene boys might later experience an "Aha!" moment. He mounted the barrel on the stock and secured it. No, that first time with his mother had been an exercise in emotion. He was young and naïve and the whore had taught him plenty. There'd been a few since, Baldwin the cop the most recent, and in the end, they'd all experienced what he'd learned from his old lady and Zach Johnson. It wasn't smart to shame and humiliate Enrique Martinez.

He peered through the attic vent opening at the front porch of an apartment building across the street. People might think his judgment of his mother harsh, but the facts allowed no other conclusion. He removed the tripod, and screwed it to the rifle. He was in the act of fitting the bolt when the door opened. He consulted his watch. No, couldn't be, he had another three minutes. Most humans were creatures of habit. He'd studied those habits in his targets and quickly learned he could set the time by them. A little girl with long dark hair walked through the door and sat herself on the top step of the cement porch.

The kid should have been in school an hour ago. What parent keeps a young girl from getting her education when she's not sick? If she was sick, she belonged in bed, or at least resting comfortably inside, not outside unsupervised. Maybe she was late for school and her mother would soon walk her to the car. The girl must not stay. Given recent events, he couldn't afford to abort another job. The Russki'd already accused Martinez of getting soft. He imagined the man's ridicule. "You passed on a clean hit because you didn't want to get blood on a little kid? I need a new man."

The Russki was a dope. Blood and spattered brains washed off. No, young kids should not have to witness a death, the trauma a scar that never fully healed. They occasionally did, though, with school violence escalating everywhere. He couldn't control the school environment, but he did this one.

Martinez wouldn't mind if the Russki were to replace him with another except for the short life expectancy of ex-employees. He planned to leave the business later this year anyway. He had two contracts to fulfill, and then he and Amy would be gone. He had to settle the Baldwin score, but that was personal.

Last week, Martinez made a compelling business case for her elimination. The Russki listened with an amused smile presaging his answer. "If I hit a state cop, I might as well hang up a going-out-of-business sign," he said. Martinez always thought the man a moron, but occasionally, he did come up with a good idea.

Martinez was not getting soft. The Russki was wrong on that count. Today was the day to reaffirm, to bury thoughts his boss might have about taking him out. The door opened. The little girl squirmed round. Martinez found Yuri Pasternov's forehead in the scope. His finger touched the trigger, and Amy's disgusted words of a few days ago filled his mind. "Look at this," she'd said. "What man does this to a child?" Martinez did not remember the photo or any of the details of the news story she'd read to him. Only her words and tone survived. He removed his finger, started his count. Forty-seven seconds later, the rifle stored, Martinez left the attic. Everything was clear. Then the cop car showed. What was he to do? Yeah, that's what he'd tell the Russki.

Martinez drove north from Watervliet to the adjoining city of Cohoes, the larger of the two, but still dwarfed by Albany and surrounding suburbs. He tooled through North Mohawk, School, Cataract and Front streets, driving the square twice to assure himself the red Corvette was not in the neighborhood. He parked, powered up his cell, and called the Russki who was not pleased but sufficiently distracted to simply order the job done ASAP. He might feel differently when he focused on Martinez's report, but Martinez would not hear the words.

Notebook and camera in hand, Martinez spent the next two hours strolling the sidewalks, streets and alleyways of the neighborhood. He met few people, none English-speaking and none even remotely curious about his presence. His business for the day complete, Martinez drove to the nearby Crossgates Mall. He ate a light lunch at Ruby Tuesdays, then stepped outside for a smoke, but called Amy at the library instead. She was proud of his progress with smoking, but too busy to chat. He told her he loved her and to have a light lunch, he had a special evening planned.

"Ooh, good. Stop at Frederick's and pick out something for me to wear for later. You know what. Have to go." She hung up.

Martinez strolled the mall, picking up roses, scented candles, two bottles of champagne and a tin of vanilla-scented body butter. He browsed music for half an hour and selected a three-CD set of strings for lovers. He spent nearly an hour in the bookstore before choosing a book of poetry with several entries he planned to read Amy. The shopping boosted his spirits and he looked forward to the evening with her.

On his way to the exit, the phone rang. The Russki called his cop story a bunch of crap, cursed his sloppy work habits, gave him 24 hours to finish and slammed the receiver in Martinez's ear. Shit! The call reminded him he'd forgotten Frederick's. He trudged back inside. Disappointing his boss didn't bother him; disappointing Amy did.

The clerk flashed him a smile of recognition, annoying him. Without a word, she led him to a computer, selected the collection of gartered lingerie and stepped back. Martinez wished she'd just pick out a couple of outfits Amy didn't already own in the style Amy liked. It wasn't as if she didn't know by now, even though she'd never met Amy. He clicked the mouse on a fishnet garter-belt outfit.

"That's a popular choice," she said.

Martinez would have asked where they listed the unpopular choices but wanted to get this over quickly. He viewed a lace bustier and a caged lace ensemble, finally settling on the ribbon rendezvous set with fishnet stockings. The clerk left to find the outfit. Martinez felt his agitation growing. He'd noticed the look she'd given him last time and she did again after he made his choice. She was thinking him one of those men with a good woman, but holding fantasies of screwing a whore, or maybe his woman *was* one and he shared her with others, or, or…who knew what else she might be thinking. Definitely this: women don't buy these styles;

they wear them to please a man. A man like you, the clerk's superior countenance said. Martinez avoided her eyes, paid for the lingerie and left.

He stopped on his way to Amy's to buy a tin of chocolate truffles, an assortment of imported cheeses and two boxes of her favorite crackers. At her apartment, he put the champagne on ice, arranged the roses in a vase and wrote a love note for the attached envelope. He lit a candle, queued one of the CD's in her stereo, then walked to the bedroom. He laid the lingerie on her side of the bed, lit a candle and mounted another CD in the Bose he'd brought from home. Back in the living room, he called the restaurant to confirm dinner delivery at seven.

Martinez was sitting on the love seat bookmarking pages in the poetry book when the door opened at 5:30 and Amy breezed in. "Hi, Rick. Nice flowers. Oh, you lit a candle too. I have to get out of these clothes." She walked to the bedroom.

"I'll open the champagne," he called after her.

"That'd be nice."

He started the love songs. "I thought we'd relax with some cheese and bubbly while we're waiting for dinner to come. I got some poems I want to read you."

"Ooh, what's this?"

Judging by her tone, Amy had discovered the lingerie. "For later, like you said. I wrote a note with your flowers."

Women loved romantic music and flowers, poetry and scented candles, champagne and massages. They loved them almost as much as Martinez loved Amy. He popped the cork and poured two glasses of the golden liquid. Amy strutted past him wearing the lingerie. She took one of the glasses, clinked it to his. "Well?"

"I thought I'd read you—"

"You know, Rick, some of the guys at work have been hitting on me, telling me they'd like to fuck me."

Martinez grunted.

"Sometimes, like today, I like to lead them on—"

"You what?" Martinez shouted.

Amy cowered before him. "Please don't yell at me."

"You're my woman and you go out of here dressed like a hooker. You think I don't know what's going on?"

"I didn't mean anything by kissing him, Rick, I swear. We were only kidding around." Her lip quivered. "Then things got out of hand. We got carried away."

"You goddamn whore."

"You're going to punish me, aren't you?"

"Damn right. You deserve it, don't you?"

"Yes."

"Get your cheating ass to the couch and kneel. I'm going to slap it until my arm is sore."

Amy scurried to the sofa and did as he ordered. Martinez didn't like the game, least of all this part. Amy was going through a phase. They would grow through it together. They loved each other.

Martinez approached her. She lowered her head to the seat.

He would make sure she read his note and listened to the poems after dinner.

CHAPTER 11

Linda couldn't remember ever missing a birthday party for Bert Bariteau, or Mr. B as she'd called him before her internship. This year she tacked a twofold agenda to the annual celebration. She'd thought about Bill often over the past month. The young couples at the Cronin party stirred pangs of nostalgia for things that should have been. She and Bill had been a couple, closer to Jenna's age, though not as advanced in their sexual exploration. They drifted apart, not by choice but because life moves on, ready or not. She'd taken years to figure that out. Too many years. Would she still light the same spark in Bill the thought of him ignited in her? Perverse as it seemed going down, her rendezvous with Jack proved she had changed. If she showed Bill, they at least had a chance to reclaim what fate had stolen. She was ready now, or almost anyway. Plus, she wouldn't leave tonight without an explanation for Bert's call the night of the basketball game and why he would ever discuss her with Eddie Cronin.

Mrs. B opened the door. "Linda! It's been a while."

"Couldn't miss his birthday. Forty-five years old, huh? How'd he land a young woman like you?"

"He was practicing for lobbying. I fell for the smooth line."

"He hasn't lost a step either." Linda kissed her cheek and glanced around the room. "Where is he? I want to wish him happy birthday." No sign of Bill, either.

"He's floating around inciting neighbor opposition to development at the end of the street." Then, as if reading Linda's mind, "I think Bill is out back."

On her way to the kitchen, Linda exchanged greetings with several of the neighbors who remembered her from her younger years, hanging around with Bill. The caterer unwrapped iced platters mounded with cracked lobster claws, split king crab legs, jumbo shrimp, shucked oysters and clams. She bent to sniff a bowl of red cocktail sauce laced with horseradish so fresh, the scent tickled her nose. "Where's the bar?"

"Out back. Self-service."

The bar setup made her smile. An assortment of red and white wine bottles littered one end of an aluminum and glass patio table, a corkscrew lying in a small puddle of red among the bottles. On the deck to the right of the table, a dozen bottles of Champagne stood at attention in a slightly rusted ice bucket the size of a baby's bathtub. To the left, a galvanized aluminum tub of ice held brown and green bottles of beer. Linda didn't have to read labels to know the beer was German and Belgian, perhaps with a couple of American microbrews thrown in. The wines were French and Italian and strictly estate-bottled, the Champagne from the tiny village of Ay, France. In short, high- quality drink served up in a setting so understated it bordered on redneck, so typically Bert Bariteau. She examined the cracked and dried label of a short, stubby wine bottle surrounded by a dozen equally short and stubby glasses set out at the far end of the table. Product of Portugal and a 1968 vintage, the label read.

She poured a splash of champagne into a flute and wandered across the crowded deck. She nodded and said hello to a group of neighbors who were talking sports in one corner. The partners and associates of Bert's lobbying firm congregated in the far corner, engrossed in conversation that sounded political. Bill stood in the center. What attracted Bill to *that* group? Her eyes lingered. He wore a pale blue golf shirt, khaki slacks and sandals. Powder blue was his color, accentuating his fair skin and highlighting the twinkle in his eyes. She recalled how Mrs. B insisted he wear sunscreen in the summer, how much she enjoyed applying the lotion for him, running her hands over his body and...

She was getting ahead of herself. It started with a hello.

Bill lifted a bottle of beer to his mouth, listening to the words of Bob Rosen, one of Bert's partners. She moved in near the conversation, not interrupting, half listening, half enjoying the rays of the descending sun and the feel of the tiny bubbles on her tongue and in her nose. The smoke from Rosen's fat cigar brought back memories of Grandpa Baldwin who smoked them out of sight of Grandma and made Linda promise not to squeal on him.

"So how'd you land that contract, then?" Bill asked. She recognized the tone of boredom.

Rosen blew a cloud of smoke. "That was a classic twofer."

"I see. Neat." Bill turned to Linda. "Hey, how you doing?"

"Great. You got a minute?"

"Yeah. Later, though. I need to make a phone call."

"This minute?"

He backed away. "It's on my internship project. I only have a small window to place this call. Sorry I missed your graduation."

So he *was* pissed. She should have invited him.

She drained the flute on her way back to the bar. The caterer had put out the shellfish. Linda filled her glass. She dipped a jumbo shrimp into the cocktail sauce, leaned her head forward and bit. Her sinuses cleared. She washed the shrimp down with a swig of bubbly. She moved to an open corner along the outside deck rail to admire the spring flowers sprouting randomly in an otherwise dormant garden. The word "basketball" drifted by from a nearby conversation. Linda tuned her ears. The reference to Cohoes High impelled her to join two of the Bariteau neighbors, Tim and George, both longtime city residents. "Hi guys, mind if I listen in?"

"Hey Linda, long time," George said. Each shook her hand.

"I'm interested in high school hoops. Maybe you can help me out with something."

"Shoot," Tim said.

"If I wanted to bet on a game, how would I?"

"You wouldn't, season's over." George laughed.

"You know what I mean."

"You're a cop now, right?" Tim said.

"Trooper. I don't want names. I want to understand how things work."

78

"Yeah, there's a couple local books who'll cover your action. Not many, though."

"But they can't get a Vegas line. They do their own?"

The men nodded.

"OK, the line is set, bets made, the game starts. Take an individual player, a Jeremy Cronin, for example. Could a player of that caliber by himself affect the outcome? When I say affect, I mean with the point spread."

"Cronin; better than Bill?" Tim asked.

"Definitely," George said. "Not Johnny, though."

"Nope, never."

"Hey guys, what's that all about?"

"We always compare local stars to the Cohoes High standard, Bill Bariteau and Johnny Marsolais," Tim said.

"Who was Johnny Marsolais?"

The men surveyed the crowd, as if the answer lay elsewhere. Tim shook his empty beer bottle and took George's. "I'll get us some cold ones."

George pointed to her glass. "Want a refill?"

"Sure, thanks. You're coming back, I hope. We were talking about Cronin and point spreads before your little detour."

"Oh, right, Cronin. Be right back."

Curious. They raised the Johnny topic, but when she followed up they reacted as if she'd inquired about their personal finances. She'd find out about Marsolais, but point spread remained her priority. The men returned.

"Thought about your question. A Cronin *could* affect whether Greenbush covered." George spoke with a hesitant tone.

"I detect a strong 'but' in your voice."

"The kid would have to know the spread. The action on these games comes mostly from adults, parents and team boosters like us. A player wouldn't normally know."

If not for the scholarship, it wouldn't be a long stretch to have Eddie involve his kid in a sleazy business.

"And don't forget sportsmanship," Tim added.

"Sportsmanship?"

"Surprised?" Tim asked. "At this level, coaches still have a strong sense of sportsmanship. If you have a team beat, you don't rub it in by running up the score. At the college level, there's too much at stake with national rankings and tournament seeding, strong incentives to chuck sportsmanship and kill the opponent. By the way, that's the reason more books won't take action on high school. Sportsmanship makes the spread calculation much more difficult."

She'd not considered that angle. "This past season, what would you guess was a typical point spread on a South Greenbush game?"

"What would you think, Tim? Good team without Cronin, dominant with him. I'm thinking a dozen or more points a game, except for West Greenbush, maybe only five or six."

"Sounds about right. Why you asking?"

"What if I told you South Greenbush only won two games by more than ten points."

"Wish I'd known." Tim laughed

"And what if I told you Jeremy Cronin didn't play in the two decided by more than 10, each a 20-plus point blowout, including West Greenbush?"

"No shit! You think Jeremy's shaving?"

Exactly what she thought. But why? "No, I can't resolve the scholarship issue. How do these bets work?"

"With the local books, you'd call and get the spread, make the bet," George said.

"No money?"

"Long as he knows you. He logs the bet in a book. After the game, he collects the bet plus 10 percent from the losers and pays the winners straight up. The ten is his vig."

"What happens if the bookie can't collect?"

Tim laughed. "Used to be, you stiffed a bookie a guy named Guido paid you a visit. Today the muscle has a name like Ivan or Vlad."

An Ivan or two probably lived in her neighborhood. Perhaps that explained the photos.

"Forget the nationality. These people make you squirm just by looking at you," George said.

Linda thought of the Hispanic man with Jeremy, how he'd made her want to look anywhere but in his eyes. Jesus! Had she messed up a bookie's muscle? Linda reviewed the coincidences. Greenbush never covered a point spread except two games Jeremy missed. A man attacked Jeremy hours before a crucial sectional game. The man fit the profile of an enforcer. Two students at the Taconic game, Jeremy fans, bet on the opponent she inferred. Dammit! Why wouldn't LeBeouf let her ask a few questions?

She'd kept an eye on the door but hadn't seen Bill return from his phone call. "So tell me about this Johnny Marsolais."

Again the exchanged look that said, "Let's get out of here." George answered. "Big star in the early '70s. Best player Cohoes High ever produced. Your Bill was good, don't get me wrong, but Johnny Marsolais was in a class by himself."

Her Bill. She liked the sound. He wasn't her Bill, though. Not these days.

"No shit. How often you think Coach Wooden flew across the country to recruit a kid?" Tim's voice was reverent.

"Shame," George said and walked away while Tim's eyes threw daggers at his back.

"What happened?

"Bert was Johnny's best friend back then. I think you'd better ask him."

"But—"

"Ask Bert!" He stalked off after George.

She wandered off to find Bert, wondering what happened to Johnny Marsolais, and why did Tim and George not want to tell her.

Mrs. B approached her in the living room. "Police work must be interesting."

Less so when stuck at a desk studying insurance forms, as she'd done for the past two uneventful weeks. "It can be." A hand touched her shoulder. She turned.

"Hey kiddo, heard you moved to my old neighborhood. Must be killing your mother."

Linda hugged Bert and planted a kiss on his cheek. "Happy birthday."

"You having a good time?"

"Nice party."

"I'm going to open that '68 Porto in just a bit. Got some Cubans too. I want you to try them."

Linda had never tried port, but Bert described a vintage port and Cuban cigar with a reverence she was sure he did not display in any church. Maybe tonight, when the men poured the port and lit their cigars, she would try the experience. What the hell, her whole life lay in front of her. "You owe me the Eddie Cronin story."

"Yeah, yeah, but not tonight. Kind of complicated. I'll call you tomorrow." He backed away and began to turn.

Like father, like son. Knowing Bert and his scheming ways, she expected she'd have to drag an answer from him. She didn't expect the treatment from Bill. "You're not getting off this time," she said to his back.

He raised his hands and hustled away.

Johnny Marsolais would have to wait, too. Linda wandered through the house, talked to several of the neighbors. She nearly choked when Mrs. B described her volunteer work with the State League of Women Voters, an organization with a good government agenda that promoted campaign finance reform and greater disclosure of lobbying contacts and expenses. She wondered what Bert thought of that. Not that his view would sway Mrs. B, a woman with a mind of her own.

Bill's disappearance made Linda uncomfortable. He would never blow off a party for his father. Did her presence cause the vanishing act? Or *was* it work, the internship being a large segment of his degree program in computer sciences? A Saturday night phone call didn't ring true, though.

Bert called out from the deck, "Hey Linda. Get out here. I'm opening the Porto."

She paused at the door and considered the tight circle of men gathered around Bert. The knot of women surrounding Mrs. B in the kitchen reminded her of a harsh truth, one she tried to ignore. Linda Baldwin didn't fit in. She didn't fit in her chosen profession and not in most social settings either. She considered going home, but Bert's frequent references to vintage wines and spirits drew her to the ritual. She stepped outside, now illuminated by the dim lights from inside, oozing through the vertical blinds dangling across the open sliding door. Bert handed her a cigar and a pack of matches. A dozen men ringed the deck. She lit the cigar, drawing the smoke into her mouth and immediately began to cough.

"Be like Clinton," her mentor said. "Don't inhale."

He handed her a glass. She held it up to a shaft of light as she saw Bert do. Couldn't be sure, but the dense liquid held a brownish tint. Did old port oxidize? The stuff didn't look like it could taste good. When Bert placed the glass under his nose, she followed suit and inhaled deeply through her nostrils. The scent stirred vague but pleasant memories. A moment later, she placed them. The fragrance was that of the nut trays her mother prepared for the Christmas holidays. Bert sipped from his glass. The ecstasy in his face prompted her to sip. He'd pronounced it "liquid gold." He wasn't kidding.

"Well?" Bert surveyed the group.

"Nutty," she blurted out.

A hush fell over the deck, as if someone had pushed the mute button. Half a dozen men stared at her. The others pretended she'd already left. Bert laughed. "Nutty's a good description, comes from the wooden barrels the port ages in." He raised his glass. "Here's to nutty. And to our esteemed State Legislature." Several of the men laughed and conversation resumed.

Her cigar was out and she fumbled to hold the glass while striking a match. Bob Rosen approached and offered her a light. She puffed, the way the men did and managed to keep the Cuban lit. She concentrated on the Porto and made small talk with Rosen. She went to sip and discovered her glass empty. Bert poured her another. Linda set the glass down and dangled the glowing end of the cigar over the edge of the railing. "Excuse me. I'll be right back."

A debate on the need for a new library raged in the living room. No sign of Bill. Someone occupied the main floor bathroom. When she emerged from the one upstairs, she heard the click of a keyboard coming from Bill's room, the next one down the hall.

The door stood partially open. Bill sat at his computer desk, back turned, hunched over the keyboard, studying the screen. *Video games?* She decided to sneak up behind him, tell him to come join the party', and see whether being alone together in his bedroom sparked in him the same excitement she felt. She eased her way through the narrow opening without moving the door and stepped lightly across the room. Two steps from his chair, her eyes focused on the screen. She froze.

Before her, the monitor flashed images of barely-teenage girls in various states of undress, engaged in sex acts. Bill casually scrolled through the electronic smut, freezing frames in the most disgusting places, quickly copying the URL's, pasting them into a spreadsheet before moving on to the next video.

A man's naked back appeared on the screen. He pried open the legs of a nude young woman. The camera zoomed to her face, fear written all over it. When the man mounted the young girl, Bill froze the action. Linda fought off the shiver. The air was suffocating.

She wasn't sure how much time passed watching the sleazy porn, but her growing shock must have seeped through her skin. Bill turned.

Linda stepped back. She extended her right arm and middle finger. "You fucking bastard!"

He turned off the monitor, casting the room into darkness except for a slender shaft of light slashing across the floor through the narrow door opening and cutting his torso in half diagonally. If it were a laser scalpel, she would gladly perform a vivisection. He leaned forward as if to stand.

"Linda, I can explain." She stepped in his path. Her straight-arm thrust rocked Bill backward onto the swivel chair nearly toppling him and chair onto the desk.

"Fuck you, Bill." She muttered the phrase to herself repeatedly, down the stairs, and onto the deck.

"Hey, Kiddo, you're back. Grab your glass, I got-"

"Sorry. I have to go." Bill stepped through the door, moved toward her. She seized her full glass of port from the rail and tossed the liquid in his face. She jumped the four steps, crossed the lawn to the 'Vette. Her heart raced with the pace of her movement and her breath quickened. Bill followed, his sandals flap flapping, his breathing heavy too. Probably from the digital fuckfest.

She sensed him closing, the breathing heavier. If the pervert touched her, she'd take him down. She had a good mind to stop and deck him anyway. What an asshole!

She glanced over her shoulder when she reached the car. Bill had stopped. She got in and locked the doors. He approached, motioning her to open the window. Linda started the engine, and drove off. At the head of the street, she stopped, opened the windows and sucked down a giant breath of evening air.

Underaged girls! *You bastard.*

CHAPTER 12

For the fifth time that morning, the phone rang. Linda lay on her back, staring at the white ceiling and walls. She rolled from her bed, the events of last night's party swirling in her mind. Her eyes looked as if she'd spent the night crying. She hadn't; not a single tear shed. The ringing stopped. Her face resembled her mother's, a good reason to avoid mirrors. She stepped to the window and stared at the back yard. Linda thought about what she had witnessed in Bill's room. Someone once said a person revealed his true character by his actions when no one was watching. Last night, in the quiet and darkness of his room, when he thought no one was watching, the real Bill came out. She was a fool for going to the party, mooning after him in his light blue shirt, deluding herself they might be together again.

Reminded her of another time she'd been played for a fool. It happened on a Saturday night in November, years ago. Her mother had revealed *her* true character in the quiet and dim light of Linda's bedroom, when she sat on the edge of the bed, stroked Linda's hair and promised everything would be all right.

She stretched on tiptoes, reached for the room shade, pulled down, and then released. True to form, the vinyl recoiled with a familiar "sproing." Time to rewrite the reminder note stuck to the refrigerator with a magnet, the one her father put up the day she moved in: "Buy New Bedroom Shade." She needed a larger note in block red letters. That should solve the problem. Now if she would only remember to bring home a red pen.

She slipped into a silky robe, fastened one button to cover her breasts, tied the sash around her waist and then realized she'd chosen the color because it matched Bill's eyes. Linda pulled the robe off and tossed it into the closet. She donned a worn terry bathrobe, plain white. She padded barefoot over worn linoleum from the bedroom through the kitchen, a room three times the size, the space largely wasted, what with her reliance on freezer, microwave and coffeemaker for her daily nourishment.

The phone sat on a five-foot section of Formica countertop, whose nicks, slices and gouges shattered what little remained of its stone image. The phone's display flashed the number two. The caller ID revealed the last five calls had come from the Bariteau home. She jabbed the message delete button, clearing the memory. She retrieved the bag of Starbucks from the refrigerator and started a pot. She fetched the Sunday Times Herald from the hallway, poured herself a cup of coffee and settled at the table with the paper.

After sports and national news, she unfolded the local section. An article on a brutal rape on Albany's riverfront bike path unsettled her. The photo showed crime-scene tape hanging from thick brush and undergrowth while Albany PD personnel in rain gear examined the area. The reporter described the early morning attack of a woman jogger. The assailant wore a ski mask, but the victim described his skin as white and deeply tanned. Linda thought of Tillinghast's unseasonal tan. Prowling a bike bath didn't fit his MO, but with Dolan on the bench, he had a free pass to rape as long as he stayed in Albany County.

Until Albany cops nailed this guy, the newspaper would fret about a pervert on the loose. Wonderful! Meanwhile, a rapist like Jeremy Cronin roamed the streets and she was the only one who cared. It was maddening, but without Jenna as a cooperative witness, she had no chance of making even a statutory charge stick. The girl struck Linda as too sensitive and caring about Jeremy's well-being to cause trouble. Within an hour of the rape, she'd reaffirmed her love. No, Linda would not nail him on a rape charge, not this rape, anyway. Even her eyewitness account meant nothing. It would require stealth, but he *would* go down. Jeremy Cronin was deep into something and she would find it. Jeremy would not escape without consequence. Tillinghast was two too many. *Strike three, Jeremy.*

The sharp knock on the front door startled her. She crossed the kitchen and peeked around the corner of the shade. Bert stood in the hall, his eyes scanning the pocked plaster walls covered with last decade's clearance sale paint. She unlocked the dead bolt and opened the door. "What?"

He shook his head. "These places never change. I called you twice this morning, thought I'd stop by."

"Why?"

"I didn't leave a message, sorry. Did I wake you?"

"No. Why are you here?"

"Can I buy you a cup of coffee?"

"Bert, you came because you want something. What?"

"To tell you about Eddie Cronin."

Bert's true agenda had as much to do with Eddie Cronin as Steve Paquin's with viewing a waterfall. "OK. You want to come in?"

He looked around the hall. "I'll wait in the car."

"Suit yourself."

Linda closed the door and returned to her bedroom where she straightened the sheets and bedspread. She put on a pair of worn black jeans and a faded Cohoes High sweatshirt. She slipped a pair of battered running shoes from under the bed, pulled them over her anklets and tied the frayed laces.

The drive to the Stewart's convenience store passed in an uneasy silence. They poured their coffees and sat in a booth by the window. "What happened between you and Bill last night?"

"I'm here to talk about you, me and Eddie Cronin."

"You were upset. So was Bill."

"Why would Eddie call you, of all people, the night of the Sectional game?"

"These things never run smooth, and you'll have arguments along the way, but love's like that."

"Eddie's phone call?"

"He's a pol, a good one. He got where he is by understanding connections. I must have mentioned you to him. His memory is uncanny."

This was pure bullshit in the classic Bert the Lobbyist mode. He'd probably said nothing untrue, but that didn't mean she got closer to the truth. His casual "maybe I mentioned your name," stood in stark contrast to Eddie's clear recollection that Bert had told him about her.

"So, you want me to believe the night of the Sectional game, when Eddie learned my identity, he searched his memory banks of thousands of names and came up with yours."

"You got a better explanation?"

"No, but you do."

"Look, I'm a lobbyist. I keep friends on both sides of the aisle. My biggest visible connections are to the party." "The party" referred to the Albany County Democratic political powerhouse. "I've cultivated Eddie to help me out with my Republican connections. It's been a good relationship. We've helped each other."

What he said made sense. The governor was Republican as was the Senate, although narrowly. "Yeah, you never know when you might have to cash a chit to get your kid out of a rape charge. You still haven't closed the triangle."

Bert jerked his head. "Is *that* why he called?"

"What'd he tell you?"

"He told me he understood you were doing your job the night of the party. When you showed at the game, though, you brought a personal vendetta. The case was closed."

"Closed? Thanks to Eddie it never opened."

Bert glanced around the store, his voice hushed. "You sure about this?"

"Why?"

He shook his head slowly. "I know Eddie's kid. Nice boy. Not like him."

Bert might feel differently if he'd walked in on Jeremy and Jenna. The girl's scream still echoed in Linda's mind. "Yeah, well, listen, while we're on the topic of Eddie and Jeremy, I'd like a favor."

"Yeah?"

"First off, find out who's treating Jeremy for his shoulder injury." Linda went on to describe the incident outside South Greenbush High, the

Hispanic man, her intervention. She revealed what she'd learned about betting and her speculation that Jeremy might be entangled in a point-shaving scam. "I'd follow up, but if they catch me, my career is over. I'd like to learn what happened, but not that badly."

"Why would a kid risk a college ball opportunity?"

"He may not be a willing participant. Might explain what I saw with the man choking Jeremy. Or maybe he's like his old man, so full of himself he can't imagine getting caught."

"Unwilling, I'd buy, not the other. About you and Bill, give it some time. These things work themselves out."

There was nothing to work out. She'd seen the real Bill and wanted no part of him. "Thanks for the advice. I'll give him time." A century or two. "What's this I hear about reformer challenges for committee posts?" Putting politics and reform in the same question to Bert guaranteed a 10-minute monologue. True to form, off he went.

On the ride home she asked, "Who was Johnny Marsolais?"

He turned his head toward her. She called Bert Bariteau Mr. Answer man because questions didn't surprise him. Linda had seen the expression on his face only one time before, at a public hearing, when a legislator asked him about insurance company agent appointments in minority communities. He turned his eyes back to the road. "What brought him up?"

"I heard the name last night. Great player, right?"

He stopped at a traffic signal. "I told the mayor a dozen times, this is the dumbest traffic light in the city. You think he'd take it down? Not on your life."

"Johnny Marsolais?"

The light changed. "Back in the early '70s."

"I know."

"Big enough for UCLA. Coach W recruited him personally. Heady stuff."

"I know."

"Back then, Wooden coached the college basketball equivalent to a Yankee baseball dynasty. His blessing was almost a free pass to the NBA."

"I know all that Bert. So how'd Johnny do at UCLA?"

Bert pulled his car to the curb in front of her apartment. He stared through the windshield. "Johnny never got there."

"What?"

"Police report said three men wearing ski masks mugged Johnny coming out of a bar late one night. They stole his wallet and all his money. One of the assailants used a metal pipe to splinter Johnny's right kneecap. Report said one of the guys told Johnny he should be thankful they didn't cut off his..." He drew his lips taut. "Well, you get the idea."

"Who did it?"

"Police never made an arrest."

"Bert, this is a small town. Who?"

"Police report said three men wearing ski masks mugged Johnny coming out of a bar late one night. They stole his wallet..."

Linda pushed the passenger door open and jumped out. When she slammed it shut, the recording stopped. Bert's refusal to share what he knew stirred her curiosity. She had no interest in Marsolais, but why did no one want to talk about him?

She closed her apartment door, stood in the center of the kitchen, slapped her forehead and laughed at herself. The little weasel had not explained what linked her to his relationship with Eddie.

CHAPTER 13

Monday morning, Linda made an uneventful presentation to a Cohoes High career day audience. During the Q&A, a young woman with a near cherub face confessed she could never be a trooper because she could not shoot anyone. "But you can, can't you? How do you do it?" The somber expression and the woman's questions haunted Linda the rest of the day.

She assured the students the rigorous academy training prepared her for all situations she was likely to ever encounter. Linda didn't want to lie to the crowd, but the truth was too unsettling.

By Wednesday, she was itchy and persuaded Ewing she should try to track down the victims from the insurance case. Vance warned her of the probable result, but she needed a respite. Chained to a desk was unpleasant; chained with insurance forms, torture. The beer sting limped to a close, failing to find the flagrant violation its instigators imagined. Turned out, most liquor licensees were careful about proof of age. The State Liquor Authority made a few busts and held press conferences to highlight the violations, largely to justify the expense of the sting. Internally, most conceded New York's liquor-sales compliance rate among the highest in the nation.

She'd served out her sentence for the visit to South Greenbush, and the brass should reassign her to patrol, at least part time. LeBeouf would probably agree to part-time patrol, but the desk punishment originated with Walker, and he just didn't like her. It was imperative that

LeBeouf convince Walker about patrol. She learned a good deal about sex predators' favorite places by being around when school let out.

As Vance predicted, her search for accident victims produced nothing. The final apartment door slammed shut. Linda crossed the last name off the list and stashed the notebook under her arm. A musty basement odor oozed from the walls of the dimly lit hallway. A large mouse, perhaps a small rat, darted from a crack in one wall, scooted across the hall and vanished into a baseball-sized hole in the opposite. Outside the tenement door, she drew a long cleaning breath of outdoor air. When she'd played baseball, she often approached the batter's box full of confidence she could hit the pitcher, only to strike out, as she'd just done.

At no door did anyone confess to even speaking or understanding English, the same reaction she got on her own block when she tried to introduce herself to neighbors. No one recognized any of the names, fostering an illusion that the accident victims never even existed. The two eyewitnesses who bolstered the accident report had both moved and provided no further address information. The move supported Vance's claim. Caused accidents were shows, with every detail scripted, every participant a paid actor except the target driver and usually, but not always, the police.

Back at Troop Headquarters, she placed the call.

Vance was too polite to express the "I told you so" he surely thought. "Sometimes you get lucky. Somebody trips up, wrong person comes to the door, you never know. But these people are well trained and give you nothing."

"How do we crack these facades?"

"Need to get to them sooner. The phony clinics can take up to 180 days to bill for services rendered and they routinely wait that full six months before presenting a claim. Our lobbyists have been trying to cut the billing time frame to 45 days to give us a chance to find the injured parties sooner."

Linda recalled a meeting with the governor's chief of staff during her internship with Bert. The meeting eventually led to a new no-fault regulation. Reg. 68, she recalled. "Didn't the Insurance Department change the rule?"

"Yes, but the courts suspended enforcement. Doctors, chiropractors and lawyers want the new rule tossed. Can't say I blame them. They've been plundering no-fault for years. Shoot, some might have to start working again."

"So how do we find them?"

"Follow the money. I don't know where the trail leads in this case, but this I do know: the so-called accident victims you're trying to track down are not the people getting the real money."

"I'm listening."

"I can't do this over the phone. Can you be at my office at 2:45?"

Troy High dismissed students around that time. Tibbs pulled up a chair and sat, his face looking as if he'd come from a grisly crime scene. "Who?" he mouthed. She held up a finger, her interest in the Vance conversation suddenly gone. "You're out by the airport, right?"

Vance gave her the address, 10 minutes from Troop G, half an hour from Troy High. "Not before four. OK?" Vance agreed, and she hung up. "Jesus, Tibbs, what's wrong?"

He nodded toward the corridor, stood and began walking. When they reached a safe distance from the bustle around her desk, he said, "There's something you need to see."

"What?"

"Pictures." The dread on Tibbs' face was contagious. She wished he would smile.

"Who?"

"Homicide vic."

There'd been another murder, this one by sniper in daylight. "They finally ID the guy?"

"Yuri Pasternov, small-time bookie and loan shark."

She wondered if Pasternov took action on South Greenbush basketball. She thought of the man with Jeremy, a bookie muscle perhaps. "What about him? Did he have pictures of me?"

He shook his head and she felt relief. "Worse, Linda. The file was open on Ewing's desk. On top were three pictures of this guy that look exactly like the ones you showed me."

Her throat tightened. What the hell? A sniper target made no sense. Hit men didn't announce their visits. "Surveillance photos, Tibbs. If the locals had a bead on him, they would have photos."

"I asked. They found them in his personal effects. You need to go in with your photos. LeBeouf's with him. This is some serious shit."

"I've got to find them."

The dread finally left his face, replaced by a look of disbelief. "You're thinking of not reporting them."

"I didn't say that."

"I'm a friend, Linda. I know you."

"Do you mean friend, as in one who does not betray confidences?"

"Yes, but for the record, I don't like your idea."

"Relax, I'm just not running in this minute. I want to think some things through."

"You do that." He left.

Her school surveillance lagged. In the six weeks since Michaud warned her out of Cohoes, she and Lilith had trolled only twice. Desk duty ravaged her one-a-week schedule. Trolling without reconnaissance increased the chance of detection and career end. No, surveillance remained essential. She didn't believe in taking unnecessary risks. If Walker had a reason to keep her behind a desk, he would. Damned if she'd hand him one.

The photos troubled her on two counts. However weak the connection, she didn't like the idea a murder victim with an unidentified killer owned surveillance photos similar to the ones sent to her. More troubling, though, was her growing suspicion that Jeremy had sucked her into his venture. She'd risked her career doing the right thing to spare Jeremy a beating even though she'd seen him rape a girl. He deserved the punishment and more. Now it appeared likely a bookie's emissary had dislocated Jeremy's shoulder, his visit either warning or payment. Regardless, Jeremy stood at the center of a betting scam somehow gone wrong, her intervention rewarded with a warning of her own. Jeremy and she were alive, and the bookie was dead. That would comfort, except she still held photos similar to the dead man's. Why? Jeremy had the answers.

She may have been willing to postpone justice for the rapist to save her career. Now her life might be in jeopardy. *Time's up, Mr. Cronin.*

Her visit to Ewing's office confirmed what Tibbs reported. In addition, the envelope beside the photos bore the same kindergarten-style block lettering as hers. LeBeouf responded to her patrol request by saying he would consider it, and assigning her to help with a Saturday night DWI sweep.

"Who has Pasternov's gambling records?"

Her nonchalant tone didn't sell the way she hoped. Ewing glanced at LeBeouf who was now glaring at her. "Not our case," Ewing said. "Strictly Watervliet. We're coordinating on the homicide, but that's all."

LeBeouf's eyes narrowed. "Why are you asking about gambling records?"

"Seemed a logical thing to say. Gambling is illegal. Wouldn't law enforcement be interested in the records?"

"In other words, you're not."

"Interested?"

"For a second I worried you were about to utter Jeremy Cronin's name, and if so, I would tell you to just leave your shield. A lot neater than going through Walker's meat grinder and then handing it over."

"Sorry, I didn't catch the name. Jimmy who?" She turned and left the office.

Sergeant Rick Michaud took her call with "Baldwin, it's been nice *not* seeing you."

"I try to please. Your guys get anywhere with my neighbors and the photos?"

"We think we found the house. Figure he shot from a third floor window or an attic vent. Daytime, I'm betting attic. Interviewed everyone best we could. Top-floor tenants have access to the attic through the house. There's access from outside. Back of the building, a series of metal rungs cemented between bricks."

"So it may have been anyone. Great!"

"I'm afraid so."

Michaud expressed concern at her news of the photos found with Yuri Pasternov. He said he would step up patrols in the area. "What do you think connects you to the bookie?"

Leaving out Cronin's name, she told him about her fight with a bookie muscle, her suspicions of a link to basketball and some variant of a betting scam. "I'd be real curious if Pasternov's records showed action on South Greenbush games."

"Let me call my buddy, Joey Fruscio, over at Watervliet PD. I'll call you back."

"You got buddies everywhere, don't you? Fruscio, Bigwater..."

"I try not to talk to Bigwater anymore. Every time I do, he brings up your name and off he goes. You sure you didn't sleep with him and dump him?"

"You start that rumor, you're dead meat, my friend, and I don't give a shit what you think you've got on me."

Michaud laughed and hung up. Half an hour later he called back to say Pasternov coded his client lists. The decoding effort had begun. The bookie had not coded the betting events and had indeed taken action on South Greenbush for the past two seasons.

She'd expected that to be the case, the link tying up the threads posing as coincidence, the brush highlighting the bull's eye on her forehead. The one Jeremy helped paint.

"Fruscio just told me something else you might find interesting."

"Like?"

"Remember the vigilante?"

"No."

"She struck. Messed a guy up good, broke his leg."

"Why you telling me?" *I warned you about this, Lilith. We have to stop.*

"Turns out the guy is a repeater and registered. Chief Gilchrest's nephew. He's pissed at his nephew but ballistic over the vigilante. Calling all the chiefs in the county."

A registered sex offender prowled Watervliet school grounds, and the police chief's main goal was to nab the woman who stopped the pervert. Alfred Brown would love the story, but she had no interest in further publicizing the incident. She expected she'd get enough heat without publicity. The broken leg was not intentional, but the man wouldn't listen. Had she been aware of his record, she would have broken both. "Sounds like they're going to get her."

"Don't know. Thought you might like to know he's also alerting the County Sheriff and Troop G. Just a heads-up."

"Thanks." *Wonderful. That does it, Lilith.*

By early afternoon, she'd finished analyzing the situation and developed a damage control plan. Small cities like Cohoes and Watervliet were proving too risky. A stranger might as well wear a neon sign saying OUTSIDER. Furthermore, all of Albany County was now off limits. All the evidence, logic and reason said stop, and that's what she would do.

At three, she drove the 'Vette across the Hudson River into Troy, a city with twice the population of Cohoes and Watervliet combined. More importantly, the city lay in Rensselaer County, Eddie Cronin's turf.

Half an hour of reconnaissance around the school neighborhood yielded ample evidence of the game she sought. She found no evidence of a game warden, though, and that presented a problem. There was at least one warden watching, but she'd yet to identify the individual or individuals. She outlined an approach requiring at least two more visits before activation. After Troy, she visited the South Greenbush Library and found the high school's most recent yearbook. The familiar face with the single earring from the Sectional game belonged to Mark Segretti. A check of the phone directory showed two Segretti listings in the town.

She parked in the MAIA Insurance Company lot at four and went inside. A young man escorted her past an office with Vance's name to a door labeled Conference 3. The scene inside reminded Linda of a movie classic. "You look like General Patton, Sam."

A whiff of permanent marker floated over the solid maple table. Vance had converted conference space to a situation room, where a military strategist might map out a course of action. About a dozen markers, of various shades of the rainbow, many without caps, littered the conference table along with index cards and flip chart pages, containing multicolored cursive text. Five stacks of blank cards stood on one uncluttered corner of the eight-foot-long surface. Hundreds of cards, attached with masking tape, papered three walls of the room, a kaleidoscope of color. Vance stood at the head of the table, silhouetted by the one bare wall, holding a wooden pointer.

"We're in a war, we're losing, and I've got bosses ready to surrender."

"Why would they?"

"Money. We pay the claim, record the expense as a paid loss and pass it on to customers in higher rates. The Insurance Department won't allow us to recoup the late payment interest penalties. The hotshot CFO is telling everyone my stubborn ways are costing shareholders money."

"Are they going to pay?"

"Not yet. My CEO trusts me. Give him another month, though. He'll cover his backside and hang me out to dry."

"So let's crack this thing. Why do you say you're losing?"

"It's so easy to loot no-fault insurance, drug dealers are changing professions. Every crook wants in on the action, and why not? Deal drugs in New York, you'll do state time right out of the box. Commit insurance fraud or stage a phony accident? First time, you'll get a stern warning, maybe a fine. Second time, worst case, you plead to a misdemeanor, pay a $5,000 civil penalty."

"Don't talk to me about punishment not fitting crime." Vance ranted about the theft of money. Sex crimes stole much more and no restitution possible. "What gives with the wallpaper?"

"Remember the Brooklyn ring I told you about the day we met?"

Linda recalled his describing the massive $3 million a month fraud NYPD had shut down nearly two years earlier. "Yes."

"This is what we pieced together. Each card represents a professional corporation. Without getting real technical, each is a doctor or a chiropractor or physical therapist or aroma therapist, MRI clinic and the list goes on."

"Aromatherapy?"

"Correct. Your insurance premiums pay for quacks who light candles or burn incense to heal people."

The cards were spread in a horizontal pattern along the walls, with only three prominent vertical interruptions, one on each wall. "Why the flat organization?"

"You noticed. Pretend that's the enemy troop alignment and we penetrate. What do we have?"

"Nothing." The long horizon of white cards blurred and her focus sharpened on one of the three vertical stacks.

"You're headed in the right direction," he said

"That where the money is?" She pointed to a column.

He tapped the wall six times with the pointer, once on each card in the column. "You're probably too young to remember the old shell games they used to play at carnivals. You still find them occasionally on a street corner around Times Square. The con man has a dried green pea and three thimbles. You watch his hands move the thimbles over the pea. When he stops, you put your $20 bill down and point to the thimble with the pea, certain you're about to win 20 bucks. The con man lifts it and takes your money."

"If you guess wrong."

Vance pointed to the wall behind her where the column stacked eight cards high. "But what if the pea landed over there?"

"How could that happen?"

"How *could* that happen? Now you're thinking like a fraud investigator." He nodded toward the third wall. "Or maybe the pea is over there."

Eleven cards in the column, added to the six and eight made for 25 possible places. She knew the answer but asked anyway. "How many of these places had money?"

Vance turned a chair around and sat facing her. He looked weary. "One. Took us two years to find it and build the case. While we chased them, the crooks netted more than $3 million a month. Three mil, after expenses, per month. Now you tell me. You think a $5,000 fine serves as a deterrent? Five grand isn't even petty cash."

The picture sharpened. "The key is quantity. The greater the number of unconnected shells, the harder it is to find the pea."

"Exactly. We nail a phony medical practice," he pointed to one of the hundred or so low-lying horizontal cards, "the clinic closes up shop and reopens the next week a block away under a different name but same medical license. Closing the phony clinic does nothing. We have no evidence the operation is part of a ring, and the medical provider still has a license to steal."

Linda raised her hands. "These guys are regulated. Don't they yank their licenses for a fraud conviction?"

Vance shrugged. "Nah. We argued the case, but the Health Department bureaucracy is all about protecting doctors. Medical fraud is not part of the equation. There are days I suspect the bureaucrats view no-fault fraud as a subspecialty, not a crime." He tapped his lips. "But that's me speaking, not my company's official position. God forbid we should point out the obvious."

"How'd you find the pea?"

"A single person or corporation controlled all these entities. In this case a guy named Victor Zalenko. He was a thug with the temperament of a third world dictator but smart enough to hire a brain by the name of Ivan Karpov. He's the one who set up the organization. I was impressed and wanted to catch him so we could hire him. Ivan Karpov was a genius." Vance's tone turned reverent.

"Was?"

"A few days before we took the ring down, we got word Zalenko had Karpov killed."

"Zalenko behind bars?"

"No, but his picture is up in the post office. I figure he left the country."

"So, where do we go from here?"

"Find the control. Build a case, like we did in Brooklyn. If I'm right, they're not picking on just my company, they're fleecing everybody. A 250 grand rip-off sounds like a lot of money to the average person. For these rings, it's a good day's gross."

"Follow the money. I presume you know how?"

"It's all about proving common ownership. They try to mask the links. We start with the clinics, focusing on newly licensed in the tri-County the past 18 months."

"Public information. State Health Department."

"Not so simple."

"What?"

"You ever hear about foil?"

"Not the kitchen wrap, right? You mean Freedom of Information Law?"

Vance preached a blessedly short sermon on state government agencies' blatant abuse of the loopholes in the New York FOIL law, ending with "Health Department is one of the biggest offenders."

"I'm State Police. I'll get the stuff without your having to file a request and wait."

"Oh you will, will you?"

"I detect a trace of doubt."

"You know what a mechanic does?"

Bert had defined the term for her during her internship. "Dispenses green grease."

"Right. When this ring came down and people started singing, we got an education in grease. They'd penetrated two insurance companies, three police precincts, and five city and borough government agencies. They even infiltrated a DA's office. Money talks."

"Your point being?"

"The Health Department. Turned out the records they produced during our investigations were incomplete. A Bureau Chief later resigned and pleaded to a single felony obstruction count. See what I mean?"

"Yes." If the ring kept an informant at the Health Department in Albany, any request for clinic information, especially one from the State Police, would raise red flags and sanitized records.

"Any bright ideas?"

"Yes" but none involving the chain of command. "Let me get some advice. I'll get back to you in a day or so."

CHAPTER 14

At Bert's house on Saturday, Linda finally had the face-to-face she sought. They'd spoken Thursday but she'd been unwilling to discuss even the nature of the request over the phone. Now, sitting on his deck in unseasonably warm April weather, Linda explained the information she needed.

"What do you want? The commissioner is a friend. I play golf with her, met all her top deputies. I'll get you what you need."

"I'm not interested in people in high places." She outlined the corruption Vance described from the Brooklyn case. "Who do you know in low places?"

His perplexed look lasted about 30 seconds. His eyes widened, he thumped his fist on the glass tabletop and pushed his chair back. "Hang on, I'll be right back." He disappeared into the kitchen through the sliding screen door. Several minutes later, he tossed a dog-eared black spiral binder of the table in front of her.

She laughed, "Bert's little black book. Can I get a copy?"

He shook his head. "This has every contact I've made in the last 23 years. Today people put this stuff on computers. Not me."

"What if you lose it?"

"What if I *need* to?"

"Ah!" It wasn't a pretty sight, but she'd viewed the lobby game from the inside and had grudgingly come to recognize the legitimate need to conceal strategy from press, public and opponents. The nature of the business demanded secrecy. That would never change. Digital files posed a huge risk to the concealment business.

Bert picked up the book, scrolled down the alphabetical page tabs and flipped open a page near the middle. "A few years ago, I helped a friend whose daughter is a single mom and needed a job to get herself and her kid off welfare. She passed the civil service exam but scored too low for any state agency to hire her. I made a phone call. The commissioner got her a temporary position, and when they could stretch the list to reach her, she got a permanent clerk job with pension and medical benefits." Bert beamed. "I like to help people. This young woman couldn't have been happier. She expressed her gratitude so often, she embarrassed me."

"How is your story relevant to my problem?"

"She's a file clerk at the State Health Department."

Linda resisted the urge to shout "Halleluiah." She sprung to her feet and planted a kiss on his cheek. "How would this work?"

Bert raised an eyebrow. "It might not. The Health Department has policies and procedures for access to records. Any clerk who violates them is subject to firing. A single mom who needs the job wouldn't risk it, if you ask me."

"But you'll ask her?"

"I'll call her. What's your schedule?"

"I'm off Tuesday."

"OK. Let me check."

"Did you ever talk to Eddie?"

"Yes. Hold on." He opened his wallet, removed a folded yellow note, and handed it over. "The physical therapy group treating Jeremy."

"What else?"

"Thinks Jeremy's lying about the shoulder. Orthopedist says the story is dubious. Eddie's worried, wondering why Jeremy needs to lie to him."

"He should worry." Linda outlined the Pasternov murder, his taking action on Greenbush games, her suspicion his enforcer had dislocated Jeremy's shoulder. "If Jeremy was involved with Pasternov, he needs help. If he's not smart enough to realize the danger, Eddie is."

Bert agreed to call Eddie. When he turned the topic to her and Bill and began his relationship advice, she politely took her leave.

***

At 12:15 a.m. Sunday, she'd been working the DWI detail for over two hours. The roadblock at the southern entrance of the Adirondack Northway provided an ingenious trap. The interstate's access ramp stretched for a half-mile. Drivers entering could not see the jaws of the snare until too late. Unmarked cars accosted the folks foolish enough to back up or turn on the one-way ramp.

The sheer volume of cars had surprised her, but not as much as the flurry of DWI tickets she had written, seemingly nonstop in the first hour. Later she had given blood-alcohol tests to people who shouldn't have been driving a tricycle, let alone a motor vehicle. In this, the final hour, she served as the greeter, a simple job inspecting cars and drivers. Good evening, sorry for the inconvenience, flashlight on the windshield for current registration and inspection, shine light in a driver's eyes, check for dilation, ask questions, listen for slurred speech, then direct each car into one of three lanes: DWI follow-up, registration-inspection follow-up or freedom. This would be a breeze.

After the first 10 minutes, the job held all the excitement and challenge of gluing an "inspected by" label to a product moving down an assembly line. Her actions switched to automatic pilot while her mind worked on the information she'd gotten from Bert a few hours earlier.

His Health Department contact would cooperate but would be out a week on vacation. Bert had gone the extra mile and tracked down Eddie to deliver the speculation on Pasternov and the man with Jeremy. Eddie reacted with nonchalance. He said he finally had a serious talk with his son and got the full story. The fight with the Hispanic man was just horseplay. As for the shoulder injury, Jeremy jammed his hand between backboard and rim. Eddie said he believed the boy. Bert told her Eddie's body language broadcast the lie. She smiled at that one. Eddie was a politician and his lips were moving. No further body language necessary.

Eddie had done a complete turn on Jeremy's story despite the evidence. What changed his mind? Pasternov's murder could have been Jeremy's wake-up call. Maybe he told his father the truth. But if Eddie

105

knew, why did he lie to Bert? To protect Jeremy? Eddie was one of the most powerful people in the region. If someone intimidated *him*... The Hispanic man's cold, dead stare provoked a shiver.

LeBeouf had warned her off the Cronin case, but the kid had drawn her into his web and her life might be in danger. This was now the Baldwin case. Jeremy left her no choice.

Linda lost herself in thought of bookies, enforcers and scammers. The parade of vehicles continued. She checked a windshield and then turned her flashlight on a pair of familiar eyes, best remembered from the day they'd gazed into hers under a tree near her house. That snapped her out of autopilot. *What was he doing driving this car?* Inspection and registration stickers checked out OK. She shifted the flashlight to the front of her face. Didn't surprise her the eyes checked out, these the pupils of Mr. "Safe Is Best." She skipped the apology and shone the light on the passenger seat. Leg. Female leg. Bare leg. A lone hand tugged at the morsel of fabric masquerading as a skirt, a vain try to cover the black panties on display. An arm dangled between seat and door.

The woman looked mature, not like a frightened teenager. Linda was tempted to ask Bill when his tastes had changed. They probably hadn't. He probably found it a bummer screwing a young teen and getting her home before curfew. An adult had no such restriction, but the sexual gratification wasn't the same. No, this woman was in Bill's "better than nothing" category.

The textbook said she should detain the car for a possible Section 1227 Vehicle and Traffic Law violation. She played the scenario out. "Ms. Bimbo, let me introduce you to my ex, Trooper Linda. She's the one who threw the book at you," Bill would say.

Bad ending. The driver was sober. This detail concerned public safety. A half-nude bimbo in a passenger seat with an open container, although technically a violation, posed no threat to the public. She had a surprise coming. Wait until she discovered Bill's fetish for exploiting frightened teenage girls.

"Is there a problem, officer?"

She held the light on his eyes. *You bet your ass there's a problem.* Then she called up the voice his father had taught her about, the voice of authority, the one lobbyists used to impose their will on the state capital. "No problem, sir. You're free to go." *Go fuck your bimbo while you fantasize her as a 15-year-old. Jerk!*

The car drove off. Linda imagined the pair's next couple of hours and etched the license plate combination in her memory bank as deeply as her initials on a big tree in a ravine, not more than a few miles away.

CHAPTER 15

Linda parked in the strip mall lot within view of the physical therapy office. She surveyed the other cars, trying to guess which one belonged to Jeremy, settling on the red Mustang convertible. So typical: a privileged kid driving an expensive sports car he didn't pay for, a magnet to lure young girls to his secluded camp where they chose sex with him or rape. She had a good mind to drive away, leave the little prick for the Hispanic man to finish. But that wouldn't be right. Jeremy was her job, and she intended to see justice. Meanwhile, the kid knew the man's identity, the man she now believed sent her photos and killed Pasternov. Today she'd find out.

She'd steered clear of Jeremy for fear of his father, but given Bert's conversation with the man, she doubted Eddie Cronin would risk drawing law enforcement attention.

A few minutes before noon, Jeremy emerged from physical therapy. Linda's early-morning phone call, posing as Mrs. Cronin, had confirmed Jeremy's 11 o'clock appointment. Jeremy looked preoccupied as he walked past the Mustang to a beat-up Subaru. His regular car must be in the shop. He reached for the door but stopped short when she approached. He recovered and pulled it open. Linda kicked it shut. "How's therapy going? These guys any good?"

"What do you want?" His eyes surveyed the parking lot.

"A name. I was the target of an attempted sexual assault. You were witness."

108

"Can't help you."

"You mean *won't.*"

"I don't know it."

"Same guy who cracked your shoulder?"

"An accident."

"Sure, and I'm Hillary Clinton. Tell me about the argument?"

"Who had more game. We were fooling around."

"The guy had you in a serious choke hold, not horseplay. Plus, why did you run from a joke?"

"I ran from you. I figured you'd trump up some other phony charge so you could arrest me again."

"What's his name?"

"I told you I don't know."

"Come on, Jeremy, you can lie better than that."

"I played city league ball in Albany's South End last summer. Coach wanted me to get a taste of the physical nature of the college game. I came up against this guy a few times. He's good, but he likes to talk trash when he's playing. I never knew his name, but I recognized him."

"So he's in the school parking lot looking for you because…"

Jeremy paused long enough to betray the lie. "To wish me luck in the tournament. He said he was the better player, by far, and we started horsing around. Then you showed up. Now excuse me. I'm late for math."

Linda stood aside and allowed Jeremy to open his car door. He slid behind the wheel.

"You're in something way over your head, Jeremy. You won't talk to me, fine. But you ought to contact some law enforcement agency. I got an up-close-and-personal look at the guy who attacked you. He's not somebody to be messing with. Am I right?"

"Thanks for the advice." He closed the car door.

Dammit! She should have followed the guy out to the parking lot and gotten his plate number. She wasn't thinking clearly. His unblinking stare had rattled her. She still had no name and maybe Jeremy didn't either.

But she had no doubt the man had threatened Jeremy the day she'd intervened and carried through on the threat a few days later.

***

That evening, Linda cradled the cordless phone between ear and shoulder and kicked off her shoes. She sipped the pinot grigio from the black-stemmed wineglass and swatted a pillow off the easy chair. She traced a fingertip over the scratches in the maple end table of the living room set she'd picked up at the Salvation Army. Her mother would be as horrified by her furniture as by the apartment location, not that she'd be visiting any time soon. She'd offered to pay rent for a "nice" place in a different part of town. Linda refused. She owed the woman nothing and intended to keep it that way.

She set the glass down, her ears not believing the words. A puff of dust rose from the chair when she sat. She sneezed.

"'Zuntight. What do you think? Will you do it?"

"Did you try Julia Roberts? She's done it before."

Jonathan laughed. "She's busy Saturday night. Come on, Linda, this would be a big favor."

"I want to make sure I got this straight. Your date dumps you four days before the ball, the Pretty Woman turns you down, and you call me up as a last desperate measure, and ask if I mind being third choice. What woman could resist?"

"You'll do it?"

"Let me check my shift schedule and I'll call you back." She tapped the off button and dropped the phone into her lap.

Saturday was a night off, and she'd certainly not have to rearrange her social calendar. He was a decent man; no, more than just decent. They'd had a pleasant dinner a month ago, lost in conversation, as if they dined alone, not at a table for six with both sets of parents looking on. Jonathan had shed his nerd image. He was smart but also funny and self-deprecating and interested in her career. And then there were his eyes. She had to admit, despite her distaste for her mother's and Becky's machinations to get the two of them together, Jonathan had intrigued and enchanted her that evening. He had also confirmed her suspicion of something odd about a basketball team never covering the spread with its star player in the lineup.

On the other hand, four days advance notice for a black-tie charity ball for Albany's major hospital was a tall order for any woman, even one owning a formal wardrobe. Linda had none.

She carried the empty wine glass to the kitchen, opened the freezer to a refreshing blast of cold air. Tonight she grabbed a Frugal Gourmet classic beef stroganoff dinner from an array of options stacked in the compartment. She tore open the cardboard box. Beneath the cellophane, flaccid noodles floated suspended in a crust of gravy. Maybe her recurring dream of being trapped under ice had something to do with the number of frozen dinners she ate alone. The microwave beeped once when she tapped the TV icon. The carousel spun. She wondered about the circle of life. Was she destined to live hers alone? She bet Bill's new girlfriend, Kathleen O'Keefe, didn't eat frozen dinners.

Linda had initially considered not running the license plate number she'd gotten at the traffic stop. Since she no longer cared about Bill, better she not know the name of the woman he now deceived. The following morning she pulled the motor vehicle registration information, although she didn't know why.

No, it wasn't likely Kathleen O'Keefe ate alone this evening. She probably didn't drink or sleep alone either. Now that she had Bill, why would she? Presuming she was unaware of his appetite for minors, a woman would have to be nuts to pass up the opportunity, the equivalent to her sitting here dithering about a date with Jonathan.

Bill was gone. Good riddance. Linda stared at the fading light outside the kitchen window, thought about Jonathan's eyes and the way he looked at her. Despite loathing the idea of doing what her mother wanted, she lifted the cordless phone. She drew a deep breath, exhaled and dialed Jonathan's number.

The Loudonville Salvation Army clothes racks dripped with "gently used" designer fashions contributed by the upper crust of Albany society. She would stop tomorrow and pick up a long black dress and a matching pair of shoes.

***

The following night, Linda stood before a full-length mirror appreciating how Cinderella felt, or would have felt, if she'd been dressed for the ball by a pimp instead of a fairy godmother. Two bedrooms in her parents' house held cavernous walk-in closets. This one housed formal attire. The master bedroom, across the hall, had two closets. One was an overflowing walk-in that held her mother's everyday wear, the second, a space the size of Linda's work cubicle, confined her father's entire wardrobe. She leaned forward, focused on a décolletage plunging so low she might be arrested for indecent exposure.

Earlier in the day, she found three dresses at the thrift store, each perfect for the occasion, but in someone else's size. The trip to Macy's also proved a waste of time, the prices obscene even without considering the fact she'd wear the dress only once.

"This one doesn't fit me." Her mother appraised Linda's image. "I've been getting weight training so, I expect one day it will. You take it meantime." Yes, Linda just bet Arcuro gave her a workout. The woman's reflection shimmered. Saint Michelle, patron saint of adulterers.

Linda had stopped at the gym before her visit with Jeremy. She'd found Arcuro training a different woman, unquestionably one of his harem. The woman glared when Linda approached Arcuro and encroached on his intimate zone. Linda stuck a finger in his chest and told him he had 24 hours. On her way out she'd ripped, from an entrance foyer wall, a large head shot photo of Arcuro.

"Ma, I can't wear a dress like this. It's too revealing. What would people think?" Linda turned and unzipped the back.

Her mother fluttered two fingers and exhaled a "tsk." "Who cares what anyone thinks? You're dating Jonathan. His opinion is all that matters. There's nothing wrong with showing a little neckline."

Linda stepped from the closet and shielded herself with the door. She pulled the dress off and hugged it to her body. "First, I'm not *dating* Jonathan. I agreed to be his escort to the charity ball. Nothing more."

"I know. Becky explained the whole thing."

That smile, same one her mother had worn the morning Linda woke to find a $5 bill under her pillow from the tooth fairy. Linda peeked around the door. "And second, I *do* care about what others think of me."

"You're wasting your time if you think Bill Bariteau will even see you." She searched the rack. "He has a new girlfriend. I hear they're serious." She selected a dress and crossed the closet. "Try this."

Linda reached around the door and took the garment. She handed her mother the one she'd taken off. Serious? A half-naked Kathleen O'Keefe tugging on a skirt flashed in her mind. Linda inspected the frock: long black, silk, a neck-level front, a big improvement. The back plunged, but hell, if it fit and covered her behind, she'd wear it. She pulled on the dress, searched out the low back zipper and stepped back into the closet. Her mother chortled, "I've heard, from reliable sources, Bill's new love interest is talking about a diamond for Christmas." Her face dissolved to pure glee. "You know, don't you, Bert and her father hate each other. This is delicious. Romeo and Juliet. Only this time, instead of the young lovers, I'm hoping the fathers commit suicide."

Linda had no trouble raising the zipper. She traced the fabric line along her lower back. Revealing, but not scandalously so. What was her mother blathering about? Bill...engaged? Kathleen could have him, the jerk. Her stomach churned like the night she'd found him reveling in computer porn.

Part of the story didn't add up, though. Linda had learned the woman's name and made a few calls to confirm her suspicion: Kathleen O'Keefe was the daughter of James "Big Jim" O'Keefe, Albany County district attorney. Bert Bariteau sought out people in power, befriended them. They helped his clients and occasionally even helped him directly. Why would Bert engage in a hate relationship with one of the most powerful men in the county? It made no sense; no doubt another in a long string of "not-exactly-the-truths" from her mother.

She turned, eyes focused on the mirror. The side slit up to the thigh was not her style. Neither were the angel-hair spaghetti straps plunging to support the fabric just barely covering her behind. But, she'd run out of options. Arcuro wouldn't have had his hands on this one. "I'll take it."

Her mother's eyes looked like a pair of full moons rising. "What a gown." Her voice dropped. "This will have Jonathan drooling."

When Linda tried to escape the closet, she stepped on the dress and nearly fell. "Oops!" She lifted the hem from the floor. "Do you know anyone who can shorten this thing by Saturday night?"

"I'll have it ready by Friday."

Bill was about to be engaged. Well, good for him. Pervert. "Ma, I'll need a bag and a pair of earrings, small plain ones."

Her mother crossed the hall to the master bedroom. Linda watched her open the top drawer of what she liked to call her jewelry case. Cabinet was more like it, the piece of solid cherry furniture about the size of a chest of drawers. When she returned, she displayed three pair of diamond earrings on a black velvet cloth. "Any one of these will go nicely."

"Let me try the studs." Small and unobtrusive, good.

"No. I brought those out as a last resort. This is a black-tie affair. The stones should dangle." Her mother handed her the three-stone drop pair. "Try these first. I think they'll work with your face and ears. I hope they'll go in. It's been a while since you've worn earrings."

Linda wriggled a post around an earlobe before finally jamming it through the barrier grown over the piercing. She turned her head away from her mother and winced. Jesus, that hurt like hell.

"Exactly what I was afraid of. I told you not to stop wearing jewelry. You're a woman. You should act like one."

She wanted to tape the woman's mouth shut. Linda jabbed the second earring through, staring directly in her mother's eyes. She responded to the searing pain with a broad smile. She screwed on the backs, convinced the dangling stones would look silly.

"They're perfect."

Linda glanced in the mirror and caught her breath. The earrings radiated understated elegance, even considering the bright red splotches for background. Wearing them for a whole evening would be uncomfortable at best. Probably cost a half-year of a trooper's salary, too, but what the hell. She hardly ever went out and wasn't likely to be attending events like this on a regular basis. Why not wear the good stuff? "Sold. Now the hard part. I need a pair of heels that won't make me a klutz when I walk."

"I have what you need. Let me find them." Her mother knelt, searching a row of shoes lining the floor under the hanging dresses. "I'm just now realizing how perfect the gown is for the occasion."

"What?"

"When you're dancing with Jonathan, all Bill will see of you is your bare back. A reminder of what he lost. Just like his father, a loser." She handed Linda a pair of dainty uppers with thin straps but short sturdy-looking heels.

"You never liked Bill, did you?" Linda had chalked it up to normal parental reaction to a young couple getting too serious, too soon. Her mother shrugged. Maybe it wasn't Bill at all, but Bert. Linda bent over, reached between her legs, and caught a glance of her inner thigh in the mirror. She forced her right foot into the shoe, fed the tiny strap through the tinier buckle, and wondered if looking good was worth all this trouble. The heels fit. Checked the reflection several times before concluding she could, indeed pull off this caper. "Ma, what do you have against Bert Bariteau? What did he ever do to you?"

Her mother knelt, pinned the dress to the correct length for the heels. No answer. Had she even heard?

"Take the gown off. I'll call my seamstress tonight."

"Bert?"

Her mother stood. "I just don't like the man."

***

Next morning's rush hour traffic on Albany's Central Avenue crept along toward downtown, still a few miles to the east. Slower than normal because of a fender bender blocking one of the eastbound lanes, according to the dispatch radio. The envelope containing Arcuro's car sales records partially concealed the face in the photo she'd pilfered from the gym. Her visit yesterday must have gotten his attention. The time/date stamp read "Tuesday, April 27; 9:28 p.m."

A few people stared when she approached the door of the Dunkin' Donuts shop, the first of three logical staging areas for the November "show," Vance's jargon for a staged or caused accident. An hour of flashing the photo at customers provided her answer. None of the males recognized the man. Among the females, however, more than a half-dozen remembered Arcuro. Of those, three recalled seeing him standing outside, as if he were a doorman. Two others remembered him sitting alone in a booth gazing out the window and writing in a notebook. She pressed each about the identity and got a slight variation of the same theme: no mistaking those eyes. She had to agree with that assessment: definitely bedroom eyes. A woman surely couldn't help but notice those chiseled forearms and sculpted body either. Linda could certainly understand why a woman would be attracted to Arcuro. He was probably a magnet for the shallow ones, like her mother, and those with low self-esteem. Heck, even Lilith had to admit a roll with Arcuro might be a satisfying experience. Of course, Lilith's and Arcuro's ideas of a roll were probably worlds apart. He'd presented one opportunity and she'd passed. It wasn't likely he'd offer another. She'd have to make her own.

CHAPTER 16

Enrique Martinez stared in his rearview mirror, watching for the headlights of the red Corvette, thinking of his baby sister, a woman now and near the same age as Baldwin. She'd been devastated when their whore mother had split, ruining the family finances. Martinez would not tell her why they were better off, no reason to burden her with his shame.

Martinez had finished his accounting degree and pitched in to help his old man out. He'd gone on to get his CPA, but his real earnings skyrocketed when his father introduced him to his Russian clients. Martinez had learned his techniques for creating corporate structures to support their enterprises. He soon learned the Russians had other needs and were willing to pay well for someone who could meet them. Enrique signed on for what proved a mutually beneficial relationship. They were thrilled. Martinez was punctual and meticulous. Not one of his jobs had ever led anyone back to them.

At 75 grand a job, he had soon dug his old man and family out of their financial hole and had even financed a Columbia University education for his sister. The rest he'd secreted away in an offshore account for the day he got out of the business. He harbored no illusions. No matter how thorough, no matter how careful the planning, eventually something went wrong: someone made a mistake or a detective got lucky. No, this was a short-term proposition. The Russki presented a problem to his leaving, but he had some ideas.

Headlights filled the mirror and a moment later the convertible tooled down the street. He turned his face away and lowered his head. The car rolled by his Honda Civic. He resumed his vigil. The car disappeared around the corner. He clicked the button on his stopwatch. Three minutes and 20 seconds later Baldwin appeared on foot. At four and 15, her apartment door swung shut behind her, and Martinez stopped the watch. Humans were such creatures of habit.

Martinez lifted the gym bag off the passenger seat and got out of the car, easing the door closed. He crossed the street and headed toward the cement porch Baldwin had used, his black attire providing only minimal protection from the overhead lamps lining the treeless thoroughfare. At the foot of her stairs, he paused and fought off a powerful urge to pay her a visit. She was beautiful and downright sexy, once he got past the uniform. He'd seen her naked once and had not been able to shake the image of her perfectly shaped breasts, erect nipples and pussy. God, how he'd relish having her pussy. This Baldwin woman was no bleached blonde. He caught his lust. Baldwin was not his woman. He loved Amy, the Baldwin sex a matter of honor, nothing more, he reminded himself. No one shamed and humiliated Enrique Martinez without consequence. Not anymore.

That first time, his junior year of high school, he'd thought he might combust from the humiliation. He'd blown off his after-school job and come home to find his mother kneeling at the edge of his bed. Zach Johnson stood buck naked behind her, thrusting himself against her bare ass. "Fuck me, hurt me," she begged. He backed away from the door.

He left the house for the park across the street where he sat, burning with shame, trying to make sense of what he'd witnessed. The more he thought, the angrier he got. That Zach seized the opportunity to screw his mother bothered him a little. Shit, he'd have done the same to Zach's mom if she gave him the chance, although with misgivings, Zach being his friend and all. Zach bragged about screwing a few girls from school, claiming some begged him. The gang pronounced those girls pigs. So, by begging Zach to fuck her, his mother had become just one more of the world's sluts. He would have never put her in that category, but that's where she fell. She was the cause of the shame consuming him. One minute she'd been his father's loving wife and Enrique's own mother, took care of him when he was sick or injured, baked cookies and bread, served tasty meals. Next minute she was just another whore.

He should have made Zach pay that day but hadn't known how. When he tried to make his mother pay, his father ignored the evidence. Martinez had left that world behind. In his new one, the Cronin kid paid for the shame he'd caused, Natasha and Yuri for the humiliation they'd brought him. Better yet, in all three cases Martinez had gotten the Russki to pay him for administering the punishment. Baldwin's turn next. He couldn't expect the Russki to pay for this one though.

He continued past the porch to the end of the brick row house where he entered a short unlit alley connected to a longer one running along the back of the buildings. Martinez peered through a chain link fence bordering the yard Baldwin shared with three other tenants. She moved about the kitchen and poured from a bottle she took from the refrigerator. Mezzacorona pinot grigio, he guessed, based upon his knowledge of the contents of her recycling bin. She carried the glass into the adjoining room. Light flooded out through the bedroom window. He crouched behind the fence. She put the wine down and began unbuttoning her uniform. Blood rushed to his head. He kept his eyes focused on Baldwin, unzipped the gym bag and reached inside. His fingers touched the tripod he wouldn't need for this job. She threw the shirt to one side, exposing a skin-tight white undergarment. He began to stiffen. He groped in the bag. Where was it? She picked up the glass, took a sip of wine and put it down. If he didn't hurry, he would miss what he came for.

He seized the telephoto lens, yanked the camera out, and powered it up. He trained the lens through an opening in the fence, finger on the shutter button. Baldwin pulled the camisole up and over her head, tossing the undergarment in the direction of the shirt. He snapped photos throughout, continuing as she picked up the wine glass and left the room. He lowered the camera and watched her naked back as she walked through the kitchen to the bathroom. He started his stopwatch. Sometime between the 10-and 11-minute marks, she would emerge, her body wrapped in a towel, and return to the bedroom. He knelt behind the fence, watching and waiting.

When they'd met, he'd been so humiliated, so intent on restoring some dignity, he'd failed to notice her ears. He later discovered they were naked. In the pocket of his weather coat, his fingers caressed the tiny jewelry box in his hand. He removed the cover and fondled the dangling jewels he'd bought for her. Soon she would wear them for him. Before she died, Baldwin would have the experience of being a real woman.

At 10 minutes, 24 seconds elapsed time, Baldwin stepped out of the bathroom, body and hair wrapped in towels. She refilled her wine and returned to the bedroom. She set the glass down. Martinez raised the camera once again. She unwrapped a towel, dropped it to the floor, and then the other. He clicked the shutter nonstop.

***

Martinez liked to surprise Amy on Fridays when he could. He would show up at the library unannounced and take her to lunch. Most times, like today, she rearranged her schedule and they enjoyed a leisurely meal at a downtown Troy restaurant. They clinked glasses but Martinez did not drink, drawing pleasure from watching Amy move the glass to her lips. When she put her wine down, the serious face she'd been wearing since he showed at the library was still there.

"Something's bothering you, love."

"No, not really."

"The newspaper?" She'd taken the Times Herald to their lunch. She'd never done so before. The Russki had called earlier to tell him about an article, and Martinez had purchased a paper. The story was troublesome, but not the type of news to upset Amy. Stories of violence to children or the elderly bothered her most, but so did reports of the strong preying on the weak and disadvantaged of society.

Amy nodded, and placed the newspaper on the table.

"You shouldn't read so much."

"I'm a librarian."

"Bad news sells newspapers."

"I like to be informed."

"Reading that crap would put anyone in a bad mood. Was it the parental neglect story?" A mother had left her three children, ages two to five, alone in a rat-infested apartment for two days while she partied with several boyfriends.

"No, the mafia."

She'd read the story. Martinez thought his heart stopped. "Mafia?"

"The Times Herald is doing a three-part exposé on the Russian mafia."

"There's no mafia here, Russian or otherwise."

"You think the problem is only down your way? Read the paper. Drugs, prostitution, gambling. You name the vice, they've been in it. The news is the professional hit men."

He wiped his palms on his pants. "I understand why you're upset."

"Police won't say, but the reporter claims the murders of the three Russians in the past two months are connected and may have been done by the same person."

Was she just upset, or did he detect an accusation in her tone? "If cops aren't talking, could be the newspaper is wrong."

"I don't think so."

"Let's order. I'm starved."

"This is Troy and Albany, Rick, not New York or Chicago or Los Angeles. The thought of contract killers walking these streets creeps me out." Amy looked at him intently as she spoke, or maybe it was his imagination.

"You watch; the cops will get them. Killers always make a mistake." His forehead felt feverish and his head light.

"It's still very...Are you all right, Rick? Your face looks flushed."

"Hungry I told you." He motioned a server and regretted snapping at Amy. "I think it's the wine on an empty stomach."

After they ordered, Amy dropped the news story, and they chatted comfortably about nothing for a while. The food and second glass of wine lifted Amy's spirits and emboldened Martinez. He told Amy he'd been considering a move even before the mafia news. Maybe now was the time. He made his pitch for Santa Fe, a place she loved and whose size would appeal to a small town girl like Amy. Martinez liked that people there knew one another but didn't pry into a man's past. He cited FBI statistics on violent crime showing Santa Fe with a per capita rate less than half that of Albany. He searched for a reaction as he spoke, her face silent as she. "Anyway, I'd like you to consider the idea. I love you and I want to spend my life with you."

Martinez did not use the marriage word with Amy. Her last relationship had ended badly. Some asshole who didn't deserve Amy had deceived her regarding marriage. It would take time before she was ready to trust again, but Martinez knew he was the one. Amy deserved a man with honorable intentions.

Amy fell silent for a moment after he finished, her eyes focused on the newspaper, as if weighing the merits of the crime rate argument he'd made. "Wow, Rick, I didn't know you were thinking of leaving so...This is all rather..." she finally looked at him "sudden."

Dammit! Just what he feared. "Amy, I..." He took her hand, his mind searching for the right words.

She pulled away.

"I'm not leaving you. Ever."

She stared at him with eyes that said, "You lie. You're the same as the last guy."

"It's something I could see us doing in the future."

"But—"

"But only if you wanted to."

"Oh."

"I brought this up because it's been on my mind and I think we should communicate."

"Santa Fe is so far away."

"It's everything you want."

"My job is here."

"They have a library in Santa Fe." The librarian was scheduled to retire within six months, and Santa Fe was preparing to launch a search for his replacement. When Amy saw the job posting, she would remember this conversation. "Give it some thought, and then we'll talk, OK?" He took Amy's hand and pressed her fingers against his cheek. "Don't worry, Amy, I'll protect you. I'll take care of you forever."

CHAPTER 17

Jonathan pulled his car into a metered space on Washington Avenue across from the Fort Orange Club.

"They have a valet. Pull in the driveway across the street."

He laughed, clicked his left turn signal. "You sound like a regular." He checked the rear view mirror and negotiated crossing the four lanes. "I've never been. You?"

"Yes." Not that Linda ever felt she belonged. The Fort Orange wasn't much different from anything else. She didn't know where she fit. Nothing she tried, no place she ventured ever seemed to fit comfortably. Her lot in life: never fitting in, never belonging.

The club stood as testament to the money and power of the people, still mostly old white males, who dominated New York's capital city and ran state government. Established in 1880, when the founders purchased an early 19th century building in Albany, the three-story brick structure faced Washington Avenue, a block from the Capitol and the Legislative Office Building, two blocks from the high court, county courthouse and City Hall. Anyone who was anyone, or aspired to be, either joined the club or made a point to be seen there, particularly when the Legislature was in town.

"Small place. Do they have enough room to hold everybody?"

"Sort of." Jonathan was right. The dinner would require the use of a dozen different rooms and every square inch of floor space to accommodate the guests. By contrast, any one of several hotels bordering the outskirts of town would have held the event in a single ballroom, and without valets sprinting three blocks from a parking garage to the front door. When she questioned Bert, he laughed, rubbed his thumb over his first two fingers. Everything in Albany happened for a reason, he told her. Didn't take her long to figure out the best reason of all.

The valet opened the passenger door, blocked Linda's exit until Jonathan came round to assist her. She fought the instinct to knock him down. Too bad chivalry wasn't dead.

Jonathan's faded red Camry floated like a fish, belly-up, in a sea of luxury cars overflowing the parking lot. Linda noticed the two attendants roll their eyes at each other, a silent argument over who would be stuck with disposing of the vehicle. Kids! In a few years, their younger brothers or cousins would be "Yes sir, right away, Dr. Deschampes" jumping to park his Mercedes or Lexus. That's how things worked in this town. With little effort, she'd be a part. He'd never win a most-sexy-man championship, but he was Final Four material. He liked her, and she liked him. Jonathan was cute, smart, ambitious and possessed a decent sense of humor. All attributes she desired in a man.

Until recently, she'd always measured a man by comparison to Bill, her gold standard. Having discovered her touchstone to be fool's gold, it was time to adopt another. Jonathan Deschampes was not a bad place to begin. Though it pained Linda to admit, her mother was right. A woman could do a whole lot worse.

Linda was pleased to find her steps in the heels almost normal. She experienced little difficulty keeping pace with Jonathan, though, with her on his arm he was obliged to shorten his step. They waited in line to climb the wood-columned front porch. Jonathan squeezed her arm. "This evening won't be awful, I promise you."

They chatted about the weather with an elderly couple in front of them and, within minutes, were inside the front door. A stubby man, bald on top, white hair on the sides, greeted guests beneath an oil painting of ancient Roman ruins ornately framed in a metal that, hanging almost anywhere else in Albany, she would have wagered was painted gold. Here, the bet would be a sure loser. Victorian style carpeting covered the floors of the foyer and, Linda knew, much of the rest of the club. In the corner by the door stood a bronze Japanese urn with dragon handles, which Bert claimed had been donated by a club member who'd served as ambassador to Japan. Christ, an ambassador, what the hell was she doing here? This was her mother's world, not the one Linda lived in. A leather armchair stood beside the urn, a subtle reminder the Fort Orange was a men's club now admitting women. Why a woman would *want* to join the club remained a mystery to Linda. Maybe many of the women were in the same situation as Bert.

Accessing the club was a business necessity. Therefore Bert held a membership. He had no illusions he actually belonged. She recalled her first visit to the club and his leaning over during lunch to whisper something surprising. He'd repeated variations on the theme a couple times since. What Linda recalled from Bert's waxing on membership and belonging went something like: "I know where I came from, and I'll never pretend otherwise. Where I grew up we didn't measure people by what prep academy they attended or which Ivy League school admitted them. If you stayed out of reform school, that was a plus; finishing high school, a major achievement; if you got into the community college, you were going places. And if you got accepted by the State University *and* graduated? Same as hitting the lottery jackpot; no one there had ever done it. Winning happened only to people in other parts of town. That's me, Kiddo, and why I'll never belong here."

She'd remembered the confession, in part, because Bert the lobbyist was a master of illusion. If the facts were indisputable, his interest waned. Fortunately, he'd told her, the truth was rarely black and white. Lobbyists earned their money in the gray, manipulating the shade into black or white, depending upon the client's needs. Bert Bariteau had no trouble manufacturing truths for clients from inconclusive data or questionable theorems. When it came to himself, though, he tolerated no illusion. He'd grown up in the same neighborhood as her mother, the contrast glaring. He stubbornly clung to his roots, almost like a badge of honor, and the woman acted as if she'd never been anything but the spoiled rich bitch she'd become upon her marriage to Linda's father.

Jonathan tugged her arm, and Linda was startled to find herself facing the greeter. She almost laughed when she imagined the man wearing a smiley face button, like the one the greeters at Wal-Mart wore. Linda guessed there weren't many Wal-Mart regulars in the crowd. No, they, like she, probably shopped Wal-Mart as a last resort, the difference being that with Linda, the Wal-Mart visit came only when she couldn't find the item at the thrift store. Jonathan shook the man's hand. "Good evening, Mr. Fischbein. I'd like to introduce my friend, Linda Baldwin."

She shook the extended hand, trying valiantly to ignore the yellow button not pinned to his lapel. "Pleased to meet you..." Crap, she'd missed his name. "Sir." The sweaty palm sliding along hers felt like a kitchen towel that had dried one dish too many. She dropped his hand and resisted the urge to wipe hers on the side of the gown.

"We're pleased you joined us this evening, Miss Baldwin. Your mother and father are generous benefactors of the hospital." The greeter in the tuxedo gushed words as sincere as his handshake. Who picked him to welcome guests?

"My pleasure." Fish something? Yeah, that was it.

The man's gaze shifted to someone standing behind her, as if he were a Department of Motor Vehicles clerk announcing, "Next in line." Linda attempted to step around him, but his hand touched her arm. "Miss Baldwin, wait." His gaze returned, his face lit up as if he remembered the name of a song he'd been humming all day. "I meant to tell you Jonathan is one of our rising stars. Bright future. I bet you're as proud of him as we are." He winked. "You two have a lovely evening."

Something in the tone and wink gnawed at Linda. She nodded at people they passed and, when they were a safe distance, whispered to Jonathan. "Does Fishbait have something on me?"

"Fischbein. Leonard Fischbein, chairman of Tech Mountain Corporation and also chairman of the board of the hospital. Can we drop this for now?" Jonathan nodded at a man walking toward them. "Hello, Dr. Cavanaugh."

Linda stopped, dropped her whisper. "No we can't. What does Fischbein think he knows?"

Jonathan tilted his head toward her ear. "Your mother serves on the planning committee for the ball. You can bet by yesterday afternoon, everyone on the committee knew the identity of my date for tonight. What spin she may have put on the information, I'll leave to your own imagination."

Her mother stood at the far end of the spacious foyer, next to the brick fireplace, one hand resting on the carved mahogany mantel, back turned, in conversation with Mrs. B. Bill's mother waved and smiled. Linda's mother turned, the glee on her face downright evil. She took Mrs. B by the arm and steered her across the foyer.

"Hello, dear. I was just now telling Mrs. Bariteau about your new boyfriend." She smiled at Mrs. B. "You know Dr. Jonathan Deschampes, don't you?"

"Of course. It's been a few years. I'm not sure I would have recognized you."

A hand squeezed Linda's elbow and from behind rang the voice of Bert Bariteau in its familiar command-and-control mode. "Jonathan, you don't mind if I have a private word with my all-time-favorite intern, do you?"

Bert steered her off through the doorway to the nearby reading room before Jonathan had time to answer. Once across the threshold, Bert whispered, "I'll make this quick."

Linda jerked her elbow from his hand. "Next time, ask if *I* mind."

"Sorry, Kiddo, you know how I am. I wanted to tip you off that Bill is here tonight. Didn't want you to be surprised."

"And is he with Kathleen O'Keefe, daughter of big Jim O'Keefe, our illustrious DA, who puts sex offenders back on the street the same night we haul them in?"

"You know her?"

"Let's say I do, but we've never been properly introduced."

Behind Bert, a familiar voice said, "Hey, Bert."

He turned and Eddie Cronin's eyes immediately shifted to Linda. "Excuse me, trooper, I didn't mean to interrupt."

"Well, since you did, let me repeat some advice I gave your son a few days ago. See, I'm betting he didn't tell you about our conversation, did he?"

Eddie answered with a blank stare.

"Your kid is in some deep shit. He's not a convincing liar, either. I had my own run-in with the man I think rearranged Jeremy's shoulder. He's nobody to be messing with. If he were my son, I'd be worried. Get me a name, maybe I can help you. If not, he's on his own."

She stepped around him and headed back to the foyer. Bert caught up. "Jesus, Kiddo, can't you at least *try* to be nice to Eddie."

"The guy has given me nothing but grief."

"Uh, not exactly true."

"Oh?"

"Can't get into it now. Back to this O'Keefe airhead. Pay her no mind. He isn't serious."

She stopped. "A diamond is."

"Where'd you hear that crap, your mother?"

"What's with you and my mother?"

Jonathan strode across the foyer, Linda's mother on his heels. Bert laughed. Jonathan wedged his frame between her and Bert. He draped his arm over her shoulder. "Ready for a drink?"

Bert scowled.

Her mother beamed. "Bert, you remember Jonathan..." She paused, looked at Jonathan and back to Bert. "I'm sorry. I meant *Doctor Deschampes.*"

Bert extended a hand, gave Jonathan's a quick shake. "Nice seeing you again." He whirled around. "Senator Solomon, could I have a minute of your time?"

Linda shifted her eyes between Bert's retreat and her mother's triumphant grin. A game was afoot between those two, and although she'd no idea what or why, she was involved: as willing a participant as the rope in a tug o' war. She linked her arm through Jonathan's and squeezed. "A glass of wine would be nice."

They made their way through the reading room and into the adjoining west parlor, another high-ceiling space. Walls of intricate carved wood surrounded them. Plank flooring, a three-foot chandelier and a grand piano underscored the opulence of the club. A man in a tuxedo sat at the piano playing tunes from "Phantom." Linda eased into an armchair and crossed her legs. Jonathan picked his way through the crowd toward the bar. Her father waved from the center of the room and took a step in her direction, but Fischbein accosted him. Her hands gripped the arms of the chair. Behind them, Bill surveyed the crowd.

Bill's eyes met hers. He shifted his gaze from her to the woman clinging to his right arm and said something. His companion shook her head. Bill shrugged and released her arm. He took a single step in Linda's direction, and she latched back to his arm. They moved toward her, Bill walking like an inmate dragging a ball and chain.

Where was Jonathan? Should she stand? She appraised the approaching pair. Red hair, freckles and a body to stop traffic, especially in that dress. Kathleen's gown was black sequined, low-cut in the front, offering a generous view of her ample breasts. She was taller too, by at least several inches. Linda resolved to remain seated.

Damn, Bill looked handsome. She'd once imagined him in a tuxedo. Now he stood before her, the way she'd imagined all those years ago, but the woman at his side was another, not the Mrs. Linda Bariteau of her youthful fantasy.

"Linda, I didn't expect to see you. Kathleen, this is my friend Linda. Linda, Kathleen. You owe me a phone call, by the way."

"A phone call?" Kathleen blanched.

"Have no fear, honey, he's all yours."

Bill frowned. Kathleen smiled, hugged his arm, her thigh now resting against his. "I'm pleased to meet you, Linda. I've heard a lot about you. You're a policeman, right? Sorry, I meant officer."

Like hell she was sorry. Where did this bitch get off calling her a policeman? "Trooper."

Kathleen looked at Bill with cow eyes. "An unusual career choice for a woman, don't you think, dear?"

"Actually, my *dear*, I find the job exciting. You pull a car over, late at night, you never know who or what you might run into."

Bill blanched. Was he worried his current and his ex might get into something?

"I have a government job, too."

"Isn't that nice?" Linda had gotten hers by busting her ass, Kathleen no doubt courtesy of a phone call from her old man. Linda uncrossed her legs and stood. Jonathan approached, drinks in hand. She reached past the woman for Jonathan's outstretched arm, took the glass of wine and drew a long sip. When Jonathan was beside her, she twined her arm through his. "This is my date, Jonathan Deschampes. Jonathan, I believe you know Bill, and this is Eileen…Oh, I'm sorry, *dear*, what did you say your last name was?"

"O'Keefe. Kathleen O'Keefe."

Linda summoned up her most convincing embarrassed-face mask. "Ah, yes. Now, if you'll excuse us." She turned a hard stare on Kathleen. When the woman blinked and looked down, Linda tugged Jonathan's arm and walked away.

Arm in arm, they wandered through the main floor of the clubhouse, Jonathan sipping a ginger ale, Linda her glass of wine.

"My mother tells me they're getting married," Jonathan said.

"So I heard."

He squeezed her arm. "One man's loss can be another man's gain."

"Time to change the subject."

Jonathan remained quiet for a moment and then exhaled a low whistle, raised his eyes as if calculating. "Bet they clear three-quarters of a million."

Linda touched her glass against Jonathan's with a clink. "Money bores me. Let's talk about something else."

Jonathan released her arm, leaned his back against a wood banister, railing worn smooth by more than a century of moneyed hands skimming its surface. He cocked his head back wearing the know-it-all face they teach in Medicine 101. "Now why does that not surprise me?"

"What?"

"Ever wonder why money bores you?"

"No." There were too many interesting things to wonder about. She was about to tell him to drop the attitude when he did, as if he had read her mind.

A stream of people made their way to the main dining room. A server, holding a tray of filled glasses, offered them champagne. Jonathan declined. Linda glanced at her half-full glass and resisted the urge to take a full one. The server left. Without warning, Jonathan reached for her hand, pulled her closer. "Care to hear what I think?" Their cheeks nearly touched, his voice a whisper.

Had she taken a refill, there'd be bubbly dripping off his tuxedo. As it was, she barely avoided dropping the glass. His warm breath breezed over her neck, and the tip of his nose grazed her ear lobe, nudging the dangling diamonds. A faint scent of distantly familiar cologne drifted up and fluttered in her chest. "I do."

Someone in the crowd bumped her into Jonathan's embrace, his arms circling, steadying her. He sighed in her ear, moved his head back, his cheek grazing hers, but his hands remained at her waist. Jonathan's closeness, scent and firm arms overwhelmed her, stirred a memory of things past. Did her cheeks and ears look as red as they felt?

He studied her face. "I think money bores you because you never went without."

She sighed, leaned against his chest. In this town, it always came down to money. Jonathan knew; her mother and Bert knew; everybody knew.

"Did you hear your parents argue constantly because there wasn't enough money?" He touched her cheek, his hand cool and refreshing against her fevered skin. "Did they mortgage their house to provide your education?" She fought the urge to kiss him. "Linda, you OK? You look warm."

"Warm" didn't begin to describe her temperature. What was going on? It was as if Jonathan had sprinkled melt-away on the tundra encasing her feelings toward male advances. A man was touching her and she wasn't seeking an escape route, had no plans to take him down. The man wasn't Bill, though, and that made her wonder. Maybe this whole thing *hadn't* been entirely her fault, her aversion to Bill a perfectly natural reaction. If she'd sensed the nature of his fetish, that would explain her intuitive reaction. Must be the case. She sure wasn't shrinking from Jonathan. In fact, if he kept this up he could probably talk her into skipping dinner. Gradually, the truth of Jonathan's observation seeped through her. "I'm sorry. Maybe I misunderstood. Are you saying I'm a spoiled brat?"

Jonathan kissed her cheek at the edge of her mouth, released her and moved from the banister. "No. I'm saying money matters more to those who don't have it than those who do."

"Yeah?"

"I appreciate what my parents sacrificed for me. I wonder if you do." He shook his head the way Grandpa Baldwin used to when she fielded a ground ball without first getting her body in front of it.

"My father worked long, hard hours to make our family financially secure."

"What about your mother?"

"Don't go there, Jonathan."

"I bet money doesn't bore her."

"I'll say. The woman has a one-track mind."

"*The woman* is your mother. My mom's told me about their growing up together. I probably know more about her than you do."

Becky thought Linda's mother walked on water, rendering her account of things suspect. "Good. Let's go. People are heading to dinner."

Beth, the hostess, stood sentry at the door to the main dining room. She glanced at Jonathan but focused on Linda. Bert had told her Beth possessed an uncanny ability to put names and faces together. "Hello, Miss Baldwin. Are you one of Mr. Bariteau's guests this evening?" She ran her finger down a sheet of paper.

"No, I'm the guest of Dr. Deschampes."

Beth glanced at the sheet. "Might it be under a different name?"

"Maybe under the hospital name?" Jonathan sounded worried.

"I'm sorry, Dr. Deschampes. Hospital employees have tickets paid for by one or more benefactors or corporate sponsors. Wait one second." She scanned the list. "Ah, there you are. You and Miss Baldwin are the guests of Mr. and Mrs. Baldwin."

Jonathan's puzzled face indicated he was as surprised as Linda was. A thought crossed her mind and she wondered if her law enforcement career would render her eternally suspicious. Probably, at least in situations involving an individual who was inherently suspect. Linda extended a hand. "Beth, would you mind if I took a quick look at that list?"

"Not at all."

Linda scanned the sheet, smiled and handed the list back. "When did you print this list, Beth?"

"I don't recall. About two weeks ago. Why do you ask?"

"No reason. I noticed that some printed names are crossed off and replaced with handwritten ones." Linda could barely contain her laughter.

"Yes. I handwrote all the name changes from the last two weeks."

Linda peered into the dining room. Her father stood talking to her mother by a large table set for 10. "Ah, there's my father's table."

Beth touched her arm before she moved. "Your father and mother have two tables in the main dining room. You and Dr. Deschampes are seated upstairs in the Corning Room, a small dining room set with tables of four."

Jonathan shot Linda a quizzical look, which Beth must have intercepted. "The planning committee thought it a good idea to seat the younger couples together, in a more intimate atmosphere."

Her mother's handiwork. If she could have arranged it, she'd have a private room, table for two and a sofa bed. Subtlety was not her strong suit. "Thanks, Beth."

As they mounted the stairs to the second floor, Jonathan said, "What was the deal with the invitation list?"

"When did you know I was coming with you to the ball?"

"A few days ago."

"My name is printed beside yours on the list Beth ran off two weeks ago."

"How could that...?" Jonathan's confusion evaporated and he laughed. "Mothers!"

At the top of the stairs, Linda told herself her fears were baseless. Not even her mother would be so diabolical as to seat her and Jonathan in the same room as Bill and Kathleen. They were the final couple. No Bill. Linda exhaled.

***

They shared a table with a colleague of Jonathan's and her husband, an aspiring novelist who expressed fascination at Linda's career choice, asked her questions and jotted notes on a sheet of paper he stashed in his inside jacket pocket. The dinner conversation was friendly and the husband didn't call her a *policeman*. Linda devoured the tenderloin and lobster tail and wolfed down her baked Alaska. It wasn't Frugal Gourmet, but then again her father had paid $2,500 for the meal. After dinner, a waitress served coffee.

The sound of the orchestra tuning their instruments floated up the stairs. Jonathan glanced at his watch, nodded at the woman across the table. "Are you on tomorrow, Ellen?"

The corners of her mouth turned down. "Don't remind me. Seven a.m. to 11 p.m. in ER." She stifled a yawn. "It's too bad. We'd like to stay, hardly ever go out together without the kids."

Jonathan began a yawn but covered his mouth, turned to Linda. "My shift starts at seven, too. Sixteen hours in maternity."

The afterglow of their brief tête-à-tête lingered. "Come and dance a couple of dances with me, Jonathan." She put a hand on his arm, rubbed the black silk fabric of his tuxedo. "Then you can take me home."

Downstairs, spectators ringed the west parlor, the center jammed with couples waltzing to the strains of The Blue Danube. They edged through the gawkers and Jonathan folded an arm around her, pulling her close. She took his hand. Their feet moved in time with the beat as if they'd been born to waltz together. When she saw her mother in the front row of onlookers, she closed her eyes and floated off on the melody. They stopped when the waltz ended. She rested her head on his chest. The orchestra struck up the next waltz, and she opened her eyes in time to catch her mother's beaming smile before Jonathan whirled them away. A moment later, she wished she'd kept them closed. Not three feet away, Bill's graceful body melded with that woman's. He seemed oblivious to her presence in Jonathan's arms. Understandable because Kathleen's breasts threatened to overflow her gown. No, that wasn't it. Worse, much worse. His eyes seemed lost somewhere in hers.

What did Bill see in the exhibitionist? At first, she thought the answer obvious: Anatomy for Dummies. That look, though, had nothing to do with anatomy. She closed her eyes, rested her head against Jonathan's shoulder. When the waltz ended, she traced an index finger down the buttons of his shirt, brushed at a stray hair she imagined in his eyebrow. "I'm ready to go."

***

Jonathan parked across the street from her apartment and cut the engine. "Thanks, Linda. You bailed me out. This has been fun."

She leaned across the center console and kissed his cheek, touched his thigh gently. "I had a good time."

He shifted from behind the steering wheel, draped an arm across her shoulders. A set of urgent currents sparked down her exposed back. She leaned forward, shifted around to face him. His lips found hers, lingered, tender and polite. She traced her tongue over his lips. His kiss lost its manners. He pulled her close, and her thigh jammed against the center console. He stroked her shoulder, paused briefly to cup her breast, journeyed to the slit in her gown and inched up her thigh. She parted her legs, the way she had for Bill, all those times, all those years ago.

Bill's gone. Grow up. She was with Jonathan now. There was no mistaking the tingle from the scent of his skin, his warm breath on her cheek, his unhurried hand caressing the path she suggested. She'd not planned on this, though, and worry slipped into her mind. If she invited him in, logical given the cramped quarters, Jonathan would interpret the invitation only one way even if she were to preface it. Not that she minded that interpretation, but what if it happened again? Would Jonathan understand? "You blink, you lose." Sensei Allan's words echoed in her ears. She pried her lips from his. "Jonathan, why don't we…" The console vibrated against her thigh. Jonathan pulled back. The vibration stopped.

"Shit!" he muttered. "Why don't we what?"

The vibration returned. He fumbled in his coat pocket, pulled out a slim cell phone, and examined the screen. "Hold that thought." He punched a button. "Deschampes here." Jonathan listened. He rolled his eyes. "I don't suppose this can wait a few hours?" He grimaced. "I didn't think so. Be there in a half-hour." He slipped the phone back in his pocket. "Sorry, we're having midnight madness in maternity tonight. They need an extra body to deliver the merchandise."

A tension she'd not recognized drained from her body. "Duty calls."

He drew a deep breath, exhaled. "Just thinking, I won't need coffee to keep me alert tonight." He laughed and kissed her cheek. "We should do this again, when I'm not on call."

"I'd like that, Jonathan." Something tugged at the back of her mind. She felt as if she'd re-lived the night she'd realized Bill was the one and planned to make love to him. She wondered if this reaction was to

Jonathan or to the ghost of Bill Bariteau and things that might have been. Would she really like to do this again?

Jonathan walked her to the door, pulled her tight against his body and kissed her, his tongue on her lips. His mouth moved along her jaw line. She licked her lips, tasted salt, his breath on her neck and ear, damp and clammy. He whispered, "When can I see you again?"

"You better get going." She pulled away gently. "Babies don't wait. I'll give you a call, OK?"

Halfway across the street, he turned. She waved her fingers at the kiss he blew, then opened the door to the front hall. Behind her, a car door shut. She closed the door, muting the sound of an engine cranking for life, as if not quite ready to run. Linda slumped against the banister guarding the stairs to the second-floor apartment. She drew a deep breath. It had been a long time since an encounter with a man left her feeling moist and rubbery. Before tonight, he had always been Bill.

A giggle floated down the stairs. A grunt followed and a deep male voice uttered a short phrase in a foreign language, Russian, she surmised. Linda smiled. Her new neighbors. A door upstairs creaked, then banged and the hallway fell quiet. They were newlyweds or new lovers, she'd guessed, but not from anything they'd said. What passed for conversation in this neighborhood maxed out at a nod and a greeting that might or might not be returned. No, she figured the relationship from the ceiling noises in her bedroom at all hours of the night and early morning. A thought of Bill and Kathleen flashed in her mind and, just as quickly, she banished the image.

***

The second pinot grigio went down as cold and crisp as the first. Linda poured a third and returned to the living room. The opening bars of Moonlight Sonata floated in the dark. Her jaw tightened. She figured Kathleen had her own place, her address different from her father's. No doubt, Bill was there now. She dropped her chin to her chest, held it for five seconds and leaned her head as far back as possible, savoring the stretching of the disks. Moments later, the tension spread back up her neck into her skull. She downed two ibuprofen and the rest of the wine and went to bed.

At one a.m., Linda turned the pillow over for about the fifth time since midnight. The room was stuffy, but no worse than it had been Friday night.

She sat up and tossed her pillow at the mirrored dresser, where, a few hours earlier she had checked her appearance before opening her door for Jonathan. She'd looked into the mirror and seen her mother's eyes. When she'd blinked, her mother's face had superimposed her own reflection. Like mother, like daughter, the saying went. The thought appalled her.

She sprang from the bed, and landed a step from the bedroom window, which opened onto a tiny fenced plot of green and brown weeds the landlord called a back yard. The rear fence bordered an ash and cinder alleyway that separated the plots of weeds and rows of apartments on her street from those facing the next street over. The neighborhood kids played kickball and other games on the cinder during the day, and the teens, paired off, monopolized the alley after dark, sheltered from the halogen lamps that shed incessant rays on every square inch of the stark, treeless street.

Linda raised the window. A hint of fresh air fluttered in, but the night was still. No wonder the room was stuffy. The waxing half moon beamed into the clear night, projecting a shadow line that ran through the center of the alley. A couple leaned against the side of a shed in a back yard across the way. They kissed, their hands wandering all over each other. She smiled and shook her head at the thought of the spark Jonathan had ignited. Jonathan was everything a woman could reasonably hope for in a man. True, he wasn't Bill, but that was a plus, now that she no longer wanted the pervert.

She retrieved her pillow from the floor, removed her nightshirt and lay on the bed, face up, in her underwear. A few minutes later, the noise started and she imagined the ceiling vibrating to the rhythmic beat of bedsprings overhead. Eventually, quiet returned.

When the shivering began, Linda covered herself with the sheet and wondered about the chill. The tears arrived without warning. She willed them to stop. Linda Baldwin didn't cry. She was past that phase. Last time was Grandpa Baldwin's funeral. When she left for six days in Aruba on spring break, Grandpa had been healthy as they came. Two days later, he had an aneurism and died. She arrived home in time for the wake and funeral. Her Grandpa had been a friend; a cheerleader and mentor. He taught simple moral and practical lessons and reinforced them with his familiar admonition. Whether it involved not getting her body in front of a ground ball or not speaking to others with respect, his "No!" served as a powerful reminder to do things right.

His death punched a hole in her life, and she raged he'd been taken without her permission. He'd never gotten to explain what he meant when he'd spoken of her need to find the real Linda Baldwin. She felt guilty she'd never said a proper goodbye. She blamed herself for waiting too long to tell him what he meant to her. Yes, she'd wailed futilely, cried herself dry over her loss.

That was then, though. Linda Baldwin didn't cry anymore, going on what, six years now. Her tears turned to sobs. She slapped her face. She told herself to grow up and stop acting like a helpless little teenage girl. Like other vices, crying created a temporal respite from the eternal aching of the human condition, a guilty pleasure she could ill afford. In the end, she rolled over on her stomach, hid her face in her pillow and gave in, the way she had that night after they buried Grandpa.

CHAPTER 18

On Sunday morning, a pair of argumentative crows, perched on the ledge outside her window, woke Linda from a restless sleep. She blinked crusted eyes against the daylight washing through the dusty screen. She wandered to the kitchen to find she had run out of coffee. A quick scan of the cabinets, refrigerator and freezer reminded her she was out of just about everything. Linda hated grocery shopping and had always blamed it on the monotony of the activity. But she'd come to realize the routine exposed the bleak truth of her existence: she slept alone, ate in solitude and had no one to share her life. Kathleen had Bill, but that was her problem. She thought about Jonathan and their good time together. The man certainly had what it took to arouse a woman. She should call him. Her mother would just love that. Linda dressed and grabbed a few sheets of blank notepaper and a short pencil.

At the local Stewart's, Linda paid for her coffee and the Sunday paper and settled into a booth near the window. She pulled out paper and pencil and quickly created a grocery list. Setting it aside, she removed the comics section from the newspaper, exposing the news. "Second Rape." The headline perched atop a photo of four people in slickers. Two of the figures had backs to the camera, the words "Albany Police" printed on the rain gear. The opening paragraphs told of the early Saturday morning assault of a woman jogger on Albany's riverfront bike path. A near carbon copy of a rape two weeks earlier, according to police. The MO appeared the same, both victims giving similar accounts of an attack by a man wearing a ski mask, leading the press to conclude Albany had a serial rapist on its hands.

The lead story concluded on page 10, adjacent to a sidebar "woman-on-the-street" interviews inquiring about how safe they felt. What did this dipshit reporter expect their answers to be? *What do you think, Lilith? Do reporters ask dumb questions, or what? Would you be safe jogging on the bike path?*

What was that?

Really?

She folded the newspaper back to page one and stared out the window. A few minutes passed and she glanced down at the photo. She inquired at the counter about unsold newspapers. The clerk gestured at a stack in a far corner and told Linda to help herself. Within minutes she'd located the relevant edition and confirmed her recollection. The first rape occurred on a rainy day, a Saturday. She left the Stewart's for the supermarket.

After grocery shopping and restocking her refrigerator, freezer and cabinets, Linda thought the apartment almost looked lived-in. She ate lunch, then drove to Crossgates Mall, which had several shoe stores. Within a half-hour, she found what she needed.

Linda tightened the laces on the running shoes. The Shoe Locker clerk smacked bubble gum and crooned. "They look so cool. They're, like, so you."

"Hang on," she said to Miss Bubble Gum and trotted away. Damn-near like jogging on air. Expensive at 70 bucks – sale price. Linda motioned to the pink bubble at the far end of the aisle, pointed at the shoes, turned a thumb up. Her cell rang.

The girl pulled an earphone from her ear and said, "Huh?"

She flipped the phone open. "I'll take these. Hello?"

"You'll take what?" Bert asked.

"New running shoes."

Bert was silent for a moment. "I don't like—"

She snapped the phone shut. He called again. "I got the Health Department thing lined up. We'll meet at Stewart's tomorrow morning. I'll have the details by then. Listen, this jogging idea is a bad one."

"I didn't ask your opinion."

"Don't do this."

"Bye, Bert."

"You'll think about it, right?"

'Right." *You thinking about it, Lilith?*

What?

Yeah, I thought so.

***

Monday morning, Linda inched along below a frozen crust, observed the apparition above, always at her feet. A form took shape through a thinning veil. She conserved her energy, refused to flail against the immovable, confident of her eventual freedom. The figure lunged. The ice parted and a body slammed hers, hands and arms clutching her, pulling her close. She rolled, trying to shed the weight, but found it locked to her. An anchor plunged past her head and dragged them to the black icy depths, entwined as though one. A solemn voice in the distance pronounced, "Until death shall you part."

She blinked her eyes open and the images receded, but she had a strange sense this was not the first time she'd had the dream. She rarely recalled dreams, even immediately after waking, and was sure that was a good thing. Linda dressed and headed out to the bike path.

Twenty minutes later, sweat trickled from her hairline and stung her eyes. She swiped a hand across her forehead. Her chest heaved and her lungs felt as if she were jogging toward hell. The I-90 Bridge over the Hudson loomed in the distant haze, the span sloping skyward over the bright red disk peeking above the trees lining the east bank of the river. She glanced at her watch. Damn, just started, and she was already struggling to keep her normal pace. That was the price for her nearly one-year layoff. Five minutes later she stopped, not just for the sake of the fire in her lungs, but more importantly to record observations in the two-by-three notepad stashed in her arm pack. Sweat dripped from under the armband.

The path was marked with half-mile distance posts. The first mile from the main parking lot offered two interesting possibilities. Thick brush on both sides afforded the seclusion a rapist needed, and the steady hum of vehicles on the nearby bridge access ramp would dampen a cry for help. The Hudson waters were visible from each. She marked their descriptions and assigned an "A" label.

Over the next three miles, Linda identified five A and a half-dozen B locations. Along the route, she encountered a score of runners, walkers and cyclists, male except for the two women jogging together. She stopped to rest at the Watervliet parking lot. Vehicles occupied every space, overflowed to a narrow street under the interstate that connected city to riverfront.

"Excuse me."

She snapped her head in the direction of the sound. A man approached: about Bill's height, but jet-black hair, gray jogging shorts, white Nikes, black T-shirt, dry. He was trouble. She walked away. The steps closed behind her. She began to jog.

"Ma'am, please stop."

She spun to face him and raised her two hands. "Don't hurt me."

He stumbled back, as if she'd fired a nine millimeter into his chest. "It's OK. Calm down."

Linda glanced around the parking lot. "I noticed I was alone in here. A woman can't be too careful. Sorry." She bit her tongue to keep from addressing him as "officer," which she was almost certain was correct.

The man backed up another step. He was late 30s, early 40s, and his mannerism suggested professional reaction to a frightened female. Now if only finding the rapist were as easy. He moved his hands behind his back. "Yeah, careful. That's what I wanted to mention." He shrugged. "I didn't mean to frighten you."

"Careful?"

"You're jogging alone. Do you have a partner you could jog with?"

Partner? *Gee, officer, like a husband or boyfriend to protect me?* "I'm in town on work." Technically true. "I've used this path before and never had any problems." Ditto. "Should I be worried?"

Christ, she'd become Bert Bariteau's clone. Make two true statements, however irrelevant, then follow up with a solicitous question. "Power shifts from the inquisitors to you." Bert had uttered the maxim as

Galileo had pronounced the world round, not an opinion but irrefutable scientific fact.

"No need to worry. Police have been urging women to use the path with a friend. If you're from out of town, you probably didn't know."

No need to worry? That was a bald-faced lie. This cop needed a seminar in Bariteau truth-isms. "Why, has there been trouble?"

"Everything's under control."

The guy's name had to be Peter. One more assurance like those two and the cock would surely crow three times. "Thank you for the advice."

She turned and jogged southbound, in the direction from which she'd come. Rounding the first curve in the path, she slowed her pace to a brisk walk. On the return, Linda stopped at each of her A locations to record supplemental information in the notepad and to snap mental photos of the surroundings.

She returned home and showered. The phone rang as she wrapped a bath towel around her body. She hurried to the kitchen, checked the caller ID. "Bert?"

"Eight-fifteen at Stewart's." Click.

She glanced at the clock. Fifteen minutes, plenty of time.

She tucked the $4 cotton blouse into the designer jeans she had also picked up at the Salvation Army thrift store. She slipped on a pair of leather sandals and headed out the door. On the drive across town, she found herself smiling at the thought of her mother's horror should she discover her daughter dressed in a $20 SA Boutique spring outfit.

The 'Vette fit easily in the sliver of space between a black Dodge Ram pickup and a panel van with the lettering "Albany Auto Glass Repair." No sign of Bert's car. Linda paid for her coffee and newspaper. She perused the front page. "No new leads in rape cases." *New* leads? Based upon what she'd read, it didn't appear they had much to go on from the start, although that didn't necessarily mean anything. Maybe Bert would know. The newspaper quoted Detective Leonard Volkan. "Albany Police are conducting a methodical and thorough search of all the leads provided by physical evidence, victim interviews and other possible witnesses."

She slipped the sports section from the paper and scanned the front page for baseball scores. A headline in the lower left corner grabbed her attention. "S. Greenbush hoops coach resigns," followed by a classic news account covering who, what, where and when, but not why. Boys varsity basketball coach Derek Reynold abruptly resigned his position on Sunday afternoon, shocking the local high school basketball community. South Greenbush school officials confirmed the resignation but offered no details. Reynold was not available for comment. Linda stared out the window, mulling over the story. A horn blared, interrupting her musing. Bert motioned from his car for her to join him. She pointed at her coffee, raised her palm. He shook off her inquiry and gestured for her to come out.

As soon as she closed the car door, Bert said, "About this jogging thing…"

"Health Department, Bert."

"Can't talk you out of it?"

"You said you had details."

"Be careful, Kiddo. I don't want anything happening to my future daughter-in-law."

The man was delusional. "Done, now how do I get in?"

He pulled a folded paper from the inside breast pocket of his blazer and waved it. "You have no idea how much I don't like this. If it goes bad, another innocent person will get fucked. I won't be able to stop it. You get it?"

Another? "Got it."

"Look at me. I don't think you do." His face was so close she could see a tiny nick with dry blood below his cheekbone. His breath smelled of mint. "This is not some rich kid, fuck 'em all crapshoot. I've got a real person, needing a real job, putting her ass on the line for you. If she knew what I knew, she wouldn't."

"Jesus Christ, Bert. I get it. What doesn't she know?"

"Ancient history. No matter what happens, you'll inherit a zillion dollars from your father." He raised an index finger and touched her nose. "Because of circumstances beyond her control, my contact is not quite so fortunate. I need you to protect her identity."

"Done."

"No matter what it takes?"

"No matter what."

The tension drained from Bert's body. "Pay attention. This goes down at 12:15 tomorrow and exactly according to the script. No deviations, no improvisation. If anything happens, you promise to walk away."

"Of course. Why would you think otherwise?"

His head cocked like a professor peering at her over half-rimmed spectacles. "Because I trained you."

***

Linda parked the 'Vette and started across the Troop G parking lot.

"I hear they're watching you." The voice was Bigwater's.

She stopped, turned. He sat on the front fender of a patrol car. "Nice to see you too, Bigwater." *Asshole.*

"They're going to get you. Just a matter of time." He nodded toward headquarters.

Her blood heated and she approached him. Two nearby uniformed troopers stopped walking. Bigwater didn't move, a grin frozen on his face. She stopped within reaching distance. "What I *do* know is whether they get me or not won't change the fact you're a fucking weasel, a chicken-shit too scared to stand up and fight like a man."

His grin vanished and his eyes narrowed. He slid to his feet and clenched his fists. She'd made a tactical mistake in spacing, but would not back away. She trained her eyes on his hands and flexed her knees. "You got lucky that day, Baldwin. I should've kicked your ass when I had the chance."

"You name the day, Bigwater."

His fists unclenched. She stepped back. He opened the car door without a word, got in and drove off. The onlookers continued walking down the row of patrol cars. Bigwater's car retreated and Linda watched the two troopers until each had reached his assigned vehicle. She walked slowly toward the building, thinking about the exchange and wondering what it would take to shut the jerk up.

Inside, she sensed it immediately. The atmosphere reminded her of the morning after the Tillinghast sting operation, before the governor sold the agency out. Something big had happened; she felt it. She stopped at Ewing's door and asked what was going on. He motioned her in. His eyes twinkled and his hand slapped a file folder on his desk. "This is big. We cracked an international identity theft ring early this morning."

Linda settled into a folding chair. "I remember your mentioning that case. You finally nailed it?"

"Not me. A U-Albany computer geek."

"Geek?"

LeBeouf leaned back in his chair. "We paid an IT professor to help us. He had three grad student interns working the case. One of the kids solved the connection."

An Albany IT grad student intern. The universe contracted. "Connection? What connection?"

"You know what an algorithm is?"

Linda stared blankly.

"Me neither, but this kid does. He calculated a freaking algorithm between a series of interconnected teen-porn websites offering free membership and a bunch of web sites stealing bank and credit card information. Even his professor was impressed." Ewing pulled his feet off the desk, leaned forward. "Most of these suckers had their bank accounts drained or their credit cards maxed out. The ring had thousands of hits a day, most for at least a few hundred bucks."

Oh, shit! She didn't like the sound of this. "Got a name?"

"The draft press release doesn't identify the civilians involved. That's SOP. These mob bastards are vindictive."

"You didn't answer my question."

"Hang on. This goes nowhere. You hear me?" He opened a folder. "Kid named Bariteau is the genius."

The Saturday night teen porn flashing on Bill's computer screen now appeared in a different light, Bill's explanation offer sincere, and her reaction so foolish she doubted she'd ever have courage to face him again. "That's great."

"It gets better."

She was afraid to ask.

"Since the Pasternov murder, the locals have been trying to break his code. We told them to give this Bariteau a shot."

"And?"

"One hour, he had it done. Name that stuck out was a surrogate for the Greenbush coach. He resigned yesterday."

"I saw the paper. So that's why."

"Always bet his opponent and always won his bet."

"Quite the coincidence for a team with an undefeated regular season."

"What's going on with the insurance case?"

The abrupt change of topic did not surprise, but caught her unprepared. She couldn't report on the Health Department. "The company fraud guys are looking at clinic links. Slow going, but I think we're making progress. If the captain needs to tell the mayor something, it's safe to say we think the claim is fraud."

"I'll pass it along."

On her way to her desk, she detoured to the coffee brewers where Tibbs was filling a cup. He filled hers and nodded to a quiet corner, his face somber. They moved off.

"What gives, Tibbs?"

"You heard about Watervliet?"

"The bookie and the coach?"

"No, the vigilante."

Linda hoped her face did not show the internal shock. "What vigilante?"

"I'm hearing the brass got word from Watervliet of a vigilante action."

"Racial?"

"Don't fuck around, Linda. This is serious."

"OK, what?"

"A woman schooled in martial arts and posing as a student beat the crap out of some guy and busted his leg?"

"That's outrageous. The guy was minding his business and a nut job kicked the shit out of him? Any witnesses?"

He shook his head slowly. "I don't know why I bother. You know damn well the man wasn't innocent, and there were no witnesses. My reason for telling you *as a friend* is twofold. One, I understand they're working a composite from the vic; and two, your buddy Bigwater and some of his pals are spreading the rumor it's you."

Bigwater's comments began to make sense. "And what do you think?"

"You're not listening, friend. What I think is immaterial, but I'll tell you anyway. You're a dumb fuck who's about to get her ass kicked out of here, and I'm going to miss you when you're gone." He stalked off.

Linda couldn't afford to lose friends, but Tibbs was wrong on both counts. He mistook calculated risk-taking for dumb, and he thought they would hang the incident on her. No, the Watervliet vigilante would never stick. Anyone who thought otherwise was the dumb fuck. She was through with Watervliet. The idea of holding off on Troy also had a certain appeal. No point taking unnecessary risks. Today's sound and fury would soon fade away. The bike path rapist deserved her full attention.

***

After her shift, Linda changed out of uniform and paid Mark Segretti a visit. His mother answered the door of the attractive split-level house. Linda identified herself as a friend and declined the invitation to come inside. Mrs. Segretti disappeared. A moment later footsteps approached. Mark peered through the screen door. He recognized Linda, his eyes widened and his mouth opened.

"I need some information."

"What kind of—

"Get out here."

Mark stepped outside and followed her to the 'Vette. "You're a cop, right?"

"Yep. And you were joking about having weed. Possession of marijuana is illegal."

"Right."

"So is making book." The shock in his face told her she'd guessed right. "We got Coach Reynold. I think you figured it out before we did."

"Kenny's the math whiz." Mark clamped his mouth shut.

"How'd your scheme work?"

"How did what work?"

"Listen, Mark, I'm not after you and Kenny. Give me a line of crap and that'll change in a hurry."

He drew a deep breath. "Here's the thing. A whole bunch of us in our class liked to bet the games. Last season, we did good. This year, we kept losing. Kenny guessed the pattern by the fourth game. Me and Kenny started collecting all the bet money. We didn't make the bets. Our team won but our classmates lost. We split the winnings."

"Was Jeremy in on this?"

"Heck, no! Jeremy was pissed at Reynold for limiting his playing time. Coach told him he had to practice sportsmanship by not running up the score. I guess we know why."

"Anyone else aware of your scheme?"

"No."

The reaction of the kids at Cronin's camp remained unexplained. "The night of the Sectional game, you and your friend mentioned how Jenna always sat behind the bench when Jeremy played. You didn't see her, though. She broke up with him, didn't she?"

"Where'd you get that?"

"I'm asking the questions."

"You got the story wrong."

"Oh?"

"Jeremy broke up with Jenna."

"Jeremy's version?"

"Jenna's. She's pretty tight with my girlfriend. Jenna was upset."

"When did this happen?"

"Right after we got knocked out of the Sectionals."

Jeremy dislocated his shoulder and could not play. The following night South Greenbush lost its first game of the year in the Sectional semifinal round. "You sure about this Jenna thing?"

Mark shrugged his shoulders. "About as sure as you can be about any emotional reaction from Jenna. Like I said, my girlfriend heard Jenna's reaction. But then, I figure..." He looked off somewhere behind her.

"You figured what?"

"You never can tell with Jenna. She's in Drama Club and she loves to act. I've seen her turn a simple classroom exchange with a teacher into high drama. It's all an act. Some teachers get annoyed and others just ignore her. I'm no critic but she sure can be convincing. My girlfriend still insists Jenna was really upset."

Had Jeremy told the truth? Jenna's reaction an act, the sex consensual? Highly unlikely. Given her declaration of love for Jeremy, a breakup would have had an emotional impact on Jenna. In addition, Linda had witnessed the action on the bed. Definitely sex and clear signs of a struggle with Jenna's head jammed against the brass tubing of the headboard. Finally, the sheer terror in the scream still haunted Linda. A professional actor playing to an audience might replicate the cry. Jenna was a high school sophomore with no audience. When she screamed, she could not have known of Linda's presence. No, she had witnessed a rape, and the perp had escaped punishment.

Segretti's story didn't help explain what the rest of the party kids were hiding. It wasn't his betting scam, and Jeremy not likely involved in any case. She'd gotten about all she figured to get. "Thanks for the help, Mark." She winked. "Be careful what you say to strangers."

"I will."

"One other thing. Does Jeremy have a regular girlfriend?"

"Geez! What, you got a thing for Jeremy?"

"Answer the question."

"He went back with his old one."

"Who is?"

"Heather Gaines. She's a cheerleader."

Linda drove off thinking about the answers Heather had given at the camp. She'd have to check her notes and re-evaluate the information from the perspective of an angry or jealous ex. The more she learned, the less she understood the reaction of the kids at Cronin's camp.

CHAPTER 19

Tuesday morning, Linda strode through the rows of cars parked in the cement vault below Albany's towering South Mall office complex. The State Department of Health Records Bureau occupied a subterranean level of the 40-story Corning Tower, the tallest one in the complex. The fire exit for the agency was situated somewhere past the orange row of concrete piers marked 14. The door would be steel, with no external handle and bearing the small black letters "DOHRB." Bert had instructed her to knock twice at 12:15 and wait up to two minutes. If it opened, she was to follow instructions, no questions asked. If no one responded within the time frame, she was to leave.

A car door slammed and an engine roared. A blue Taurus station wagon approached and Linda moved from the center of the aisle. In the distance, a steel door came into focus. The engine hum faded to the sound of voices. She darted behind a concrete post and froze, seeking the source of the conversation. Quiet. Had they heard her? Seconds ticked by. Her watch read 12:12. Not much time, but she couldn't risk exposure. Nothing showed when she craned her head around. The voices returned. To her left, a man and woman embraced and kissed beside a cement pillar. The man touched her cheek and she pulled away, holding his hand to her lips. When she released her hold, she turned and marched purposely in the direction of the 'Vette. An elevator binged and a door closed. Twelve-fourteen. *Come on buddy, your lover is gone.*

As if the man had read Linda's mind, he opened a car door, started the engine and drove off. Linda strode double-time to the entrance, her eyes scanning the parking lot. No one in sight. Her heart pounded. She knocked twice and stared at her watch. Twelve-fifteen and 50 seconds. The sound on the other side caused Linda to step backward, seconds before the door swung out. She stepped inside and a woman with chestnut hair eased it closed, tugging gently until the latch produced a soft click.

"I appreciate your doing this, Miss…" Linda whispered. The woman wore an ID badge pinned to her blouse, but it faced in. She searched the brown eyes and found nothing but fear.

"No names," she hissed. "Friend of Bert, friend of mine. 'Nuf said. Show appreciation here." She pressed her index finger to her lips.

Linda nodded. The woman's taut lips curled up ever so slightly. She motioned Linda to follow and then entered a corridor of light tan cement walls and black-specked white linoleum tiles whose corners flaked.

They entered a cavernous room with neat, uniform, rows of black filing cabinets. By the fourth turn, Linda was lost. She hoped Bert's friend planned to lead her out of the place. The walls above the cabinets provided little help, three of them radiating with a red emergency exit sign. Her guide stopped and, without looking at the label, opened a file drawer crammed with manila folders marked with neatly typed numeric code. Linda hadn't expected to find a folder marked "Fraudulent Clinics, Past 18 Months." She *had* expected to be able to read the labels, though. She might need her allotted time just to decipher the code.

Linda turned her head in the direction of the soft "sis." The woman tapped a finger below her eye. With thumb and index finger a fraction of an inch apart, she nodded to the open drawer. Linda bent to scan the horizon of the drawer and found the solution to her code problem. Several dozen thin folders sat with their tabs protruding above the others. She grinned and turned to show her appreciation. The woman had vanished.

Linda extracted the three sheets of copy paper she had folded into the back pocket of her jeans. She pulled a pencil from her side pocket and began a methodical review of all the elevated folders, quickly recording names, addresses and dates, peeking at the time when she returned each file. At twelve-forty, with a full five minutes left in her allotted time, only three folders remained. A male voice jarred her to attention. "Brenda, I asked for those files this morning." *Shit!* This was not in Bert's script. The voice sounded close.

"I'm sorry, I thought you wanted them this afternoon. I'll get them now," a woman said.

"Never mind, I'll do it myself."

The woman's voice rose. "I've reorganized the Albany County records. It will be quicker if you let me."

No reply but for approaching footsteps. Linda tapped down the remaining elevated folders and eased the drawer shut. She scurried away from the sound. At the end of the aisle, she took shelter beside the last cabinet and waited. A man rounded the corner, followed closely by Bert's friend, Brenda, she presumed. Was it mere coincidence the man wanted the files Linda had been examining?

Linda looked around. The only exit in sight stood some 50 feet away, a fire door that read EMERGENCY EXIT ONLY-ALARM WILL SOUND. She'd gotten what she came for.

"I've experimented with a new organization scheme by region." Brenda's voice muffled the sound of a file drawer rolling on its tracks. "This cabinet contains a year of records for the five-county Capital District. I thought if you liked my idea we could reorganize the rest of the state."

So, Brenda had reorganized files to expedite Linda's search. Risky business on her part. Linda thought the situation through. An exit now would preserve her cover, but expose an intruder's presence, potentially fatal to her mission and Brenda's job. As much as she'd like to leave immediately, there was little advantage. If the boss discovered Linda, it wouldn't be much worse than her leaving now. He'd know they had an intruder, but since he'd be unable to detain her without help, that's all he'd have.

A drawer slammed shut. "Put them back where they belong, Brenda."

"But—"

"Next time, get my approval before you try something you know nothing about. I went to college for this stuff. And turn your ID around."

Linda made a mental note to get the name of Brenda's boss from Bert. What an asshole. She welcomed the sound of retreating steps.

"Will you sign out the files, sir?"

"You leave the file register alone. I'll have these back in a couple days." A door slammed.

Moments later, Brenda walked past Linda, a stack of folders in hand. "Pst." Linda hissed.

The woman snapped her head back, her cheeks rosy.

"I'm sorry to put you through this," Linda said.

Brenda's lips curved to a tight smile. "Not your fault. He's a jerk. Now get out of here." Linda followed. Brenda walked past the closest exit door to the corner, turned, hustled to the next and eased the door open. "Hope you got what you needed."

"I did. Thank you. Does he do that often?"

"Lecture me?" Brenda nudged her through the opening.

Linda stepped outside, but held the door open. "No. I mean take files without signing them out."

Brenda brushed Linda's hand away. She made no reply. In her eyes however, Linda found her answer. She definitely wanted the boss's name. Brenda began easing the door shut, and Linda noticed her ID badge. Marsolais, Brenda R., read the name above the photo.

***

Later that afternoon, Linda lounged on the sofa, her bare feet propped on the coffee table, listening to the voice on the phone and relishing the fruits of her day off. The jog had proved informative, and the exploration in the bowel of state government at the Health Department produced a wealth of data. Bert had signed up readily for the research into Brenda's boss and now Vance elaborated on tactics used to identify a bogus clinic. Linda felt an itch in her nose, rubbed the bridge and sneezed.

"God bless you," Vance said.

Fat chance of that happening. Where was God when she needed him? Turned a blind eye, didn't he? Like her mother. "Thank you, Sam."

"You said you scored at the Health Department. You got names for me?"

"Not over the phone."

"Come on, Baldwin. I'm stuck in the Bronx taking depositions."

She sipped from her glass of ice water. "Wow, insurance fraud in the Bronx. Who would have thought it?"

"Sarcasm doesn't fit you. By the way, we've got a state senator involved."

"Mary Seale?" Before they yanked her off patrol, Linda had nailed the chair of the Senate Appropriations Committee on a DWI for refusing a Breathalyzer, only to have the brass drop the charge for fear of retaliation on the State Police budget.

Vance laughed. "Wrong party, wrong gender, wrong color."

"Who?"

"Let's swap names tomorrow at 10. My office, OK?"

"See you tomorrow." Linda punched the off button, thought for a minute and dialed Bert's home phone. She'd leave a message. He would call back when he got home. The familiar voice answered. "Hi, Mrs. B. Is Bill home?"

"Linda, good to hear from you. Hold on."

She was tempted to hang up. The phone clicked. "My mother told me Linda, and my first reaction was, 'Linda who?'"

She felt like he had punched her in the stomach. "It hasn't been *that* long. A couple weeks."

"Well, which of my two dozen phone messages are you returning?"

"Ouch. Come on, Bill, you know why I was upset the night of your father's party."

"I tried hard to explain. So now..." His voice dropped to a whisper. "Let's just forget it, OK?"

"No, I owe you an apology for acting like a shit."

"Apology accepted."

"I want to buy you a drink, tell you in person, and ask your forgiveness."

Silence. What did she expect? She pushed him away and he took up with others. He wasn't the type to play two at a time, though, and he certainly knew she didn't want to see him merely to apologize in person.

The mental admission shocked her, much like the confession of a murder suspect who maintains his innocence for months only to blurt out "I did it" to a packed courtroom midway through his trial. Nevertheless, there it stood, out from behind the wall of her subconscious where it had been lurking since the moment she learned about the identity theft case. Amazing. She knew what she wanted. "OK, I'll take that for a yes. I'm off Sunday night. What do you say?"

"You sound like my old man. No."

This wasn't Bill. "No, not Sunday night? Or no, leave me alone?"

Bill sighed and she wondered whether from indecision or pity. "No, as in no."

She forced a perk into her voice. "Sounds like a definite maybe. I'll call you again. I do owe you an apology."

"Not anymore. Thanks." The line went dead.

She sucked on the remaining ice cube from her glass. Not too bad a start; he hadn't told her to leave him alone.

The phone rang, startling her.

"Your line's been busy for the last half hour," Bert growled. "Who you been talking to?" He laughed. "More important than me, I mean."

"Your son."

"Really." The "I'm curious" tone dripped in her ear. "Did he call you?"

"Hardly."

"How'd it go?"

She swung her feet from the sofa and stood. "Given what's gone over that dam, about what you'd expect. Is Brenda Marsolais related to Johnny?"

"Daughter. Want some advice?"

"No."

"OK, here you go."

"I can't wait." A lesson in love and emotion from Bert should prove about as useful as one in lobbying from Dr. Joyce.

"In many respects, you're so much like your mother it's uncanny. Scary, almost."

"How do you know my mother so well?"

"She doesn't like to admit it, but I knew her when. Back then she was just like you."

Linda straightened her back. "I'm nothing like her."

"Wrong. When your mother wanted something, nothing stood in her way."

She padded barefoot to the kitchen. "I'm like that?"

"Yes. You see what you want, you go get it. You did it in school and with your judo thing and the troopers. What, you think love is any different?"

How about lust? She imagined unbuttoning Bill's shirt the way she used to and running her hands over his bare chest and shoulders. Maybe, if she ever got Bill alone again. "It is."

"You'll see."

She refilled her glass from the kitchen sink, opened the freezer in search of ice. A stream of cold air flooded her face. "Even if I were like my mother," Linda shivered at the thought, "given the current situation, I think even the great Bert Bariteau might consider the obstacles formidable."

"Nope."

"That was a pretty quick answer."

"Yeah, but there's a basis." He paused. "Shit, I lost track of the time. I have to run, but this topic reminded me why I called."

"You got a name that fast?"

"You ever hear the saying, 'Blood is thicker than water?'"

She plunked three cubes into the glass. "Yeah?"

"In some families more so than others. And in a few, more like an adhesive."

Whose family? Definitely not the Bariteau. "Brenda's boss?"

"Name is Daniel O'Reilly. Danny O, they call him."

She dipped her index finger into the glass and stirred the cubes. "What's that got to do with blood and water?"

"Danny's a brother-in-law to an obstacle of yours and son-in-law to big Jim O'Keefe. Should give you plenty to think about on a personal *and* professional level." The phone clicked before she had the chance to ask about Johnny Marsolais. Linda stared into the open freezer, a stiff icy breeze tightening the skin on her face. She tried to imagine Kathleen telling Bill to do her father's bidding, but all she could envision was the red hair, green eyes, freckles, perfect body and boobs spilling from her gown. District Attorney James "Big Jim" O'Keefe was about to own Bert Bariteau's son, a situation she was in no position to change. She pushed the image of Bill and Kathleen from her mind. There was work to do.

Linda called Michaud and asked if he would get certain information on the Reynolds gambling case from his Watervliet PD contact. Two hours later he called back to report what he'd gotten from Detective Fruscio. Like most bookies, Pasternov kept his records in code names. Sifting through the records, Fruscio had found a curious pattern with one particular bettor who only bet on South Greenbush games. He made bets in the range of $1,000 to $1,500 per game and always won. As the season progressed, the spread trended steadily downward, from a high of 20 points early in the schedule to a low of seven. That made sense. Fans who'd been burned, despite the school victory, needed lower margins to entice their betting interest. To shield his identity from the bookie, Reynolds had used a surrogate to do his betting. When the law showed up, the proxy collared Reynolds. He wouldn't take the fall for a lousy 10 percent commission.

She winced silently when he described the way they'd cracked Pasternov's code. Bill was on the good side once again. He didn't belong in bed with the O'Keefes, but he was on his way. Michaud did relay two other items of interest. The next biggest bet on a Greenbush game was under $100, most of them under $50. Pocket change in today's dollars. Jeremy Cronin's name did not appear in Pasternov's records. The second item was Pasternov's most recent love interest, the now deceased psychologist, Natasha Borisova. The romance raised the possibility of a love triangle, not a contract hit, as explanation for the two murders. Borisova had been raped, presumably by the murderer, adding credence to the triangle theory.

A betting scam no longer explained the look on the party kids' faces. The wagers were too small and Segretti had likely taken the bets, not Pasternov. Nothing linked Jeremy to the betting. Something had gone down, but she still didn't know what. She was determined to find out, certain Jeremy fit at its center.

***

Two days later, Tibbs stopped Linda on her way into headquarters. He handed her a tri-fold sheet of paper. "How'd you do it?" he asked.

The sketch bled through the back. "What's this?"

"Don't you want to open the vigilante composite?"

"No use to me where I'm working."

"You're not curious?"

"Don't I look interested?"

"I was pretty sure it was you, a woman who passed as a teenager, schooled in martial arts and targeting sex predators. The name convinced me. Who else but a lit major versed in mythology comes up with a name like Lilith? How am I doing?"

"Lilith? Wasn't she the psychologist's wife on the sitcom, *Cheers*?"

"Adam's first wife in mythology, the one he divorced because she refused to lie beneath him submissively?"

"What a bitch. Lucky for Eve, though, huh?"

"I subscribe to the Baldwin theory of coincidence: two or more ain't. You might as well have left a business card."

She waved the folded sketch. She stuck her face in front of his. "So, how'd the artist do with my picture?"

"Not you. I repeat my original question. How did you do it?"

"Let me ask you a hypothetical question, Tibbs. Let's pretend you're a registered sex offender and the nephew of the local police chief. One day you decide to go trolling by the high school when classes let out. You get lucky, only your luck turns bad and you end up with a broken leg because the young girl you intended to fuck wasn't who you thought. Now, Uncle Police Chief doesn't like your trolling for young girls. What he hates even more, though, is a vigilante on his streets. So he sweats you and he convinces you to help produce an artist rendering so law enforcement can nab the vigilante. You with me so far?"

He nodded, a faint smile on his face.

"For the sake of argument, let's pretend I was your attacker, and burned my face in your memory. You sit with the artist, describe your assailant. You inspect the resulting sketch and say OK. Do you know my hypothetical question?"

Tibbs took the folded sketch from her hand and shook open an image of a young woman with short hair. The resemblance ended with the hair. "What was my interest level in having police find you?"

"I was going to ask if your recollection of my face would look like hers, but that's a good one."

"I suppose it would, with that fact pattern. How often do you expect those circumstances to repeat?"

"That's not a hypothetical."

Tibbs crumbled the sketch and tossed it at her. "Hypothetically, you're still playing a dangerous game that won't end well. That's my hypothetical prediction."

***

Martinez studied the face of his executioner and damned near laughed. The clown frowned when trying to concentrate, like now, unlocking the car door. Executioner? What a joke. The Ivan wouldn't last a month. He lowered the binoculars, replaced the vent and rolled from his stomach to his back. He began assembling the rifle. This attic was cramped compared to the one around the corner where he studied Baldwin. Just the thought of her produced an electric spark.

The Russki had shown himself a complete fool, hiring Leonid Volodina. The Ivan might be able to wash and polish his car, if the man gave him all day. Instead, the other Ivans whispered, Volodina would replace Martinez.

He found no surprise in the rumor. In this business, a man did not choose a woman over a job and expect longevity. The day he realized he'd fallen in love with Amy, he knew this would happen. For the past month, the Russki had been hinting Martinez was through. The inevitable didn't bother him. He'd been preparing. But Volodina? The choice insulted

Martinez. They would find out soon enough Martinez *was* through. Almost.

The Baldwin score needed settling first. He would do her strictly for its lesson value, but the image of her in his bed still set his pulse racing. The thought made him feel guilty, as if planning to betray Amy, something he could not contemplate. No, Baldwin would be a one-night stand. He'd chosen the place and now only a few details, like the invitation, remained.

Martinez rolled back on his belly. The logistics of Volodina, however, were proving difficult. Like all the others, this Ivan was a creature of habit, but using the front door not one of them. He parked on the street and left his apartment for his car every morning at about the same time. Habit made the Ivan weak, and Martinez believed he had found a fatal vulnerability. He removed the vent and focused the riflescope on the dumpster standing in the alley next to Volodina's apartment building. Yes! He imagined pulling the trigger, started the stopwatch, and began the rehearsals.

CHAPTER 20

An arm reached over Linda's shoulder on Friday afternoon and a report dropped to the center of her desk. She spun around in her chair. Bigwater backed up. "I want this ASAP," he snapped. She stood. He took another step back and grinned. "You seem to be adapting well to this job."

Linda was making progress on the anger front. Her first reaction was not to seize his wrist, twist his arm, bend him over her desk and jam a knee up his ass. No, her anger was definitely under control. She picked up the report and placed it at the top of the pile. "I'll get to it as soon as I get back." She brushed past Bigwater without another word and headed to the coffee brewers. When she returned, she shuffled Bigwater's report to the bottom.

After a month of her bugging LeBeouf about wasting personnel, he relented and assigned her part-time patrol that, thank God, would begin in a few hours. The insurance case treaded water while Vance's crew analyzed the clinic data she'd pilfered from the Health Department and figured out their next step. Meanwhile, LeBeouf announced, no doubt at Walker's insistence, her availability to assist with reports. Troopers hated the minutiae of reporting and many sought her help, the stack on her desk growing all week.

The drizzle began that evening while Linda's patrol car idled in the center median on I-90 in Rennselaer County. She prayed the rain would last at least 12 hours. She'd jogged every morning this week, but the weather was far too good for her needs. The Cronin case had come to a sudden stop. Linda had yet to determine her next move. She guessed Jeremy and the unidentified Hispanic man figured prominently in what had happened at the camp, the betting scam the obvious connection, but she had nothing linking either to the dead bookie. Or did she?

She'd been focusing on the bookie angle and lamenting what it failed to tell her, while overlooking what it did reveal. She'd been operating on an assumption that the Hispanic man worked as Pasternov's muscle and what she'd witnessed between him and Jeremy was an offshoot of their relationship. What if the man had no business connection to Pasternov? She'd dismissed the man with the unnervingly dead eyes as the source of her photos, reasoning he would not have murdered Pasternov. She now considered the possibility, no, the likelihood, she'd been wrong. Linda began feeling ill. She was a murder target.

Murder in the Capital District was uncommon, and three in a matter of weeks would normally raise a popular outcry pressuring law enforcement to show quick results. A recent exposé by the Albany Times Herald diminished public concern. Attributing the killings to the Russian mafia allowed people to perceive them as gang warfare. Who cared if one lowlife murdered another? Homicide detectives needed the break, given they worked with nothing but a single strand of pubic hair from the Borisova corpse, and the DNA did not match anything in the database. Natasha Borisova and Yuri Pasternov were lovers before death. Borisova was raped. Detectives liked the mafia news story for easing the pressure but doubted the pair was a mob hit. More likely it was a jealous lover. No comfort to Linda. Whoever sent Pasternov the photos probably killed him, and she his next target.

When her shift ended, she returned the patrol car and drove home. She trolled down Cataract Street half a block past her apartment before shoehorning the 'Vette into a parking spot. She swung the door open and stepped out. Her foot landed in a puddle. Jesus. Linda gripped her unzipped raincoat together at the chest and sprinted toward the porch. She dodged puddles and threaded between parked cars but still managed to soak her other shoe and pant legs. The hall door creaked closed behind her. She removed her raincoat and shook the water on the cracked linoleum of the dimly lit hallway. From upstairs floated the melody of a song she could not identify, though it sounded like a Santana.

Linda unlocked the deadbolt, swung her apartment door open and locked it behind her. With a flip of the switch, the overhead kitchen fixture illuminated the room, spilling light on the entrance to her bedroom and the short corridor leading to the living room. She crossed the kitchen. Something wasn't right. She passed through the alcove to the back door: intact. She hung her jacket by the door, returned to the kitchen and checked the window: also intact. Dammit, she wasn't imagining things. What? *Think*.

The air, something unusual: the place smelled damp and musty, like the entrance hallway on steamy nights. She'd experienced heavier rain since moving in, but the apartment never smelled this damp. The Glock slipped from her holster with a move so reflexive she almost convinced herself she might use it. Holding the gun at eye level, she tiptoed to the front of the house, living room and second bedroom. Nothing there, not even the dampness.

She returned to the rear of the apartment. Pressing her back to the wall, she reached for the handle and pushed the bathroom door in. The knob struck the wall pad. She wheeled around into the doorframe, trigger finger at the ready. An open shower curtain hung innocently from the rod. She stepped toward the tub and moved the vinyl aside with the gun barrel: nothing. She moved from bathroom to bedroom and swung the door open. It bounced off the wall softly, cushioned by the clothes she'd hung on the hook inside. She raised the gun, rounded the doorframe, panned the room: again, nothing. The tiny open closet space held her entire personal and professional hanging wardrobe with plenty of gaps to reveal that no one stood behind the clothes. She holstered the gun and turned her attention to the lone window, covered by the new room shade: as she'd left it. Yet something was off. What?

She tugged the room shade and eased it open, taking note of the wet sill. Her chest tightened. How did that happen? The lock stood at the halfway position. Until recently, she'd been careless about locking windows, a habit formed from years of living in a neighborhood where folks often didn't lock doors. Lately, she'd been vigilant. She pulled the handle, the window slid open. *Shit*. On the sill between window and screen lay white paint chips, some with traces of wood.

She retrieved a kitchen chair and climbed up to examine the lock. A series of narrow gouges etched the bare wood along a strip about six inches in length at the top of the lower window. Linda imagined a coat hanger or a wire car-door opener similar to the one in her patrol car working its way through the seam and then snaking upward to slide the window lock. Mystery solved.

Someone had unlocked and opened her bedroom window, and recently, based upon the start of rain. She switched on the lamp atop the mirrored dresser. In her top drawer, her underwear and socks were neatly stacked, her middle drawer also untouched. The envelope of cash she kept hidden beneath her sweat pants in the bottom one was intact.

Linda stepped back into the kitchen. She drew deep breaths to slow her heartbeat. She opened and closed cabinet doors and drawers looking for signs of an intruder. In the end, there was no evidence anyone had come in. Why not? Linda conjured up several scenarios in which someone opened the window but did not come in, leaving the scene pretty much as she'd found it.

She locked up. The spring creaked when she drew the shade closed. She undressed and slipped into a thin nightshirt. She washed, returned to the bedroom and placed the gun on the nightstand next to the clock.

Linda pulled back the comforter, her eyes still scanning the window and adjacent walls. She arranged the cover at the foot of the bed and glanced at the pillows. A three-by-five photo of herself lay on each. Goosebumps sprouted on her arms, her skin as grimy as the night she'd arrested "Jack" the sex predator. Now everything from the evening made sense. Except how had he gotten those photos? She bent to look, taking care not to touch them. Unlike the first batch, taken as she exited the building, these were interior shots. In one, a nightshirt covered her head, and she stood wearing only a pair of white panties. The second photo was a full frontal nude, her hair wet, a towel hanging from her hand.

How the fuck did he…? But she knew. For 21 years, she lived in a second-floor rear bedroom overlooking woodlands and with direct access to a bath and shower. It took some months in her new digs to realize she had more privacy living with her parents than in a big apartment alone. She pulled back the shade and peeked out the window. The row of buildings across the alley whose backs faced her window was at least 30 yards distant. She'd never figured to be seen from those windows. Her gaze shifted to the vine- and weed-choked rusted fence bordering her yard, a barrier she'd presumed offered an extra element of privacy. At six feet in height, the fence obstructed a view of her window to the casual passerby but also served as a perfect blind for a hunter intent on shooting his quarry unobserved.

Her stomach churned. The man who took those pictures had been in her bedroom, his hands on her pillow. She massaged her temples. She needed a drink. Every attempt at logic or rational thought derailed in the pure essence of violation seeping through her pores. In the kitchen, Linda poured herself a generous glass of wine then returned to secure the photos in plastic sandwich bags, though she doubted they contained prints. She carried glass, photos and gun to the living room.

Once seated, she gulped a full mouthful and then a second, tasteless. She drew some deep breaths. Her mind slowed a bit and she began a review.

Two new pictures, these in the nude. Maybe the same photographer, but maybe not, though the evidence pointed to the former. They'd not found photos with the Borisova woman, but that didn't mean she'd not got them. There were too many coincidences between her and the Pasternov-Borisova case to dismiss the theory.

Linda listened to the splatter of rain on the window behind her and considered a second possibility: her photographer was the bike path serial rapist. Had he been stalking *her* while she thought she'd been stalking him? What if he had figured out her intentions and then waited for rain to leave his calling card? She considered the sender could be one of Lilith's ex-boyfriends, her relationships always ending abruptly on a sour note. She couldn't even smile at her own attempt at humor.

Her immediate problem was the jogging routine. If the rain persisted, tomorrow morning would be the best day of the week to be on the bike path. She should alert Ewing but played the scenario out. In every configuration, the two photos passed through the hands of male detectives. From there, she could only guess but wasn't about to become the Troop G centerfold of the month. She imagined Bigwater's assessment of her ringing down the corridors of headquarters. Like hell! Those photos would never circulate around Troop G or anywhere else. A second option was to do nothing, abandon her morning jogging routine and stay home where she would be safe and dry. She had enough problems without heading out to search for more.

While mulling the do-nothing course of action, she walked to the kitchen and refilled her wine glass. Back in the living room, her mind began to focus and clarity emerged. The new photos did nothing to change the risk she'd assumed when she decided to start jogging. The man on the bike path was a sex predator. Whether the same person left the photos made no difference. One man or two, they were sex predators and she had to stop them. She'd chosen to pursue perverts. Whether she did so in uniform or otherwise, she would not allow them to intimidate her. Their threat presented an opportunity to prove herself equipped for her career. Besides, the bike path had become her home field, always the better place to confront an opponent.

The morning she'd waited for loomed in a rainy mist only a few hours away. She would gain no advantage backing down now. A man had messed with her once, and she'd vowed never again. The man who broke into her bedroom was messing with her.

Linda drained the second glass of wine and went to bed. Her mind began to review bike path details and rehearse attack scenarios. At some point, she slept, but lightly. She woke, covered with sweat, and glanced at the clock illuminating the gun on the nightstand: 4:12 a.m. The room was suffocating. She heard a creak and reached for the gun. When the creak became a steady rhythm above her head, she smiled and put the gun down. She opened the window and a cool damp breeze stirred the dead air. Comfort argued she leave it open. Caution dictated otherwise. She positioned the window and shade six inches open, propped herself into a sitting position on the bed, gun in her lap, and listened to the frenzied creak of the ceiling.

CHAPTER 21

Saturday morning, Linda woke to the sound of rain splashing on the sill.. She sat in bed, again rehearsing scenarios she'd fallen asleep with. Her thoughts turned to a man: nameless, faceless, snapping photos, climbing through her bedroom window in a pouring rain, peeling back her bedcover. Hopefully, he too awoke this morning, welcoming the sound of falling rain, playing scenarios of his own. The fear gripping her last night showed no signs of leaving. Sensei had taught her to deal with her fears by confronting them. For many people she knew, fear induced paralysis. Others papered them with a veneer of bravado. Linda had learned to harness hers and to focus their awesome powers into a narrow beam of energy that reflected back, laser-like, upon their source. She was afraid. She was ready.

She dressed in white tank top and black nylon running shorts. The 'Vette covered the short drive to the Corning Preserve in a pummeling rain. The parking lot held 6 other cars, not the usual 30 or so. She guessed at least two were undercover, the perp knew which ones and where their occupants hid. She snapped the Velcro band tight around her arm, tapped the pouch cover secure and slopped across a deep puddle on her way to the bike path entry. Water lapped over her running shoes. At the "0.0" signpost she began to jog.

Half a mile out, she rounded a sharp curve and nearly collided with a man running toward her. She pulled up, straight-armed, fists at the ready. The man jerked to a halt, eased off the path, eyes on her. "Jesus, lady! I didn't mean to scare you." He passed. Linda watched him return to

169

the paved surface. "You shouldn't be out here alone," he shouted before jogging off.

Hear that, Lilith? The man thinks I'm alone. Her cop-cut hair and equally skimpy outfit absorbed their capacity of rain. The excess leaked into her eyes and ears, into her bra and panties, down her legs, into her shoes: a veritable male magnet. An old mantra cycled through her mind. "Rape is not about sex. It's about power, domination and control. Sex is the vehicle." What was it with men?

A stretch of dense brush covered both sides of the path ahead. Of all her A-list locations, this one was the most likely. Peripheral vision at full scan, muscles tensed, pulse pounding, she slogged along, the Hudson now in sight through the tangled vegetation.

A blur of motion over her shoulder loosened a shock of adrenaline. She fought the instinct, pretended she'd not seen. *Good job, Linda. Here he comes.* The undergrowth rattled and thrashed. A pair of wild turkeys sprang from the thicket, wings flapping. She lowered her head and veered off the path as if they'd attacked her. They glided low over the brush and landed in the open field in front of her. She stopped to give her heart time to slide back from her throat and stretched her quads. The turkeys paraded across the field of grass and wildflowers stretching beyond the I-90 bridge, its arch now visible in the distant haze. *Shit! Where is he?*

The path broke from the undercover, meandered away from the river, toward the concrete columns supporting the bridge. The hiss of tires spraying water from up on the ramp grew louder, stamping out the squish-squish of her running shoes. An open field stretched ahead, the next A-list location, a patch of brush on the far side of the bridge still five minutes away. She would have bet anything on the turkey hideout. Maybe the press and the cops had spooked him from the bike path. Or he'd taken his game somewhere else and she'd read about his latest victim in tomorrow's paper. No, he was here. She sensed it.

She passed the first bridge support pier, traffic now a din. To her right, a small flock of Canada geese waddled across the field toward the river. Something brushed her left shoulder. An arm wrapped around her neck, yanked her back. *What the fuck? Attacked in an open field?* A hand covered her mouth, the scent of gasoline in her nose. She bit. The hand flew off.

"Fuckin' bitch," the deep guttural voice was barely audible above the din of traffic. The chokehold tightened. The taste of salt and petroleum lingered on her tongue but she couldn't spit. Her esophagus constricted.

Her breath labored. Sensei Allan's commands appeared in her mind. Swivel head to restore breathing, deep breath, fist, hip slide. She slammed a fist to the opponent's groin. No contact. She'd spent months learning the maneuver to evade the hip slide, groin punch. Her attacker had executed the move perfectly.

He spun her around. Ski mask. His fist smashed up into her chin. Her head snapped back, knees buckled, but she managed to stay on her feet. Her tongue burned. Her skull was ready to explode. She wiped a hand across her mouth. Blood. She spit. He grabbed the back of her hair, dragged her behind the column. He pinned her against the concrete, jammed a shoulder in her back. "Gonna be my way, baby." Shit! What did Jeremy say to Jenna before he raped her? Something about his way. This bastard sounded like he'd not yet exerted himself. An athlete's conditioning, like a basketball superstar. Jeremy didn't strike her as that stupid, but she never underestimated the arrogance of the privileged.

His hand pressed against her ass. A finger probed between her legs. She screamed. The sound whimpered into the black hole of I-90 bridge traffic. A hand tugged at the waistband of her nylon shorts. She kicked a leg backwards: Again, no contact. *Big mistake, Lilith.*

She'd not considered the possibility of an assailant better schooled in martial arts. Too late now. She struggled for balance. Her legs disappeared from under her and she collapsed, her cheek scraping the concrete. She landed face down in a bed of crushed stone and gravel and rolled to her back. The man pounced, brushing aside her straight leg kick, spreading them. He shifted forward, a hand on her shoulder. Jagged edges bit at her back and butt. She twisted her head but froze when a cold metal pressed against her neck. He leaned back, held the knife high: double-edged blade, hunting variety.

The man wore a camouflage shirt and had the forearms of a steelworker, not a Jeremy Cronin. He tugged the crotch of her shorts with one hand, slipped the knife between her legs and sliced. He yanked the waistband of her panties, tearing into her belly. The cold metal against her groin aroused a fear he might cut her. The remote possibility of rape she always pushed from her mind in the planning stages now loomed as both real and imminent. The pressure of the waistband released. Bastard! He'd have to kill her first. He pulled at the waist of his shorts and they opened with a Velcro rip, exposing an erect cock. "Cunt."

171

That word. Again, that word. *Did you hear what he called you, Lilith?* The man lowered himself. His cock prodded. She launched a handful of straight fingers at the eye slits. One finger found a socket. He yelled, pulled himself upright. She swung at his knife arm, jarring the blade loose. It fell to the dirt beside her. She rolled back on her shoulders, kicked her legs over her head, landed on her feet and searched for the knife. He had already recovered, grabbing at the handle. He lumbered to his feet.

Linda sized him up: bigger and stronger, better conditioned, trained in martial arts, holding a knife. She ripped her torn underwear off, turned, and ran for the bike path, the waistband of her shorts intact, torn crotch flapping in the breeze. Nothing registered but the hiss of the traffic and the burn in her lungs. She reached the path, headed back toward the parking lot. The footsteps announced his presence. Just a matter of time before he caught her. She slowed, limping and gimped forward, counting; *One thousand one, one thousand two...*He entered her peripheral vision. *One thousand—*

Linda stopped and spun. Her thrust kick landed squarely, the ball of her heel finding the soft center of his crotch. The collision nearly toppled her, but the knife clattered to the macadam. She struggled to stay on her feet. He began to double over. She thrust a straight-armed open palm under his nose. The ensuing crack jolted her, sharper and more ominous than she'd imagined in the hundreds of practice sessions. He fell, face first, into a muddy puddle. Linda gasped for air and willed her pounding heart to slow.

A man wearing a navy blue rain jacket, handgun drawn, appeared in full sprint on the path under the bridge. There wasn't much time. She dragged her attacker's head from the puddle and yanked off the mask. Caucasian, about 30, light brown hair with a military cut. From the arm pouch, she extracted a foil packet of ammonium carbonate.

She snapped the foil between her fingers and jammed the smelling salt beneath the man's bloodied and misshapen nose. He stirred. "Can you hear me?" No reply. Her palm throbbed and her arm ached up to the elbow. She hoped she'd broken his nose. Sure sounded like she did. She slapped at his cheek. "Come on, wake up!" He moaned.

"Talk to me."

"Wuzza?"

"Did I make you feel like a man?"

Nice work, Lilith. This fucker's going to jail.

Engines droned in the distance.

"Are you hurt?" The blue jacket gasped for air. His eyes darted around.

"He jumped me." Her attacker now writhed on the ground, moaning.

"I'm Detective Myers. You got a nasty bruise," he wheezed. He slid the gun inside his jacket and produced a set of cuffs from the pocket. He knelt to shackle the man. He stood and pointed at her head. "We'll have that looked at." He glanced at her torn shorts, averted his eyes and unbuttoned his rain slicker. "Here, take this." The gun bulged in the shoulder holster lying over his black T-shirt. He scanned the open field toward the river and back under the bridge. He pointed to the attacker whose nose continued to trickle blood, which washed off his cheek into a puddle the shade of deep pink. "Who did this?"

She snapped the jacket buttons over her torn shorts. "We better stop that bleeding. He might have a broken nose."

"Who did this?"

"I got lucky."

"You did, did you? Who are you?"

"Off duty trooper."

He jerked his head up. "I knew it. Where'd they go?" His eyes swept over the field. "You state fucks ain't supposed to be in here."

"It's just me and I don't want credit. Your bust, OK?" The sound of the engines grew to a roar.

"I'm listening." Myers yelled.

"He jumped me. I struggled free." A helicopter circled above. She screamed. "You saved me."

Myers's eyebrows arched. He shook his head and knelt beside the rapist. His lips moved, but Linda could hear nothing over the drone of the chopper: some Miranda warning.

Half a dozen cops swarmed over the scene. The helicopter hovered. In the initial rush to secure the site and protect the evidence, Albany's finest temporarily lost track of her. Just as well. They didn't seem to be in a very cooperative mood. Her mission complete, she backtracked slowly and when no heads turned, she did, through the turkey hideout and into a full run. Her jaw ached, tongue burned and the throbbing in her head would not clear. Try as she might, she could not stop the trembling that had started after Myers cuffed her attacker. Halfway to the 'Vette, she heard the ATV engine, considered ducking off the path but stopped.

The man pulled the bike up and cut the motor. "We should talk."

Oh, shit. She'd encountered this guy in the Watervliet parking lot, the first day of her jogging routine. Maybe he wouldn't remember her. "About what?"

He extended his hand. "I'm Vice Detective Leonard Volkan."

Ah! The man quoted in the newspaper story. That was a start. At least he had some media savvy. Myers showed zilch. She stepped backward. "You want the jacket back now?"

Volkan glared. "Don't fuck with me, trooper. What went down?"

"I explained the situation to Myers."

"He's new. Try me."

She'd planned to be in and out without a trace, hadn't counted on a prolonged encounter with the rapist. Time to improvise. "Let's start with your victim." The words burned through the residual constriction in her throat.

"Victim?"

"The guy looked to me like he was attacked. Makes him a victim, no?" Delivering the line made her want to puke.

"What the fuck did you say?"

"Simple: If I'm not a victim, this rapist walks. You need a vic, and I need you."

Volkan took a step toward her. She stepped back. "Let's get something straight, trooper. At the end of this day, you're *going* to be a victim." He pointed in the direction they had come. "The only question is whether you'll be his victim or mine."

"What? You'll arrest me?"

"Whatever it takes to put this guy away. I got to bust you, bet your ass, I will." He nodded his head. "You need something from me, start talking. But this sucker's no victim. Got that?"

She'd laid the whole thing out in her mind, a tightly woven script, but nothing had gone as planned. She'd been damn near raped, almost killed, and now Albany police acted as if she cost them a collar, not handed them one; messy business, but she got the bastard, took out a sex predator, and this one would do time. Not even Judge Shane Dolan could save his ass. "OK, my name is Linda Baldwin. Let me explain what I need."

***

The phone rang for the umpteenth time in the last hour. Once again, the machine answered and another media outlet left a message. The deal she negotiated sucked, but only in part because Volkan was a pro and she a novice. Her identity, the only thing that mattered, was a deal killer. The defense attorney would be all over it. Crap, she thought that part through about as well as she calculated the ease of taking down the rapist. All she got was a story. Albany cops had rescued her from an almost certain rape, or death. A fig leaf, no doubt, but far better than facing the Troop G hierarchy in the buff.

LeBeouf's voice spoke to the machine. "Baldwin, call me ASAP. Captain Walker wants to—"

She answered. "Sorry, my phone is ringing nonstop with people wanting an interview. I haven't answered any of them."

"Good move. Jesus, you OK? Walker got word from the Chief. Sounds like you got beat up pretty good."

"I took some shots."

"There's more coming. Captain wants to see you."

"I'll be in after I shower and change."

"No, now!"

She wanted to ask for a DNA match against the hair they found on the Borisova woman but thought better of it. No point tipping her curiosity when they would perform the test anyway.

"I'll tell him you'll be here in 20 minutes."

"Or after I shower and change, whichever comes later." She hung up, searched her case for the Joplin CD. The phone rang. Ah, there it was. Caller ID showed Bariteau. "Hello."

"Are you out of your mind?"

"Hi, Bill. Did you call to tell me you'll meet me for that drink?"

"My father told me what you did. He tried to talk you out of it."

"Same guy taught me sometimes you just got to do what you got to do." She loaded the CD.

"We need to talk."

How about our tree, Sunday afternoon? You bring the blanket, I'll get a bottle of wine and we'll talk about us. "Great."

"Sunday night, 7:30 at Kelsey's, OK?"

"Sure. Hey, I—" Click. They were making progress. They'd made a date, of sorts, and he certainly cared. Otherwise, why call? She punched start, scrolled to the song. "Busted flat in Baton Rouge, waiting for a train, and I's feeling near as faded as my jeans…" In her bedroom, she flopped on the bed. Swimming in the oversized sweats Volkan had given her at the station, she joined Joplin in the refrain. "Freedom's just another word…"

"Set it up over here," a voice outside the window ordered. Linda rose from the bed and reached for the edge of the room shade. She peeked out. The rain had tapered to an Irish mist. A camera crew in the back yard fussed with tripods and cables. A perfect hair brunette huddled under an umbrella talking into a microphone.

Linda walked to the kitchen, stopped the CD and switched on TV. "…our reporter, live on the scene, Victoria Murphy. What's going on Victoria?"

The screen zoomed to a close up of the 'Vette, then faded to a woman reporter wearing a rain slicker with the hood up. "Alicia, we believe the red Corvette you saw belongs to the victim of the latest attempted rape on the Albany bike path. Albany police have a suspect in custody."

"Any word on what happened?" The camera zoomed on her front door and back to the hooded rain jacket.

"Albany police are saying very little except that an off-duty female state trooper was attacked but managed to get free long enough to alert police. The attacker was subdued, arrested and brought in."

"Victoria, have police released any names?"

"Not yet. However, we do know the suspect was rushed to Albany Medical Center for treatment of an unspecified injury. Sources have provided Channel 11 news with the identity of the victim."

The scene from the street outside cut to the studio anchor. Her facial expression suggested she was about to read the contents of stone tablets, not a teleprompter. "As our viewers know, Channel 11 subscribes to the highest level of ethics in television news."

Linda choked back a laugh. How high was slug-high?

"Our policy is to never release the name of a sex-crime victim."

Unless your competitors do.

"In this case, Albany police assure us the intended victim refused medical attention, and no sex crime was committed. Therefore, after considerable deliberation, we have concluded the woman is not a victim. This has been a difficult decision for us, but the trooper is a public servant and the public's right—"

The phone rang and she snapped the TV off, glanced at the ID. Bill calling back. "Hi, handsome. Can I buy you a drink?"

"Some other time. They got you surrounded, Kiddo."

"Hi, Bert. I was going to call you before I left the house."

"You know the drill. Remember the rules?"

"Two message points, short sentences, no word bigger than two syllables."

"You'll do fine. Listen, if you need a place to stay for a few days, while this blows over, you're always welcome here."

Any chance Bill put him up to the offer? "Thanks, Bert. I'll let you know."

The offer twisted in her head while she showered and dressed. The invitation was a tempting opportunity to spend time with Bill but might also lead to a discovery he spent every free minute and all his nights with Kathleen. She'd called her father earlier to tip him off to the impending media splash and to ask that he offer no comment. Maybe she could reclaim her old room for a few days, if her mother hadn't already turned it into another walk-in closet.

An hour later, Linda left the apartment. Strobe lights slashed at her face. Floods atop tripods blinded her. A swarm of bodies crowded the sidewalk and blocked the porch steps. "Trooper Baldwin." "Trooper Baldwin?" "Trooper..." She started down the steps sideways, elbows clearing a path. Someone jammed a microphone under her chin. She brushed it aside. A woman's voice broke through the din. "Were you frightened by the attack?"

Not as much as by this school of piranhas. "I'm late for a meeting. I have nothing to say." The curb loomed ahead.

"Is it true you assisted Albany police in apprehending the attacker?" A man shoved a microphone in her face.

"I'm late for a meeting. I have nothing to say." Free of the throng, she sprinted across the street to the 'Vette and unlocked the door. A man holding a microphone rushed the car. She recognized the reporter from the Albany affiliate of the Wolf Network, tabloid sleaze on your TV.

"Miss Baldwin, as a young woman jogging alone on the bike path, do you accept any responsibility for the events?"

Should we answer the question, Lilith? Better not, since the proper response involved shoving his microphone up the reporter's ass. Half a dozen cameras trained on her like a SWAT team on a hostage taker. If she gave in to the urge, she'd become red meat in a fish tank of public relations sharks. Besides, the reporter was right. As insinuated, she'd asked for it. Moreover, she'd gotten what she wanted. She smiled at the cameras. "I'm late for a meeting. I have nothing to say."

***

"You can't act like this and continue to be a trooper. What bothers me is I don't think you understand." Walker wrapped up a lecture sounding as if he were deeply concerned about her career.

She understood perfectly. A woman couldn't stop a rapist all by herself without a Dudley Do-Right. That didn't make for good public relations in an organization with a testosterone level swelling larger than its annual budget. Her reflection stared back from the polished mahogany surface of his desk. "I was off-duty. I went jogging. A man tried to rape me. Albany cops saved me. Thank you for your concern."

"You ran every day, didn't you?"

"I'll have to check my personal calendar."

"Undercover boys said a woman jogged the path alone every morning this week."

That bastard, Volkan. They had a deal. "Yeah?"

"Claimed it was you, all except the one who saw her close. *He* said the woman came from out of town and knew nothing about the bike path trouble. He couldn't remember her exactly, but certain it wasn't you. How'd you manage that?"

Volkan may be a hard-ass, but a man of his word. She shrugged.

"You're lucky you weren't killed."

True, but only because she'd encountered a man schooled in martial arts. She needed all her cunning and skill to bring him down. The key point being she ended his rape spree. This aftermath crap was a nuisance she must endure. She had Walker boxed, and he knew it. No wonder he was pissed off. He had no proof, and media sympathy lay on her side. Bert would be proud. She'd done it on her own. Cool. "I feel very fortunate today, Captain."

Walker shook his head slowly and deliberately, and all Linda could think of was Grandpa Baldwin's disapproval when she fielded a ground ball without the proper form. Comparing this sexist peckerhead to Grandpa Baldwin bordered on obscenity.

Tomorrow at three, you'll report right here, at a desk where you'll have adequate supervision. You're off the road. LeBeouf will keep you busy."

His words landed like a kick to the groin. She resumed patrol yesterday. One day and off. Back to file clerk duties. "What about the insurance case?"

"Ewing thinks there's something to it. Help him out, but don't leave your desk without his OK."

***

"You have three reporters camped on your front stoop and one watching the alley." Bill reported his reconnaissance, his face anxious.

"That does it, you'll stay here tonight." The finality in Bert's tone annoyed her almost as much as Bill's anxiety. No room at the homestead thanks to her father's college roommate and family who were visiting for a week.

"Hey, Bill, I need to cancel our date for tomorrow night. Can we reschedule?"

"How about now?"

The walls of the room contracted, much like the ones in Walker's office a few hours ago. "I wanted to do this over a drink."

Bill glanced at his father. "Help yourself. We have Champagne, wine, port, beer, whatever you want."

"Rain stopped. Want to go down to our tree?"

"No."

Whoops. "OK, what are you drinking?"

"I'm not."

Bert glared at Bill who had turned to climb the stairs. She shrugged and followed.

Bill leaned against the headboard of his bed, his long legs stretched out. "Until a few months ago, I never thought I would say these words."

What would he do if she rose from the desk chair and jumped on top of him, the way she used to? Probably toss her off. How could he know about the change? How could she explain the itch Jonathan raised but only he could soothe? "Don't. Things have changed. I'm different."

Bill shook his head. "Nothing has changed."

But it had. If he gave her a chance, she would show him. He could touch her now and she wouldn't freeze. She imagined herself, lying on the bed melting in his arms. "You're wrong, Bill."

He stared off into space. "The stunt you pulled this morning proves I'm right."

What did that have to do with her readiness to make love to him? "I don't follow."

His eyes caught hers. "For almost seven years, I've watched your anger eat at you. They told me you'd get over it and I believed them. After this morning, I don't believe any more."

"Anger?" What happened to sex? He wanted sex. Finally, she felt ready. Where'd this anger complication come from? This was simple stuff, as basic as a catcher waiting for a Nolan Ryan fastball, nothing to do but show him a target. Of course, if Ryan delivered a knuckleball instead, the catcher was bound to look like the fool she felt. Bill fed her the curves and knuckleballs. He saved the straight hard stuff for Kathleen.

"Linda, you're pissed at the world. Maybe you have a right to be. But it doesn't change what your anger is doing to you." He shifted his eyes. "Not to mention the people around you who lo... care for you."

Did he say "love?" "Anger? You think I'm angry?"

"Jesus, Linda, where do I begin? You've alienated all your girlfriends. You created a media splash with a sting operation after taking on the DA and judge, and you stalked a serial rapist. That's only what I know about. I'm betting there's more."

In each case, there were mitigating circumstances. "I'm not angry with you."

"Yeah, right. Then why'd you stomp out of here the night of my father's party?"

"I said I was sorry."

"Not the point, but this is. Your anger allowed you to think of me as...God knows what. Even worse, you believed whatever without giving me a chance to explain."

"I'm sorry."

"So am I, Linda. Sorry to watch you destroying yourself." He swung his legs off the bed and stood, towering over her. "It hurts, and I can't do it anymore."

She looked up into his eyes. "Do you love her?"

He blinked repeatedly. "Don't change the subject. We're talking about you, not me."

"So we are. And it's me who wants to know. Do you love her?"

He turned his back, pulled the door open shaking his head, and disappeared.

Linda sat still. The memory of Jonathan's kiss made an inexplicable appearance. She should call him. The front screen door screeched open. A car engine coughed to life. She slipped off the chair and into Bill's bed, buried her face in his pillow, drinking in the scent of his skin, like a desert wanderer slaking her thirst from a mirage.

CHAPTER 22

Tuesday afternoon, on the way to a meeting with LeBeouf and Walker, Linda saw Ewing greet a man at his office door and usher him inside. She paused before entering Walker's office. What was Cousin Joel doing at Troop G?

Walker began before Linda had time to take a seat. "The DA's not a happy camper." Walker's tight face suggested he felt the same. "What went wrong?" The captain sat ramrod stiff behind his desk. He directed the question at LeBeouf who sat next to Linda in a matching black leather upholstered chair facing Walker.

Linda had a good idea what had gone wrong, but this was neither the place nor time to offer her theory. After several days of bureaucratic wrangling, they'd finally obtained a warrant for a suspect medical clinic late Monday evening. Vance woke her shortly after midnight to report two men with a van moving three file cabinets from the target clinic. There was a leak. But who? From the state, Major Casey, Ewing, LeBeouf, Walker and herself knew of the raid. At the DA's office, an ADA had likely drafted the warrant, no doubt with the knowledge of Kathleen's father.

Linda recalled her first meeting with Val Hoinski the day they'd fought over the Tillinghast sting. "He may be good buds with the boss, but friendship only goes so far," Hoinski had said, referring to Captain Walker and the DA. Given what she'd subsequently learned about Danny O'Rielly, O'Keefe's son-in-law, and his handling of clinic licensing records, she kept quiet about the removal of the files. Her hunch about the leak required better insight before she opened her mouth. The raid took place. As expected, they found nothing suspicious.

"Maybe nothing went wrong, and the place is legit," LeBeouf said.

"OK, but let's play what-if-not," she said.

Walker glanced at her across the huge mahogany desk, as if discovering her in the room, his face looking like the "Who asked you?" question she guessed he suppressed.

"Possible, I suppose." LeBeouf shook his head. "Might have been the locals."

In many instances, State Police notified local police of an impending action as a courtesy. LeBeouf confirmed they'd done so in this case. "Next time, we should cut them out," she said.

"If we even get another shot," Walker said. "The DA had serious reservations about this warrant. He's not going to rush to give us a second."

Linda expected LeBeouf to argue the case, but he remained silent. He may have had his own suspicions about the source of the leak.

After leaving Walker, Linda asked LeBeouf for a minute. They walked back to his office, and he closed the door. Before they'd even sat, Linda said "Two guys with a van moved files from the clinic hours before the raid."

Halfway to his chair, LeBeouf froze. He stared at her. "What?"

"You heard me."

He sat. "How do—?"

"Vance had a man staked out. I got a call at one a.m."

"And you forgot to tell me?"

"Why would someone move files at one in the morning?"

"Why would someone not tell her boss their mission would surely end up as a fiasco?"

Linda was not yet ready to disclose her suspicions about Walker and the DA. Not until she talked to Bert. "I figured you wouldn't want to tip off the clinic."

LeBeouf fell silent. A few minutes passed. He offered her a tight smile. "My call, not yours."

"Agreed."

"It's what I would have done."

"I know."

"Better not happen again."

"You told Walker you suspected the local cops. Do you?"

He appeared surprised by the question. "Makes the most sense to me. What are you thinking?"

She chose her words carefully. "A lot of people were involved, and almost anyone could have been the leak, intentionally or unwittingly. The local cops are a good place to start. I have a friend who knows the politics of the county and local governments pretty well. I'll ask him about the Watervliet force."

"OK, and get back to me. I think we cut out the company fraud boys, too. If we try this again, I want it air tight. Oh, one other thing. Troop C needs a few bodies, and Walker has to provide one. Guess whose name came up?"

Troop C covered New York's Southern Tier along the Pennsylvania border. Knowing Walker, that figured. "The boonies can't be any worse than being chained to a desk in Albany."

She left LeBeouf and headed straight to Ewing's office. His door was open and he was alone. She asked about his recent visitor.

"You know him?"

She nodded. "My cousin."

"He's got information on a big regional gambling and loan sharking operation."

"Another upstanding, concerned citizen, huh."

Ewing laughed. "Yes, plus he's in to these guys for about 10 grand."

Now Joel's visit made sense. She eyed an empty coffee carton sitting on Ewing's desk near the straight-backed chair that normally housed files but was currently uncluttered. "His cup?"

"What of it?"

Would the saliva on the cardboard contain any usable DNA? She considered the risks of asking, picked up the empty container and crushed it. "My cousin is such a pig."

She tossed the trash and returned to her desk where she re-examined the detailed information Vance's investigators had provided. They'd given her plenty of evidence to justify a second search warrant, but she couldn't disclose her Health Department trip to LeBeouf, not yet. The most pressing issue in the fraud case was Vance. He had to break this case soon or likely face demotion. Linda couldn't let that happen to a decent man like Vance.

Something nagged at the back of her mind. Vance had told her taking down a fraud ring required figuring the connections. He and his team had done a good job with the clinics. The missing connections required a different kind of expertise. She dialed Bert's house and snapped to attention when Bill answered.

Shifting plans, she said, "Hey, Bill. How you been doing?"

"You looking for my father?"

"Well, actually, I thought, since—"

"Hang on, I'll get him." The phone on the other end clattered on a hard surface.

"...I had you, we could talk about anger. I've been thinking about what you said and..."

"Linda? Who you talking to? Hold on a second." Bert's voice muffled. "I'm back." Something slammed. "Sorry about that. What's up?"

Good question. What *was* up with Bill? "I need some political insights, but not over the phone. I'm off at 11. Will you still be up?"

"For you, always. Come on over. Wine?"

"White Burgundies?"

"No, but I'll get some."

***

Linda sat at the Bariteau kitchen table facing Bert. The scent of mineral deposits, limestone and calcium, filled her nose. The amber liquid swirled around the walls of the glass as if in a centrifuge. The vortex mesmerized, like the hypnotist's spinning disk.

She swirled a sip of the wine over her tongue, swallowed and drew a deep breath through her mouth and out her nose. "Wow. This stuff has body." She clicked her glass against his.

Bert peered through his glass. "What did you call me about?"

"I need some political insight, starting with County Judge Larry Rosenfeld." He had signed the warrant.

"What about him?"

"Can he be bought?"

"No." No hesitation, no preface. A stellar endorsement coming from a man who believed everyone had a price.

"Positive?"

"Absolutely. Why?"

She explained the problem with the first warrant, the speculation it might have been local police or the judge who tipped the targets. They intended to cut out the cops next time, and she wanted to rule out the judge.

Bert stood, sidled to the kitchen counter. "OK, so you eliminate cops and judge. Any other suspects? Shit. Where'd she move that notepad?"

"Yes. That's why I'm here."

"Do you rule out the State Police?"

"Except one."

"Your boss?"

"Yes."

"Who else?" He asked this in a tone more akin to a teacher quizzing a student.

"The DA's office."

"Ah, yes, the DA's office." He rummaged through a cabinet, glasses clinking against each other. "Here we go. I don't think your problem is State Police." He tossed the notepad on the kitchen table and dropped back into his chair. "Can you explain to me why someone would put a scratch pad I use every day behind the water glasses in the back of the cabinet?"

"You want my services as a relationship counselor? You crazy?"

He wrote something on the pad, then paused. He tapped his temple with an index finger and scribbled again. He dropped the pen on the pad. "No, you'll make Bill a wonderful wife."

If nothing else, the man was persistent. "If not the judge and not State Police, you're left with a pretty short list. Who?"

Bert raised his glass to the overhead light, twirling the vessel by the stem. "I can't get over the deep golden hue of this stuff. The owner of the wine shop told me to try a couple bottles. I'm going back tomorrow to buy a case or two." He sipped, then pushed the sheet of notepaper across the table. "Here, two more judges, one in Albany County, one over in Eddie's neck of the woods. They can't be bought, either."

She didn't look at the paper. "Who?"

The front door opened with the familiar creak, then shut with a forceful bang. The sound of steps in the hall grew closer. She glanced at her watch: 11:45.

"You're home early," Bert said

Bill's face had a pink tint, or was it the light and shadowing? "Yeah, well, you know…" He glanced at her. "Oh, hi." He turned. "Good night."

Bert's told-you-so smirk looked ready to explode. "Trouble in paradise. Shame, huh?"

She dragged her heart back to its professional position. "I seem to recall, before the interruption, I had asked a question. Who?'"

"I'm sure I don't have to say this, but I will anyway. What I'm about to tell you-"

"Is between you and me and no one else." She refilled his glass, then her own. "Talk."

***

It looked like 2:17, but the damned clock wouldn't stand still long enough for her eyes to focus. She lay in bed, in full uniform, waiting for the ceiling to stop swirling. Definitely was a mistake letting Bert open the second bottle of Mersault, but the tale he spun so fascinated she didn't want him to shut up. The cabbie had laughed when he picked her up at Bert's, said he'd *got* more rides from uniformed troopers than he'd given. She took no notes while Bert talked, fully intending to record her impressions when she got home. Now her ambition was to remember some of the conversation in the morning and hopefully, not fall off the bed.

Five hours later, after a dreamless sleep, Linda woke and found the substance of Bert's tale largely intact. According to Bert, District Attorney James "Big Jim" O'Keefe was the most corrupt public official he had ever met. Five years ago, Bert had tipped the federal prosecutor to allegations that Big Jim extorted cash for the reduction of felony charges to misdemeanors. Somehow, the DA learned of the probe and the source of the information. The DA had confronted Bert and threatened his livelihood directly, his personal safety indirectly. She smiled when he told her that part. The DA obviously didn't know Bert well. But a few weeks later, the federal prosecutor called Bert to say his office lacked the resources to pursue the allegations. Even Bert had to admire the kind of juice necessary to pull off a feat where the kill order must have come from a place within spitting distance of the Oval Office.

Bert's interest in the DA reawakened a week after Linda's visit to the Health Department, when Brenda's boss began a campaign of harassment. The situation had escalated, and Bert arranged with the commissioner for Brenda's transfer and promotion to a new bureau in the department. Given what Linda had told him, he found the timing of the harassment by the DA's son-in-law intriguing. The news on the leak of the warrant added credibility to Bert's suspicion of O'Keefe's involvement.

Linda wondered how best to use the information? Furthermore, did Bert have an overactive imagination, or had something gone wrong between Bill and Kathleen? Why wouldn't Bill answer whether he loved Kathleen or not? One thing was sure. Neither father would be bestowing a blessing on their union. In addition, it was probably just as well she hadn't talked him into telling her the Johnny Marsolais story. Bert claimed he hadn't drunk enough to tell the story, a tale better told in a sober state.

That afternoon, while working on reports, she practiced what she would say. The hour approached six before she got Ewing and LeBeouf together in a private setting. They met in Ewing's office and Linda made her pitch.

"No way!" LeBeouf's response was swift and stiff as the lines in his brow.

"We'd need a good reason to do this, and the final decision gets made upstairs." Ewing's tone was more receptive. His face had a look of curiosity. "Give us a solid argument and we'll pursue it."

"Let's start with the judge," Linda said. "My source tells me he's clean. Let's take him and any of us out of the equation. Where does that lead us?"

LeBeouf frowned. "Fuzzy logic and not necessarily leading to the DA's office. There are at least two other viable theories."

Linda had thought of one. "Vance's investigators were watching five clinics." She couldn't tell Ewing and LeBeouf the five were all on the list she'd gotten from the Health Department. "We raided a different one. Vance told me when an opportunity comes up, he extends his resources by paying someone near a suspect clinic to keep an eye on the place. In this case, the tip on the moved files came from a clerk at the late night pizza joint across the street. His deliveryman tailed the van up to Cohoes where they unloaded the file cabinets in the alley behind the Cohoes No-Fault Clinic. Vance has had the place staked out since then."

"Could be him." LeBeouf played devil's advocate, she guessed, anticipating the arguments he was likely to get.

"His career is on the line over this case. He says fraud, he's straight and I believe him."

"The clinic may have been clean to begin with."

"Sure, and two men moved files eight hours after the place closed because...?"

"What I'm missing is an angle for bypassing the DA." Ewing sounded willing to pursue the clinics based purely on the suspicious file move, Linda guessed. LeBeouf appeared reluctant for some reason. Both men were aware of the political minefield they would encounter if they angered O'Keefe. By articulating the real issue, Ewing provided the opening she'd been looking for. Bert had laid it out for her last night. Amazingly she remembered the details when she woke in the morning.

She stood. "How about this? We change the warrant location to the Cohoes Clinic where the suspect files now reside. Then we take the new warrant to the same judge and tell him we observed men moving files hours before we executed his original warrant. Presumably, he'll sign."

LeBeouf shook his head. "When the DA finds out and blows his cork, you don't have to answer him. We do."

"Here's what you tell the DA." Bert had made her recite this twice last night before she'd gotten totally wasted. "We're sorry. We didn't think you'd want to be bothered. Witnesses told us someone moved records before we executed the warrant. This was basically a warrant for the same records but at the new location."

"O'Keefe's not going to buy that," LeBeouf snapped.

"Won't matter because it will be done," she said. LeBeouf was being more difficult than she'd expected, perhaps intimidated by Big Jim?

"We apologize. Promise it won't happen again," she said.

"Won't be necessary because we won't do it the first time," LeBeouf stood abruptly.

"Let's talk tomorrow, Marty. I want to think about it." Ewing remained seated.

LeBeouf turned to Ewing. "You serious?" When Ewing smiled, LeBeouf shrugged. "OK, we'll talk."

CHAPTER 23

L inda sat at her desk working on reports and weighing the wisdom of re-enlisting for sting duty. Two months earlier, she begged off stings. Ewing replaced her with Ellen Durocher, a competent trooper and beautiful woman, but a tough sell as a young teen. Durocher's photo on the net produced some interest but no sting. In the first week the shrinks had flashed Linda's photo, the vermin slithered out from under their cyber rocks to chat her up. Yes, Ewing would be eager to take her back. She preferred not to do stings because of the risk, but the boredom of paperwork was driving her insane. She had no substantive duties except the insurance case, which was at a lull while her bosses tried to shed the fear of their own shadows.

Sting duty offered a relief from the tedium but came with enormous career risk. In the Capital District, chance of a repeat of the Tillinghast case was ever-present, the likelihood higher than she liked. That was the problem. Should anyone try, there would be casualties, her career being one. No, better she stick with Lilith, the safer alternative.

Captain Walker's phone call interrupted her musings. He wanted to see her. No good would come of that meeting.

"Where's my fucking report, Baldwin? I've been waiting since Friday." Bigwater planted two hands on the edge of her desk and loomed over her.

"Shit, I didn't get to your report yet? I swear, just the other day the thing sat on top of this pile."

He straightened and looked down at her as if he the master and she his slave. "Find it!"

"I'll check while you get me a cup of coffee. Black will be fine."

He glared at her and muttered something under his breath she interpreted as, "Fuckin' cunt."

She engaged his eyes, stood and moved around the desk toward him. Bigwater stepped away. She followed. "You got something to say to me, say it out loud."

He stared.

Linda took a step back. "Now, I've got something to say. I'm sorry for kneeing you in the balls. You deserved what you got, but you were in no position to defend yourself and that's not fair, the way I play." Bigwater gaped at her the way her Russian neighbors did when she asked them about the neighborhood. "Here's the rest. You're going to apologize for what you said that day in the gym. We'll shake hands, and we can at least act like colleagues. You follow me, Paul?"

"Ain't happening. Nothing to follow."

She shrugged. "Your choice. Tomorrow afternoon I'm posting an invitation for Troop G to come watch us have it out, man to man. You can show up or not. Won't matter to me. You following now?"

Bigwater's eyes widened. His mouth opened, but no sound came out. He stalked off.

Walker rose when she entered and motioned her to sit in one of the leather armchairs. "Before I get to the personnel matter, I want you to know we're seriously considering your idea on the second warrant. Everyone is warming to the idea. You display political smarts well beyond your years."

Everyone? As if some brass other than Walker impeded the warrant. The compliment had to be trouble, though. "Thank you."

"Marty tells me you're interested in an opening down in Troop C."

Now it was clear. The bastard had called her in to rub her nose in what he intended to do and lay his decision off on her and LeBeouf. Took balls. "He did? Funny, I never asked. *He* raised the issue with me."

Walker frowned. "Well, maybe I misunderstood him."

Dubious. She'd caught him in a lie, and he'd need to find a cleverer one. "That must be it."

"In any event, based on seniority, your name would be in the mix. I want to talk to everyone under consideration first. We'll decide in about two weeks."

Yeah, right. For all practical purposes, he'd already revealed his decision. She stood. "How about the warrant?"

"Soon."

She wouldn't take that bet.

***

The following afternoon, Linda shuffled through the stack of reports. Bigwater approached, glanced down at her desk but passed by without a word. He should have been on patrol. What was he doing here? She wondered what she should do about her challenge. Walker would ream her out if she followed through on her threat, but if she didn't, Bigwater would spread the word. He'd got under her skin and she'd said something dumb. She reached for the phone and dialed. When would she learn? The line rang at the other end.

"Sam Vance."

"Four o'clock at Cohoes No-Fault. Bring your crew." The warrant surprised her. She would have bet Walker didn't have the courage to do what she'd suggested. The fact he'd done the unexpected made her uneasy.

She opened the center desk drawer and retrieved the file folder with the signed warrant. She raised her head to find a cardboard coffee carton hovering over her desk. "Did you find my report?"

"Jeez, Bigwater, thanks." She took the cup and pointed at the folder. "I'm going out, but I'll find your report before the close of the shift."

"OK, I'll check back around 10. Hey, before you go." He stuck out a hand. "I want to tell you I'm sorry for what I said. OK?"

She damned near dropped the cup. Had she heard right? Mr. Macho turned down an opportunity to have at her? She stood, extended a hand, shook his and found his grip firm. "OK."

He didn't let go. "We start over today. That right with you?"

Linda nodded. "Deal. Sorry to run. I got a guy waiting for me."

Her heels clicked against the marble floor and echoed off the concrete walls of the empty corridor. In the patrol car, she propped the coffee carton on the dash. She engaged her shoulder harness and wondered if there was any way to bronze cardboard.

***

The moment the receptionist glanced at the warrant, shrugged and showed them in, Linda had a premonition about the outcome. They walked along a narrow corridor lined with doors, each identified with the letters ER and a unique three-digit number. Linda learned from the first raid these were examining rooms. She stopped halfway down the corridor. Vance had disappeared. Company fraud investigators and troopers methodically knocked on doors and inspected rooms. Someone tapped her shoulder. "Nothing here, gut instinct," Vance whispered, "but play it out, anyway."

After three hours, Linda and five other troopers had combed every square inch of the clinic. Bigwater took part, which explained why he had been hanging around headquarters earlier. He probably didn't know the assignment until everyone moved out. He was cordial and helpful and asked her many questions about insurance fraud. Vance and his crew of investigators pored through the records, none difficult to find, thanks to a cooperative clinic staff. Each time Linda looked at Vance, she found him either frowning or shaking his head. She asked him to step outside.

Across the street stood Smith's Restaurant, where she'd dined with Jonathan and their parents a few months earlier. Linda nodded at the clinic door. "They expected company."

"Yes."

"Where'd the dirty files go?"

Vance stared across the street. "They could have shredded them, I suppose, but I don't think that's what happened."

"No?"

"They moved the files before our first raid, which means they still need them. I think they walked out the front door."

"How? Where?"

"I've been wondering since we got here. If I had three cabinets of files to move, and I thought the place was under surveillance around the clock, what would I do?"

"And the answer is...?"

"I'd move them in broad daylight and right under the surveillance team's noses."

"Huh?"

"Did you notice the briefcases?"

She'd asked several specialists to open a briefcase, in each instance finding the case devoid of files. She'd thought nothing of a medical professional carrying a briefcase. Neither would the surveillance team. Inspection preparation would have taken only a few days if every briefcase left each evening stuffed with dirty files, and returned the next morning empty or with clean records,. "I see your point. Clever."

Vance articulated the real question. "How did they know?"

Linda now had a solid theory and only a few things to check out before nailing it down. "That's what I'm going to find out. Excuse me for a few minutes."

Vance returned to the clinic, and Linda walked away from the entrance. She punched up directory information on her cell. An operator answered. Linda gave him the last name Hoinski and the location Valley Falls, a small rural town where, she'd learned from Bert, the ADA lived. She was almost certain there would only be one Hoinski in town. The operator connected the call. The prosecutor answered on the third ring.

"Val Hoinski, this is Linda Baldwin, a friend of Bert's. Remember me?"

Hoinski laughed. "Let's say you made a lasting first impression. Changed the system yet?"

"Working on it. Sorry to bother you on a Friday evening, but I need some information. How's the baby doing, by the way?" Bert had told her Hoinski had a five-month-old, her first.

"She's fine. She's so cute and so smart." Hoinski launched into a summation of baby antics sounding as if the kid were on trial and Linda the holdout juror.

Linda rolled her eyes and listened. Mothers! A unique breed. She wondered if she'd ever be one herself. Linda interjected some appropriate "wows," but said nothing else to encourage Hoinski, who finally said, "Sorry, I get carried away. What's up?"

"Was the DA's office aware of a search warrant for the Cohoes No-Fault Clinic?"

"Recent?"

"Today."

"No, we weren't, and Jim's going to be pissed."

Linda didn't want to tell Hoinski she suspected the DA knew before the raid. "I didn't think so."

"You called to say you guys screwed us?"

"No. Do you remember telling me that Captain Walker and your boss were good buddies? Could you elaborate on the nature of the relationship?" A long silence ensued. "Val?"

"No."

"You don't remember?"

"I remember clearly. I told you Marty LeBeouf, the sexist shithead, and Big Jim were good buddies."

Linda recalled the conversation and tried to conceal her shock. "Actually, Val, you used the term 'your boss,' not LeBeouf."

"Who do you report to?"

"LeBeouf."

"Ah. For a minute, I thought I'd made a big mistake."

Linda got the message loud and clear. She'd screwed up again by making an assumption. Not Hoinski's error, hers. She was accumulating a growing trail of mistakes and little evidence she'd learned anything from them. "Have you had any dealings with Walker?"

"Only a few. He struck me as tough but fair, a man who let you know where you stood."

Before the phone call, Linda stood on firm ground with a substantive theory and a good grasp of the terrain. Hoinski's revelation was an earthquake, a seismic shift. Linda felt the land rumbling under her, the solid footing dissolving to quicksand, and expected at any moment she might be swallowed up. Everything she thought she knew was wrong, her answer no closer today than on the day she'd met Vance, the truth even more elusive than what happened at Cronin's camp. Hoinski's voice snapped her back from her musings. "Linda, you still there? Are you OK?"

"Yes, I'm fine. Thanks for your help, Val."

"Any time." Hoinski ended the call.

Linda leaned back against the brick wall of a boarded-up building, determined to reconfigure the fraud case. The implications of LeBeouf being the DA's connection were enormous. LeBeouf was an ally, a supporter, the one who suggested she help with the investigation. Yes, the guy who offered her services on the insurance case, much to her and Ewing's surprise. Why?

Was it possible for Walker to *not* be involved in this at all? Didn't seem likely. Walker was on her case from day one, twice pulled her off patrol and was now about to ship her off to Troop C. She thought about Walker's surprised reaction to her saying she'd not requested the transfer and realized much of what she attributed to Walker she did only because LeBeouf had told her. Given her new doubts about LeBeouf she was tempted to view Captain Walker in a different light. For now, she would trust no one. It was time to shake some trees.

She returned to the front of the clinic, where Vance and his crew huddled, the dejection on their faces undisguised. She pulled Vance aside. "We're going to get these clowns. I'm starting to get a picture and it's not pretty. There are some holes and I need your help."

"Shoot."

"If I asked you for a list of all your company's no-fault claims for the past two years that involved more than three claimants and $50,000 in payments, what would you say?"

"I'd say you're starting to think like a fraud guy, but your threshold is too low. I'd go to four passengers and at least $75,000. I'd also want the data from our four largest competitors."

"How soon?"

"Middle of next week. Give me a letter showing State Police requesting the information. That will help with our competitors."

"No letter."

"Why not?"

"Because if my theory is correct, this case will be closed in a few days, if not sooner."

Vance's jaw dropped. "Closed?"

"Probably, but I'll use your research to reopen it."

"We better be quick."

"Trouble at the office?"

"We get a new interest penalty tacked on early next month. I figure I've got to the end of the month to crack this."

"Won't be good for you if they pay."

"The CFO has already shown the boss an attractive 'retirement' incentive for me."

"Forget it, you're not retiring."

CHAPTER 24

Linda paced back and forth across her kitchen floor. She stopped, filled her empty coffee cup, took a sip and resumed pacing. She now knew the meaning of "twist in the wind," what she'd done for the past week, since she'd learned the truth about the DA and LeBeouf.

On Monday, LeBeouf did as she'd expected and convinced Ewing to close down the insurance fraud case. Linda argued with both men that she should use her idle time to pursue the case and prayed neither would detect her lack of conviction. On Tuesday, she and Lilith blew off some excess energy mauling a 50-year-old guy who took what he thought a middle school girl for a ride. There was no elation after this experience as there had been with the first ones. No, the encounter left her with a depressing emptiness and numbness.

Last evening Vance called her at Troop G with the coded message they'd agreed upon: he had completed work on the jewelry cabinet she ordered and would deliver it to her place in the morning. *Come on, Sam. Where are you?*

The exterior door creaked. Linda opened her apartment door. At the far end of the hall, Vance stood examining the dingy surroundings. In his hand, he held an accordion binder stuffed with file folder. "Hey, where's my jewelry cabinet?"

He tapped the binder and laughed, stepping cautiously down the hallway. "No cabinet, but a few jewels."

She closed the door. "Coffee?"

"Nothing, thanks." He seated himself at the table.

She sat beside him and reached for the thin file folder he'd pulled from the binder. He spread his hand over the folder. "Not so fast. Let me explain. The data derives from accident reports filed with the proof-of-loss claim form. The individual files are stuffed, so we took a day to summarize the most germane factors for each accident. Believe it or not, only 27 accidents in the two-year period met our criteria. Here's our summary." He handed her a four-page document in table form, printed horizontally.

Linda began scanning the first page. Vance continued. "The accidents are in date order. We captured vehicle ID and description, driver surnames, passenger surnames, investigating officer, summonses issued, date of first claim for payment and a column for notations of anything that struck us as odd."

Near the bottom of the first page, the surname Arcuro caught her eye. She checked the date: January of the previous year. The passenger surnames were all Russian. No surprise, but a monster one in the next column. NYS Trooper M. LeBeouf investigated. "Jesus Christ!"

"Pardon me?" Vance's face was redder than normal.

"Sorry, Sam."

"You found your boss's name?"

"Yep." She scanned the second and third pages of the report. Nothing jumped out at her except the preponderance of accident victims with surnames sounding of Eastern European descent.

At the top of the fourth page, she found a group of familiar names. She glanced at the date, then crossed the kitchen to the wall calendar. March 5 was a Friday. She was onto something big. Her notebooks were in her desk at Troop G, so she couldn't be certain. Not yet. But she'd bet her 'Vette the date was the night of the party at Jeremy Cronin's camp. The guilty faces flashed in her mind. The scene downstairs began to make sense.

"What do you see?" Vance asked.

"A handful of weak links, all English-speaking. I'll know much more when I get to work this afternoon."

"How can I help?"

"For one, do you have details on the nature of the injuries?" Linda pointed to the line with the surnames Cronin, Jarosz and Maillot along with three others she did not immediately recognize. Heather Gaines was not listed.

Vance inspected the entry and began shuffling through file folders. He opened one up. "Here we go." He read a bit. "Six victims, three male, three female. All claimed severe soft tissue injury." He paused and scanned several more pages. "Each victim received multiple treatments at least three times a week for 10 weeks."

"Have your guys interviewed any of the victims?"

Vance glanced at the report again. "It's not our case, but probably not. This was filed just last week. I'm sure the company fraud guys will have some questions."

"I want them to hold off for a week. Who should I call?"

"I'll do it."

"But you're competitors."

"Allies over fraud. I'll have him call if he has questions. What else?"

"I want the name of the most suspicious clinic you've got in Rensselaer County. I need it ASAP."

"Within the hour."

"Call my personal cell," Linda gave him the number. "One other thing before you go. These rings are effective because of the cooperation of the accident victims and the medical professionals who supposedly treat their injuries."

"Right, everyone is paid by the ring."

"If someone decides he no longer wants to cooperate?"

Vance stood and walked to the door. "We don't sell life insurance to those folks." He left.

Linda's head swam in connections. A week ago she had none. Now so many, it was hard to sort them out. The homicide of the Russian chiropractor, whose first name she recalled as Sergei, and that of the female psychologist, Natasha something, who'd been raped, now appeared to make more sense. Neither listed employment, but both had money to live and pay rent in decent neighborhoods. In addition, she now viewed Jeremy's shoulder injury in a new light. If Jeremy was not involved in a betting swindle, but *was* involved in a fake auto accident, that might explain the injury. Maybe Jeremy realized, after the fact, the threat to his college career should he be caught making fraudulent insurance claims. That would explain the man she saw roughing him up. Jesus! Had she bloodied the nose of a Russian mob enforcer? Did he now think her a threat to the fraud ring? "We don't sell life insurance to those folks." Vance's words chilled her.

There was too much to think about. She had to take things in order, starting with the accident involving Jeremy and Jenna. If it had occurred on the night she'd broken up the party, there was a minor logistical oddity: four couples at the camp and three cars. She'd presumed the teens traveled in pairs, the transportation configuration of the vehicles being two, two and four. But if six kids occupied one vehicle, the only way for three vehicles to be present was if the other two kids each drove. Heather Gaines was not a victim. Therefore, Heather must have driven one.

Linda drove to Loudonville. She slipped in and out of Troop G without encountering LeBeouf, Ewing or Walker. She verified the accident date as the night of the party at Cronin's. Comparing her notes to the summary sheet she'd gotten from Vance, the time of the accident, if indeed there had been one, was little more than 90 minutes before she arrived at the camp. Based upon the activity in progress upon her arrival, it was hard to believe anyone qualified as recently injured.

Fifteen minutes later, Linda pulled her 'Vette into the driveway of the Gaines residence and parked behind a metallic red Chevy Malibu. She rang the front doorbell and waited.

About 30 seconds after the second ring, Heather opened the door. "Yes? Can I help...?" Her voice trailed to a whisper.

"Do you remember me, Heather?" Linda opened the screened storm door and stepped inside to a carpeted foyer.

"Yes."

"We had a deal."

"So?"

"You lied to me."

"No I didn't. About what?"

"How's your boyfriend?"

"My what?"

"I've been asking myself why a young woman would date a man she thought a rapist and finally concluded she wouldn't. You never thought Jeremy raped Jenna Jarosz, did you?"

"No. Jeremy's not like that."

"Why did you try to make me believe otherwise?"

"I didn't."

"Jealousy? Revenge? He was your ex at the time, wasn't he?"

"Jenna was too immature for a man like him."

"So you think that's why Jenna screamed?"

Heather looked at the ceiling, as if her answer might be printed there. "No."

"Why not?"

"Jeremy broke up with her a couple weeks later. I never knew why, but I think something happened around the time of the party."

"What happened?"

"I don't know, but I don't think it involved sex."

"Because?"

"Jenna tracked me down after Jeremy broke up with her and went crazy. She called me every name in the book and accused me of stealing her boyfriend. She scared me, being so filled with rage. She told me she was the only woman who could satisfy Jeremy. I tried to walk away, but she followed, giving me TMI."

"Of the graphic sort?"

"Let's just say I don't think Little Miss Innocent screamed because Jeremy wanted sex."

This was similar to Mark Segretti's story. "Do you think she put on an act?"

"I asked Jeremy. He told me it was a long story he didn't want to talk about."

If the sex was consensual, what else explained the scene on the bed and the scream that still haunted Linda, a harrowing plea as authentic as any she'd ever experienced? Rape still offered the most logical explanation, but Segretti and Heather had created enough doubt to require she explore other possibilities. "I showed up at the camp, and a bunch of you looked nervous as hell. Why?"

"I wasn't nervous. I was annoyed. I mean, we weren't bothering anyone so why'd somebody call a cop?"

"How about the other girls? Did they seem nervous to you?"

"No." Heather snapped the answer, and her face betrayed her.

"What were they nervous about?"

"I said—"

"Heather, I let you slide once because you promised to tell me the truth. Now I find you lied. You'd better start talking. Next time I have to come looking for you, I'll be holding a warrant for your arrest. Understand?"

"You don't have to get all pissed about it. After you ran upstairs to rescue the fair maiden in distress," Heather rolled her eyes, "we finished dressing. The two other couples huddled in a corner of the room whispering about something. Me and my boyfriend tried to join them, but they stopped talking and asked us to leave them alone. I got mad at them and went outside. He came after me and we had a fight. I wanted to go, but he was afraid, so I left him."

That explained the whispered conversation Linda had heard from upstairs. Tiffany Maillot had participated in the conversation, and knew a lot more than she had told Linda. "You drove to the camp alone, didn't you?"

"Tiffany asked me to drive her car because she and her boyfriend wanted to go with Jeremy and Jenna. They were stopping somewhere on the way down. I thought it was just to buy beer. My boyfriend had his car, so he followed me. Everyone else piled into Jenna's car. Jeremy drove." Heather snorted. "The girl was so young, they wouldn't even let her have a full license, so she couldn't drive. We got to the camp, and I unlocked the door with the hidden key. We went inside and started the music. We had a few beers. The fridge was stocked."

"Then why would they stop for beer?"

"I don't know. Anyway, we hung out about 45 minutes before they showed up."

Undoubtedly why Linda had found Heather and her boyfriend involved in some leisurely post-coital activity, while the other two couples were more feverishly engaged. "Did they have beer when they came in?"

"No."

"Did you ask where they'd been?"

"They had a flat tire."

"That sounded true to you?"

"Why would they lie?"

Because they'd cut Heather out of the action. "Didn't you wonder why they'd all gone together in one car?"

"I figured because they wanted to talk about me and my boyfriend. Before I made the mistake of breaking up with Jeremy, I was tight with the other couples. Me and Jeremy decided who else to invite to the parties and whether they would be regulars or not. Jeremy insisted on no more than eight at the camp. I hadn't been to a party since I broke up with him, but Jeremy invited me and my boyfriend. I imagine Jenna was not happy about it."

"No one was hurt when they arrived? Everyone seemed fine?"

"Everyone except Jeremy. I'm sensitive to his moods. He had something on his mind."

"It wasn't your clothes in a heap on the floor and you under a blanket with another guy?"

Heather smiled. "I sure hoped so."

"In the weeks following the party, did you notice any unusual absences from school by anyone who'd been there?"

"Jeremy had the shoulder injury. He missed some classes for doctor appointments."

"Anyone else?"

Heather thought a moment. "No. I'm in at least two classes with all those guys. I didn't notice anything like that. Why?"

Linda would have been shocked if Heather had said yes. What the party kids had been hiding all along was their role in a nearly quarter million dollar insurance fraud. They probably didn't know the dollars involved, but the runner did. According to Vance, the runner recruited the actors, or crash dummies as he called them, staged the event, arranged for the victims' signatures on the phony no-fault claim forms.

This was a pack of high school kids, Jeremy their leader, and as much as she'd like to believe otherwise, the role didn't fit. Who then? Eddie? No, Jeremy's injury was related to the phony accident, and Eddie knew the truth.

"Jeremy's scared, isn't he?"

"What makes you say that?"

"A woman knows if her man is scared or not, so don't answer my question with a question."

Heather flashed her green eyes, and all Linda could think of was Bambi in the headlights. Finally, she nodded her head. "He won't talk to me, though. Can you help him?"

"I'm trying. Meanwhile, let's keep this conversation just between us. Not even Jeremy, OK?"

"OK, but—"

"No buts, Heather."

"All right."

"Good. If you think of anything else, give me a call." Linda left her cell number, thanked Heather and left.

***

That evening, Enrique Martinez sipped his Champagne, the strains of a Ravel composition engulfing him, his eyes hypnotized by the flames dancing on the wood in the fireplace. An unexpected cracking sound jolted him to attention. He jumped to his feet and scanned the dark recesses of the log cabin. No one, of course, there being one entrance, and he'd bolted the solid door shut. Besides, the cabin sat in the north end of New York's Adirondack Park. The nearest paved road was more than five miles away. He heard a second crack and spun back to the fireplace. A piece of wood collapsed into the embers sending a shower of sparks up the chimney. Nerves. He should relax. He'd made his decision.

Martinez had never wrestled with a problem for so long, but then a woman like Amy never factored into a decision before. He spent two weeks sorting through the complexity of his life and longed for a return to a simple existence. His peace of mind demanded he eliminate the Russki and Volodina. They presented no problem. Baldwin did, damn her.

Why couldn't she have obeyed when he'd told her to run along? Had she done so, none of what he'd planned would be necessary. Instead, she interfered in his business and managed to shame and humiliate him in front of another man in the process. And for what? Because he tried to give her the finger and tell her to fuck off? For days afterwards, Baldwin's action burned, a taunting reminder of that day all those years ago.

Two days after catching Zach with his mother, Martinez had listened, in the boys' locker room, as Zach boasted to the gang of his latest conquest, whom he didn't name, and how she'd begged him to hurt her. Everyone laughed with vicarious pleasure at the part where Zach described bending her over, slapping her ass and taking her from behind. Martinez had turned, his face burning.

He looked around the room, admiring his selection for its romantic ambience. He'd picked the place out with Baldwin in mind. He planned to show her what happened to a woman who humiliated a man. Although he belonged with Amy, he would have enjoyed teaching Baldwin a lesson. Eventually, though, he came to realize he could not touch Baldwin and be true to Amy. Given a choice between the two, he would choose Amy every time. He'd tried to figure a way to achieve both objectives and finally realized he was deluding himself.

Baldwin was not just any ordinary woman. She wore a uniform, and not just any ordinary uniform. He knew from its reputation he did not want to test the patience of the New York State Police. The organization was smart, competent and relentless, especially when it came to one of its own. He'd followed statewide manhunts for those suspected of murdering a state trooper. They never ended well for the hunted.

He had been so consumed with revenge for Baldwin, he failed to see the truth. If he wanted to spend his future with Amy, he dare not tempt a confrontation with the State Police organization. Killing a few Ivans or a Russki didn't cause much of a stir, much like tapping gently on the casing of a hornet's nest with a long stick. Taking out Baldwin was the equivalent of sticking a screwdriver in the nest and prying it open. There was a chance no harm would come of the action, but he wouldn't bet on it.

He certainly wouldn't gamble his future with Amy for the satisfaction of avenging the shame Baldwin had caused.

Yes, Baldwin was fortunate. Enrique Martinez was a changed man. Baldwin had Amy to thank for her luck. He would destroy the photos he kept on his nightstand. Though he loved seeing Baldwin nude, his obsession was now over. The surveillance photos would also have to go, as soon as he found the one he'd misplaced somewhere in his apartment.

He'd gone to a good deal of trouble and expense to stash a second car at the nearby quarry, a vehicle he no longer needed now that he'd changed his plans for Baldwin. Martinez preferred to work alone whenever possible, but the auto business was a specialty, and the two wise guys he employed had a reputation for delivering untraceable merchandise. If he'd thought this through sooner, and had not been so driven by revenge, he might have saved himself a good deal of money. Lesson learned.

A pleasant sense of well-being engulfed him. Everything flowed according to plan. Volodina and the Russki would be his last two, and then he would be free. He and Amy would move to Santa Fe if she decided she wanted to, or they might stay in New York. Anywhere would be fine as long as Amy was by his side.

The Capital District was growing on him. He could get an accounting job in Albany. Life had been good. It was time to think about giving back. Maybe he would go into public service. He might even offer his expertise to the Tax Department, teaching them how to collect revenue from the shadowy enterprises he had helped create. By God, the time had come for Enrique Martinez to even the scales for the wrongs he had done in his life. He owed it all to Amy.

He rose and walked to the bedroom where he experienced a touch of shame. He had prepared the place for Baldwin and now realized how wrong he was. Still, he'd created a romantic setting for such a rustic place, and wasting it would be a bigger shame. That settled the matter. They would celebrate after he finished with the Russki and his Ivan killer-wannabe. He would surprise Amy with an intimate weekend at the cabin. The owner would never know. He lived in Jersey and only used the place weekends from mid-June through Labor Day. Hunters like Martinez's father rented the place from October into December.

A late May romantic getaway would fit in nicely. He owed it to Amy. The woman had fallen in love with him. She chose her words carefully, as a librarian would, never actually using the three-word sentence. He understood. She'd been burned and would give her trust cautiously.

She didn't have to speak. Her eyes revealed the truth. Enrique Martinez had learned to read women, and Amy's eyes read like one of her library's large print books for old folks. He breathed in the scent of burning firewood and considered himself one lucky man.

***

The aroma of brewing coffee wafted in from the kitchen on Saturday morning while Linda dressed in jeans, sweatshirt and sneakers. Time was up. She'd agonized more than 24 hours trying to figure out what to do next. Friday afternoon, she'd re-examined Vance's research, checking what she could without raising suspicion. LeBeouf stopped by her desk twice, indicating either unusual curiosity on his part or paranoia on hers. In her haste and excitement Thursday morning after seeing Arcuro and LeBeouf's names on the same accident report, she'd initially overlooked another. On her second pass, the Jarosz surname caught her eye. The driver's first name was identified with the initial A. One of the five passengers was a J. Jarosz. Jenna? Fortunately, she'd been stuck working on accident reports, providing some cover for her inquiries into the identity of the investigating officers listed in Vance's report. In two cases, the police agency reported no officer by that name. Only the LeBeouf report failed to show on the DMV records; odd but no more so than seeing a sergeant as a traffic accident responder. Something wasn't right, and when she added in all the other things she now suspected about her boss, courtesy of Val Hoinski, the case against him was strong. Circumstantial, but solid. Her dilemma was where to take the information.

If she went over Walker's head, the major or anyone else would push it down to him anyway. Then Walker would be pissed at her. Ewing presented another possibility. But as LeBeouf's peer, he would need a captain's OK to act.

She called Bert seeking advice. He concurred with her analysis. She had a true dilemma. Big help. No, Walker was her only choice. She worried Walker and LeBeouf might be partners, but she had to take the risk. She sat on a major fraud case. Inaction was not a viable option, even though it represented the safer career choice. Vance was a decent man. If she cracked the case, she might save his career.

The last person in the world Captain Walker would be expecting on his doorstep on a Saturday morning would be her. She found his address in the phone book, filled her travel mug with hot black coffee and headed to the 'Vette.

A half-hour drive brought her to a sprawling two-story stone and wood house sitting back a good 100 feet from the road. A pond fed by a running brook sat in the center of the yard. Four trees at least a century-old shaded the house. Neatly trimmed grass covered the expanse from road to house and wound around both sides. Landscaping reminiscent of Mrs. B's back yard garden adorned the foundation. Three cars stood on a long and wide blacktop driveway.

A tall slender woman about Linda's own age answered the door. Linda identified herself using the trooper title and asked to speak to Captain Walker.

The woman smiled, her brown eyes alive with mirth. "Come in." She ushered Linda into a hallway, turned and yelled up a stairway. "Hey, Captain Dad, you got a visitor." Turning to Linda, she said, "We keep my dad's ego in check by calling him Captain around here. He knows what his title is worth in this house."

An upstairs door opened. "Who is it?"

"Trooper Baldwin," the woman said.

No answer. Linda imagined nothing good going through Walker's mind.

"Dad?"

"I heard you, Laurie. Show her in and offer her some coffee. I'll be down in a few minutes." A door closed.

She followed Laurie into the kitchen and accepted the cup of coffee she poured. They sat at the table.

"Listen, before my father comes down, I want to ask you a question."

Linda could not imagine what came next. "Sure."

"You're a woman in a man's profession. What's it like? Any words of wisdom?"

Walker's daughter sure wasn't shy, a good start, and Linda told her so. "You thinking of following in your father's footsteps?"

"No. I'm third-year law. I want to be a prosecutor. Women are more widely accepted in law, but you've still got to deal with the macho males who think you're an airhead because you got tits." She glanced back to the hallway.

Linda wondered if she put her father in that category of males. Until recently, Linda had pegged him there, but Val Hoinski had cast some doubt on her assumption. "My best advice is to always act like you belong. Never defer to a colleague because he's male. Exude confidence in yourself by being prepared and knowing your stuff. Speak directly and forcefully and look people in the eye. Most importantly, never ever act intimidated by anyone, even if you are. Intimidation is a favorite technique of the macho boys who feel they have something to prove to you. Tell them by word, deed and body language to fuck off, and don't back down."

Laurie stayed silent for a moment, staring into the hallway. "Thank you. My dad told me the same thing in different words, but you know, he's a male in a male profession. Plus he's my dad, and he's kind of protective. Hearing the words from a professional woman means a lot to me."

"Baldwin, what brings you out here on a beautiful Saturday morning?" Walker's voice boomed down the hall.

He entered the kitchen. Laurie stood and pecked him on the cheek. "I have to run." She turned to Linda. "Thank you."

Linda wished Laurie had kept quiet. Walker watched his daughter leave the house. He poured himself a cup of coffee and carried the pot to the table. He filled Linda's cup. "Thanks for what?"

"She asked for some advice."

Walker sat across from her. He nodded. A bright red speck dotted the center of his chin. "I see." His tone turned somber. "This must be serious."

Linda nodded. For the next 20 minutes, she laid out for Walker everything she knew from Vance's research, the two warrants, the friendship between LeBeouf and the DA, what she'd learned about the DA from Bert. She covered the odd connections between the accident victims, the Cronin family, her suspicions of the party kids and the staged accident. She threw it all at him, emptied both barrels. Throughout her monologue, she had a sense of talking to a mannequin someone had programmed to raise and lower a coffee cup to his mouth.

Walker remained silent for a moment after she finished. "You understand the political implications of what you're saying."

She nodded.

"I don't care about the power brokers." His eyes narrowed forming spider webs in the corners. The dot on his chin had turned dark. "My only concern is my personnel. You've leveled some serious charges at a superior officer. If founded, they could result in a criminal indictment."

"I know. I hope I'm wrong."

He stood, and crossed his arms. "If you took this evidence to any objective DA, what would happen?"

Linda recalled the advice she'd given Laurie. She rose and looked Walker directly in the eye. "She would tell me it was all very interesting and to come back when I'd finished investigating and had something concrete."

"Right."

"I've gone as far as I can, given LeBeouf is my report sergeant. Someone at your pay grade has to authorize completion of the investigation. That's why I'm here."

His face remained taut. "What do you need?"

She fished in her jeans pocket for the notepaper with the clinic name and address Vance had provided, along with the name of the Rensselaer County judge Bert had given her. She handed the note to him. "I want a search warrant for this Troy clinic, signed by that judge, and without the DA's office knowledge. I'd like this kept as secret as possible until the last minute. If the leak connection is what I think, that will cut off both ends."

He refolded his arms across his chest. His mouth said, "I've got to think about this." His body language said, "No fucking way, Baldwin."

What the hell. She'd rolled the dice in desperation, and they'd come up snake eyes. It was better than not trying at all. "I'd also be curious about any and all communications between LeBeouf and the DA or anyone in the DA's office. If there's a connection, you should find proof." Linda walked past him down the hall to the front door, heard him following behind and wondered if she'd been smart to turn her back on him. She reached the door and pulled it open quickly. She turned, surprised to find a lost look on his face. "Thank you for listening, Captain."

"No problem," he said.

She closed the door. He lied. She'd just dumped a gigantic problem in his lap. One day next week, she'd learn the penalty for ill-advised dumping. She felt sorry for Vance.

CHAPTER 25

F ive days after their meeting in his kitchen, Walker summoned Linda to his office. The atmosphere around headquarters had changed subtly. Everyone seemed on edge. LeBeouf barely spoke to her. Walker passed her several times with no more acknowledgement than a nod. It may have been her imagination, but Linda drew an impression she was being shunned. If Walker and LeBeouf were partners, as she now suspected, the treatment would be a logical interim step while they figured out how to dispose of her.

Walker's arms were crossed, his face as rigid as when she'd left his house on Saturday morning. His body language betrayed the words. He would transfer her to Troop C. She would be out of his hair forever. Vance would likely be eased into retirement. LeBeouf and Walker's scam would go on until someone bigger than she ended up nailing them.

He slid a thin manila folder across his desk. The folder bore no markings and needed none. How fitting he should deliver her transfer papers in a plain wrapper. She didn't move. No need to look. She knew the contents.

Walker pointed at the transfer order. "Your warrant."

Linda covered her internal double take without missing a beat. She gave away nothing. On the outside, she played cool and suave. "Great."

"You seem shocked. Is there a problem?"

No problem other than the distinct possibility Walker and LeBeouf were setting her up. "Sergeant LeBeouf?"

"…is in Syracuse today. Any other questions?"

Linda examined the warrant, which was exactly what she'd asked for and signed by the jurist she'd requested. "Who else knows—?"

"I want this executed at 10 a.m. You and I, the commander and the judge are the only people who know about this. Let's keep it that way until just before we move out. I'm giving you plenty of backup."

Linda recalled the conversation on Saturday and Walker's skeptical reception. "So, you think…?"

"I think you asked a lot of good questions the other day. I have some answers. Now shut up and go get the rest."

***

"Sorry for the ride. The unmarked wouldn't start. This is mine." Linda stole a glance at her watch, 9:45, and then at Vance, whose knees rested below his chin. His lanky frame, like Grandpa Baldwin's, was not designed for a Corvette. "Push the seat back. That should help."

He fumbled with the control. "Where we going?"

The 'Vette flowed into the eastbound traffic on Route 7, picked its way clear of the laggards in the two right lanes and joined the leftmost stream of cars going places with purpose. "I have a stiff neck. I thought I'd get treatment." She glanced at him.

The seat slid backwards, Vance stretched his legs, and his eyes lit up. "Really!"

Her eyes focused on the road ahead. "Take out your cell phone and turn it off."

"Well, sure, but…" Vance extended the phone, into her line of vision. The display was blank. "You think I—?"

"What I think is irrelevant. We have a leak. Don't take it personally." The 'Vette approached the Collar City Bridge into Troy. The morning sun danced on the Hudson River. To the south, fishing boats rocked in the wake of a tug-escorted barge.

They crossed in silence and Vance said, "Collar City No Fault is the best bet on this side of the river."

She angled the 'Vette right on River Street, crammed the car into the lone open segment of curb, beside the hydrant, three doors down from the clinic. "So you said."

"A lot of billing activity the past three months, scant evidence of patients coming and going. The place looked more like a billing mill than a treatment center."

"Let's find out."

He stretched his legs outside the car. "Who's watching the exits?"

"Relax, will you?" The latch on her waist pack clicked in place, the pouch sagging from the weight of the Glock.

They approached the glass entrance door. Vance stepped aside. She pulled on the door. It didn't budge. She pushed. Same result.

A woman's voice from overhead asked, "Can I help you?"

She located the speaker in the upper right corner above the doorframe and noticed the mini cam. "I hurt my neck in a car accident, and my lawyer told me to check out your clinic."

"Sorry, we take new patients on written referral."

She turned to Vance, searching for an appropriate response, but he looked like he had discovered his lottery ticket matched the winning numbers. "OK, sorry to bother you."

She jogged back to the 'Vette. Vance loped behind. She unlocked the trunk.

"What are you doing?" Vance asked.

"I forgot my key."

He glanced inside, laughed and removed the sledgehammer, setting it on the blacktop. "Big key." Vance seized the wooden handle. He stepped onto the sidewalk and began the walk back. The hammer swung like a pendulum. "Do you always drive around with a sledge in your trunk?"

"Only when I expect I might have to reason with unreasonable people."

Vance stood to the side. Linda approached the door, warrant in hand and pounded the glass.

"I said you need a written referral, lady," the voice said through the speaker.

"I'm not a patient. I'm a State Police officer, and I have a warrant to search the premises. Open the door." She held the warrant out for the surveillance camera's inspection.

"All legal documents must be presented to our lawyers. Call them at 1-800-LOTTOLAW. They'll verify the validity of your document and arrange a convenient time for your search."

She smiled at the camera. "OK. I'll be back. 800-LOTTOLAW, right?"

"You got it."

She stepped away from the door and edged Vance several steps farther from the entrance. She pulled her cell phone and punched a programmed number. The call connected. "Sixty seconds, we're going in," she stage whispered. Linda grabbed the sledge from Vance and began her silent count.

Across River Street in an area called Monument Square, a marble column stretched skyward. High atop the obelisk, the statue of a woman stood sentry over the city. The focal point of the sculpture was the clarion the woman pointed heavenward, her face positioned to blow into the mouthpiece. Less obvious was the sword in her other hand dangling at her side. Neat. Not only did the Trojan women call the townsfolk to arms. Having declared the battle imminent, they drew their own swords and took the fight to the enemy.

Linda turned her eyes back to the entrance and set the hammer in motion in an ever-higher arc. She stepped in front of the door, and fired her missile. At the periphery of her vision, gray uniforms scurried down the sidewalk in two directions, guns drawn. The maul landed inside the clinic in a hail of safety glass and skidded to a stop against the leg of a desk. She pulled the Glock from her waist pack, and touched Vance's arm. "Stay close. I don't know what to expect." She stepped through the open doorframe, her shoes crunching beads of glass.

A corridor extended to the right, beyond the unattended reception desk. A cacophony of voices worried down the hall, but there was no sign of human life. A door slammed. The voices receded. The first door in the corridor opened to a room about 12 feet square. Unoccupied. Vance's face registered a fat smile at the rows of file cabinets. In the distance, a muffled voice, "State Police. We have a warrant." A gunshot, small caliber she guessed. Then two pops, no mistaking the 9 mm.

She pushed Vance into the file room. "Stay put." She closed the door behind her.

Gun raised, she started down the hall. From a second doorway emanated an urgent sounding "Purr, squish; purr, squish; purr, squish." The handle refused to yield. She tried again and thought she saw Vance in the corner of her eye. "Get back!" She kicked. The door flew open to reveal a man jamming a pregnant file folder into the jaws of an industrial-sized paper shredder sitting on a steel shelf. "State Police. I have a warrant."

He glanced over his shoulder, grabbed another file and turned back to the shredder.

Linda took two quick steps across the room and stabbed a foot into the back of one knee. He stumbled, then regained his balance. He spun, slammed a fist into her cheek, snapping her head back. Her legs weakened. The gun fell. Only her sensei's lectures on visioning prevented her from falling to her knees before a man the way she had that afternoon all those years ago. Her voice also teetered near collapse, gasped for footing. "You're obstructing a police investigation."

"Get lost, cunt."

The word unleashed memories of a blue number 10, the stench of chlorine, the feel of grout lines cutting across her ass. *Can you believe this guy, Lilith?* Her sweep kick snapped his feet from under him. The man landed ass first, legs spread. His head thumped the floor. Eyes trained on the center of his crotch, Linda planted her left foot, raised her right leg, imagining a 50-yard field goal attempt to win the Super Bowl. *OK, Lilith, relax, lean into it and follow the kick through, straight up over the goal posts.* From behind her, Vance's voice rang in a tone she'd not heard from him before. "No!"

Her focus snapped from crotch to the Glock. *Not today, Lilith. We have company.* She lowered her leg, retrieved the gun, and trained it on him. "Listen, shredder-boy, you are under arrest for obstruction of a police investigation, destruction of evidence and assault. You have a right to remain silent. You have a right…" She finished the Miranda, cuffed him, yanked him to his feet, and pushed him through the door. In the corridor, something moved behind her. She spun around, Glock raised.

"Behind you, Baldwin." She'd never been so relieved by the sound of Bigwater's voice. "Entrance secured. Rear exit sealed. Where to?"

She nudged shredder-boy forward. "Head of the corridor."

Before she'd taken two steps, a man stepped into the hall about 20 feet in front of her. Linda raised her weapon. Shredder-boy wheeled and spun himself back into her outstretched arms. The gun flew from her hand and clattered to the floor. The man facing her raised a gun in two hands.

"Down!" Bigwater screamed. She dropped to her knees, reaching for her weapon. There was an explosion. She seized her gun and aimed at the shooter who now lay motionless on the floor, gun several feet out of his reach. She glanced back. Shredder-boy disappeared around the corner toward the front entrance. She kept her gun trained on the man lying on the floor

"Paul?" Linda got to her feet slowly. Bigwater did not reply, his face expressionless. Not a muscle moved. "Everything's OK, Paul. It's over."

"I killed him."

Linda moved to his side. "I don't know, Paul. I'll check on him. But *he* raised the gun. You did what you had to do."

"I killed a man." His eyes shone glassy. A tear leaked from the corner of his eye and ran down his cheek and over his jaw.

A gray uniform appeared in the corridor, gun aimed at the shooter. He looked at Bigwater and immediately flattened himself against the wall. "Everything's under control inside. You all right out here?"

"Check the perp," Linda said.

"The gun," he replied.

Linda recognized him, but his name escaped her. She touched Bigwater's outstretched arms and pressed down gently. He offered little resistance and the muzzle soon pointed to the floor. The trooper knelt by the shooter. Linda sought Bigwater's eyes and found a trace of recognition. "Let me hold your gun for a minute, Paul. OK?" He handed her the weapon as if it were a hot coal.

"He's alive. Serious shoulder wound and bleeding, though," the trooper said.

"Hey, Paul, you didn't kill him. You stopped him, took him out."
A faint smile appeared on Bigwater's face. "You saved my life, too." His
smile spread. Jesus, she owed her life to Bigwater.

"I did, didn't I?" He nodded to his gun. "I'll take that back."

Figueroa and Vanier appeared from around the corner, shredder-
boy sandwiched between them. With only a word to Figueroa, she could
have a private moment with shredder-boy in the records room. "Hey,
Tibbs, do me a favor, will you?"

"What do you need?"

"You and Vanier and Bigwater, take this scumbag," she pointed to
shredder-boy, "down to the secure room and read him his rights again."
She stared directly into his eyes. "I don't think he wants my version of his
constitutional rights." All three troopers laughed and proceeded down the
corridor, stepping around a man and woman in white uniform who knelt
attending the shooter.

The door to the records room screeched and Vance poked his
head out. "OK to come out?"

Linda nodded. She'd not noticed his return to the file room. When
he reached her, she said, "Didn't I tell you to stay put?"

Vance cocked his head but said .nothing.

"Anyway, I want to thank you for what you said back there."

His brow knitted. "Say? What did I say?"

"When you shouted 'No.'"

"Huh? I never left the file room. It's a gold mine."

"But you said…" Linda glanced over her shoulder to the door
leading to the room with the shredder.

"Whatever you heard didn't come from me." Vance laughed.
"Must have been my ghost."

CHAPTER 26

Enrique Martinez had cruise control set at 74 and Beethoven's Ninth on the CD player when the call from Joe Arcuro came. He listened to the runner's report without comment, thanked him for the information and hung up. Six miles south, he exited the New York State Thruway at Kingston, made a U-turn beyond the tollbooths and re-entered the highway northbound. He called the two clients and rescheduled for Monday. The only benefit in Arcuro's troubling news and the sudden change of plans was the opportunity to spend the night with Amy. An hour later, he parked at the Crossgates Mall and went shopping.

He returned to his car 45 minutes later carrying all his purchases in the oversized shopping bag the clerk at Frederick's had given him. Amy would not leave the library for another hour. He would surprise her, and they would have a drink at a nearby pub while he described her new lingerie and his plans for her. He killed some time driving to Troy by detouring through Cohoes, passing twice through Volodina's neighborhood and still arrived at the library half an hour before Amy's quitting time. He was in the process of backing his car in a visitor space when he noticed Amy's car had pulled out from her reserved spot and was turning on 2nd St. They wouldn't be having a drink at the pub, but he could still surprise her. He followed the car.

***

221

At 4 p.m., Troop G headquarters buzzed with activity. Detectives had begun questioning the two dozen medical professionals they'd arrested at the Troy clinic. Troopers had run down the clinic owner who slipped out of the building moments before the raid and led both local and State Police on a high-speed chase for nearly an hour. Troopers in Syracuse had arrested Sergeant LeBeouf earlier in the day.

Vance and Linda were sitting at her desk when troopers marched in with the clinic owner in custody. Vance's face registered shock. "Victor Zalenko?"

The name sounded familiar. "Isn't he the guy who ran the Brooklyn ring?"

Vance nodded, eying Zalenko.

"Same guy who had your idol, Karloff, killed, right?"

"Karpov; Ivan Karpov, and I did not idolize him. He might have been a genius, but he was a criminal. I can't get over Zalenko, though. The FBI has been looking for him since we closed down his Brooklyn operation almost two years ago."

One detective ushered Zalenko into a room and closed the door. Another stood outside. Linda stood. "Excuse me, Sam, I'll be right back."

"Go ahead. I need to get back to my office." He smiled. "I have a hotshot MBA's nose I want to rub in something."

Vance left. Linda walked to Ewing's office. She stuck her head in the door and said, "Our ring operator is an FBI wanted named Victor Zalenko. Ran a similar gig in Brooklyn a couple years ago."

"Where'd you get that?"

"Vance ID'd him."

Ewing picked up a sheet of paper. "He's using the name Albert Jarosz. Sounds familiar."

Linda stared at Ewing in stunned silence. The remaining elements of the party scene at Cronin's camp began to sharpen. She thought it strange Jenna's mother hadn't come in the camp and wondered why they refused to press charges. It wasn't because of Eddie Cronin's political clout. Albert Jarosz/Victor Zalenko had a more powerful motive to keep law enforcement at bay and would even if Jeremy *had* raped Jenna, which Linda seriously doubted. She felt like a fool. Jenna had played her, pushed all the right buttons, made herself the poor victim. *The little shit fooled us, Lilith. What do you think of that?*

Rape was a heinous crime, and victims struggled to maintain credibility in the face of sleazy defense lawyers. Every time a woman claimed rape falsely, she dealt a blow to the legitimate cause of real victims. Jenna had played the rape card to cover the real crime. Linda intended to have a conversation with the girl about responsibility.

"Hey, Baldwin, you still with me?"

"Yeah, sorry. Jenna Jarosz is the girl I thought Jeremy Cronin raped. I'm betting Albert Jarosz is her father."

"You think she's in on this?"

"Not a doubt in my mind." One thing remained unexplained. Linda refused to believe Jenna had manufactured the scream.

Linda returned to her desk. She played back the phone message that came while she met with Ewing. She returned the call. The guard at the front desk told her she had a visitor waiting, a young woman who would not give her name and insisted she speak to Trooper Baldwin and no one else.

Linda walked to the lobby where a stunning brunette, possessing a body as felonious as Kathleen O'Keefe's, paced between the guard desk and the door. Linda studied the woman's eyes. Most people would take her for mid-20s. Her eyes said 30. She extended a hand. "I'm Trooper Baldwin. Can I help you?"

The woman gave a having-second-thoughts nod.

Linda pointed to the guard. "You'll need to show him ID and sign in. Your name is…"

"Amy Farraday." She finished with the guard and walked aside Linda. Amy rifled through her handbag. "I'm sorry to bother you, Trooper Baldwin; I'm probably just being silly."

They arrived at Linda's desk. "Please call me Linda." She pulled out a chair for Amy. "This conversation is just between us. If it turns out to be silly, there's nothing lost, and I'll forget we ever met."

Amy glanced around at the other troopers sitting nearby and those passing by the desk. Linda pointed at a closed door. "Let's go in here."

Linda closed the briefing room door and sat at the small table opposite Amy, who now held a small Kraft envelope in her hand.

"I thought I recognized your picture from the newspaper." Amy put the envelope down and tapped the center with a finger. "So I checked the archives. That must have been awful."

Amy had to be referring to the bike path incident. "What happened to the other two women was awful. To me, no. It's what I do."

"You're very brave."

Some would say foolhardy. "Thank you. You said you recognized my picture by looking in the newspaper. Is that the picture?"

Amy's countenance turned sheepish. "My first reaction was *'The other woman.'* Then the more I thought the less certain I became. So I came to find out."

Linda seriously doubted she'd ever be "the other woman" to the likes of Amy or Kathleen. She reached for the envelope. "May I?"

Amy nodded.

Linda mustered every ounce of fortitude she had to conceal her horror. The envelope held a 3x5 color photo: a copy of one of the photos she'd gotten in the mail from a so-far anonymous sender. She wanted to scream, "Where the hell did you get this?" but said, "I assure you I'm not the other woman. I'm curious though. Where'd you find this?"

"In a book of short stories I let my boyfriend borrow. A couple days after he returned it, I went to put the book back on the shelf and the picture fell out."

"And you thought he was cheating on you."

Amy shrugged. "It's just a strange photo, don't you think? I mean you're in uniform, and the picture taken from a distance, like a surveillance photo on a cop show. Don't be offended, but I wondered why, if he had another woman, he wasn't carrying a more flattering picture of her."

Like the nudes on her pillow. "What's your fiancé's name?"

"Enrique Martinez. And he is *not* my fiancé. Lord no."

"Would you happen to have a photo?"

Amy produced a candid shot of her in Martinez's lap. He was the man Linda had seen roughing up Jeremy Cronin. Another puzzle piece fit into place. Linda pretended to study the photo. Martinez was connected to the fraud ring, probably as an enforcer. That would explain his interest in her, believing Jeremy had already talked to State Police about the phony auto accident. It would also explain Jeremy and Eddie's uncooperative attitudes, a shoulder separation all the warning necessary to buy their silence.

"Do you know him?" Amy asked.

Linda put the photo down. "We're going to want to talk to your boyfriend. Does he live with you?"

Amy shook her head. "The Bronx."

"Do you have an address?"

Amy wrote out Martinez's full name and address on a sheet of notepaper and handed it to Linda who copied the information into her notebook.

"Is he at home?"

"Maybe. He left Troy a few hours ago."

If he'd left Troy. If he'd not noticed her suspicions. If he'd not realized he'd left the photo in the book and gone searching only to find the picture missing. If, if, if: too many for comfort. "I'm going to arrange police protection for you until we've had a chance to talk to Martinez."

"Why?"

"Do you have somewhere other than home to stay for the next 24 hours?"

"I'm not going anywhere or doing anything until you tell me what you're not telling me." Amy's voice had turned hard.

"The man in the photo with you tried to assault me sexually. I witnessed his assaulting another individual. I believe physical abuse and intimidation are his specialties." Linda paused to let her words sink in. "Let me ask you, Amy, does any of what I'm saying come as a surprise?"

Amy didn't respond, her face expressionless.

"How often did he get rough with you?"

Amy appeared surprised by the question. She blushed. The fact the woman had to think before responding provided Linda the answer she'd suspected. Amy would now lie to cover the abuse, the way so many victims did. "Never. Not that way."

Jesus! Didn't this woman understand abuse? There was no "that way" about it. "Oh, good. He must be a real peach. Do you realize we have three unsolved homicides in the Capital District?"

Finally, fear appeared in Amy's eyes. "I know, but what's that got to do—?"

"I think your boyfriend might be responsible for at least one, possibly all three. Now do you understand why I want police protection for you?"

Amy's stunned reaction was perfectly normal for a woman who just learned she'd been sharing her bed with a killer. She gave Amy time to process her new reality. Several minutes of silence passed before Amy said, "What am I going to do?"

"Can you arrange for a place to stay? Perhaps a friend you've not mentioned to Martinez?"

Amy thought a moment. "Yes."

"Do you need a phone?"

Amy shook her head and reached into her purse. She pulled out a cell phone, flipped it open. She pressed a button and studied the screen. The color drained from her face. "He called 10 minutes ago." Amy stared as if the object in her hand had turned toxic.

"I didn't hear anything."

"I muted the ringer when I..." She dropped the phone and put a hand over her mouth. Linda thought the woman might vomit. A moment passed and Amy appeared to regain a degree of composure. "I have a new voicemail."

Linda picked up the thin cell. "Put on speaker and play the message."

"No." Amy snapped her response.

"What?"

Amy reached for the phone. "I said, no. I want to delete it."

"You're not deleting a message germane to a homicide investigation."

"You can't listen." Amy was growing agitated.

"Why is that?"

"Sometimes his messages get a little personal, if you know what I mean."

"Lives may be in danger. I don't have time to waste on modesty. Here are your choices: We can listen, just you and I; or I can take this down to a group of male BCI detectives who will break your access code and play it." Amy seemed unconvinced. "Look, Amy, I'm a woman. I'll bet I've heard the words before."

"OK." Her tone was one of resignation.

Amy played the recording which consisted of a cheery-voiced Martinez telling her he enjoyed the previous evening, he was stuck in a traffic jam about five miles from home and he missed her already. Linda's pulse quickened when he told Amy his boss had just called to tell him he needed to return to Albany tomorrow. He wondered if they might get together in the evening. Her heart skipped a few beats when he said, "I know you've been a naughty girl. You like to take my love and then betray me. I'm going to tie you down and punish your two-timing ass. I'll make you beg for me, you little whore." The message ended. Damn! Her fears had proved right. Martinez had figured Amy out. He wasn't calling from the Bronx. He was probably across the street.

"Do you need any more proof?" Linda asked.

"Proof of what?" Linda expected a face filled with horror. Instead, Amy's cheeks glowed the crimson of pure embarrassment.

"How dangerous Martinez is."

Amy laughed dryly. "He always leaves me messages like that. If he suspects something, he's not letting on."

Now it was Linda's turn at stunned speechless. Amy turned her head away, but even in profile, her cheek radiated scarlet. The truth about Amy Farraday shocked Linda's senses. Amy wasn't with Martinez *despite* the fact he treated her rough. She was with him *because* of it. "It's none of my business, but do you love this guy?"

"He thinks I do."

"You don't think that's a dangerous game?"

"You're right; it *is* none of your business."

Linda stood. "You make arrangements for a place to stay while I go talk to a detective about picking up Martinez and getting you protection for the duration." Linda left Amy alone in the conference room and headed to Ewing's office.

Ewing was standing, jacket on, looking like a man about ready to leave. "What's up?" he said.

"I got a lead on the three homicides."

"No shit!"

"Remember the photos they found at the bookie's place?"

He nodded. She handed him the note and photo. He examined the picture. "Same as the bookie." He glanced at the name and address. "This your photographer?"

"Yes."

"What's your connection?"

"Martinez is the man I saw roughing up Jeremy Cronin, the guy I believe responsible for Cronin's dislocated shoulder. I thought it was about a betting scam. Now I'm convinced it's related to the crime ring we just busted."

"Because of Jarosz?"

"A couple hours before I broke up the party at Cronin's camp, six of the kids were involved in a fender bender. No one was injured, but the insurer was billed a quarter million for medical care."

"How'd you get the photo?"

"His girlfriend."

"Women. They'll turn on a boyfriend for a little thing like that." He laughed at his own attempt to ease the tension. "We'll want to talk to her in the morning."

"I think Martinez served more as a boy toy."

"Really?" Ewing sounded eager for a lurid story.

"I'll give you the juicy parts later. I want protection for her from the time she leaves here until we pick him up. She's in an interview room arranging for a place to stay."

"I'll take care of it now." He glanced down at the address and winced. "NYPD."

Linda knew the jurisdiction and the potential for bureaucratic delay while requests flowed through channels. Good detectives like Ewing maintained an informal network of peers in the NYPD. An official request might take days. The unofficial route often reduced waits to hours or shorter. Ewing removed his jacket. "I think I can spring Figueroa. I'll have him find you." He waved the note with Martinez's address. "Then I'll get to work on this. What about you?"

"I'll stay with Amy until he gets here."

"You know what I meant."

"I've been on his list for a couple months. I'm sure I'll last another day. I've got a place to stay and my own protection." She fingered the handle of the Glock. "Put your manpower where you need it."

"I will. You're getting protection."

She backed away from the door. Ewing picked up the phone. Like hell she would take a babysitter home. The jokes would never end.

Linda spent the next half-hour with Amy Farraday in strained conversation and awkward silence. She'd learned more about Amy's personal life than either of them found comfortable. Tibbs showed up to take Amy off her hands.

"Who drew you?" Tibbs asked.

"Ewing's working on it."

Worry clouded his face. "You're sure Ewing's got somebody?"

"It's under control, Tibbs. Now get out of here before you piss me off." Linda wasn't sure what Amy made of the back and forth with Tibbs, but finally they left, and she breathed a sigh.

She returned to her desk and thought about Tibbs's solicitude. He'd become a good friend, and like any good friend, he could be a royal pain in the ass sometimes. He worried too much about her, wanted her to play by the same rules he did and usually pointed out the risks of doing things her own way. She didn't need his lecture tonight. She knew the rap by heart.

Tibbs's words contained much truth. Martinez was a contract killer, not some sleazy scumbag prowling for young flesh. She had no experience in Martinez's league. The smart move would be to accept the protection Ewing insisted she take. She was part of a team and needed to trust her teammates as she had done with Walker.

She straightened up the top of her desk feeling a sense of relief. She walked to Ewing's office. His animated voice carried down the hall. The door stood ajar. Ewing spoke into the phone trying to persuade someone of something: a visit to Martinez's apartment, no doubt. Linda continued on to the coffee brewer and poured herself a cup. A heavily photocopied cartoon of a busty woman with a phallic-shaped object protruding from her mouth hung taped to the wall above the machine. Beneath the figure were the words of a dumb blonde joke. She tore the cartoon down and tossed it in the trash.

She wondered about the man who had taped it up. If he were in Linda's position, would Ewing insist he take home a protector? Reality check: she was a woman in a profession heavily dominated by males, the crude joke a part of a male environment. The sexist attitude might not be deliberate, but a fact nevertheless, requiring vigilance that she not buy into it, however well intentioned. The men would never view her as equal if she didn't act it. Coffee in hand, she returned to her desk, breezing past Ewing's office double-time. She called for a taxi and exited through the front lobby to wait.

Linda had the cabbie drop her off on North Mohawk Street, where she ducked between two buildings and drew her gun. She crossed the alley that ran behind her apartment. She strode through the yard. Something moved in the corner of her eye. She swiveled around, gun trained on the motion. A cat scurried under the fence.

She entered through the back door and searched the apartment thoroughly, without lights. When she found no intruder and no sign of attempted entry, she allowed herself to relax a bit. She uncorked a California Zinfandel and carried bottle and a glass into the dark living room, where she sat sipping her wine and sorting through the flurry of events from a day that now seemed like a week.

Everything was coming together, the insurance fraud case nearly complete and Vance's job safe. Most importantly, though, was the imminent end of the stalking ordeal. She'd handled it fairly well, but the endless vigilance, the constant worry someone watched or waited for her, took a toll. The prospect of letting down her guard a bit was inviting. Martinez would be in custody in a matter of hours. Amy would be safe and

Linda's ordeal would finally end. Jenna, Jeremy and Eddie Cronin as well as the party crew represented loose threads but minor ones.

At some point, Linda fell asleep in the overstuffed chair. She woke with a start to the sound of the front door squeaking closed. From the hallway, she heard giggling, followed by the sounds of footsteps on the stairs. Linda wanted to go to bed but was certain a creaking in her bedroom would soon remind her she slept alone. Besides, an intruder would not come looking for her in the living room first. She removed her belt, shirt and pants, stretched out on the sofa, rested the Glock on the floor within easy reach and eventually fell asleep.

***

Enrique Martinez stretched out on the bed at the Marriott. The classical music playing on the radio did nothing to ease the rage that had been building since Amy's car first entered the State Police parking lot. He loved Amy as he had loved no other woman, and she betrayed him. She was no different from all the others.

She'd left in a patrol car with a male trooper. Martinez had not followed. He had no need to hurry. He had a lifetime. They wouldn't guard her forever. Baldwin's red convertible was in the side lot where uniformed troopers parked patrol cars. He wondered if she had met Amy. Not likely, there being no obvious connection between them. He had failed to see Amy's deep concern about the Russian mafia as a budding suspicion about him. Like every woman who would betray a man, Amy hid her true self from him, pretended nothing was amiss. Martinez knew Amy well, and she'd given no sign of the treachery in her heart. If she were an actor, she might have won an award for her performance. He'd deal with Amy eventually. His immediate concern was tomorrow morning.

CHAPTER 27

Linda woke shivering to the sight of a half-empty bottle of red wine staring at her from the coffee table. The apartment had cooled overnight. She rose from the sofa and rounded up her uniform. She took a hot shower and dressed in sweatshirt, jeans, thick cotton socks and sneakers.

She wolfed down two Frugal Gourmet macaroni and cheese entrees, realizing she'd skipped lunch and dinner yesterday. Between bites of brunch, she put on a pot of coffee and played the phone message she'd not noticed last evening. Jonathan again, the message a familiar one. Linda jabbed the delete button. Her elbows rested on the kitchen counter. The final drips stalled their way into the pot. She slid the filter holder out, placed a cup under its center, swung toward the sink and dumped filter and grounds. Jonathan had called several times since the night of the Charity Ball, and she'd returned each one. She wiped the coffee drips from the counter. At first blush, she'd thought their vastly different work schedules conspired to keep them from a follow-up date. Now she knew better.

The comforting aroma of fresh-brewed java filled her nostrils. She took her first sip, and the heat dispelled the slight chill of the kitchen. Coffee in one hand, cordless phone in the other, she walked to the living room where she resisted the urge to raise the room shades and allow the morning sun to bathe her favorite chair. When Martinez was in custody, she'd raise them and let the warmth in. The thought reminded her of the Glock hanging in her bedroom closet. She fetched the gun and settled into the chair. She dialed Ewing's office, but hung up when his message recorder picked up. He should arrive shortly. She'd try him again.

She now recognized the problem with her elaborate waltz with Jonathan. They waltzed and waltzed, both parties unsure they wanted the dance to end for fear of what came next. The situation reminded Linda of the agony her high school girlfriends endured. When the big dance came, they suffered, waiting for an invitation from Mr. First Choice while simultaneously stringing along Misters Two, Three and Four, just in case. Heaven help the poor girl who had to "settle" for a third or fourth choice because she'd held out too long. The exercise drove her girlfriends mad with frenzy.

Up to now, Linda's life had always been simple. When the big dance came, she went with Bill, until the day she stopped going altogether. She learned valuable life lessons about friendship and loyalty back then, when Bill immediately became Mr. First Choice for most of her former friends. To a woman, they pursued Bill like doe in heat. She'd stood by, a cool observer, nothing more, making notes, taking names. How ironic, after all the machinations, Bill should end up with a mate from the big city, Albany. Mr. First Choice chose an out-of-towner, and the joke was on them. What foolishness.

Now she positioned herself for a repeat. Jonathan was her second choice as, she suspected, she was his. How long should she hold out? She wondered whom Jonathan wanted instead of her. Did couples who settled for second choices make for lasting relationships? Her thoughts turned to Bill, Kathleen and their shared look at the Charity Ball. Little wonder about *their* first choices.

Jonathan wasn't exactly "settling." Her first choice was gone, elevating Jonathan to the top. He offered promise for a solid long-term relationship. What else could a woman reasonably ask? The time had come to end the waltz and get on with life. She'd slept alone too long. She picked up the cordless handset, scrolled down to Jonathan's number and pushed the call button.

The phone rang. A gunshot exploded behind her. Linda sprang from the chair to her knees, dropping the handset. For a fleeting second she was paralyzed. She'd placed Martinez in the inactive file of her brain, but she may have been premature. Maybe he'd finally finished toying with her and come to get her. Like hell. She grabbed the Glock and crawled to the window. Peeping around the shade, she examined the windows and rooflines across the street. Nothing unusual. Of course not. Shit, she'd been sitting near the front window. The shot had sounded muffled, not the crack and explosion of a nearby rifle.

She dashed to the back door, opened it and scanned the yard, alleyway and buildings. A second shot cracked, drawing her attention to her left. In a narrow alley between two brick row houses, a man crouched behind a green dumpster filled nearly to the top with black, green and white garbage bags. Crowning the heap were a blue webbed lawn chair and a TV without a face. The man appeared to be unarmed, his hands resting along the corner of the dumpster. His head leaned to one side as if peering through the alley to the street. Linda visualized the houses on the opposite side of Front Street, three stories if memory served.

She rushed across the yard, her pulse pounding. What the Christ was going on? A sniper in the neighborhood and she was not his target? A mixture of relief and tension filled her. Target or not, she had work to do. She tore open the rusted gate and sprinted down the cinder alley toward the dumpster. Another shot. She pulled up short. A puff of cinder erupted from the ground behind and to the left of the man. The angle put the shooter on an upper floor across Front Street, positioned right of the alleyway. She raced the final 25 yards toward the building to the right of the alley. At the back wall, she paused to catch her breath.

"Don't look at me." The man snapped a head of wavy brown hair around. "Turn around! Watch the shooter." The man complied.

"Good, you understand English."

"Nyet."

"Are you hurt?"

He shook his head.

"Do you see the rifle?"

The man nodded.

"Third floor, right?"

Another nod.

Remarkable for a man who didn't understand English. "Good. I'm going around. When you hear three quick shots that sound like pops, not cracks, you run back this way. You follow?"

"Da."

Linda circled the building and approached the front from a narrow alley. At the head of the alley, she flattened her stomach to the brick. It took a moment to locate the rifle muzzle extending from a rectangular opening above a third-floor window across the street. She raised the Glock, steadied it and trained her eye along the sight. When the opening appeared, she fired. The gun recoiled. She aimed again and fired and then once more. Her ears pounded from the explosions, more piercing and ominous than shots directed at a paper target while wearing ear protectors. She moved her eyes from the barrel and stared at the opening, the gun now gone.

Linda stepped across the sidewalk and crouched behind a van. No movement. She stood, Glock trained on the house. Still nothing. She recalled the neighborhood reconnaissance she'd done the day the first batch of photos arrived. If the shooter intended to escape undetected, he had to use the alley behind Cataract Street, which meant he would cross the foot of Front Street. She sprinted to the corner.

Two months ago, her survey of alleys and tunnels helped form a theory. She stopped, her pulse pounding. Hard running footsteps approached. Theory gave way to the reality of what came next. A flash of terror ripped through her. She raised the Glock with two hands. Without warning, the somber cherub face from Cohoes High career day appeared, and the young woman's haunting questions followed. "You can, can't you? How do you do it?" The pounding steps neared. A figure emerged.

"Police. Stop!"

In a fluid movement that seemed like a slow motion replay, the figure wheeled to face her, gun raised. There was no mistaking the eyes of Enrique Martinez. Linda flung herself against a chain link fence overgrown with weeds. His gun exploded, the sound of shattering glass registering behind her. Something scratched the back of her hands. She tried to raise her gun, but found her arm movement slowed by the weight of the blackberry vines adhering to her sweatshirt. She yanked the Glock to eye level, ready to fire. Over the strands of dead weeds draped across her arms, Martinez was gone.

She'd had him in her sights and not fired. Why? The question troubled her. Yesterday, Paul Bigwater fired to cover her without hesitation. When her turn came, though, she blinked. At Martinez, of all people. The man had tried to molest her, stalked her, invaded her bedroom and, for all she knew, planned to kill her. The sound of his retreating footsteps floated up from the dirt path. She brushed the weeds from her arms and stepped clear of the thicket.

***

Martinez slowed on the narrow path, easily navigable the last time he used it, now nearly overrun by weeds and brush. He stopped to listen. No sirens, at least not yet. Soon, though. Timing was everything in this business. He planned everything down to the second. Then Volodina bent over as he squeezed the trigger. The lucky bastard had dodged his destiny, for now.

Martinez had allowed himself two minutes from the first shot before exiting the attic. Seconds after retracting the rifle from the vent opening, a shot exploded, followed by two more quick blasts. He'd scrambled down the back wall wondering why Volodina had waited so long to return fire. Baldwin's surprise appearance answered his question.

Shooting at a brick wall was as easy as executing a paper silhouette of a man. When Baldwin had an opportunity to kill him cleanly, though, she blinked. That didn't surprise him, the work of ending lives being a man's job. The female started and nurtured life. The requisite body chemistry largely precluded a kill instinct. The feminists argued they could do any job a man could, but nature repeatedly proved them wrong. Women who killed were extremely rare. Baldwin wasn't one.

He'd miscalculated this morning, concluding Baldwin was not home because he'd not seen her car in the neighborhood. Had he known otherwise he would have never tried to take out Volodina. He made a habit of not conducting business with law enforcement around, woman or not. Damned Baldwin, messing in another one of his jobs. The woman was feisty, a royal pain in the ass, but God was she beautiful. Like the unfaithful wife in the Hemingway lion story, he wanted her. It took a real man to tame a woman like her, a challenge he would welcome.

Behind him, he detected a distant but urgent rustling of dried brush. Martinez shook his head, not believing his ears. He had decided to let Baldwin be, but she wouldn't let it rest. She wanted more. He smiled at the thought. Fine, he would give it to her. He sprinted down the path. He'd have to improvise. There wasn't much time.

***

Linda wiped at the sweat on her forehead. Her pulse hammered from the running, this no jogging pace. She didn't know how long she could endure but was determined to catch up with Martinez. That his intended target was not her but the man in the alley puzzled her. Was it a ruse to flush her out, and, if so, for what purpose? What was the connection between her and the man? Martinez had the answers and she intended to get them.

Ahead a car engine started, the sound accompanied by a distinct echo. Linda slowed. Damn! He must have driven back here through the tunnel. She ran hard. There wasn't much time.

She wished she had her cell phone. The lack of approaching sirens indicated no one had reported the gunfire.

A muffled gunshot rang out. She slowed, wary, the lure of the running motor drawing her forward. The idling engine grew louder and finally she located the source. A black SUV stood parked under the mill building, front passenger door open. She stopped and looked around. Why was the car still there? At least a minute had passed since the engine first cranked. The vehicle faced away from her, toward Harmony Street. Martinez should have left by now. Why hadn't he?

Gun trained, she closed the remaining 40 yards, sweeping her arms right and left along the thick brush lining and in many places encroaching the canal bed. Her body had cooled since she'd stopped running, and despite the sweatshirt she shivered. She recognized the Mercedes Benz logo on the back of the SUV and noted the New York license plate: a dealer plate. Like the car, probably stolen. A faint sound of classical music reached her ears. She had a sense of the surreal, this not really happening, she a mere spectator. She'd come to recognize the feeling: fear, nothing more. Sensei taught her to channel her fears into constructive action. Martinez would soon learn how that worked.

At the mouth of the tunnel, she paused. The vehicle was no more than 20 feet distant and she saw, through the glass on the rear hatch, what looked like a figure slumped over the steering wheel. What the hell? He'd committed suicide? She craned her neck, peering intently at the figure. Something about the scene didn't look quite right. An alarm flashed in her brain. She tore her eyes away in time to catch the blur on her left. A cold metal pressed against her temple. Linda froze and realized her failure to react instantaneously had immobilized her agility, her most potent defense.

"Drop it!" a male voice growled.

She lowered her arms. A peculiar odor drifted past her. "What do you think you're doing?"

Something soft brushed the back of her neck and a strong hospital odor reached her nostrils. A cloth covered her mouth and nose. She tried to wriggle her head, but found it pinned against his body. Her legs soon felt rubbery and her mind drifted off thinking it strange Martinez had not answered her question.

CHAPTER 28

Linda rode in the back of a horse-drawn covered wagon making her way west, a rugged individual striking out on her own to explore new frontiers. The bump, bump, bumping of the wagon over the rough and uneven trail penetrated her bones. She ached. She'd fallen asleep at least a couple of times, but the horses must have known enough to keep to the trail because the bumping never stopped. A fly tickled her nose. She reached to slap it and found she could not move her arms. She'd had too much to drink, her mind a blank. Alcohol did that to her. Why drink otherwise?

Her eyes blinked at the darkness and she gradually became aware of the cloth covering them. The forward movement gave her a sense of progress, but the bumping, the erratic, incessant bumping drove her mad. She tried to scream to make it stop. Her mouth would not work. Hangovers were like that. Her ears functioned, though. She heard music, classical music, perhaps Mozart.

The fog in her head began to lift. She remembered hearing music coming from a black car with an open passenger door. But she'd not gotten in the car, at least she didn't think so. So where was she? Linda focused as much as the thinning fog in her brain would allow. The images returned: a gunshot; the driver slumped over the wheel, a suicide. But no, the picture was not quite right. She realized this at about the same time the cold metal touched her head, the hospital odor and the cloth over her mouth. Slowly she reconstructed what had happened.

There'd been shooting. She fired her gun at the shooter's position. She ran, her gun raised. Someone shot. Who? Linda recalled the eyes and the rest of the scene snapped into focus as sharp as the terror spreading through her being. She tried to yell, found fabric tied tight between her teeth and mustered a grunt. She reached to pull off the blindfold and panicked when she found her arms stuck to her sides, her wrists bound. She lay on her side, her head resting on something soft. Her legs curled tight, her ankles also bound. She was a prisoner, Martinez's prisoner. The terror cleared the haze much as a stiff blast of icy wind overpowered a lingering fog. Almost as quickly as her mind had cleared, her self-defense and survival training kicked in. Linda calmed herself, focusing on the details she recalled and calculating how she might escape.

Thanks to her foolish pride, she'd rejected police protection. Had she done otherwise, this may not have happened. She worked for an organization dedicated to protecting people. Its public outreach message urged citizens in need to seek help. Now she served as poster child for what happened to a person who ignored the extended hand. She was on her own. Nothing new. Martinez, though, *was* something new, a contract killer. The fact she remained alive provided no comfort. He'd raped Natasha Borisova before killing her, and he intended to rape her. She shuddered. Like hell. Not if she could help it. She made a vow back then: never again.

***

A stiff wind had chilled her that November Saturday afternoon. It would hurt. She'd known it for sure. Always hurt the first time, her friends had told her. Linda had lowered her head against the breeze biting her cheeks on the walk to Uncle Frank and Aunt Lydia's house, the garment bag flop-flopping her back in rhythm with her step.

The late afternoon sun dissolved in the approaching waves of gray and black clouds. The air foretold the season's first snow, a blotter for the lingering scent of decaying leaves. A car horn blared and tires screeched when she crossed Simmons Avenue at Columbia Street without raising her head. Shit.

Her faded black corduroys and Cohoes High sweatshirt proved no match for the advancing storm, despite the lined windbreaker. She shivered, from the weather or the prospect of the pain she could not be sure. She jogged the last four blocks to warm herself, taking care her change of clothes remained on the hangers.

She let herself in and shouted into the stillness. "Anybody home?" She dropped her gym bag in the front hall closet, hung the garment bag. Although she'd rather hang out at the mall with her friends on Saturday afternoons, the extra money she earned cleaning her Aunt's house came in handy when she wanted to splurge.

While she passed the feather duster over the mantle, she imagined Bill's tender caress on her arms, on her back and on her thighs. When the vacuum cleaner roared to life, nagging doubts crowded out the pleasant images. Would she be any good at this? Would Bill be disappointed afterwards? Would anyone be able to tell, just by looking at her, what they'd done?

A cold draft tickled her ankles. She turned in time to see her cousin push the front door shut. A real jerk, Cousin Joel, so proud he beat her out for the baseball team, even after he knew what her mother had done. His teammates heckled the crap out of him. Everyone knew she was the better player, by far. She offered a small wave. He pursed his lips and opened his mouth. If he said something, the vacuum motor ate the words. He climbed the stairs and disappeared.

An hour later, she stored cleaning equipment and supplies in the broom closet; retrieved her change of clothes. She showered and dressed in the basement bath and smiled at her image in the mirror wearing the black silk panties and matching bra. She'd blown a whole week's pay on the underwear because she'd fallen in love with the embroidered intertwined red hearts on the bra and panties. For their first time, everything must be perfect.

She tugged the tight black skirt over her hips. After buttoning the red blouse, she regretted not having brought a heavier jacket. The skin on her arms tightened at the prospect of the 15-minute walk to Bill's house. Although sleeveless was not her first choice for winter weather, Bill loved the blouse on her, and she loved how he looked at her when she wore it.

The whirring buzz of the hair dryer filled the room. In the upper corner of the mirror the door moved. She'd locked it, hadn't she? In the reflection, Joel's grinning face peeked around the opening. He might be a relative, but he could be a real pain in the ass sometimes. She patted her head and flicked the dryer off. She turned to face him. "Ever hear of knocking?"

"It's my house."

She stashed her dryer in the gym bag with her work clothes and zipped it. "Good for you. I have to run."

Joel eased his shoulder inside. The blue number 10 leered at her.

"See what I'm wearing, Cuz?" Joel pushed the door from his chest. It crashed with a thud and bounced back. He stepped inside slammed his fist against the door, as if a hammer nailing it to the wall. Linda's throat tightened. One exit. Occupied. "Well, hey, you made the team and I didn't. Congratulations." She glanced down then willed her heart back to her chest. Joel's legs were naked below the jersey.

***

The bumping had stopped and so had the music. A car door opened and slammed shut. A click near her head was followed by a "whoosh" and cool air. She wriggled around face up to the fresh air. Something scraped the surface she lay on. She tried to ask where she was, his reply swift. "Shut up, bitch."

Linda tried again but got no immediate answer. She smelled a faint trace of the hospital odor. His breath was warm on her cheek. "Want more?"

She jerked her head away, turned her face down. She couldn't afford to be drugged, needed to be clear-headed for whatever opportunities he opened up for her.

She heard the hatch close. Linda squirmed around the space on her back using shoulders and buttocks to maneuver. Her fingers explored the carpeted bed of the vehicle for an object to cut the binding around her wrists. She found nothing, not a stray nail or paper clip, not even a hard, straight edge. She'd been flexing her arms and trying to stretch the restraints since she'd become conscious, with no useful results so far. The effort had created a tiny bit of separation. At this rate, it would take hours. That didn't likely fit Martinez's time frame.

The click, the "whoosh" and cool breeze announced his return. Linda lay still. His hands seized her ankles. He dragged her and lifted, tossed her body over his shoulder, like a butcher hauling a side of beef. Martinez walked with her slung over his shoulders for a distance she estimated at about 100 feet. Along the way, gravel scraped followed by soft padded footsteps and finally a series of steps up. The air was crisp with a hint of moisture and scent of pine, wet grass and burning wood. She strained her ears for clues about her location, but only a full chorus of crickets accompanied his footsteps. After another half-dozen steps, he eased her off his shoulder to a soft surface, a couch or chair she guessed. A door closed, the cool air receded and soon his hand fumbled at the back of her head.

He pulled off her blindfold. She blinked. Her pupils reacted to the light. Once they'd adjusted, she took stock. A small fire crackled under a large teepee of firewood in a stone fireplace occupying much of one wall. The head of a buck hung above the fireplace. To the left lay a corridor, in shadow except for the shaft of light flickering from an opened door at the far end. Two other doorframes were visible in the corridor. The wall to the right was rough-hewn plank with a large bay window located high above

242

eye level. No light shone through. She'd encountered Martinez sometime between 9 and 10 in the morning. At least 10 hours had elapsed, perhaps more. She twisted around in the chair. Behind her, a solid wood door with oversized black hinges and a large black lift latch stood inside a log frame, bolted shut by an iron shaft as thick as a crowbar. The owners must have been expecting an invasion by barbarians. To one side of the door stood a long rectangular pine table with pine benches on the sides and matching pine chairs at each end. Beyond the table was a kitchen, its Formica counter, sink, microwave, electric range visible.

"Nice place, huh? I thought of you when I picked it out."

Her eyes fixed on the hunting rifle mounted on the wall behind the large table. "Useless," he said. "The trigger mechanism is jammed." He approached her. She recoiled. "Aw, I thought you liked me. Let me free up those wrists and ankles."

Martinez walked to the kitchen, fumbled in a drawer and returned with a small pair of scissors and a large black garbage bag in one hand. In the other, he held a Colt semiautomatic pistol. "Stand up." She did, barely able to keep her balance. He could have knocked her over with one finger. "Not such a tough bitch now, are you?" He stood behind her and pressed the tip of the gun barrel into her neck, below her jaw. She flinched. "Careful, Linda." He whispered in a solicitous tone, his mouth near her ear. "A sudden movement might cause my finger to slip, and that would be a shame. We haven't had a chance to get to know each other." His tongue touched her earlobe. "Yet." A weight registered on her ear. The pervert had put earrings on her.

The binding around her wrists loosened. She fought the urge to smash his face in. Martinez stepped back, gun aimed at her chest. "Finish it." She eased the tape off, the hair follicles protesting. She was making progress though. Her hands were free. The gag remained in her mouth, and probably for the better. Martinez wouldn't want to hear what she might say. Better she act, not speak her mind. "Move slowly now. Bend over and undo your ankles." Linda motioned for the scissors. He smiled. "Do I look stupid?" She picked at the edge of the tape and unwrapped a length that coiled around about eight times. When she'd finished, Martinez said, "Off with the shoes and socks." Linda did as instructed, and he tossed them into the garbage bag. He pointed the gun toward the shadowed corridor. "Let's go."

Linda moved slowly, her mind racing. Her legs and arms were free for now but probably not for long. She'd been deliberately avoiding the thought of Martinez's endgame. Now she confronted it head on. Martinez knew she was a trooper. For all her grievances with the State Police as an organization, she could not fault the professionalism and the methodical way the agency went about pursuing criminals. Unfortunately, relentless determination was also her big problem. He had to realize by now he'd made an irreversible mistake, even if he freed her unharmed.

She'd been in uniform long enough to know she never wanted to be the target of a State Police manhunt. Her colleagues would make his life pure hell when they found out he'd kidnapped one of their own. They took those things personally. No, at this point Martinez had nothing more to lose if he raped and killed her, the course of action she expected he would attempt. She wished she'd told Ewing the whole story. They would find out eventually and descend upon Martinez like fire ants on bare flesh. It might be too late for her, though. Linda weighed her chances of taking Martinez in the corridor and found them slim at best. He was bigger, stronger, wary and holding a gun. This was not the place.

"To your left," Martinez said. She stopped at a closed door in the hall. "Bathroom." She turned the doorknob and pushed the door open. To her left stood a toilet, beside it a sink mounted to the wall with metal brackets. Below the sink, water lines and drain stretched down into the floor. A mirror hung above. She stepped inside and reached out to close the door. Martinez stood on the threshold. "Don't be modest. I've seen your pussy." She would have loved to kick him in the balls but didn't relish the prospect of ending her life in a 6x6 john. Plus she needed to pee. She unzipped her jeans, bared herself to her knees and sat on the surprisingly clean white seat. A shower stall, partially hidden by the open door, faced her. Martinez stared at her exposed flesh. He wore a thick leather belt with an engraved metal belt buckle bearing the image of a monster truck. "You can't wait for me, can you?"

She stood and turned her back on him. The roll of toilet tissue felt a bit clammy. She wiped herself and pulled up her jeans. She opened the hot water tap to wash her hands. Martinez reached past her and shut it. "Never mind. You won't be touching anything. This way." Martinez stepped back from the doorway and nodded toward the end of the corridor.

She reached the end of the hallway, peeked into the lighted room and turned as cold as the ambience was warm. Martinez had outfitted the space as a rustic honeymoon suite. The four-post bed of light pine was queen-sized and covered with a bright red bedspread. Two bouquets of red roses in slender glass vases sat atop the nightstands at the head of the bed. Three red candles in glass formed a semicircle around each vase. A bottle of Champagne sweated in a bucket of ice on top of a small pine bureau to one side of the door. Two Champagne flutes and another three candles flanked the bucket. At the far end of the bureau sat a Bose Wave machine, its CD compartment flipped up, the time flashing 12:22. The only other piece of furniture, a small wooden rocker, stood to the right side of the bed. Martinez could not have done all this in the short time he'd left her in the car. He'd been planning for some time, though nothing about the abduction made sense.

Martinez nudged her into the room, slipped in behind her and closed the door. This was no time to be thinking about how she'd gotten here. Her sole focus had to be getting out, no matter what it took. He pointed to the closed door where a pure white skimpy negligee hung from a hook. The flimsy see-through material was clearly not meant to be worn. It was designed for a woman to model. To dress for her man so he would lust after her, undress her and take her. Christ, he wouldn't even have to undress her. The bottom consisted of a scant triangle of satiny material and a couple of strings. Not counting the pervert, Jack, she'd dressed for a man only once. That hadn't worked out so well. This time didn't appear any more promising. Did he really think she would wear lingerie? For him?

"Do you like it?"

For the first time since he had removed the blindfold, she looked directly at him. She shook her head.

"Put it on." He pointed the gun first at her, then the peignoir. There was not a snowball's chance in hell she would strip and dress in wedding night wear for this lunatic. He could kill her.

"What's wrong? Here I thought we were getting along so well. I know we got off to a bad start with the bloody nose incident. I figured I'd give you a chance to make up with me, show me the respect a man deserves. You want to do that don't you?"

She stared at the lingerie, wanting no part of Martinez and his delusions.

He sat in the rocker, gun aimed at her, and shook his head slowly. "You disappoint me, Linda."

Well she'd been disappointing men's expectations for a long time. Martinez had begun to rock, head back and eyes wide and glassy.

"You're all the same, you know: a pack of whores who will betray and cuckold a man at the drop of a dime." His voice rose and his eyes glazed. "All the same. Natasha slipped out to fuck a two-bit bookie, thought I wouldn't find out." He paused a moment and Linda noticed his lips were wet. He cackled. The sound rattled her, like the laugh of the insane. "They got theirs. Amy's next. I thought I loved the bitch. No, you're all the same, aren't you?" His face had flushed and bubbles of spit had formed on his mouth. He spoke loudly now, like a preacher making a moral point to the congregation. "And you." His eyes were now lost in a place Linda hoped she'd never find. "To think I used to call you 'Mommy.' Whore was more like it though, telling Zach to call you 'Mommy' while he slapped your ass and fucked you from behind. You fucked my best friend and on my bed." He practically sprang from the rocker. "Get undressed!"

Linda recoiled, her mind still trying to process what she'd learned. Martinez had mother problems. Who didn't? His mother whored around with younger men. Linda could relate. Natasha Borisova was Martinez's work. Probably not a paid job, though. Linda had been able to link Natasha, romantically, to the murdered bookie, Pasternov. No doubt another vengeance murder.

Of more immediate interest was the fact Martinez knew about Amy, which meant he knew State Police had learned his identity. If she were Martinez, she'd have been packing her bags and planning a quick route out of New York and out of the country. Of course, for all she knew, they were already in another country. Her reasoning rested on an assumption Martinez would act in a rational fashion, but based on his ravings about his mother, that was a shaky one. Still, his survival, the most basic of all human needs, depended on immediate flight.

"You don't listen, do you?" Martinez rifled through the drawer in the nightstand. He removed a cloth and a small brown bottle with a cap and drop dispenser. He unscrewed the cap and splashed liquid on the cloth. She shook her head. No! No more drugs. Her survival depended on being able to think clearly. She snatched the negligee from the hook and dangled it in front of her. Martinez smiled and seemed satisfied. She feared a drug dose far more than wearing lingerie. Suddenly his smile vanished and he waggled the gun barrel at her. "You had your chance. Now we do it my way."

She kicked out, aiming at his groin. He sidestepped; swung his gun arm up under her extended leg. Linda landed flat on her back. Her head thudded against the wood floor. He was on her in a second, muzzle against her neck and the cloth covering her mouth and face. The pain at the back of her skull faded away. That was a relief.

***

Linda woke to the distant sound of a classical music composition. She smelled perfume. Her eyes blinked at the light dancing on the ceiling. Her mouth felt dry, as if stuffed with cotton. She surveyed the room and her memory returned in a rush. Her arms stretched to the corners of the bed, her wrists taped to the head posts. Her legs splayed in a similar fashion. Unlike her wrists, her feet did not reach the posts, but he'd taped and tied them in rope-like fashion underscoring the versatility of duct tape. He'd dressed her in the lingerie she refused to wear. On the floor next to the bureau lay a black garbage bag, a leg of her jeans protruding from the opening.

Martinez had stripped and dressed her. Her flesh crawled. *Stop it, Linda. No time for emotion.* She breathed deep to quell the terror and expel useless thoughts. Her pulse slowed and she focused on her central problem. At some point Martinez would decide he was through with her and would kill her. A glass clinked. The Champagne bucket, bottle and one glass were gone from the dresser. The time on the Bose blinked 12:48. She'd been unconscious no more than 30 minutes and had no hangover. She wondered why.

Martinez had spent part of the time undressing and dressing her. He'd taken the Champagne to the main room where he no doubt sat sipping, waiting for her to regain consciousness. She had to use her precious time to explore the weak spots, to create an opportunity where she had a reasonable chance at escape, regardless of the risk. She began to test the vulnerabilities in the bonds and hoped Martinez would take the time to drink the whole bottle before returning. Maybe she would surprise him. She worked feverishly and methodically on the binding to her left wrist, the place she'd identified as the weakest link in Martinez's bondage scheme. While she struggled with the tape, she began to acknowledge Martinez might rape her. When he'd finished, she'd live with it or...

Linda had spent the last seven years rebuilding her self-esteem, creating a level of self-confidence that allowed her to function in a dangerous world. She'd done so while avoiding conscious thought of the humiliation and degradation rape brought, believing it not possible to do so otherwise. Now her self-assuredness crumbled no doubt because of the shaky foundation of denial she'd built on. Tied to this bed, struggling to get free, the details now assaulted her as unrepentant as Martinez would be when he came for her. Cousin Joel's naked legs had protruded beneath the baseball jersey that afternoon. Then it had started.

***

He stepped toward her. "You dress real sexy. Shame to waste it."

"Out of my way, Joel." Her fist collided with his shoulder like a gnat against a windshield. A surge of adrenaline shocked her nostrils.

He pressed her back against the vanity. His breath reeked of beer. "You been getting' ready for me?"

"You're drunk. Get out of here before I call your mother." Her voice was failing.

Joel probed under her skirt with one hand; the other squeezed her breasts. "Yeah, you call my momma and tell her how I fucked you and made you smile. She'll be proud." He lowered his voice to a whisper. "You're just a girl. Men play baseball. That's why I beat you out."

"Get your hands off me." Her words rung in her ears as a plea.

He grabbed the hair on the back of her head and yanked. Her knees buckled and she collapsed as if in prayer. Joel raised his jersey. "Oh, yeah, baby. I knew you'd want to kneel for me."

His cock stood erect, exposing his balls. Linda took dead aim, swung her elbow. He twisted sideways, pulled her head forward, rubbing himself on her cheek. She spit.

He stepped away, slapped her face with the palm of his hand. "Nice Catholic girl. No mouth sex. So take me bareback like the Pope says."

"Don't you dare," she gurgled.

Joel laughed, jammed her back until she lay prone on the tile floor. He yanked her skirt up to her waist, ripped her blouse open. Buttons pinged on ceramic. He pushed her bra up, grinned. "Nice tits."

"Here's the deal." His fingers reached for her silk panties, split them as if they were rice pancakes. "I fuck you and you beg me for more. You will, you know." He knelt between her legs, stroked the insides of her thighs.

She wiggled backward, and succeeded in pinning her head against the base of the toilet. The grout lines of the ceramic tile dug into her skin. The stench of chlorine from the bowl freshener mixed with the perfume she'd secreted from her mother for this special day. She tried to kick free. As in a dream where the monster chased, she found herself unable to move her legs, her muscles aching with the tension. Her brain screamed, "You're a pig. Let me go." A squeak passed through her throat.

"I like feisty pussy. Let me show you what girls are good for. 'Cause it ain't baseball." He spit into his hand, rubbed the saliva into her vagina and repeated the action.

She wanted to scream, "No!" But her voice had run off to hide. Joel prodded, fumbled and cursed. The pressure between her legs grew. He thrust his hips, the pressure released, replaced by a searing pain.

He sneered. "Cunt."

His body rocked back and forth, and she wished the nightmare would end. His movement quickened, the sneer dissolved and his eyes rolled. He groaned, lowered his head to her ear. "I make you feel like a woman?"

***

The memory of that night had aided her determination. Her struggle had created enough separation around the one wrist to pull free. She resisted the urge to do so. Starting with one hand, she guessed it would take her at least a minute, maybe two, to free herself completely. If Martinez discovered her in the process, she'd lose the only opportunity she figured to have. The second problem involved leaving the cabin. She'd seen only one door. Martinez was armed and presumably sitting within sight of it. The bedroom had no windows. Should she try now, creating a confrontation heavily stacked against her? Or wait, gambling her life that a better opportunity would arise? The classical music stopped. So did Linda's heart. Something scraped the floor, followed by footsteps. There was no decision to make. She rolled her head to one side and closed her eyes, hoping he'd look in and leave.

The faint opening strains of Ravel's Bolero reached her ears. The bed sagged between her legs. A hand rubbed her breast and a momentary panic gripped her. *Concentrate, Linda. He's going to rape you. Focus on the end game.* Her cheeks compressed between a thumb and finger, the hand rotating her head face up. Linda blinked her eyes open. Martinez was naked. He released his grip and slapped her face. "I've been waiting for this."

Martinez explored her body with his hand and fingers, pinching her nipples until she winced. He rubbed her clitoris, slapped her thighs. He commented on her perfume and the scent between her legs. She turned

249

away, imagining herself in a future time, figuring the most efficient method for freeing her ankles and wrists. The tempo of the music increased. His hands grasped the V-strings of the negligee bottom. He must not have realized the bottom would not come off when she was spread-eagle. He leaned over her to the nightstand drawer and removed the scissors he'd used earlier. He snipped the strings, returned them to the drawer and knelt straight up brandishing a condom. Martinez smiled. "No telling where you whores have been."

Linda focused on the positive. Those scissors might buy her precious seconds, maybe a full minute. He fumbled a bit locating her crease, but gradually penetrated her. She moaned from the pain of the friction. Martinez smirked. "I knew you'd like it, Linda." Ravel's composition built to its cacophonous climax while Martinez raped her, whispering a stream of hate-filled invective toward his mother and women in general that penetrated deeper than the physical violation he visited upon her. Martinez spoke almost nonstop throughout, whereas Joel had said little. Martinez's words did not shock as much as the emotion behind them. It flowed like bile.

She found her eyes drawn to Martinez's and saw in them the same hate and rage that spewed from his lips. The music's volume and tempo built feverishly and his words began drowning in it. Still his eyes drew her as if magnets. He rested his hands on either side of her head and lowered his to within inches. Although the words had stopped, his eyes spoke volumes about anger and hate and the internal poison the emotions bred. His eyes appeared glassy with it.

His frenzied pumping signaled he was nearly finished. Linda wanted to turn away. She really did, just as she had the afternoon she'd rescued Jeremy. He'd intimidated her that day. Today, although she had plenty of reason to be intimidated, she found herself unable to pry her eyes away. Now she knew why. Through his eyes, she glimpsed the deadness in his heart strangled by the emotions of hate and rage. She could not look away because in them she detected a mirror reflecting her own soul drowning in the sewage of anger and vengeance she'd flushed there. Did her soul differ much from that of Martinez or Joel?

Martinez grunted and lowered his head beside hers. He gave a series of powerful climactic thrusts and shouted, "Take it, whore." He shuddered once. His weight crushed her chest. She shifted her torso a bit and lay perfectly still. A moment later, Bolero ended. The track changed to something less sexually charged. Martinez raised himself to his knees. "Did you like that?" She did not move. "Sounds like you enjoyed yourself." He spit on her breast. "Pig." He removed the condom and drained it on her pubis. He tossed the latex at her head. She squirmed. It landed to one side. Liquid began to leak down between her legs. He stood and walked to the bureau, switched off the Bose.

Martinez turned. A jolt of adrenaline spiked her. He held the Colt. This was it. She'd vowed she would go down fighting. Time for action. Only his words prevented her from tearing her one hand free and reaching for him. "Don't worry about the underwear. I've got something a little more whorish for you to wear next time."

Linda tried to conceal her relief. Martinez planned an encore. Maybe she'd get lucky. *Right. There wasn't going to be a next time, shithead.* Standing in the doorway, he waved the barrel at her, the way a teacher wagged a finger at an unruly student. "Stay put, now. You can shower when I'm done. We got more fun coming. I want you fresh."

He left. She listened to the quiet for several minutes. The toilet flushed and shortly thereafter, the shower began running. She slipped her wrist free and reached down to open the nightstand drawer. The scissors sped the tape removal. Linda grabbed the garbage bag and started down the hall. Something banged inside the bathroom. Her heart stopped. Martinez cursed. The water kept running. She hurried to the door, slid the bolt free and paused. The shower still sprayed. She considered searching the kitchen for a long knife. Just as quickly, she conjured an image of a nude Martinez emerging from the bathroom while the water continued to run. She bolted out the door and down the steps, running to his car, wearing nothing but a see-through gown held up with string straps.

The air nipped and tightened her skin. Her feet hurt from the gravel on the drive. She checked the ignition on the off chance he'd left the keys. No. She had no time to waste disabling the car, which would be of no use to him in the surrounding woods, anyway. Besides, maybe he would yield to the temptation to leave town before law enforcement started looking hard. Maybe he'd leave her alone. She peered into the back of the SUV for something she might use to defend herself and found nothing. Shit! She ran down the gravel drive toward a dirt road, trying to recall which way the vehicle had turned before stopping. She reached the rutted road and turned left.

Linda sprinted as fast as her lungs and aching feet would allow. The surface was sand and grass with occasional potholes, tree roots and a few stones. Light reflecting from a thin layer of clouds illuminated the road sufficiently to allow her a decent pace. She ran much longer than she'd expected. When she heard the car engine, she veered into the woods.

CHAPTER 29

Linda cursed the dark. Not 20 paces off the dirt road, and she could barely identify what was underfoot, let alone what lay ahead thanks to the shadows of the trees and their foliage. She wished for a flashlight. Her right foot squished on something wet and spongy. She recoiled. A dead animal, or worse, a live one? No time to look back. Just run.

Moments later she stepped on an object shaped like a covered tree branch and stumbled sideways. She struggled to maintain her balance. Something tugged at the flimsy gown. The image of a clawed bear paw leapt to her mind. One adrenaline-fueled spin move freed her from his clutches. The fabric tore. Her violent move propelled her into a thicket of thorns that grabbed at her bare skin and stuck to the falling shredded garment. She surveyed her surroundings: no bear, no wolf, not even a chipmunk; nothing but a copse of vines and her overactive imagination.

She needed to get a grip, but that would not come easy. The hate-filled rage from Martinez, his hands all over her body, the tenderness between her legs, they were not products of her imagination. She was entitled to the jumbled emotional state of violation, rage and terror now possessing her like a trinity of self-righteous ogres. She tore off the remnants of the gown; and stuffed them into the garbage bag. The action produced a calming effect, almost as if removing the garment might remove the memory of the rape. Fat chance. Still, if she expected to get out of the woods alive, she would need her wits, not her emotions. Her survival depended upon holding at bay the demons she now realized had governed her for nearly seven years.

Her body itched all over from the scratches. A small clearing appeared, and she carefully edged toward it. She originally planned to put a good distance between herself and the road, then stop and dress. Bad idea. The sooner the better. The car engine sounded distant but growing closer.

The light at the edge of the clearing was marginally better. Crouching behind a monstrous fallen tree, Linda opened the garbage bag and dressed hurriedly in the jeans, sweatshirt and sneakers she'd been wearing when the first gunshot sounded outside her living room, an event that now seemed eons ago. She removed the earrings. With each piece of clothing, her mood improved. The few mosquitoes buzzing about would soon have to work to find bare flesh. Only the most industrious would suck blood. The sneakers would allow her to move at a faster pace. The dark clothing replacing the white gown would make her harder to spot. For the first time since encountering Martinez in Cohoes, things began to look up. She stuffed the tattered gown back into the garbage bag and lifted.

The weight of the bag surprised her, filled her with hope. Sure, it would have made sense from Martinez's viewpoint. She reached inside. At the bottom Linda found her Glock, clip intact. Dammit! Had she known, she would have waited in the hall for Martinez to step from the bathroom and ended his terror spree. This time she would have gotten justice. In her haste to flee, she blew a great opportunity to end this nightmare. Instead, she still ran from Martinez.

Linda thought a moment. She was armed and he knew it. That made the fight almost fair. Bullies and intimidators like Martinez shied away from fair fights. They preferred their prey tied down and spread eagle: easy pickings. If they got a little resistance, they slithered off looking for an easier mark. Yes, Martinez no longer viewed himself as predator. Now he realized every New York State trooper would make him his prey, every trooper except her. Based upon his psychotic ranting about women, he expected her to run and hide. Martinez would be surprised to learn her running and hiding from men like him and Joel, from the memory of what they'd done to her were no more. Those days were over.

You think we should track him down, Lilith?

Speak up, would you?

Not like you to be quiet.

A flash of light split between the trees. Linda held still and listened. The sounds of the car engine and the bouncing of the frame over the rutted road came close, closer. Ahead, the shadowy outline of a massive boulder offered a good spot. Suddenly the road swam in light.

She broke into a sprint, imagining a clear shot at the driver window, or, with any luck, through an open one at Martinez himself. Just short of the boulder, she stumbled and fell, crashing to earth on a thin layer of leaves and pine needles covering a bed of rocks. She managed to protect her head but her elbows, knees and hip caught the brunt of the fall. The gun slipped from her hand. She grit her teeth and pretended she wasn't worried about broken bones. She scrambled to her knees and groped the ground. Light slashed across the front edge of the boulder. The gun, where was the gun? She bent over, sweeping a forearm over the leaves and finally found it; pulled back to a kneeling position.

The light had passed and now bounced along to her left. He'd driven right by her, not more than 10 paces away, and she'd not gotten a shot off. Damn. She picked her way carefully and sat behind the boulder. The car sounds were fading, headlamps now only occasional distant flashes, like heat lightning. A dark damp splotch appeared on her jeans over her left knee, from either the damp ground or broken skin. She wasn't about to take them down to find which. Her body ached as if she'd spent a half-hour in the sparring ring with Sensei. She was hungry and thirsty. The last food she'd consumed was the two frozen dinners for breakfast, possibly today but perhaps not. She tried to sort out her next move.

Martinez was gone, and she sat alone in an unfamiliar forest without a light. Daylight might not return for several hours. The cabin held bad memories but also electricity and running water. She would likely find canned goods or dehydrated foods stored in the kitchen, perhaps even a container of coffee. Following the road would be the easiest way back and shouldn't take more than 15 minutes or so. If Martinez should be foolish enough to return, she'd hear the car coming.

After five minutes of a steady pace along the dirt ruts, she noticed an orange glow above the tree line. She detected a faint scent of smoke but not the same as the fireplace smoke from inside the cabin. This smoke carried the odor of burnt laminate common to house fires. No point in going any farther. Martinez delayed setting out after her so he could torch the place, figuring to destroy all traces of his and her presence. He'd left her alive though.

That obviously had not been his intention. He had planned this well and made only a single mistake, the same one males had been making for the past seven years. He'd underestimated Linda Baldwin. Soon Martinez would recognize the enormity of his mistake.

A distant crash drowned out the chirp of crickets. A stream of sparks and a plume of smoke brightened the sky. The fire must be visible for miles around, but so far had not attracted anyone to the scene. No neighbor drove down the road, curious about the blaze. No siren screamed in the distance. Whatever the location, a vast expanse of wilderness laid between her and civilization.

The sooner she got out and to a phone, the quicker the manhunt for Martinez would begin, the less likely he would escape. She reversed direction. Soon the only sounds were the crickets and the rustle of her footsteps. Linda walked briskly, fueled by a growing desire to get Martinez and bring him to justice.

Justice. When she'd looked in his eyes, she'd recognized herself, recognized the anger and lust for vengeance governing her own personal and professional life for so many years. The rage had been burning all along for the whole world to see. Her rape counselors told her and she agreed, but only to shut them up. Sensei recognized the problem and warned her. Bill told her he'd watched her anger consume her and wanted no part. She didn't blame him, especially since Kathleen warmed his bed. Even Tibbs tried to tell her, and she practically bit his head off. She eventually recognized a kernel of truth in what everyone said. She planned to look into the issue. Someday.

That day was here. Martinez's near-lunatic rant about the evils he'd suffered from women, forced her to recognize the nonverbal, and largely subconscious, rant she'd been screaming to herself about the injustices she suffered at the hands of men. A deep look into Martinez's eyes made her realize it was time to rid herself of her thirst for revenge. Time to accept the fact she was powerless to change past events.

What she could do, though, was what she swore to do when she took her oath as state trooper: uphold the law and bring wrongdoers to justice; hold Martinez accountable for the murders he confessed. And, yes, accountable for the terror and humiliation he visited upon her and other women. Martinez wouldn't get away with his rape. Not like Joel did. The last words Cousin Joel had spoken still haunted her: "I make you feel like a woman?" *No, Mr. Martinez, this time I'm getting justice.*

***

Linda had closed her eyes, afraid to move. Joel's weight lifted from her body. The door closed and she turned her head sideways. Three red buttons lay against the baseboard. She rolled to her stomach and forced herself to a kneeling position. A pink trail trickled down her leg, joined the smeared stains on the floor.

She struggled to her feet and pulled her work clothes from the sack. A sense of shame washed over her. Shamed by her situation. She and Bill had carefully planned every detail of their special day, and she'd ruined it. What would he think of her? Shamed by her trusting little girlishness. Shamed by her helplessness. If she'd not planned the rendezvous with Bill, would any of this have happened?

Her black panties lay on the white ceramic, a stark contrast to the mixed stains of blood and semen. Joel had torn them in two place, across the crotch and up the side, the rip sundering the intertwined red embroidered hearts. She dressed in her corduroys and sweatshirt and stuffed her special clothing into the sack. Not so special anymore. Ruined clothes. Everything ruined. She wiped the floor clean with her wet bath towel and hunted down her stray blouse buttons. When she finished, the only visible trace of her shame appeared as a diluted bloodstain. She crammed the stained towel into the sack, zipped it shut, pulled on her jacket and ran from the house, slamming the front door behind her.

At the head of the block, she turned and stopped running. During the walk home, her thoughts turned to what she would tell Bill. She got sick. No, why didn't she call? She needed an excuse. This was not just any old date. Dear God, Bill must not find out. But Cohoes was a small town. If anyone knew anything, eventually everyone did, Bill's father usually among the first. That settled it. She'd tell no one. No one would know, unless Joel bragged.

Damn Joel. This was his fault. Or was it? What if she hadn't gone to all the baseball games and jeered, along with his teammates, at his errors? Maybe he wouldn't have been so angry with her. If she'd stayed away, the team captain could not have called into the stands begging her to come down from the bleachers and replace Joel at second base. If she'd tried out for cheerleader, as her mother advised, none of this would have happened. Grandpa Baldwin may have been wrong when he told her girls could play any game a man played, and she'd gotten what she deserved. The assault played back in her mind in slow motion, over and over and over.

A hot shower failed to cleanse her. She crawled into bed, yanked the covers over her head and closed her eyes. The pictures continued to scroll in the darkness. Every detail of the attack burned in her brain, bold and proud as her cousin in a baseball jersey. For all the imagery, only one sound bite survived. "I make you feel like a woman?" The question echoed until she was ready to scream.

Little bastard. Who did he think he was? She would tell his father, mother, her parents, and the cops. She didn't care if the whole city knew. He would pay for his abuse and the way he'd made her feel. Her mother had different ideas, though. When Joel had finished with her, Linda was certain no greater humiliation was possible. She'd been wrong about that.

***

A high-pitched shriek stopped Linda in her tracks. Instinctively she raised the Glock. What was that? She scratched at the tingle along the back of her neck, then rubbed the goose bumps forming on her arms. She was not alone. That shriek was human and a terrified one. She stared into the dark shadows of the woods in the direction of the sound. Someone was in trouble, possibly attacked by a wild animal. Or Martinez. Had he abducted another woman, say Amy? It didn't seem likely, but there was no way to know, and she'd given up trying to figure his logic. She fixed the location, started into the woods without thinking and then stopped.

Her emotions and gut reactions had ruled her for the past seven years. They'd led her into some dangerous situations, most of them avoidable. They'd also brought heaps of trouble on the job and nearly cost her life. Where did she think she was going? If this was Martinez, she would be better off getting away and out to civilization for help. The odds were a lot better than her chances of confronting him by herself, even with a gun. She tried once and he outsmarted her. Did she really think the second time would be different?

Besides, Martinez might not be the cause. His car passed some time ago and she'd not heard it return. Probably the cry of a wild animal, not human at all. Sure, she held a gun, but if a wolf decided to stalk her, he'd be just like Martinez, on her before she recognized his presence. Or it might be nothing at all, her mind playing tricks, seeing and hearing evil at every turn.

The second shriek was louder, more prolonged and even more terrified. It was not her imagination. She would avoid Martinez at all costs, but she needed to find out who was screaming. Linda moved back into the woods, treading slowly and deliberately, just in case it *was* Martinez, another confrontation with the lunatic no longer on her agenda.

A hundred yards in she thought she detected a clearing ahead. A thick mass of brush and vines stood between her and the clearing. A narrow path cut into the thicket. At the edge, she got down on hands and knees and crawled along, skirting several piles of small black pellets. The shriek sounded again, closer now, the screech of a frantic child.

The path widened near what appeared a meadow gradually sloping into a rocky area with no vegetation. What struck her first were the white birches among the trees bordering the open space. They stuck out like neon lights on a darkened street. Her clothing was dark, but her blonde hair and fair face would be too easy to see. Recalling images of combat soldiers, she scooped dirt from the path and rubbed it in her hands, on her face and into her hair. She got to her feet slowly behind a large tree. A quick scan of field and periphery yielded no sign of activity.

She sat at the edge of the clearing thinking about the eerie spectacle. A car engine roared to life nearby, then settled to a steady purr. Linda scrambled to her feet. Through the pounding in her ears, a car door slammed and gravel crunched. The crunching gave way to a loud bumping noise similar to that in the back of Martinez's SUV. The pace of bumping accelerated, melding into a series of scrapes and crashes, punctuated by a thunderous splash. Quiet returned.

While her brain processed the sounds, another motor sputtered to life, this engine lacking the authority of the previous one. Now it made sense. Martinez had stashed a second car in the woods and taken time to dispose of the first. Linda shuddered, realizing she was supposed to be in the SUV she presumed went splash. She remained alive and intended to keep it that way. She would play this smart. Martinez would leave, and she would trek out to a phone and start the manhunt.

A fluttering above her head stopped her heart. She swung the Glock toward the sound, her arms extended. She caught a fleeting motion and tried to identify the target. A bird floated out into the open and back to the edge, landing on a branch in a nearby tree affording a good view. His head swiveled to face her.

The owl stared at her, its face pallid as the shadow figures stalking her dreams. Its pumpkin-shaped head featured a triangular beak with a bayonet tip and a pair of black unblinking eyes penetrating almost as deeply as Martinez's. He shrieked again, and Linda finally understood his message. She shivered, lowered the gun and exhaled, wondering how a bird so small imitated the scream of a child. He flapped his wings and glided across the meadow and out of sight.

A beam of light slashed across the far end of the clearing. Gravel crunched. She began running along the tree line. Sure, if she let him go, troopers would eventually grab him, but, if he killed or raped someone in the meantime, she would never be able to live with herself.

She would have to learn to curb her emotions but not at the expense of losing herself. Grandpa Baldwin had told her many times as a young girl that she was the only one who could truly know Linda Baldwin. Not Grandpa. Not her father or mother. No one. She'd questioned him about what he meant, but he always smiled and said he had faith she would find out who Linda Baldwin was. He was right. Now she did. She also realized *that* Linda Baldwin must try to stop Martinez *now*.

In the reflected light, the outline of a small car bounced diagonally across the clearing. The car was going to reach the corner before she did. Linda pulled up beside a tree, rested the gun against the trunk and tried to focus down the barrel. Her heart pummeled her chest. Perfect, the driver side faced her.

The car entered the sight line. No, it was all wrong. She'd aimed too high. She adjusted the position, refocused, but on a rear side window. She fired. Glass exploded. The car stopped. Linda recalled the SUV idling behind the mill building. She sprinted around the back of the car, ducking behind a tree on the passenger side. Shortly she would find out if Martinez was a creature of habit. The wait seemed like an eternity, but the front passenger door flew open and Martinez rolled out to the ground, sprung to a crouch, his gun panning the area from which she shot.

She stepped from behind the tree. "Lower the gun and drop it, carefully." Martinez appeared frozen in time, the back of his head as still as it had looked after she'd bloodied his nose. He slowly lowered his arms, but his hands looked to be joined and the gun not on the ground.

"Put the gun down." She hoped her voice did not betray the shaking of her arms.

Martinez began to turn.

"Move any further and I'll shoot."

He stopped. "No you won't."

The headlights splashed against the trees ahead rendering Martinez in eerie profile, like a suspect in a lineup, like the shadowed images of gunmen she'd practiced on at the firing range. This was no cardboard cutout, though. It was human life. He resumed his turn but as if in manual freeze-frame. Everything else faded to background, the hum of the engine the only sound. She aimed at his torso. The horrible implication of what he said finally sunk in. She *didn't* have it in her to kill him. Perhaps not by herself, but...*We need to off this bastard, Lilith. He raped you.*

Lilith?

Lilith?

No answer. Lilith had not escaped the cabin. Perhaps Martinez held her. Linda's eyes never left Martinez, her brain numb at the thought of what he was about to do. She could not kill him. She was a woman. His arms began to rise. His face turned. He wore a smile.

Grandpa Baldwin winked and nodded.

The explosion jolted her.

Martinez lurched backwards. A look of wonderment replaced his smile. He still held the gun, but his arms were down. He crumbled to his knees. She kept the Glock trained on his chest. With a wheezy grunt, he strained to raise his gun. Her second shot flattened him on his back.

She counted to 100, slowly, gun trained, looking for movement. There was none. She approached him cautiously, Glock aimed at his head. She kicked his gun out of his hands and beyond reach. Resting the tip of the barrel against his ear, she checked for a pulse and found none.

She stood, a powerful wave of nausea overwhelming her. She killed a man. Hadn't even known she had it in her. The most disturbing part was that it had taken a man like Martinez to teach her the truth. Linda placed the gun on the hood of the car and doubled over, her stomach retching. Nothing came up. She stuck two fingers between her lips and tasted the grit from the dirt on her fingers. She depressed her tongue and forced herself to retch and retch until the hot acidy bile she harbored spewed from her mouth, just as she'd imagined it flowing from Martinez's while he raped her.

CHAPTER 30

Saturday's morning sun had dried the meadow dew long before the crime-scene crew and medical examiner packed up and left. The SUV remained submerged pending arrival of divers. Fire fighters found the cabin a pile of ashes atop charred appliances and a few partially burned logs.

Linda answered the easy questions at the scene. The tough ones would come soon enough. Trooper Maureen Duffy remained with Linda throughout and drove her to Plattsburgh for the "interview" as the two male detectives labeled the session. When Linda told them they could skip the interview because she wasn't looking for a new job, neither cracked a smile. Duffy laughed.

Duffy was a 30-year veteran, a graduate of the first Trooper Academy class with women. Linda tried to imagine what the experience must have been like for those pioneers and concluded she would not have made the cut back then. The environment for women had improved considerably in the intervening years, but there remained a gap between the ideal of full integration of women in the force and the reality of everyday law enforcement. Linda was beginning to appreciate she could advance the goal, keep alive what Duffy and the others started by becoming part of the team. The conduct of a Judge Shane Dolan toward a known sex predator would always anger her, but she would have to learn to trust the system to hold the power abusers accountable, as it did in Albany more often than not, according to Bert.

Linda turned down the offer of sleep prior to the interrogation. The events of the past 36 hours swam in her mind. When she closed her eyes, Martinez's came into focus, the smile on his face a haunting reminder of what she'd done. Sleep was not imminent, at least not without the aid of liquid medication Troop B wasn't licensed to dispense. She insisted they get on with the job, downing a couple of greasy bacon, egg and cheese sandwiches and what seemed like a half-gallon of crap coffee during the grilling. The detectives acted uncomfortable at Duffy's presence during the interminable inquiry. They bristled when their questioning sought a level of detail Linda didn't care to provide and Duffy forced them to back off.

The circumstances of the killing held all the markings of a vengeance shooting, and Linda would never convince most people otherwise. No, she would have preferred Martinez alive and not solely because of her aversion to killing. Life imprisonment without chance for parole dealt a much harsher punishment than the death penalty Martinez had chosen and forced her to impose.

The detectives finished late in the afternoon. Duffy drove Linda home, covering the 150-some miles on I87 from Plattsburgh to Cohoes in an hour and three-quarters. *That* was Linda's idea of driving.

During the trip home, Linda learned the brass at Troop B had briefed Walker on the events. The Troop G press office told Duffy they would issue an official statement Monday morning. Linda recalled the media circus outside her apartment after the bike-path rapist capture. She'd be better off spending a few nights away from home.

After Duffy crossed the Cohoes city limits, Linda realized she'd left her 'Vette parked at Troop G. She considered asking Duffy to drop her at headquarters, but her car keys were sitting on her kitchen counter next to the phone. The patrol car vanished around the corner. Linda circled around back of the apartment and entered through the unlocked and open back door. The simple act of retracing the steps that had begun her ordeal felt like someone loosened the tie around a super-helium balloon. Her adrenaline drained and an overpowering fatigue took its place. She wanted solitude: no press, brass, friends or family. Not now, not just yet. She needed time and space to create a reasonable perspective. She longed for a couple bottles of Bert's Mersault and a chance to forget the last day and a half.

Her message light blinked. She played them back: Ewing, Walker, Tibbs and Bigwater on Friday inquiring of her whereabouts. Each of them called again on Saturday, Walker asking her to stop by his office on Monday morning. He would suspend her with pay pending completion of the shooting investigation. By now, Ewing, Tibbs and Bigwater would have gotten the news from Walker. No need to return any calls, thank God.

She reserved a room at an Albany hotel Bert used for his out-of-town clients. The daily rate was more than she cared to spend, but the place housed a full service bar and restaurant. She called a cab and crammed some clothes into an overnight bag along with her dead cell phone and charger. The taxi pulled from the curb, and Linda again considered retrieving the 'Vette from Troop G. "Take me to the Five Star Wine shop over on New Scotland. I'll only be a minute. Then, I'm going to the Albany Hilton."

It was after seven by the time she checked into the hotel. The lobby bar was quiet. She asked for a pinot grigio and the bar menu. After downing two glasses of wine, she ordered a burger and fries, which arrived with the fourth pinot. When she finished, she settled the tab and took the elevator to her floor. After a long hot shower, she used her remaining energy to climb into bed and immediately fell asleep.

The sound of the door opening woke Linda with a start. She rolled off the bed to the floor. She reached for the gun in the overnight bag and remembered Troop B detectives had confiscated it. She grabbed one of the wine bottles and sprinted to the door.

"Housekeeping," a woman's voice announced.

She stopped the door's movement with a foot. "Get out."

"I'm sorry. I knocked twice. You should use the sign."

She prayed the door would move no further. "OK, now just leave."

The door retreated with a soft click. She checked the peephole. A young black woman stood near a cart loaded with linens, towels and other room supplies. She stared at Linda's door shaking her head and muttering something. "Crazy bitch," Linda guessed. Was this to be her future? Had she traded wondering about using a gun for eagerness to pull one at the first sign of trouble? The clock read 11:48; almost 14 hours of sleep. She must have needed the rest.

An hour later, room service delivered a large porterhouse and mound of mashed potatoes along with two bags of ice. She put the Mersault bottles in the sink and dumped the ice over them. She plugged in her cell but kept it turned off. Between bites of steak, she clicked the TV remote until she found the Yankee game and settled in for a long day of doing absolutely nothing more demanding than ironing the clothes she would wear for her Monday morning meeting with Walker.

The score was tied at the end of nine innings. Linda uncorked a Mersault and poured the exquisite liquid into a water glass. Bert would be horrified. She sipped wine while watching TV and ironing her slacks and blouse. At six, a banner scrolled across the bottom of the TV screen-advising viewers of the local news delay. The text that appeared next turned her blood cold. "Local trooper shoots, kills murder suspect. Details after the game." Leave it to the media hounds. They probably didn't have her name, though. Not yet.

By the time the Blue Jays shredded the Yanks bullpen in the 13th, Linda had drunk more than two-thirds of the bottle. The lead news story opened with a camera shot of the front of her apartment. So much for her short-lived anonymity. The scene cut back to the studio anchor who provided some sketchy details about the Martinez incident. He went on to report that although Troop G would not confirm it, they had learned the trooper's identity from reliable sources. The station ran file footage of her escaping the mob of reporters following the bike path incident. The anchor revealed her name. He concluded by saying no one answered the door at her apartment and neighbors wouldn't even say if she was at home. The final line felt like a dagger in her chest. "Channel 7 has contacted Trooper Baldwin's immediate family. They tell us they don't know her whereabouts and are deeply troubled by her disappearance."

Oh, shit! She'd intended to make that call on Monday morning before Troop G issued a statement. She powered up her phone and found seven voice messages. She opened the second bottle of wine, filled her glass and listened. Three were from her father, his tone progressing from concerned to annoyed to downright pissed off in the final one. Tibbs, Bert, Jonathan and Bill accounted for the other four. She was tempted to return her dad's call, and she definitely wanted to talk to Bill, but her tongue felt fuzzy. The few short sentences she tried to speak aloud sounded slurred, even to her own ears. Not the time to be talking to anyone except her good friend Tibbs. He wouldn't care if she slurred, and she was eager to find out what he'd learned about LeBeouf and the DA. During their 15-minute conversation, he asked three times about her degree of inebriation, which she found strange given she opened the conversation with "It's Linda and I'm drunk." She ended the call and powered the cell off. She showered, polished off the second bottle of Mersault and stumbled into bed.

***

Linda floated beneath a delicate crust of ice crystals, her breathing labored. A human figure loomed above her, threatening, but it was not male. That surprised her. Was that red hair and freckles? An owl with a pale face and piercing black eyes perched on a solitary branch that appeared suspended in air. The ice melted. The human figure retreated. The owl blinked at Linda three times and flew off with a shriek that sounded like the one that had chilled her a few nights before. She sat up in bed and rubbed the sleep from her eyes.

When she pulled her hands away, the looming figure reappeared, not Joel or Martinez but a woman. No red hair, though, not Kathleen O'Keefe. The blonde hair and the face bore a striking resemblance to Linda's mother. Linda glared, but it was not her mother.

Sensei had taught her the importance of learning as much as possible about one's opponent. Glaring directly into the mirror opposite the hotel bed, Linda realized she had much to learn about the woman who glared back at her. But she had a start because she now knew what she was made of. She dressed and went down to the taxi stand. On the way to Troop G she made the call, got her mother's voice on the answering machine and left a message saying she was fine.

Walker's main agenda for their meeting appeared to be learning about her physical and emotional well-being. He spoke of the benefits of the counseling sessions, which were not optional. He went on to tell her she'd become a valuable asset to Troop G, she'd done a commendable job on the insurance case and demonstrated courage in her pursuit of Martinez. He followed the plaudits with admonitions about using better judgment, attaching greater value to teamwork and having more trust in her colleagues. Linda had listened to the same speech from brass so often she knew the words by heart. Now watching Walker's face, she allowed the message to register for the first time. She stood when he finished. "You can tell Detective Ewing I'm ready to return to sting duty when my suspension is up if he wants me back."

Walker said he would, and she left. Bigwater leaned against the wall a few yards down the hall, a notebook in his hand. He motioned her to come, a serious expression on his face. "They told me you were here, so I came by. I only have a minute. I'll make this quick."

He probably wanted to talk about the experience of shooting someone. "What's up, Paul?"

"I got an envelope for you." He glanced nervously up and down the corridor. "I want you to slide it inside your shirt."

Linda wanted to joke with him about guys using creative lines to get women to unbutton, but his facial expression warned her off. She loosened a single button above the pants waist. Bigwater slipped a sealed Kraft envelope, about 4x6, from the notebook.

The envelope reminded her of Amy's visit. "Photo?"

He nodded.

She inserted the picture in her blouse. The secrecy troubled her. "Surveillance photo, right?"

He turned his head and shook it. "I wanted you to have it. Screw the evidence. The bastard is dead."

Her cheeks began to heat. "Where'd you get it?"

"Me and Vanier went to the Bronx on Friday. Fucking New York City, bleeding-heart liberal judge gave the NYPD a hard time about the warrant."

Bigwater avoided eye contact. His words began to rush. "Might not have taken so long if we knew Martinez kidnapped you. Anyway, we finally got into his place and a few minutes later one of the NY boys gave off a wolf whistle in the bedroom. I went to the door and found two of them ogling a frame on the nightstand. When I got closer, I snatched the picture up, called you my girlfriend."

"Wait! You told them you and I…?"

"Sorry, first thing came to mind. It shut them up. Vanier asked me about the photo on our way back. I told him if I ever heard a word about the incident, I'd come looking for him."

While Bigwater told the story, his eyes rested everywhere but on her. He finished, and Linda thanked him. He nodded without making eye contact, and headed for the door as if late for a big meeting. So much for her pride. When she'd thought of the nude photos falling into the wrong hands, Bigwater served to symbolize her fears. He'd seen them anyway and behaved like a true colleague, covering her. He pulled a page from the Baldwin playbook, though, by snatching a photo that belonged in an evidence locker. The man was full of surprises.

Linda visited the coffee makers where she filled a cup and laid claim to an abandoned newspaper. She stopped by her desk to straighten up a few things. The news highlights column caught her eye. "Feds Probe DA," the top item declared, referring the reader to Alfred Brown's column.

She seized the paper, shook the B section free and read the column. Citing reliable, unnamed sources, Brown reported on speculation that federal prosecutor Cynthia Favre had opened an investigation of Albany County DA James O'Keefe. The probe sought to determine whether official corruption played any part in protecting the large criminal ring recently uncovered by state and local police agencies in cooperation with the FBI. Prosecutors pegged the insurance swindle alone at $15 million. Favre's office declined comment. So did the DA's. Brown's source told him the connection appeared to be a now-suspended law enforcement official and a "high-ranking" official in the DA's office. A State Police spokeswoman said the governor and police superintendent took all charges of corruption seriously and investigated them aggressively. She would neither confirm nor deny an investigation. Brown noted this was not the first time rumor of official corruption had tainted O'Keefe's office, citing a previous federal investigation of extortion and bribery that ended with no charges filed. The closing paragraph left her gasping for breath.

"Longtime lobbyist and political observer Bert Bariteau said, "If you keep seeing smoke, eventually you'll find a fire." "Who knows?" Brown concluded.

Jesus, Bert knew better than that. He'd taught her that if you were the only person quoted in a story from anonymous sources, you might as well tack your name to the byline. Bert wasn't stupid. *You can't trust any reporter.* His mantra swirled in her head. Except he trusted and respected Brown. Why would Brown screw him? Answer: he wouldn't. Yet there stood the quote. Why?

No question, Bert wanted to nail O'Keefe for corruption, but that required the U.S. attorney's office. More likely, his objective was to damage O'Keefe politically, but the DA's re-election bid was two years off. What was Bert up to if it wasn't politics? She contemplated the question, and her skin turned grimy.

A quick drive downtown brought her to the Bariteau firm's parking lot, where she double-parked the 'Vette behind Bert's car. He wouldn't be going anywhere until she left. She said hello to the receptionist as she breezed by and walked into Bert's office. He looked up when she entered, and Linda would have loved to capture the expression on his face.

It was the same one worn by the kids at Cronin's camp, the big difference with Bert's being the manifestation lasted about three seconds.

"Hey, Kiddo, I tried calling you all weekend. Are you OK?" He eyed the scratches on her arms.

"Fine."

"What brings you downtown?"

"You."

He tried to hide the sly smile. "Me?"

Linda walked around his desk to where he sat. He rolled his chair back and attempted to stand. She pushed him back. "You and Brown, to be precise. Now listen. I appreciate your wanting to help, but from now on, stay the fuck out of my business, my career *and* my love life. You get it?"

"What's Brown got to do with this?"

"You only had one reason to put your name in his column. You weren't aiming a broadside at Big Jim O'Keefe. You stuck a wedge between Kathleen and your son."

Bert sat silent for a moment, rubbing his chin, his eyes fixed on her. A faint smile appeared on his face. "Yeah, I see how the quote might be misconstrued."

"This is me you're talking to."

"By the way, have you been following the Senate campaign?" His intercom buzzed. Bert pushed a button.

"Health Commissioner on line six," the voice said.

"Take a message."

"I don't give a shit about the Senate campaign. Did you hear me?"

"I heard you."

"Good. That call reminds me about Brenda and something you said a while back. What's Brenda's connection to me?"

"You know the strangest thing about Brown's column on the DA? He called me. Can you believe it?"

"No. So instead of this line of crap, why don't you tell me about Johnny Marsolais and how his daughter and I are connected?"

"It's a long story."

"I've got all day. While you're at it, you can tell me Johnny's story too."

Bert consulted his desk calendar, and stood. "I'd love to but I have a meeting uptown."

"You're going to be late."

"What?"

"Your car is blocked in and you're not leaving this office until I get the story."

He sat down. "I don't want to do this."

"Yeah, but you're going to."

"I guess I've known this day would come." He looked around the office. "Sit! You're making me nervous."

Linda returned to the front of the desk and sat. "So who did in Johnny Marsolais?"

"Frank Gordon."

"You don't mean my Uncle Frank." That couldn't be. Uncle Frankie was one of the gentlest souls in town.

"Yes, your uncle. Back in his day, he was the most feared thug in one of the grittiest neighborhoods in Cohoes. He beat the crap out of his old man, put him in the hospital."

"What did he have against Johnny?"

Bert closed his eyes, rubbed a hand over his mouth and rested it there. He appeared to be sleeping.

"Bert?"

"His 15-year-old sister told him…" His voice cracked.

She thought she detected tears. "What did she say?"

"Johnny raped her."

Linda gasped. "He raped my mother?"

Bert shook his head. "Listen, Kiddo, you suffer from a severe case of the black-and-whites. Think gray. Pay attention."

"Johnny raped her when she was 15. That's what you said." Damn, she had never given so much as a hint.

"No."

"Yes it is."

"She *said* he raped her."

Bert, the damned lobbyist and his tortured words. She told Uncle Frankie. No different from the night Linda told her mother what Cousin Joel did. Of course, nobody broke Joel's kneecaps, even though he deserved it. In fact, thanks to her mom, no one did anything. "OK, so Johnny did it and Uncle Frankie took care of the bastard."

"There you go again. Right or wrong, good or evil, black or white. How many times I got to tell you, Kiddo? The world doesn't work that way. Something *did* happen. If you check the New York statutes, it says rape."

"Cut the shit, Bert. Rape is rape."

He shrugged. "You're right. I checked."

Joel's sneer loomed in her head. "So even though not lawful, Johnny Marsolais got what he deserved, right?"

"Define justice."

"Punishment commensurate with the offense."

"OK."

"And, so Johnny got justice with a little 'j.'" Maybe, if she had a big brother, Joel would have gotten justice too.

"Here's the deal. I'll tell you the story. At the end, I want you to answer a question. Was justice served?"

Linda nodded.

"For the record, I'm telling this story for the first time and under duress."

"Save it for your political buddies."

Bert leaned back in his chair. He put a finger to his lips and remained silent for a moment, his eyes on her. Then he took a deep breath and exhaled. "From the start of her first year in high school, everyone recognized Michelle Gordon as the most beautiful girl of the freshman class. By the end of October, she made varsity cheerleader and made it clear to everyone she wanted to be Johnny's girlfriend. Johnny paid her no attention. Swarms of college scouts dropped in on basketball games and practice sessions, and any number of junior and senior girl groupies wanted him. Michelle had no chance. In March, Johnny brought Cohoes a basketball championship. Then he won a full scholarship to UCLA, a dream come true for a boy from the wrong side of the tracks.

"Johnny had a problem, though. UCLA required he graduate high school. I tutored him, unmercifully, for the last three months of our senior year. Johnny squeaked through. Your mother never dropped her pursuit. Whenever possible, she managed to be around when Johnny hung out. The upperclassmen thought she was comical.

"In August, the week before Johnny headed off to UCLA, the seniors arranged a keg party up at Sandy Bars. Do you know the place?"

Linda shook her head.

"It was an illicit but popular swimming hole on the Mohawk, just above the falls. Michelle crashed the party. No one minded, except a couple girls shot her dirty looks when their boyfriends tripped over themselves to get her a beer. She drained the first beer as if a bartender announced last call. Then she sauntered over by the keg and asked me what I was doing sitting alone. I forget what I said, but we talked about nothing while she refilled her cup. She asked if I was coming to the fire where Johnny entertained a small group with the story about talking to Coach Wooden. He'd embellished the tale to where it was almost completely fiction, and I said no. She walked over and sat by Johnny. At the end of his myth, many of the group paired off and headed down the dark path toward the tree with the rope swing, carrying blankets and beers. Michelle touched Johnny's shoulder, leaned in and said something.

"Johnny smiled and nodded, then stood. She ambled to the keg, filled the two drink cups without so much as a word or even a look at me. She returned to Johnny and they set off arm in arm. After everyone was gone, I poured a fresh beer and sat by the fire."

At this point in the story, Bert turned sideways to stare at the bookcase against the wall. Linda waited, but he said nothing. "Bert, what were you thinking about, sitting there by yourself?"

He laughed. "What do you suppose 18-year-old guys think about?"

"Were you in love with my mother?"

No answer. She reached across the desk and touched his arm. "So you were."

He didn't move. "Anyway, after a while, up the path they came, Michelle draped all over Johnny, eyes like saucers. By this time some of the other couples had come back, and we were all sitting by the fire when Michelle asked Johnny, in a very slurred voice, when they could do that again."

Bert paused, turned to face her. Linda experienced a sickening feeling about what came next. His tone shifted to that of the TV anchor reporting the evening news. "Next day, word got to Frankie his baby sister had been at the keg party playing big-girl games with the college boy. A few days later, Johnny lay in the hospital with a busted kneecap and word circulated Frankie evened the score with him for raping his sister." Bert stopped, looked into her eyes and shook his head slowly. "I give Frankie this much credit. When he learned the truth, he was none too happy with his baby sister."

Jesus Christ, her mother made the whole story up, lied to her brother and got Johnny whacked. Linda finally understood her mother's reaction to Cousin Joel's attack. The woman thought all girls lied about rape when it was convenient. What a piece of work. She wondered how much of this her father knew. "How'd Uncle Frank find out?"

"Small town," Bert said.

"*You* told him, didn't you?"

He shrugged. "Why do you suppose your mother speaks so highly of me?"

CHAPTER 31

Linda declined Bert's lunch invitation and drove to South Greenbush, her mind drowning in information. While puzzling things over and sorting out fact and emotion, one line of question pulsed like a dull toothache. How much of Bert's insistence that she marry Bill had anything to do with her or his son? Did she merely symbolize the Michelle whom Bert had failed to win? If nothing else, the physical similarities were compelling. Or had Bert designed a devious plan to stick it to a lost love? Knowing him, there would be no simple answer.

The same might be said of the Johnny Marsolais story. He was 18, his partner 15, and under a strict reading of New York Penal Law, the act constituted rape even though the girl practically begged him. Yet what was the probability an 18-year-old kid from the wrong side of town and a bare-minimum high school education even understood the concept of statutory rape, let alone the intricacies?

Ignorance of the law was no defense, they'd taught her. Perhaps not, but it was certainly a factor in weighing the penalty. What Johnny did with her mother may have been illegal, but what she did to him was downright wrong. Uncle Frank had meted out punishment but not justice. He ruined a man's life because he believed a lie. Did he still hold his sister accountable for the lie? Did the debt to her brother influence her mother's decision not to prosecute his son for raping Linda? Did Joel dodge justice all those years ago because of an unpaid debt? She found the thought as repulsive as the whole story.

The parking spot mid-block afforded Linda a good view of the Jarosz's front door. Thanks to her drunken Sunday night conversation with Tibbs, the Jenna story was nearly complete, everything but the why, which she intended to get today.

The leak in the aborted clinic raids came from LeBeouf. The Feds supplied the information from a wiretap of DA O'Keefe on an unrelated case of bribery involving a construction project. The tap caught LeBeouf warning the DA of the impending raids and O'Keefe's thanking him, promising to fix things. LeBeouf faced a disciplinary hearing, which would likely result in his termination. On the criminal end, his fate rested largely on the Feds' decision about prosecuting DA O'Keefe for corruption. Linda recalled Walker's recent words on the importance of working through the proper channels. Had she done so with her foray into the Health Department, she might have missed the information that helped move along a stalled case.

Tibbs also told her BCI detectives had revisited Jeremy Cronin and compiled a good account of events the night of the party on Crooked Lake. Once Jeremy knew Jenna's father was behind bars and Martinez dead, he became cooperative. He told detectives of a minor auto accident on his way to the camp that Friday night. He slowed when a car passed him on a country road, but the driver cut back too close and braked. Jeremy slammed the brakes but still bumped the car. The other driver apologized. He said a deer crossed the road and he braked to avoid hitting the animal. They exchanged insurance information. A police officer arrived in an unmarked car. The cop spoke briefly to both drivers. He took down the names of the passengers in both cars on a form attached to a clipboard. He returned to his car and left. To Jeremy's relief, the cop did not give him a ticket. Then things got strange.

After the other driver left the scene, Jenna suggested they all claim injuries and get money from the insurance company. There was no harm in trying, she reasoned, the worst case being the company would say no. At first, only a couple of the kids thought the idea a good one, but the more Jenna talked, the better the plan sounded. When she mentioned they might get as much as $1,500 each, in cash and without anyone knowing, the opposition dissolved. Jeremy didn't like the scheme, especially the part about signing a bunch of blank insurance forms but didn't express his reservations until after the group got to the camp.

Jeremy explained his concerns to Jenna the first time they were alone. She invited him upstairs to discuss the matter in private. Once in the bedroom, Jenna locked the door and began to undress. At some point in the foreplay, she asked Jeremy to "go along" with the scheme because she would get in trouble if he didn't. Jeremy claimed this gave him his first inkling the accident might be phony and Jenna somehow involved. He didn't want to throw his girlfriend in, but he also feared involvement in something illegal. Jenna dropped the subject for a few minutes but while they coupled she repeated her plea that Jeremy cooperate. He told her he was sure he could straighten things out with the cop. She screamed as if he'd threatened to kill her.

At this point in the retelling of Jeremy's story, Tibbs had paused, laughed and interjected. "The poor boy found himself caught in a vicious struggle between what every 18-year-old male thinks about 24/7 and his gut instinct about what was right. He probably thought it was a bad dream. Two minutes later, you kicked in the door. Then his nightmare began."

Based upon Heather's insights about Jenna and sex, one topic she thought the cheerleader had been truthful about, Linda had already concluded rape didn't explain Jenna's horror. Now the terror in her tone made sense. Despite Jenna's sexual persuasion, Jeremy said he would not participate in the insurance fraud. Her scream was for the danger to Jeremy's life. She knew what happened to people who threatened her father's business. Jenna's rape claim wasn't born of a desire to get Jeremy in trouble. She made the claim to keep Jeremy from talking and further endangering his life. Knowing Albert Jarosz was Victor Zalenko and that he employed Martinez convinced her Jeremy owed his life to Jenna. Still, the girl's use of a rape claim to cover up the truth gnawed at Linda.

Her cell rang, startling her. She glanced at the caller ID and flipped the phone open. "Hi, Mom."

"Your father and I were worried sick about you."

Linda wondered where her mother's concerns had been seven years ago, but bit her tongue. "I'm fine."

"Yes, so your voice message said, three days late."

"It wasn't three days."

"We found out from a TV reporter you were kidnapped and you killed a man."

"I'm *sorry*."

"We didn't know how to contact you."

"I didn't want to be found. Can you understand?"

"No. We're your parents. We want to help."

Yeah, right. What a big help she'd been when Linda needed her. "I learned the hard way to take care of myself."

Silence. "That was a low blow."

"Perhaps."

"My mother did her best for me. That's what I did for you."

A South Greenbush police car rolled past, the uniformed officer taking note of Linda. "Just curious, Mom. Did Johnny Marsolais have anything to do with it?"

Her mother gasped. "Who told you...?"

"Jesus, Mom."

"I can't believe Bert did this."

"I guess it explains some things."

"And to think I once had a crush on the man."

"What? *You* had a crush on Bert?"

"Freshman year, I thought Bert was cute, not like the jocks, but attractive, smart, on his way to college and a bright future. Those things weren't important to most freshman girls. Kids grew up quicker in my old neighborhood, some faster than others."

Bert and her mother once shared a mutual attraction. Incredible.

"Let's get back to Johnny."

"Bert still hasn't learned to stay out of other people's lives. Imagine the man attacking the integrity of his own son's future father-in-law, in the newspaper no less."

Yes, just imagine.

"He broke up the impending engagement. Maggie Bariteau told Becky that Kathleen came to see Bill this morning with tears streaming down her face and called the whole thing off."

To steal a phrase from Bert: "Shame, huh?" Still, the news generated a grimy and vacuous sensation. "You still haven't told me why."

"You can't imagine what it was like, living in poverty and squalor, walking on eggshells, afraid to do or say anything to displease my father. I lived my childhood scared sick he'd beat me or be the reason he beat my mother. I was young and could take his abuse, but her…he'd worn her out. The year he turned 19, your Uncle Frankie beat our old man near to death. My brother became the man of the house. I vowed my children would never suffer the violence I did growing up. The father you have is by design, not by accident. My choice."

"But why Johnny?"

"My father conditioned me to not disappoint. I figured I better not disappoint my older brother either. When Frankie asked about Johnny and me, I got scared and confused. I lied.

"And Johnny paid."

"Do you think I don't bear the guilt of what happened to Johnny?"

"Must be rough."

"His kids went to college on anonymous scholarship funds your father and I set up."

"Brenda didn't."

"How did…? Brenda was the last. Somehow, Johnny found out the funding source. He forbade her."

Johnny's kid paid for her father's pride, as if the denial might change history. No, Linda had learned a great deal about the futility of trying to alter the past. Jenna's car appeared in the rearview mirror. "So, Dad knows about you and Johnny."

"I keep nothing from your father."

"Is that so?" Linda recalled the scent of her mother's perfume wafting from Arcuro's apartment, her blouse lying on his sofa back. "Does he know about your affair with Joe Arcuro?"

"What did you say?"

Linda looked out the car window. Jenna's car passed the 'Vette and slowed. "You heard me."

"I don't have to take this shit from you." The phone slammed. The line went dead. Linda's hands shook. Crap, the conversation did not go as planned. She didn't intend to accuse her mother, but did anyway, as if a devil in her put the words in her mouth. Some alibi. Linda tried on her seven-year-old rationalization: the woman was a selfish bitch. The excuse no longer fit. To be more precise, it was irrelevant.

Thanks largely to Martinez, she had come to understand the depths of the anger she harbored toward Joel and men in general. Now she recognized confronting and controlling her wrath over sex crimes only scratched the surface. No, the wellspring of her rage lay somewhere else. The realization stung.

Jenna parallel-parked. Linda jumped from the 'Vette and approached. Jenna stepped from the car and noticed Linda's presence. The girl took a moment to register recognition, but when she did, she sneered contempt.

"What do you want? You're so low down the totem pole, the bubble gum sticking to my sneakers doesn't recognize you."

"Good. I don't want anything."

"I ain't telling you nothing."

"Right, you're going to listen."

"No I'm not."

"You lied to me about Jeremy's raping you."

"So?"

"You led me to believe Jeremy forced you."

Jenna laughed. "Led you to believe? Who you kidding? You already believed it. I mean I like to act, but come on. You fed me my lines."

Linda wanted to slap the kid. Her comfort level with lies and deception, her perceptive approach to the use of sex for persuasion, her matter-of-fact reaction to her motives and deeds, the package frightened Linda. The girl was a freaking teenager. How had she gotten cynical so young? "Rape is a heinous crime committed every day. My job is to stop sex crimes. When you cry rape falsely, you make my job harder."

Jenna looked at Linda as if she were a stray cat she'd decided not to feed. "Well isn't that nice? *My* job is to protect myself. I'd do it again."

Linda had decided some people were simply not potential candidates for redemption. Martinez had been one, but he was older and more mature. Jenna was still a kid. "The money meant that much?"

Jenna stared at her as if she'd spoken Swahili. "Money? You think what I did had anything to do with money? Tell you what. Spend a few years with a tyrant father who beats you every time you say or do the wrong thing. Have him threaten your boyfriend's life." Jenna spit on the sidewalk. "You're so lame, you make me sick." She turned and walked away.

Jenna was right about one thing. Linda *had* fed her the lines for the rape scene and bore part of the responsibility for the false claim and its aftermath. Had she not gone after Jeremy, she would not have encountered Martinez, putting her own life in danger and exacerbating the threat to Jeremy's. The truth was not comforting. She tried to imagine living in a household with a father possessing the temperament of a Third World dictator, as Vance had described Zalenko/Jarosz. She could not relate. She no longer had the urge to set Jenna straight. The task would be a good deal more complicated than Linda had thought. The girl needed help beyond Linda's ability. She would make inquiries at school and try to facilitate getting Jenna the help. It wasn't right to give up on a 16-year-old, no matter how cynical.

The parallels between her mom and Jenna were striking. Linda grew up with a father who loved and respected her, a man who encouraged her to be what she wanted to be. He wasn't perfect. He might have been less deferential to his wife in matters affecting Linda, but she'd come to realize the situation applied to most fathers. Jenna's headed a major Russian crime ring. Linda imagined his reaction when his daughter brought BCI detectives to his doorstep the day after the camp incident.

Her mother also grew up in a household where violence was commonplace. The young and weak needed to develop defense mechanisms, lies and deceptions being among the most common. She must have used them to shelter herself from an abusive father, her leap in logic to a violent older brother a sensible precaution. Linda forced herself to wonder what she might have done had she faced the choices her mother and Jenna faced just before they made their rape claims. The answer was not as simple as she would like. That the decision had to come in a matter of seconds while facing down an abusive figure made Linda's stomach queasy. Jenna was partly right. She felt lame, and the thoughts of what

Jenna and her mother must have experienced while growing up were making her sick.

She spent the rest of the afternoon at Starbucks, reading every newspaper in the place and chatting with the troopers who streamed in and out of the coffee shop. In terms of keeping up with things at Troop G, the Loudonville Starbucks was the next best thing to actually being at headquarters.

On her way back to Cohoes, her cell rang. She answered without looking at the display.

"I satisfied your curiosity. Your turn to satisfy mine."

"What do you want, Bert?"

"You going to marry my son?"

Bert "Get to the Point" Bariteau's question involved a multi-step answer with many caveats and escape clauses. In other words, a lobbyist's dream. The first step was not something she would discuss with anyone, least of all her intended father-in-law. "He hasn't asked."

"When he does?"

"You mean *if?*"

"You still got a lot to learn, Kiddo."

True, but so did Bert.

***

That evening, Linda drove across town to her parents' house. A light rain misted the windshield. Linda's father opened the door, and the look of disappointment on his face nearly made her turn around and leave. But she'd vowed to do this and steeled herself.

He hugged her. "We love you, and we'll always worry about you."

Waiting so long to talk to her parents was inexcusable. She'd acted like a shit, and now she knew why.

Her father released her. "Do you realize you've never rung the doorbell at this house before tonight?" He shook his head, the way his father used to. "Your mother told me about this afternoon."

How much had she said? Certainly not the infidelity part. "I need to talk to her."

"That's been true for a long time, Linda. I've been telling your mother the same thing: she needs to talk to you. But no, you two are so alike…"

"Where is she?"

"Do you want me there?"

"No, Dad, this is between us."

Her father pointed up the stairs. "You hurt her."

Linda started up without responding. This was going to be difficult enough. She took two steps. He said, "Linda?"

Something in his tone chilled her. She turned.

"Most Thursdays, your mother and Becky have lunch together, and then visit Becky's mom over in Valley View." He walked away. The words he'd not spoken cut far deeper than the ones he'd said.

The master bedroom door stood open, and Linda found her mom sitting in a corner reading.

She looked up from her book. "What do you want?"

"I have something to say."

Her mother rose and walked to the foot of the bed. "Oh, goodie, I can hardly wait."

Linda approached her. "I deserve that. What I said this morning was wrong and hurtful. I spoke in anger. This next bit is something I should have said seven years ago."

Her mother looked at her warily. "What's that?"

"The night Joel raped me he hurt me, humiliated me and made me feel worthless. I didn't think it possible to feel any worse. I wanted justice, wanted Joel to pay for what he'd done. So it hurt even more when that didn't happen." As she spoke, Linda watched her mother's face. The smooth mask of self-confidence she wore in public crumbled. Her lips trembled. Her eyes blinked. "But now I've come to realize what hurt me most that night. All I wanted, Mom, was for you to take me in your arms, console me and comfort me. I wanted you to explain why you thought it best not to call the police. I wanted you to act like a mother. That's the real hurt I've been carrying around all these years. I've needed to say these words for a long time. Now I have. I'm done."

Her mother's cheeks were wet with tears, her eyes red. Her body shook, and Linda thought for a moment that she might collapse. Without warning, she threw her arms around Linda and hugged her with a surprising strength. She rested her head on Linda's shoulder. "I am so sorry for everything," her mother moaned. "I thought that—"

"Hush, Mom."

"Knowing I couldn't undo my mistake only made it worse. Just like with Johnny."

Linda returned her mother's hug. She had said what she needed to say and now experienced the lightness of having unshackled the yoke. They stood at the foot of the bed holding each other. Her father came to the door and looked in. "Is everything all right in here?"

"Fine, Dad. I think everything's going to be just fine."

EPILOGUE

The Martinez killing inquiry lasted almost a month, but Walker finally called and cleared her return to duty on the coming Monday. Linda spent most of the suspension in Starbucks, keeping up with Troop G. She also had several long phone conversations with Bill, sticking to safe subjects for now. Bert arranged for her to meet with Jeremy privately. She apologized to him for her actions and wished him well at Duke. Jeremy was visibly uncomfortable with the meeting, accepted the apology, thanked her and left.

She made a tentative start with her mother. They had seven years to undo, and Linda recognized it would take time. She was now intent on doing her part and trying as best as possible to put the past behind. Perhaps one day they would develop a normal mother-daughter relationship, if such a thing even existed. Still, even if none developed, it would be far better than the one filled with hate she'd clung to for seven years.

Once a week, she accepted an open invitation for dinner at her parents' house where she savored the few hours of family time without an undercurrent of tension and hostility. Her mom hinted about visiting the apartment, but Linda didn't extend an invitation. She was ashamed to admit she'd chosen the apartment and furnishings mostly to spite her mother. She'd extend the invitation after the lease ran out and she moved to a nicer place.

Her mom gave her a recipe for braised short ribs, a gourmet one-pot meal that should be "foolproof" as long as Linda used the cookware borrowed with the recipe. Microwaves didn't have a braise setting, but how difficult could an electric oven be? A package of ribs sat in her refrigerator. Linda planned to cook them for a special occasion.

On Saturday, she parked the 'Vette in front of her parents' house and followed the sidewalk to the dead-end sign. Two hawks glided lazily over the trees. She started down the dirt path to a quiet ravine. The top of the oak appeared. An early afternoon sun filtered through the sturdy limbs, producing a downy aura about the trunk. Next to the tree sat a small stack of firewood beside a canvas transporter, both borrowed from her parents' living room early this morning. On top of the wood stack lay a worn wool blanket from the 'Vette's trunk.

The sweet scent of the previous autumn's decaying leaves reminded her that seasons change. "To everything, turn, turn, turn, there is a season, turn, turn, turn…" She recited the words she learned from a recording by the old rock group, the Byrds, who had carved a major hit singing the refrain Pete Seeger pilfered from Ecclesiastes.

A distant rustling of dried grass quickened her pulse, but she didn't turn from her examination of the tree trunk. The misshapen heart, callused by seven years' weather, appeared to have survived the seasoning remarkably well. The crackled trampling drew closer. She touched the "L" inside the heart. The hard, sharp edges of the fresh carving from her memory had rounded soft with the years.

An arm reached over her shoulder and a hand covered hers, moving her finger to the "B," top left of the four initials. Their hands traced, his body moved closer, touched, but not quite snuggled. They finished their route. She imagined he would whisper in her ear. He released her hand and stepped back. She turned to face him.

"Sorry I'm late. I got halfway here, and realized I forgot this." He held up a soft-sided wine tote and laughed. "My old man caught me searching the wine cellar. I had a '92 Mersault in my hand, and he said—"

"I can imagine."

"I told him where I was going. He wanted me to take two."

Recalling the morning after the night she'd split two bottles with Bert, she said, "Good thing you only brought one."

He gestured toward the blanket and the bundle of firewood. "You've been busy. This was a good idea."

"I wasn't sure you'd come."

"Why do you say that?" He set the wine on the blanket and moved to the bundle of wood.

"My mother told me your fiancée broke up with you. I thought you might be licking your wounds." She knelt beside the wood.

He knelt, reached an arm across the pile and touched her cheek. "The only people calling Kathleen my fiancée were Kathleen, her mother and yours." He began erecting a teepee with the firewood. "I heard the rumor and asked her to stop. Do you have any kindling?"

"What happened?"

"Earth to Linda: Did you bring little sticks to start the fire?"

"No kindling. She didn't stop, did she?"

"Told me plenty." He stared into space. "I like what my mother and father have in each other. I want a relationship like theirs. I'm going to have a say about who it's with, though."

His father predicted as much. "So when she broke up with you…"

"The day of Brown's column and my old man's 'smoke and fire' quote." He glanced at the teepee he'd built and raised himself to one knee. "I've got to get some kindling."

"No. Tell me about Brown's story."

He laughed. "What's to tell? I love my father, but he's a real piece of work. Brown would never quote him without permission. When I read the column, I knew what he was up to."

"Me too."

"Just as well, I guess. Kathleen's dumping me spared me the messy business of breaking up with her."

Linda gazed out beyond the tree. A hawk soared in the distance. She imagined herself floating overhead, eyes alert. She turned to Bill, stifling an instinct to say she was sorry. "Before we light this, I want you to do something for me."

"What?"

"There's a big fire circle, next to the path, about 30 yards down." She pointed out the direction. "I'll gather the kindling. You bring up some rocks to surround the teepee."

"OK." He rolled his eyes and started down the path.

"I'm serious about this."

"I know. I know."

She wandered down the narrow path in the opposite direction, collecting twigs and dried brush and dropping them into the canvass carrier. Her thoughts turned to a spring-like day seven years ago walking this path, collecting kindling, heart lighter than the wispy clouds racing overhead, borne on the urgent breeze.

Lost in nostalgia, she nearly filled the carrier before she realized how much kindling she'd gathered: enough to start several fires. She pulled a handful of dry grass and tossed it. The blades floated straight to the ground.

She returned. Bill stacked kindling under the teepee of wood, now securely encircled by flat stones stacked about a foot high. Linda popped the cork from the bottle of wine and filled the two plastic glasses. "Take a sip before you light that."

He clicked his glass to hers. "Here's to…" He nodded to the circle of rocks. "…safe fires and whatever the future may hold."

His father and her mother had each taught an important truth about the future. It bore all the opportunity a person dared to seize. Bill struck a match. The kindling cracked and sparked. He fussed with the fire.

She sipped some wine. "We haven't had dinner together in a long time. I just got cleared in the shooting. We should celebrate."

He stared blankly at the struggling flames, perhaps conjuring a diplomatic declination. "How about La Serre?"

She handed him her wine and knelt beside the fire. She leaned over the stones and whispered encouragement to the dying embers clinging to the kindling. They responded with a bright glow, gradually engulfing the dry firewood. She straightened, took her glass and sat with her back against the oak. "I had something else in mind."

He joined her. "You'd rather Italian?"

Smoke leaked sideways, rising up the oak as if through a chimney. "How about you come to my place? You bring the champagne. I'll make dinner."

Whether from the smoke or concern about her culinary skills, Bill choked. "I didn't know you could cook."

"I've changed. Is tonight at 6:30 good?"

The ensuing silence felt like an eternity. Finally he said, "Linda, we need to talk."

Once he realized she controlled her anger and she was ready to make love to him, there wouldn't be much to discuss. "About?"

"Me."

Him? First it was sex, then anger and now him. Or was this new complication a smokescreen for his feelings about Kathleen? Their fathers might keep them apart, but that wouldn't necessarily douse the heat she'd witnessed in their exchanged look the night of the ball. "You?"

"My loving you, to be precise."

An issue only if he loved Kathleen too. "If you love me and I love you, what's the problem?"

"Nothing to do with you. The issue is whether I can deal with loving someone who risks her life every day."

Kathleen was not a factor. She leaned her head against his shoulder. "I'll show you how."

"Seriously, we need to talk."

"Six-thirty at my place."

"I bring the Champagne. We talk."

"Sure." *Afterward.*

Linda put her hand on his knee and traced a route inside his thigh. She wondered if her upstairs neighbors would be home tonight.

ABOUT THE AUTHOR

Bernie Bourdeau was born and raised in Cohoes, NY a small city a few miles north of Albany, New York's capital. He spent the first half of his career working in government, most of it as a senior economic advisor to the State Senate, where he specialized in financial services issues. He developed an interest in property & casualty insurance while working for the senate. He spent the second half of his career as president of the New York Insurance Association, a trade group of property & casualty insurance companies. For the last 8 years he also managed the NY Alliance Against Insurance Fraud where he learned the intricacies of major league insurance fraud and the crime rings that run the enterprises.

Throughout his career he read and admired the writings of some great authors: Hemingway, Faulkner, Twain, Updike, Vonnegut and more recently Thomas Perry, Dennis Lehane, Harlan Coben, William Kennedy, Richard Russo and many more. Their writings spurred a longing to create stories people would want to read. After leaving the world of politics, he began to chase the dream. *CAUSED* & EFFECT is the result of that pursuit. He is currently working on the sequel.

A THIN GRAY LINE will reunite Linda with Bert, Vance, Eddie, Bill, Kathleen and a cast of new characters to explore the illusion we call truth. Linda is drawn into the middle of a high stakes political battle where the campaign tricks are both dirty and deadly and where the future of the country turns on the question of which version of two competing lies shall carry an election.

9088637R0

Made in the USA
Charleston, SC
09 August 2011